GRAND PRIX

Formula One in the deadly years

a novel by

Richard Melville

First published in 2014
by Richard Melville
Auckland, New Zealand
richard.mdl@gmail.com

ISBN: 978-0-473-29285-0

Cover illustration by Brett Young
Printed by CreateSpace, An Amazon.com Company

This is a work of fiction.

Reviews

I read the above story over two days, as I found it hard to put down.

The adventures of Will portrayed a lifestyle that most men can only dream about. He ticked all the right boxes with Formula One, sailing a Super Yacht and having affairs with beautiful females.

The description about racing in his machine was really excellent; you feel as if you were behind the wheel. This must be the best technical description of Formula One racing ever written.

I have to admit that I was sorry to come to the end of this story and only hope that there will be a sequel. — Roger Ashley Wilson

I was surprised how much I enjoyed this book. Will, the power struggle, politics and intrigue of F1 was interesting. The author clearly has knowledge of the F1 paddock. Great story that takes in racing, sailing and business. — Bruce Elliott

Over the years I have tried to find a good Formula One novel. I finally found it. — Douglas Harper

A fascinating insight into the exhilarating world of F1 motor racing, and the risks the drivers took to succeed. — Julie Haynes

I just finished reading your novel and enjoyed it very much. You should be very proud of yourself. I would not be surprised if it becomes a movie. I think it would make a good one. It is one of the best novels I have read in a long time, if not the best ever — Bob Costey

About the Author

Grand Prix: Formula One in the deadly years reflects the life experiences of Richard Melville. Born in Jamaica, and after winning the Jamaica Grand Prix as a twenty-year-old, Richard set off for Europe to go motor racing via the US. There he shared an Austin Healey Sprite at Sebring with soon-to-be Formula-One World Champion Graham Hill, in 1961.

Among crashes, the highlights of that year in Europe were leading the BMC Team to Team Prize and Manufacturers' Award at the Nürburgring 500 Kilometre race, and winning at Snetterton in England.

In 1962 he teamed up with Ian Walker Racing. A big crash at Goodwood in the ex-UDT Laystall Lotus Elite the morning of Stirling Moss' accident was followed by a year of mechanical failures. He was the only survivor of the Ian Walker drivers. The other three were killed over the next few years. Those were the deadly years.

Richard returned to Jamaica, where he built up a successful construction business. During the course of this, he learned to fly, flying back and forth to Central America and the US, and not racing again till 1972.

Club racing Formula Fords in Florida wasn't challenging enough: Richard soon switched to the professional Gold Star Formula SuperVee series. He found himself an amateur against professionals, while running a difficult business, in what became known as the bad years in Jamaica. The Manley socialists with all their theories had come to power, cosying up to Fidel Castro, nationalising businesses, causing capital flight, resulting in draconian laws, and destroying the economy, which never recovered.

Richard's experiences are reflected in the novel. While trying to win an extremely competitive championship, he was being distracted by the frustrations, failings, and challenges of a large cattle operation in Central America that was going wrong. At the same time Richard was running his construction business in violent times, while looking for opportunities to transfer it to Central America, extricating himself from Jamaica before the doors were closed, as had happened in Cuba.

By 1976 the risks far exceeded the rewards and after the union goons told him that they knew where he lived, Richard moved himself and his family to New Zealand, where he continued motor racing for another two seasons, finishing third in the New Zealand GP behind soon-to-be Formula One World Champion, Keke Rosberg, and soon-to-be Indy Car Champion, Bobby Rahal.

By 1980 Richard had set up the first contract processing lamb boning plant in New Zealand. The obvious inefficiencies in meat processing soon resulted in machines being developed and patented to enhance the handling and packaging of meat cuts.

Richard soon got hooked on the Kiwi sport of yachting, and after owning several yachts finally built his kauri wooden yacht *Grand Prix*, a half size version of *Imperialist*, designed and built by arguably the best designers and builders anywhere. After racing up to the Pacific Islands and Australia over the years, Richard has recently sailed *Grand Prix* to New Caledonia and across to Australia, and is now planning his next adventure.

"There are only three sports: bullfighting, motor racing, and mountaineering; all the rest are merely games."

— Ernest Hemingway

1

WILLIAM HAROLD ARCHER pulled down hard for the last time on the shoulder straps of the six-point harness. He opened his hands and flexed his fingers, as he would do many times before the race was over. Grasping the gear lever with his right hand, he blipped the throttle, pushed in the clutch, released it, pushed it in again, and pulled the gear lever against its spring loading, to the left and back, graunching it into first gear.

At six feet, he was left little space by the aerodynamicists, and sat gripped in his seat in a semi-reclining position, shoulders squeezed in by the bodywork, his head enclosed by the roll-bar supports. He could see straight ahead and a bit to the side. The mirrors were near-useless. But it didn't matter as far as he was concerned: if he couldn't see them, they weren't there.

Among all the howling engines, Will couldn't hear his own, but he could feel the vibration through the back of his seat as he blipped the throttle. He knew his engine was making a racket behind his head, but he couldn't differentiate his racket from the rest. He hoped that the little fat man standing on the rostrum would drop the flag quickly, for if he delayed, and the car engine didn't overheat, the clutch would certainly burn out.

He was on the front row of the grid, in the last race of the season, but he wasn't on pole, which meant that he was on the left-hand side of the track, going into a right-hand corner. This was both a disadvantage and an advantage. On the outside the track was clean and well "rubbered in", as that was the path all the cars took into the downhill right-hand corner. On the inside of the corner, the grip was much less, because there was no rubber left on the road by previous cars braking hard into it. However, the pole-sitter had the inside line for the first corner, which ultimately gave him the advantage. Will hoped to jump the start, but he had to do it without getting caught. He was an expert at jumping starts. Starts weren't the problem; finishes were. He hadn't finished many races this season: he had crashed in some, and had had mechanical problems in others. All in all, not a brilliant season, but at least he hadn't spent half of it in hospital, as he had in the previous one.

The starter lifted the flag over his head. Will increased the revs to 8000, and fixed his eyes on the starter's left shoulder. The instant that shoulder came up, he was going to drop the clutch. Waiting for the flag was too late; he needed to get into the right-hand corner from the left-hand side of the track, before all the others stormed up the inside. Will was not aware of the crowd in the stands to the left, nor the pits to the right. He was aware only of the roar of the engines, and the tightness in his chest. The shoulder moved! Drop the clutch, feel the wheelspin, ease off a bit, feel the tyres grip. "Get out of first gear quick, before you over-rev it," Will talked to himself: "Careful with the shift into second, don't miss it, can't hear the engine, too much noise." Total pandemonium; into third, into fourth, no time to look at the rev counter, nobody alongside.

The track sloped steeply down to the first corner. Down the hill, glance in the mirrors, just ahead of the pole car, out to the left-hand edge, brake hard, don't lock the brakes, the nose dips touching the ground, third, second, look in the right mirror, clear. Got the bastards! Up against the outside kerb, off the brakes, turn into the apex, the front wheel rides up over the red-and-white sloping kerbs, boot it, the back steps out, flick in some opposite lock, feel the rear of the car squat under power, drift to the outside of the corner, over the outside kerb, launching itself off the kerb with the engine howling. Will shifted up through the gears, third, fourth; look in the mirrors, all clear, through the long flowing esses, drifting from kerb, to kerb, to kerb, beautiful, onto the straight, into fifth.

Will checked the mirror to see what was happening behind him; he glanced at the gauges. All okay. He must plan for the end of the straight, as the bastards would be all over him by the time he got there. Slipstreaming, they would have towed each other up to him. If they got too close, he would have to use the inside line to protect his corner, forcing them to go around on the outside. He didn't want to, as this would cramp his entry, slowing him down; but he might be forced to. This was a very fast, oval-track-type corner, steeply banked downhill. Once committed, that's it, do or die, you couldn't back off, or you would lose it, and then it would be into the Armco, or into the Armco and the pine forest. Ray Milligan, the team owner, always claimed that it could be taken flat in fifth, but nobody ever had. Everybody braked; there was a limit to insanity.

They were getting closer and closer, slipstreaming up to each other, like a bunch of cyclists. He shifted to the right to protect the corner. He looked in the mirrors, which gave a blurred vision of them all over the track, fighting for position, darting this way and that. Will talked to himself, "Concentrate, concentrate, focus, forget the rest, and go for the high line." The triple Armco barrier lined the outside, with the solid wall of pine trees beyond. It was a blind approach. He glanced at the mirrors. "They are closer, wide line, careful, careful, gently, gently, just rub the brakes, carry the speed. Nobody inside, go for the apex, watch the inside kerb come up, front wheel to the edge of the striped, sloped kerbing, don't touch it, could flick you into the Armco at this speed." The G force pushed his head sideways and forced his ribs into the seat. The car drifted to the outside, up against the Armco, close, out of it, away.

Downhill, left-hander coming up, not as steep, not as fast, ignore the mirrors: if you can't see them, they aren't there. Turn in to the apex, wheel up on the kerb, and drift out to the edge, fantastic! Right-hand uphill first-gear hairpin, don't let them down the inside, wait, wait, wait, push down hard on the brake pedal, till the wheels almost lock, nose just rubbing on the ground, car squirming around, working the wheel to keep it straight. Will turned in under brakes, tyre smoke coming off the unloaded front wheel. Ease off, don't lock the inside front, use the uphill to slow down. Skip fourth, third, second, first. Careful: don't over-rev it, feed in the power. Rear end steps out, quick flick to opposite lock, feed in the throttle, rev counter in the red, second, third, fourth, fifth, every time on the red line. Short, flat, straight section; check the mirrors, not so close, good.

Right-hander coming up, brake, third; roll it in, feed in the power — smooth, good stuff. Short downhill straight rising to the next one to a left-hander, watch the kerbs, good. Talk to yourself, talk to yourself, and don't do anything stupid.

Short straight, into fourth early, sweeping right-hander, ease off, on again, from kerb to kerb to kerb in a beautiful sweeping arc. "Let the turkey eat, feel it suck down, work it, work it, balance it, balance it, don't let it get away from you." Onto the pit straight. Search the pit wall; look for the board, that's it, good. Look in the mirrors, a bit of space, turn one coming up again, over to the left-hand edge, wait to brake, wait, wait, on the brakes, squeeze the pedal till the car starts to squirm, third, second, turn in, over the kerb, the car lurches into oversteer, catch it, power on, slide to the outside, over the kerb, away, up the gears, through the esses, onto the straight, into fifth.

Will pushed himself away from the wheel, opened his hands and tried to force himself to relax, inhaling deeply and exhaling, checking the gauges: temperature okay, pressure okay. Check the mirrors, think, use your head, can't keep going like this with full fuel, tyres won't last. For the first time since the start, he was aware of the flag marshals and the crowd. He checked the mirrors. Good; they were starting to spread out.

As he blasted past, the pit board showed plus 1.5 secs. "Good, pulling away!" End of the straight; yellow flags being waved furiously. "Smoke! Jesus, what's happened now? I can't slow down, they'll close up, but track may be blocked, oil flags, oil, on the racing line? Where? Look in the mirrors; they aren't slowing, into the smoke, on to oil, shit, sliding , sliding, sliding, work the steering, don't lose it, Armco coming up, going to hit, going to hit, oh shit, oh shit. Jesus made it."

On the pit straight, pit board plus 1.8 secs, good, into turn one, white flag. Ambulance, watch it, up through the esses on the straight, waving white flags, there's the ambulance. Oh shit, who this time? Off at the fastest part of the circuit. Over the Armco, into the pine trees. Poor bastard. Okay, check mirrors, still there, yellow flags, oil flags, more than before, less smoke, into the smoke, onto the oil, sliding, sliding, work it, work it, keep it straight, out. Mirrors, the bastards are closing in, Jesus.

Pit board, plus 1.3 secs. "Got to shake them loose or slow down through the yellow, can't keep this up." On the straight, less smoke, fewer yellows, oil flags, full blast into the oil, sliding, sliding, twirling the wheel this way and that, good control, great, away!

Will knew that they couldn't pass under the yellow, but he didn't want to give away the distance in front that he had worked so hard to get. He didn't want to hit the ambulance either. That would be instant death. As the race progressed, he gradually inched away from the second car, his chest expanded, breathing deeply, filling his lungs with air. Was this euphoria? He didn't know. Did mountaineers feel like this? His mind kept flicking back to the car in the pines. Hope it's not too bad. He had seen so many people die in his career. At least one per year. And he had had so many near-misses himself.

He opened his hands on the wheel, and pushed himself back in the seat, taking another deep, deep breath. He was in total control. This was what it was all about. He was on top of the world, king of the mountain. It was all happening in slow motion. Braking into the corner, he could feel the car pitch forward, turn in under brakes, the weight on the outside front wheel, feeling the back lighten up, turning in, turning in, feel it roll, down the gears, fourth, third, second, inside front wheel on the apex, on the kerb, ease off the brakes, slowly onto the throttle, more and more throttle, feel the rear start to squat, feel the G forces, feel the transfer of weight from front to rear, rear still coming around, straightening up the wheel, powering towards the exit, perfect. How many hours had he spent testing to get this car like this?

There were no guarantees. Sometimes it would work today, and not tomorrow. But today he was on top of the world. Nobody could touch him. He would win this race, and the season was finished — the last race of a difficult season. They had had engine failures, in the mad rush for more horsepower. The more horsepower they got, the more unreliable the engines became, and the further back in the championship they fell. The further back they were, the more risks they took, which resulted in more crashes. They had finally won one. It was a high that would carry them into the next season.

They were on the rostrum, but there was no shaking and squirting magnum bottles of Moët at each other. Jean Luc was dead. Instead they toasted him.

"Why didn't you slow down under the yellow flags, you crazy bastard? Do you want to die as well?"

"Why didn't you?"

"Jean Luc is dead, and here we are celebrating. What a macabre sport; if we were at war, there might be some sense to it. Our odds of surviving are lower than fighter pilots in a war, and we call this sport. This is a good year. Only Jean Luc. Last year Louis and Taffy. Next year maybe you and me, madness."

"What are you going to do Carlos?"

"I don't know, I don't know, madness."

The pall of Jean Luc's death hung over the track. But Will knew that it would make no difference. There would be an investigation and ideas offered for improving safety, but he knew very little would come of it. A grieving fiancée, grieving parents. But it would all soon be forgotten. Next season they would be right back into it as if nothing had ever happened. The drivers were friends as far as it went, which was probably just as well. They did not socialise as much as in past years. Egos and competitiveness prevented any real relationship between them. It was too professional now, too hard, too competitive, and there was too much at stake.

"Will, did you see what happened?"

"Of course not, it was behind me. I only saw the smoke and the ambulance. I didn't even see any damage to the barriers. I only saw the smoke."

"There are some terrible rumours floating around."

"I know, I have heard. But I don't want to talk about that now."

"For Christ's sake don't pull that stunt under the yellow again — slow down, one day it's going to backfire on you!"

Back in the luxurious motor home, Will sat slouched in the leather armchair with his overalls zipped down to his waist. "Where is Angela, Ray?"

Ray looked down at the carpet. "She's gone."

"Gone where?"

"Just gone."

"How do you mean, just gone?"

"My friend, she said that she was fed up with waiting for you — you were never going to stop racing. She had been to the hospital once too often, and didn't want to go to the morgue."

"Did Jean Luc set her off?"

"Probably, she just left without saying anything to anybody."

Where has she gone, Ray?" he insisted.

"I don't know, probably New York."

"I'd better go and find her."

"Let her go," Ray said. "Angela's gone. She's better off, you're better off. Now, debriefing time."

"It's the last race. Let's skip it."

"We have to do it now, while it's fresh in your mind."

"How can I think clearly? Jean Luc is dead. Can't we put it off? Besides, it's the end of the season. There'll be a new car next year, so the information is out of date anyway."

"Will, you know as well as I do it can't wait, so let's start at the beginning."

They went through the ritual, the same ritual that they had gone through after every race, every practice and test session for the last five years. How did the car feel in this corner, and in that? What happened on the turn-in? How did the steering feel? What about the brakes? Good or bad wasn't an answer. How many revs were you pulling at a particular spot? Were the gear ratios right? What happened if you used a higher gear in a particular corner? What do you think needs improving? Nothing was left to chance. The exact feel was required. The debriefing was recorded to help with the ongoing development of the racing car. Ray would say, "Communicate with me, talk to me; if you don't we won't progress." But sometimes Will felt as though Ray was prying into his soul, so wouldn't come up with his exact feelings. It was almost too personal. But he knew it had to be done. Ray could virtually read his mind, interpreting Will's feelings and ideas to reality.

"Are you going to the party?" asked Ray after the debriefing was over.

"No, I think I'll go down to the boat for a while."

"Do you want the plane?"

"No, you keep it. See you in ten days. I'm going to try to sneak out the back."

•

The riot of colour that followed the first cold snap heralding fall in northern New York always lifted Will's spirits. On both sides of the highway lay a glorious tunnel of trees, every colour between silver and gold. It was so beautiful that it made Will wonder, "How did this happen? There must be a God." His mind drifted from one thought to another. They had finally won a race. It had been a terrible year, but finally it had all come together. Now Jean Luc was dead. But Ray never gave up, and had finally produced a race-winning car. He was a pain in the arse, but he was one hell of an engineer and organiser. He certainly knew how to get the best out of people; but he would drive Will crazy with his repetitive questions.

Ray had been a racing driver once. He had never got to Formula One, but he had been on his way until somebody ran over him. He was in a Formula Three race at the Nürburgring when the car broke down. While walking back along the public road, he was hit by a road car that he had not heard coming. Ray now walked with a stick, and had to use a hearing aid; however, he was sharp as a tack, and even with his stick he could outdrive most people. He could still be competitive in a Formula Three car if he had a mind to.

Ray's whole life was the team. He had no home life, nor any other interests. He lived in an old Georgian house just up the road from the workshop. Ray was a perfectionist. Way beyond any kind of perfection that would be expected in the normal business world, or in any other world for that matter. He drove Will crazy at times, but Will knew that he would leave absolutely no stone unturned in producing the very best of every component that went into his racing cars.

Ray treated Will like an errant son, forgiving his antics with a rueful smile; however, he was unforgiving when such antics related to the racing cars. God help anybody who left a speck of dirt anywhere on the car or in the workshop. He demanded top performance from everybody in the team, including Will. He grilled Will every time he drove, whether in a race, a practice, or a test. Ray had to know exactly what was going on, in every last detail; he left nothing to chance. Every experience had to be examined and re-examined in minute detail, corrected or built on, in his mind there was no such thing as luck. That was Ray Milligan.

Will wondered what Angela was up to. Had she really left because of Jean Luc? She didn't even know him. She had wandered off before, usually when she got the idea in her head that there was another woman around, and she was usually right. The truth was that Will was easily bored and couldn't take domesticity; besides, she wanted to get married, and Will wasn't into that. He wasn't sure whether he was glad she had gone. She had been around for so long that he had grown accustomed to having her around. He supposed she would show up, when whatever was bugging her blew over. In any case there was this spunky chick in the city, so he was glad Angela was out of the way, at least temporarily.

Will laughed, as he remembered the time Angela sent him

for her car. She said June, her little fat friend, would take him to pick it up. They left in her VW and headed for the street where Angela said she had left her car. They drove up and down the street with Will getting more and more irritated. "Where did she leave the damn car? Do a U-turn here," he said, but she hesitated, and the opportunity was lost. "Oh God," said Will, "stop, let me drive. Stop here." She was getting flustered.

She stopped, and Will hopped out, opened her door, but she was still sitting in the driver's seat. "Move over," but she didn't move. Frustrated, Will reached in and pushed the seat back and sat on her lap. Did a U-turn and drove up the street, still looking to see if he had missed the car. He couldn't see the blasted car anywhere. "Shit, where's the f—ing car?"

He was so irritated that he almost forgot he was sitting on Angela's little fat friend, squashing her. He had not meant to upset her. All of a sudden he noticed her warm breath on the back of his neck. Her breathing was heavy and he thought, "I must be squashing the breath out of her." Then he realised it was a lot more than that, and felt himself hardening. He should get out of the car. He looked down, and her little fingers were straight out, rigid, tense. Will didn't think, and wasn't sure why he did it. He picked up her right hand, and gently placed it on his stiff organ. She did not move, just left her hand there, but she didn't remove it. "Oh shit," thought Will, "what have I done, Angela is going to kill me."

Then Will felt the warm breath increasing rapidly, and a slight hesitant moving of the fingers, followed by a gentle squeezing, increased breath, heavy stroking, and then a solid grip. Not a word was said, dead silence, except for the now out of control breathing. Will climbed out of the seat. "Please, don't go," she said.

"Oh God," thought, Will, "on this street, here and now, true it was dark, and there were no lights on in the houses, but what if?"

Will gently lifted her out of the seat, pushing the front seat forward, laying her on the back seat. She lay there with her eyes wide open, breathing uncontrollably. "Are you sure that you want to go through with this?" asked Will. She nodded vigorously without a word, still staring directly into his eyes. Will couldn't remember when he had ever been so excited. He felt his organ throbbing with blood. He pulled the door shut, and gently slid her dress up to her waist, reached down, and as she lifted her fat bottom off the seat, pulled down her panties.

She lay there with her smooth white belly, with the little belly button, and straight, light-brown pubic hair, her eyes wide open staring, as he pulled off his pants, then switched her focus onto his engorged organ. Will had not kissed her nor touched her, but took his organ and rested it against her vagina, still looking directly into her eyes. She was so wet, that Will pushed his organ between her legs, sliding it along her vagina. June opened her eyes as wide as they could go and pushed up. Will very slowly slid his organ up and down her vagina, and between the cheeks of her fat bottom. Then she lifted one leg over the front seat and the other over the back seat.

Will slowly and very gently pushed the head of his organ against her vulva, feeling resistance and pulled back. Her eyes widened. "Have you done this before?" asked Will. She nodded, and then shook her head. "Oh God," thought Will, "I shouldn't be doing this; she is an innocent." She looked directly into his eyes and said, "Please." She was so wet; she glistened in the slight light. Will slid the end of his organ from her clitoris right around the back and to the front again. She was so wet now that Will slowly slipped the head of his organ into her, working it gently, very, very slowly. He inched in bit by bit, and she never took her wide open eyes off him. Will had never felt one like this before. Her vagina seemed to be clamped to his organ. It was so tight, yet so wet, he could feel every rib, every part sucking onto his organ, as he slowly slid in and out. She held onto him and came and came, time and time again. And when he went in as far as he could go, she suddenly grabbed him, and pulled him into her. No longer the compliant little fat chick, but the out-of-control woman thrashing about, grabbing, biting, kicking, scratching, bucking, kissing, till he thought his lips might bleed, her tongue searching in his mouth, as she humped up against him, willing him on.

•

Will laughed as he remembered. That was the sweetest thing that had ever happened to him. In a VW, on a side street of all places. He hadn't done it in a V Dub since he was a kid. Then he had thought that there was no better place. And now he was sure he had been right. He hadn't bothered looking for the car after that, and caught a cab back to Angela's. When she saw him she exploded. "You dirty bastard," she screamed. "You did it, didn't you? Poor June, poor June." No matter how much he lied, it made no difference. He never saw June again, and she remained friends with Angela. The dirty bastard Will had done a number on her, and both of them made sure that Will never saw her again. That was an experience that he would always treasure, and never forget. He smiled whenever it crossed his mind.

2

WILL LOOKED OUT of the window of the old amphibian, as it droned over the Bahamian shallows. The sky was light blue, with the odd fluffy white cloud about. The sea was so shallow and clear that he could see the sandy bottom through the water, looking like a bluish desert. As the pilots prepared for the descent, Will watched them push the fuel-mixture levers into full rich, and ease the throttles back. He felt the old plane tip forward as they selected half-flaps, then tip forward again as they put down full flaps. Will was paying particular attention, as he had had a bad experience with a seaplane once, when they landed in a three-foot chop. He was focused on the door to make sure where he was going if they flipped the plane.

But it was fairly calm as the pilot selected fine pitch on the props for the final approach. The old amphibian touched down, bumped and skipped a few times, with Will focusing on the wing floats to make sure they didn't dig in, as the spray flew past the window, and the plane settled down. The pilot raised the flaps, applied power and taxied over to the ramp, lowering the wheels and applying more power. The old amphibian roared and waddled up the ramp on its wheels, stopping in front of the ramshackle shed that passed for an airport building.

It was hot, and looking as though it was going to get hotter. There were several dilapidated old taxis in a row: Chevs, Fords, and a real old Caddy, as he walked into the shed across a dusty, creaky wooden floor to stand in line at a counter with a sign that read "Bahamas Customs and Immigration". As the line crept up to the official, he could feel the sweat starting to trickle down his back. Will handed over his passport and immigration form to the large, sweating black man, whose uniform had three buttons open, exposing a huge gold chain. The man did not say one word, as he slowly riffled through the passport with ringed fingers. Without once looking up at Will, he finally stamped it, and languidly handed it back.

"Goddamn drug dealer," thought Will as he walked up to the ancient black Cadillac. The old man behind the wheel reading the newspaper said, "Whey's you goin'?"

"To the marina."

"They's no marina hey, but they's a haba."

"Well," said Will, "transport me to the haba then."

With a slow grinding of the starter, the old taxi came to life and shuffled off down the potholed dirt road between the scrub pines, trailing a light cloud of dust behind it.

"You going bone fishin'?" asked the old man.

"The bone fishing any good?"

"Lots of folks come down for de bone fish." The old man looked at Will for a while in the rear-view mirror then said, "Whey's you staying?"

"I'm being picked up by a yacht, and we're leaving right away."

"You going out on de big sailboat," the man said half to himself. "Dat's what I call a real boat, yas suh, dat's a real boat, dey used to have dem aroun' in my daddy's time. Yas suh, dat's a real boat."

They hadn't gone more than a half mile when the old taxi turned, creaking and groaning, through a gate. There before them lay a grassy area with a few sea-grape trees, and a beautiful white sandy beach surrounded by a white coral wall, with pastel-coloured water, in greens, blues, and all the shades in between going off into the distance. To the right there lay a modern concrete dock, to which were tied two charter Sports Fishermen.

As he paid off the taxi, a couple of figures came running up. They were tall, blond and suntanned, dressed in baggy shorts, polo shirts, and deck shoes. "Hi guys," said Will.

"We heard you were coming just minutes ago. We would have picked you up," said Graham, the first of the pair.

"No worries," said Will, "I didn't send a message, and if I had, you probably wouldn't have got it anyway."

"Great race," said Peter, the other one. "We watched it on TV. But that poor guy. That was a horrible way to go, burnt like that."

"That was bad, but I only saw the smoke," replied Will. "Where's the boat?"

"Round the corner," said Graham. "It's too shallow in here."

"This whole area is too shallow. How did you get it in here in the first place?"

"There's an old dredged channel, and we just made it. We are all provisioned and ready to go to sea. Forecast is good;

we should get a broad reach in about fifteen to twenty knots during the day, easing overnight. It should take us about four days," said Peter.

They walked down to the pier and climbed aboard the big Zodiac rubber dinghy. Peter pulled the starter-cord on the 25 horsepower Mercury outboard motor, and Graham cast off. They zipped across the bay, the dinghy skipping across crystal clear water in shades of green and blue. Around the point, cooled by the breeze, lay *Imperialist*, 100 feet of gleaming black ketch, with a giant rig towering over her. It always pleased him to see his boat. He never tired of her. At first glance she looked as though she might be old, but she was new. She had benefited from the best of the old with the best of the new. She had acres of teak decks, a comfortable deckhouse, and a huge cockpit, with a massive stainless-steel wheel bound in leather. She was built on laminated ring frames made up of glued quarter-inch strips, while tongue-and-groove strip planking formed the hull, with triple diagonal strips on the outside, protected by painted fibreglass.

Inside, the timber glowed golden in the afternoon light filtering down through the deck hatches, prisms, and brass portholes. At the foot of the companionway was a four-foot-square teak grating, which allowed water brought down by wet crew to drain into the bilges. Beside it stood a large, heated wet locker. No wet-weather gear was permitted past this point.

There was huge walk-in galley with massive gimballed stove and deep rails to keep pots and pans where they were supposed to be, countertops with deep fiddles and three sinks: one for dirty dishes, one for washing, and one for drying. Double stainless doors led into the industrial-grade fridge; stainless covers led to two top-loading freezers, one for short-term and one for long-term storage. Opposite the galley was a sophisticated dual-purpose navigation area and office, whose desk was surrounded by the latest in navigation and communication equipment, recessed into the surrounding bulkheads. All flat surfaces had deep fiddles to prevent anything left on them from falling onto the teak-and-holly cabin sole.

Past the galley came the majestic saloon, with settees upholstered in tartan wool. The deck-head, or ceiling, was of tongue-and-groove strip planking, painted cream, with laminated beams in polished satin varnish, providing a contrast to the cream of the deck-head. With her oil lamps lit at night, there was nowhere Will would rather be.

Imperialist didn't have much accommodation: there was only one double cabin. The rest were all good, single sea berths, but then Will wasn't planning to accommodate many people. *Imperialist* was set up as a sea boat; the bunks were designed to be comfortable in a sea way, not to impress the ignorant public at a boat show. Most of his friends and associates didn't like her; they were into their jets and gin palaces, which suited him just fine. Peter and Graham had been involved in her building and somehow had just stayed on. They knew every nut and bolt, and had become his non-judgemental friends. They weren't interested in motor racing, which was just the way he wanted it.

With the aid of powered winches, the three of them easily hauled the dinghy on deck, deflated it and dropped it into the sail locker. They started the engine, raised the anchor, and set off. They had to concentrate on their navigation as they left the island because they were in the old dredged channel with shallow water all around. Using a hand-bearing compass, they took the bearings off landmarks, keeping a running fix of their position. Bearings were recorded on a chart, as they eased their way down the poorly marked channel. *Imperialist* drew a lot of water, but now that they were in the deep, they were safe.

The wind came in as forecast. With the jib, staysail, main and mizzen set, *Imperialist* was soon sliding along, lifting to the following sea and running down the face of each swell with a warm wind and rushing water. By morning they would be out of sight of land, and Will knew that that was when he would really start to relax.

Will was in a deep sleep in his sea berth, with the lee cloth making his bunk a cocoon of safety and comfort.

"Come and give us a hand, Will. It's up to thirty-five knots. Better put on your gear, it's pissing down," said Graham, shaking his shoulder.

"Okay, okay," Will said, clambering over the lee cloth.

Imperialist was heeled way over; probably thirty degrees he thought, as he struggled into his wet-weather gear. At least the gear was dry, didn't stink, and wasn't cold. There was nothing worse than having to struggle into wet, smelly gear in the middle of the night, to go up on deck in the freezing cold.

Will clambered up the companionway, reached out through the hatch, and clipped his harness onto the D-ring bolted to the cockpit floor. *Imperialist* was charging down the sea, way overpowered, with the lee rail buried. Spray was flying everywhere; Peter was on the wheel, and white water was rushing down the lee side and over the deck. It was pitch black. The moon was nowhere to be seen; the wind-driven rain virtually horizontal. Only the phosphorescence-laden wake stood out as if floodlit. It was a magnificent sight, but she was struggling. They had to reduce sail. Peter and Graham had already rolled away the jib, leaving the staysail, with both main and mizzen fully eased, but it was not enough.

"What do you want to do?" Will asked.

"Get rid of the mizzen," Peter replied.

Graham said, "I'll set the lazy jacks, you let the halyard go."

Will unclipped his harness from the D-ring and re-clipped onto the jack line, as he carefully walked back to the mizzen mast. Graham hoisted the lazy jacks to catch the sail as it was dropped.

Will let the mizzen sheet run, taking the pressure off the sail. He uncoiled the mizzen halyard and flaked it out on the deck and flipped it off the winch. Graham dragged the flogging sail down, struggling in the wind to get it flaked as best they could, while Will attached the sail ties to hold it on the boom.

"How's that?" he shouted.

"Not enough," said Peter. "Better whack a reef in the main."

Their movement on deck was a pain in the backside, as they were always attached by the safety harness impeding their freedom to move around as needed. Peter let the main sheet go and eased the vang. Will released the halyard until he thought the mainsail was down enough to set the second reef. Will and Graham pulled the luff of the sail down till he could get the reefing eye over the reefing horn; it was heavy work, hard on the fingers, and nails, with the wind and rain lashing down, fork lightning flashing the main flogging, and thunder rolling in the background. They went back to the halyard winch, ground the main back up, and then back to the reefing winch, pulled in the slack leech line, and ground down the main with a winch. They were both breathing hard by this time, and Will felt as though his fingernails were half ripped out from dragging down the heavy mainsail.

Back to the cockpit, where Peter had already pumped the vang back on and re-trimmed the main. *Imperialist* was no longer overpowered, and had definitely picked up speed with the sail reduction. Looking aft was a magnificent sight: a rooster tail formed by the wake, highlighted by the phosphorescence: a trail of fire like an outsize rocket scorching across the sea. The sky was black; flashes of lightning would turn the night into a surreal day, emphasising the sensation of an express train hurtling through the wild night.

"She is hauling ass, boy, look at that rooster tail," said Will.

"Yep," said Peter, "this is what it's all about."

•

In the morning a beautiful sunlit day had replaced last night's heavy weather, and they were out of sight of land. The jib had been rolled out, the reef had been shaken out of the main, the mizzen had been reset, and all was well with the world. There was a long, low, leftover swell running, which would gently lift the stern and propel her forward in a long slide; then she would slow down as the next wave caught up, repeating the process. The sun was out; the sky was clear; the sea was the deep, deep blue of the Caribbean. Will was alone on deck; the other two were off watch, asleep below. The autopilot was steering as he drank his coffee and ate the fresh bread baked overnight. He was at peace with the world.

Watching, Will saw some dolphins in the distance. He picked up a winch handle and tapped the rub rail to attract their attention. They came hurtling over, diving under the boat and surfacing on the other side alongside the bows, playing in the bow wave. Will went forward and leant over the rail to watch them. One of them rolled onto its side and looked up at him. He never tired of dolphins; they always seemed full of the joy of life, playing in the bow wave, diving under the boat from side to side, eventually becoming bored. The yacht wasn't going fast enough to keep them entertained. With a final flurry, they left.

Will walked around the deck checking the various fittings to see whether there were any signs of wear and tear after last night. He loved this boat; he stood there admiring the acres of teak decks, the deckhouse, the big flush hatches, the huge winches, the large dorade vents, which sent cool air down below, yet kept out the water. *Imperialist* wasn't air-conditioned, and had no generator; she had no need of these trappings. She was well-ventilated with hatches and dorades. At anchor in the tropics a boom tent could be erected, which kept the direct sun off the deck, while a wind scoop helped to funnel the breeze down the hatches.

Peter stuck his head up through the companionway. "Why didn't you call me? It's my watch."

"I was enjoying it too much. Besides, I got a chance to eat the bread while it was hot."

"Did you leave any for me?"

"Not much. You reckon we should set the lines?"

"No, we're still going too fast. Maybe later."

"Did you hear those people on the VHF this morning?" asked Will, "You would have thought they'd been in a typhoon in the China Sea."

"People like that shouldn't be allowed to go to sea with radios."

The next morning they had fresh fried fish for breakfast.

Will had lightly fried the fillets in butter, adding heaps of salsa, serving it with freshly baked bread and Cuban coffee. Will sat on the side deck, resting against the cabin sides with the plate in his lap, looking out to sea. No land, no people, and fresh fish for breakfast. What could be better? They had set a line just after the sun rose on an almost flat sea with a light following wind. Graham had landed a dorado on a light rod, displaying all the dramatics of a record-breaking marlin. They had heaved to, bringing *Imperialist* to a standstill with the jib backed, while he stood on the transom and fought the fish. It was always a shame: the dorado came out of the water coloured in bright blues and greens, but the colours rapidly faded as the fish died.

Soon after, Will took the noon sight with the sextant, bringing the sun down to the horizon, using the mirrors on the sextant. Graham took the exact time of the sight, going down to the navigation table to work out their position, and their next stop.

They were anchored in as close as possible. *Imperialist* drew fifteen feet and they had anchored in twenty-four. They were not in as close as they would have liked; however, there were two other yachts in the bay and *Imperialist* needed a lot of swinging room. It wouldn't do to bash into somebody's 35-footer with their 100-foot boat. It was a lousy day; if it wasn't raining, it was drizzling. The cockpit was wet and all the hatches were closed. *Imperialist* swung on her anchor, first this way and that, as intermittent gusts blew off the steep cliff, with long periods of calm in between. During the gusts, Will could hear the anchor chain graunching and popping in the anchor roller. With nothing else to do, he turned on the Single Side Band radio for the forecast, waiting for it to warm up. He wasn't sure whether he would pick up anything, as he was underneath the cliff, but he might as well try, although he suspected it was a hopeless task.

The navigation station was one of Will's favourite spots. It was full of the latest technology, the very best in radios and wind instruments, set in beautiful, polished timber. There were both electronic and cable speedometers, in case one or the other failed; two sets of wind instruments, one mounted on each mast with all their attendant analogue displays: wind speed, amplified wind direction, depth sounder, and radar; two radio direction-finders, both inbuilt and hand-held; electronic and magnetic compasses; and a barometer mounted on the bulkhead along with the hand-bearing compasses.

There was a huge chart library laid in wide, shallow drawers, and a flat table on which fully opened charts could be worked on. Over the chart table was a prism, which intensified the natural light, flooding it over the table. Will sat there watching the wind speed, and direction needles roll back and forth, pondering what he was going to do for the rest of the miserable day. He kept looking outside, hoping for the weather to improve, but it seemed to grow worse every time he stuck his head out. Finally, he gave up and hopped into his bunk.

Next morning the world had changed. Flat calm, clear sky, and not a breath of wind. Will took a book and went forward, making himself comfortable on a bagged sail. He found he couldn't read, however, as his mind kept wandering. His conscience was bothering him, but why? He hadn't run off, Angela had. He could never understand women; they were never happy to leave well enough alone. If there was so much wrong with you, why did they want you? There was no logic to any of it. But he should have tried to contact her before he left, even though she had left a message saying not to.

His mind drifted to the new season, and the new car that should be ready for testing in a few weeks. He had never won the championship, and some said he never would. It wasn't that he lacked desire or skill: he was quick, and he was a good test driver. It was, they said, that he took too many risks, that he didn't play the odds. He wouldn't settle for second when first was too difficult; he wouldn't play the waiting game. Okay, he thought, if it's tactics they want, it's tactics they'll get. I can play the waiting game, I can play the odds. But odds men don't build boats like this. Boats with no resale value. Boats that take skill to sail and maintain.

He stood up and walked forward to the bow, looking back along the 100 feet of *Imperialist*. He was so proud of this yacht: it was his dream come true. He knew that if he ever had to sell her, he wouldn't recover a fraction of what it cost to build. People who could afford it wouldn't want it, but then, he was never going to sell her, was he? It was a beautiful day. The trade winds would come in later at a solid twenty knots. The sky was blue and so was the sea. He wished they could go on forever, and some day they would. But right now he knew he would hanker for the motor racing. He also knew how lucky he was to be able to earn an enormous amount of money doing something that he would gladly have paid for the privilege of doing.

They left that afternoon in a fifteen-knot breeze, which held up till the following afternoon. They put up the big kite, and just rolled along. They even kept it up overnight, as the weather was so settled. As they approached their new anchorage they studied the marine chart. It looked simple enough. It was wide open; however, there were some submerged rocks on the northern side of the entrance, which they had to keep clear of. Further in was an islet off a reef. It all looked very simple. *Imperialist* was a big boat, needing plenty of water, and they had never anchored here before.

They dropped the sails at the entrance, and motored in. They needed to charge the batteries, and run down the freezers. Will took bearings with the hand-bearing compass, taking a sight on a point that he recognised on the chart. Then he took two more at different points, trying for an inverted triangle. He called out each bearing as he made it, which Graham wrote down, and then laid them off on the chart. The lines met in what was called a cocked hat, as in Nelson's time. Within that triangle was where they were: the smaller the triangle the more accurate the position. Will compared the depth-sounder reading with the position on the chart. The procedure hadn't really changed since Captain Cook's time. In fact, Will had seen charts still in use that had been drawn by Cook.

It was always a little tense going into an unfamiliar anchorage, especially an unmarked one. Even though the charts might be accurate, there was always the possibility that they could make a mistake and end up on a rock, or worse. Will slowed down to four knots, then two, and when four fathoms came up on the depth-sounder he slipped the gear lever into reverse. When the speed read zero, he signalled Graham to let the anchor go. There was fifteen knots on the wind-speed indicator, as *Imperialist* drifted back, beam on to the wind, while the anchor chain rattled out. Graham knew how much chain to let run — six times the depth was the rule of thumb.

This would allow the chain to rest on the bottom, so that the anchor shank would lie flat, enabling the anchor to bite into the sand or mud. The anchor chain had little plastic tassels in specific colours at specific distances along the chain, so that when the right colour came up Graham knew how much chain had gone. He could then tighten the windlass brake, to stop any more chain going out. When the chain stopped running, *Imperialist*'s bow was pulled into the wind. To make sure, Will applied some power in reverse, and took a bearing on two opposite hills to see whether the anchor was holding. Satisfied, he cut the engine, and started covering up the instruments in the cockpit, while the others were downstairs switching them off. "Beer o'clock, guys."

3

Two weeks later, a 747 stood on final approach into Heathrow. Among all the business-suited men and well-dressed women in first class, Will was fast asleep, sporting two weeks' worth of beard, jeans, T-shirt, and salt-encrusted deck shoes. The stewardess shook him awake. "Sir, straighten your seat back, please. We are coming in to land."

He pushed the footrest away, straightening up the seat.

"Would you like a hot towel?"

"Thanks," he replied.

She looked closely at him. "Aren't you that racing-car driver? You certainly look like him."

"Nah," said Will, "not me. They are all runts."

She walked off with a puzzled look. He watched her as she walked up the aisle. The odds men would like her, he thought. Blonde, tall and thin, big boobs, and no backside. Not for me — women have to look like women.

He cleared customs with a minimum of fuss, and caught a

taxi to his flat. It was what he called "a convenient place". He had bought it on the advice of his accountant, recommended by his lawyer, professionally decorated by a woman in a kaftan who didn't wear underwear, and looked after by a couple recommended by somebody else. It was a very sensible investment, he supposed, but he couldn't have cared less. He wasn't into sensible or fashionable investments.

He threw down his bag, picked up the phone and called Ray, who exploded. "Where have you been? Why didn't you call? The whole world is looking for you, and we are testing next week."

"Where?"

"Spain."

"Good."

"But where have you been?"

"You know where I've been."

"Why didn't you call?"

"I couldn't call."

"Of course you could. She's looking for you."

"I'll see you in the morning."

"Call her."

Will hung up.

Next morning, he drove in bumper-to-bumper traffic to the factory, where the cars were developed and built. As he walked through the front doors he was greeted in typically enthusiastic style by the receptionist, who planted a big wet kiss on his cheek. "Welcome back, Will. What have you been up to?"

"Oh, the usual. What about you?"

"Not nearly as exciting a time as you've been having," she said with a huge wink. "There are a lot of messages and mail for you."

He walked into his office wondering what all that was about. It became clear when he saw, in the middle of his desk, the local tabloid newspaper. On the front page was a picture of him with the caption, "Race ace ditches pregnant fiancée."

He leapt up from his desk and stormed into Ray's office. "What do you know about this?" he demanded, throwing the newspaper down on the desk.

Ray looked up with an innocent expression on his face and asked, "Is it true?"

"You know it's the bloody opposite."

"You mean she got *you* pregnant?"

"For Christ's sake, it's no bloody joke. How the hell did this get into the paper?"

"You know what these scandal sheets are like, they'll print anything, and the rest of the media is going to make your life a misery. There already have been several calls this morning."

"I'm going to call the lawyer now and get him to start defamation proceedings."

"Best of luck," replied Ray. "These people spend their lives fighting off legal proceedings."

Back in his office Will called his lawyer. "What do you mean there is no point suing? Do you mean these people can print anything they like and get away with it?"

"That is the net effect," replied the lawyer, "and if you ask the courts for an injunction the rest of the media will pick up on it, and there will be nothing you can do about that either, because it will be in the public arena."

"Who owns the paper?"

"As a matter of fact, I am going to brunch at Freddy Manning, the Managing Director's house, next Sunday morning. I could drop a discreet word. Not that I think it would do any good, mind you."

"That's too late," said Will. "It has to be stopped now."

"Freddy would never respond to that sort of pressure."

"Give me his number. I'll call him."

"It won't do you any good telephoning him. It might even make it worse."

"Just give me the bloody number."

Will telephoned Freddy, and got nowhere. Yes, they had the story on good authority. No, they were not responsible for hurting people; they were there to print the news. No, they would not divulge their sources.

He telephoned his various contacts in the media, whose advice was that there was nothing to be done as the paper, and its managing editor, were all without principle and the best thing to do was forget it.

He dialled her number not expecting her to be home, not quite sure whether he wanted her to be. She was home.

"How are you?" he asked.

"Fine."

'Have you seen the newspaper?"

"Yes."

"Well?"

"I don't know where that came from."

"What do your parents think?"

"They think that I have done the right thing."

"They would, but no, I mean the newspaper."

"Father thinks that it is just as well, at least everybody knows."

"Knows what?"

"That we have split up."

"That's not quite how I read it, in any case what about the rest of it?"

"The rest of what?"

"For Christ's sake, can't you give me a straight answer for once in your life?"

"Will, if you are going to be abusive, I am hanging up."

"Hang up, then."

She hung up.

Well, he thought, I guess that's that. At least her father will be pleased. A senior career civil servant, he and Will had absolutely nothing in common, mild dislike and lack of interest in each other had gradually settled into an acceptance of the inevitable. But now they were both saved from having to put up with each other for the rest of their lives. That was the upside; however, Will wasn't that sure that not seeing her again was exactly what he wanted, and he hadn't found out whether she really was pregnant.

•

On the way back to the factory, Will thought that maybe talking to his lawyer hadn't been a total waste of time; he did have a name, a home telephone number, an address, and the date and time of a party. The least he could do would be to embarrass Freddy at his own party. The house isn't far from here, he thought, I'll go and have a look. He drove through the upper-class neighbourhood looking for the address. On the corner he found a large, two-storey Tudor-style house with immense wrought-iron gates, on about a half-acre of well-developed garden, surrounded by a high concrete wall, painted white. He was sure this place would be very secure against intruders;

however, what he had in mind was not intrusion.

As he swung through the gate of the factory, he saw the chief of security. "Bill," he said, "what do you think of paedophiles?"

"You mean, a man who interferes with children?"

"Yes, especially one who has been getting away with it for years, without anybody doing anything about it."

"The pervert should be shot. Who is he?"

"No, we can't do that, but what if we could really embarrass him?"

"How would we go about doing it?"

"Well, what if he had a nice white wall surrounding his house, and some of his victims were to spray-paint their experiences on his nice, white wall the night before he threw a big society breakfast party?"

Bill looked thoughtful. "This wouldn't have anything to do with that bit in the scandal sheet, would it?"

"Could be," said Will.

"I know some young tearaways who would love a job like that. They're already spraying graffiti for nothing anyway."

Will passed over a handful of cash. "Thanks, Bill."

•

Will was at another of the endless round of cocktail parties that went with the promotion of products sold by the sponsors of motorsport. It was at a huge old country house outside London. He wouldn't have minded a house like this one, but he wasn't sure what he would do with it, if he had. He had just broken free from more journalistic questions about his impending fatherhood, and was fed up with the whole thing. He didn't know whether he was going to be a father or not, and he hadn't ditched anybody either. He stood in a corner, nursing a glass of iced water, trying to make it look like vodka, and hoping nobody was going to ask him any more stupid questions. He thought about that for a minute, concluding that if he didn't want to have to answer stupid questions, he should find some other way of making a living.

He felt an arm around his waist, and probing fingers searching under his belt. He recognised the perfume and felt the soft, insistent touch of a pelvis on his thigh. She whispered, her mouth touching his ear, "*You* did it, didn't you?"

"Did what?"

"Ruined Freddy's brunch, and the rest of his life for that matter."

"How could I do a thing like that?"

"I don't know," she said, "but it's just the sort of thing you would do."

"Rubbish," said Will, finding it difficult not to crack a smile.

"How is she?"

"You'd have a far better idea than I would. I haven't seen her for two weeks. Am I to be a father?"

He felt the tip of her tongue touch his ear. "Not that I know of. You should keep your affairs simple. Life is complicated enough as it is."

The pelvis snuggled up against his thigh, and he remembered her thick growth of dark brown pubic hair, and her total lack of inhibition.

"Will, when are we going to see each other again?"

"We're seeing each other right now."

"What about right now?"

"Where is his lordship?"

"Over there, salivating over some bimbo's cleavage."

"Okay. Where?"

"The powder room. Follow me in a few minutes."

When Will entered the room she was leaning against the sink, resting on her hands and he could see the outline of her body as if she had nothing on. She was a very tempting woman. "It's been a long time, Will." She started pulling at his belt and pulling down his fly. She was breathing hard. "Hurry Will, hurry," she moaned, as his pants dropped to his ankles. He pulled up her dress and was not surprised that she was wearing no underwear. He lifted her up onto the sink, seeing her luxurious growth of pubic hair and navel. He entered her in a rush. She was already soaking wet, as he knew she would be. There was no mucking around with this one. She put her legs around his back and supported herself on her arms. "Give it to me, Will, give it to me now. All of it. That's it! More, Will, deeper, harder, that's it, give it to me!"

He grabbed her by the cheeks of her writhing backside and pulled her in to him. He liked the feel of her, the smooth skin of her rear end, and the wetness of her. She was moving more slowly now after the initial urgency, her head was thrown back; her mouth was wide open and her eyes were closed, savouring every bit of it. His pants were down around his ankles tripping him up; trying to kick them free and keep up with this woman was a major mission. He looked over his shoulder to make sure that he hadn't kicked them into a pool of water.

"Forget the goddam trousers, Will, give to me." She was putting her whole heart into it, and he knew the counter-top wouldn't last much longer — it had started to creak and groan. "Hurry up, Will, stay with me, that's it, that's it." Her eyes had rolled back in her head and her mouth was wide open as she gasped for breath. "Oh God, oh God, I'm coming, come with me, Will, hurry, come with me!"

There was a tapping sound on the door. Panic. "Occupied!" shouted Will in his last gasp.

"Sorry," replied the knocker.

After they caught their breath, they both started laughing, as they disentangled themselves. "It's a good thing that he didn't knock a second sooner," she said.

Will walked back into the party and saw Ray. "Where have you been? I've been looking all over for you." Ray looked at him closely. "You look a bit flushed. You haven't been pegging her ladyship again, have you? Aren't you in enough trouble as it is?"

"You are just jealous," Will laughed. "Why were you looking for me?"

"A couple of journalists want a ride down with you."

"Which ones?"

Ray told him. "Yeah, that's okay."

"Will, why don't you call her?"

"I've already called her. It's all over."

"I don't believe that," said Ray.

4

WILL WAS IN the factory for a seat fitting, sitting motionless in the chassis of the new car, wearing a green plastic garbage bag, and waiting for the gooey-looking two-pot mix to harden around his body. When the seat was finished, it would be the mirror image of his back and sides, and would hold him securely like a fist in the cockpit.

The seating position was one of the many fine details that made up the preparation of a racing car. Nothing could be left out. The placing of all the pedals had to suit him exactly. Despite the six-point harnesses, if the seat fitting was not right, the G loadings in the corners and under-braking would force him to one side or the other. Everything had to be right: the seat, the pedals, the relationship between brake and accelerator; the foot rest had to be the same height as the accelerator pedal, the heel stop had to be right so that he could brake using his ankle as a fulcrum. Braking had to be controlled, with his heel on the stop, allowing him to push down on the brake pedal with the ball of his foot, giving him total control over the braking force. The accelerator pedal had to be placed so that by rolling his foot, he could blip the throttle on down-shifts.

The steering wheel was tiny, bound in leather. On the right and very close to the steering wheel was the gear lever, short and stumpy at elbow height, almost touching the bodywork. In front was a tiny screen, not to look through, but to deflect the wind over his head. Above the wheel and directly in front was the rev counter, a large chronometric dial with a needle that flicked back and forth, showing the engine revs. Attached to the rev-counter needle was the tell-tale, which swung with the rev counter, leaving behind a record of the highest revs, telling on the driver if he over-revved. Will seldom looked at the rev counter, unless he wanted to see how many engine revs he was pulling at a particular spot — he could hear when to change gear. He had to keep the engine operating in its narrow performance band. Any mistake or deliberate over-revving could result in damage to the engine. On one side of the rev counter was an oil-pressure gauge; on the other side a water-temperature gauge. There was no point having anything else, as there was no time to read it. In truth, he hardly ever looked at either the oil or water gauges after the engine warmed up, unless he suspected something was wrong.

On the right-hand side of the dashboard were his three most important switches: the master switch, the oxygen supply, and the fire extinguisher, with the manual backups. Will had trained himself that if he lost control of the car and a crash was inevitable, he would hit the master switch and kill the electronics. He had also trained himself not to panic, and not to push the fire extinguisher until he actually saw fire. He had done that once, before a fire had started. Later, when he had needed the fire extinguisher, the bottle was empty. Luckily he had got away without being fried.

He sat in the seat with his bottom virtually on the floor of the riveted aluminium monocoque chassis, his legs straight out in a semi-reclining position. Between the double-skinned outer and inner panels were the fuel bladders. Beneath his knees was the fire-extinguisher bottle, and above was the instrument binnacle. Over his head was the roll bar; bolted to the back of the chassis was the Cosworth V8 engine. Attached to the back of the engine was the Hewland gearbox, with the rear suspension and wing mounted off that. The engine was part of the chassis. The engine and gearbox were the connection between the rear suspension and the chassis.

Over it all was fitted the fibreglass bodywork, with the nose section and mid-section over the cockpit, and the rear section over the engine and gearbox. Attached to the front bodywork was the front wing, and hanging off a support above the gearbox was the rear wing: like upside down aircraft wings, producing downforce instead of lift. He was almost entirely enclosed, with his head just sticking out of the cockpit. On either side opposite the instrument panel were the rear-view mirrors, for what little good they did. He was in a cocoon of fuel, with a shrieking 465 horsepower V8 behind his head, a missile, waiting to transport him to his doom if he wasn't careful.

A Formula One car was built to its limits. It was as light as the rules allowed, as aerodynamic as possible, as low to the ground as practical, and with as much horsepower as possible. Everything was at its maximum. The G loads on the driver were huge. Braking was a science in itself. Like everything else, it was at the maximum. The tyres were at their limit. The driver's neck was under massive load, with the weight of cornering, acceleration and deceleration. The driver's head would be subject to three-dimensional G forces that would cause the average person's neck to collapse within a couple of laps.

5

WILL WALKED AROUND the twin-engine Beechcraft Baron, checked the fuel and oil, moved the control surfaces back and forth to make sure that they were free, checked that the pitot tubes were clear, and checked the propellers for any sign of damage. He opened the front locker and stowed their baggage in the nose compartment, opened the rear door, and let in one of his passengers. He climbed up on the wing and eased himself across into the front left seat. The other journalist followed him in, closing the door behind him. Will reached across to make sure that the door was securely locked. "Put on your seat belts," he said.

Will flipped on the master switches, reached over with his right hand, pushing the mixture controls to full rich, pushed the propeller-pitch lever to full fine, and set the left-hand throttle to quarter. He turned the starter for the left engine. As the engine turned over, he jiggled the throttle lever back and forth till the engine caught. After it had settled down, he checked the oil pressure, then pulled the lever back to low idle, before starting the second engine. When he was satisfied that both were running properly, he switched on the avionics.

Will looked over the array of instruments carefully, setting the required frequencies on the radios. He enjoyed looking at the instrument panel, with all the gauges and switches beautifully laid out on the silver-grey panel. He always appreciated quality. He held the solid white moulded control wheel in his left hand, rotating it left and right and pulling it fully back into his stomach, to make sure all the controls were free. The wheel was contoured to fit his left hand perfectly: it even had a thumb rest. The middle held a clock with a stopwatch mounted in it. At his thumb was the transmit button for the radios, another one for the auto trim. He put on the headphones and pushed the transmit button. "November 6883. Taxi instructions."

"November 6883. Cleared to one-three, hold clear of the active runway."

"Roger, cleared to one-three."

Will released the brakes and eased the throttles forward. The engine noise built up and the plane waddled out on to the taxiway. He steered with the rudder pedals, making judicious taps of the toe brakes as they rolled down the taxiway. Just short of the runway he stopped, locked the brakes, and started the final pre-flight checks. He ran up one engine and then the other, checking the magnetos by switching off one and monitoring the drop in revs. Satisfied, he repeated the procedure with the other engine. Then he cycled the propeller pitch to ensure that the propellers would change pitch as required. He noticed that his passengers were slightly apprehensive about the drop in revs as he switched the magnetos on and off; particularly the "waa

waa waa" noise as he cycled the prop pitch.

"You're a bit brave flying with a racing car driver. You know they don't have much of a record as pilots," he said to relax them a bit.

As this didn't seem to relieve their apprehension, he continued with his pre-flight drill. He pulled the control wheel back again and rotated it left and right to double-check that all control surfaces were free and clear. Will was a careful pilot. He never forgot the sayings that had been drilled into his head by his instructors when he was a student pilot. He never forgot that there were old pilots and bold pilots, but there weren't any old and bold pilots.

He reached down by his right leg, checking the trim wheel, and called the tower. "November 6883 ready."

"November 6883 cleared onto one-three for immediate takeoff; call at three thousand."

"Roger, cleared to three thousand."

Will checked that the mixture was full rich, the props were full fine, and the flaps set to takeoff position. Turning to his passengers, he asked, "All strapped in?" He released the brakes, and slowly pushed the throttle levers forward to full. He checked the instruments again as the plane accelerated, keeping his right hand on the throttle levers, his left hand on the wheel, lining the plane up with the white line in the centre of the runway using the rudder pedals. At 90 knots he slowly pulled back on the wheel, and she left the ground. He flipped the gear lever, and the wheels came up. A moment later he raised the flaps, and pulled the throttles back to cruise climb. At 3000 feet he called the tower; they cleared him to his next check point.

As they climbed, Will engaged the autopilot, gradually

pulling back on the mixture levers, leaning out the fuel as the altitude increased, and the atmospheric pressure dropped. At 9500 feet they levelled off and he pulled the throttles back to 65 per cent cruise power, reset the prop pitch, and synchronised the engines. They were over the cloud base. Up here it was a beautiful day with a clear blue sky. "Like flying over cotton wool," said one of the journos.

Will found flying peaceful, enjoying the technicality of it, and flew within the bounds of what he considered safe, not totally agreeing with the bureaucrats' view of safety. The time passed quite quickly as his passengers lost their apprehension and chatted about motor racing in general. Will couldn't resist asking what could be done about the scandal sheets, which created a lively discussion till it was time to land.

Will called the tower, which responded immediately: "November 6883 cleared to descend to level 5 QNH 1002, winds from the north-east at eight knots. Advise at level 5."

He disengaged the altitude hold on the autopilot, and rolled the pitch wheel forward. Setting the rate of descent at 500 feet per minute, so as not to be too hard on their ears, he watched the airspeed build up as they lost altitude. As the altitude decreased and the atmospheric pressure increased, he pushed the mixture control lever forward, enriching the fuel.

The countryside was dry and sparsely populated. There appeared to be clusters of small villages with very little traffic on the roads. "November 6883 at three thousand."

"November 6883 cleared to land on two-five," came a voice with a heavy Spanish accent. Will clicked the transmit switch twice, flicked off the autopilot, pulled the throttles back to half, and pushed the mixture levers to full rich. A couple of minutes later he reduced power again, pulled down the gear-selector lever and heard the clunk as the wheels locked in place. He checked for the three greens, indicating that the wheels were down and locked, selecting half-flaps. He re-trimmed the aircraft, setting up his rate of descent. Will took great pleasure in making his landings with one power setting, not having to increase and decrease power to maintain his glide path. Few pilots, even the ones flying the commercial passenger jets, seemed to be able to judge an approach, and keep the rate of descent steady, without increasing and decreasing power. He could easily tell the good pilots from the bad by the smoothness of their approach. As the speed bled off, he selected full flaps. His final act was to push the propeller controls to full-fine pitch. The book said that full fine was one of the first settings on approach in case a go-around was required. Will did not like hearing the revs surge up as he pushed the levers forward. It was too crude. It was like some incompetent stuffing a car into a lower gear, without equalising the revs. He touched down right on the markers. His passengers had no idea how pleased he was with himself, and had no appreciation of the skill involved.

Ray met them at the airport, and on the way to the hotel said, "We have a barbecue invitation for this evening at a Señor Santiago's," he said. "Everybody's going, so you'd better come."

"Who do you mean by everybody?"

"Us, the team, everybody."

"Oh," Will said. "Us, the team, everybody. That's fine. It's those other everybodys that I can't hack."

"You didn't seem to do too badly at the last one. I don't know how you get away with it."

"Skill, Ray, skill."

They turned off the main road in a high-speed convoy of team cars, arriving at stone gateposts, and an ornate, black iron gate leading into a driveway bordered by poplars. In the distance stood a massive single-storey stucco hacienda, with red-tile roofs, surrounded by large verandas, supported by white columns. Off to the side were several outbuildings of a similar style. As they drove up to the house, the horses in the paddocks started to gallop alongside the cars, their tails up and their manes flowing in the wind. It was a wonderful sight, the horses pounding along beside the car, and Will was immediately glad he had come. They drove up to the magnificent house, turning into a brick courtyard covered by large, shady trees, where they were instructed to park among the many cars already there. "Now this is what I call a real house," said Will.

They were escorted down a tree-lined path to a huge swimming pool, bordered by a large flagstone patio and a magnificent brick barbecue. Off to one side was a young cow on a spit, being attended by two men using large paint brushes to baste it with sauce from a stainless-steel pot hanging from a black steel tripod. The spit was surrounded by people drinking margaritas, and slicing off titbits, as the meat became crisp on the outside.

"We'd better go and make ourselves known to our hosts," said Ray.

"Okay," said Will. "Let's get it over with." They walked up to the front steps where they were received by a couple who could have been any age between late forties and early sixties. Ray said, "Will, I would like you to meet Señor and Señora Santiago."

Will bowed slightly and said, "Señor, Señora."

"Welcome, welcome," said Señor Santiago.

"Thank you for inviting us," said Will.

"It was our pleasure, Señores."

"You have a magnificent home," said Will. "It is one of the most beautiful places I have ever seen."

"Thank you, it was built by my great-grandfather over a hundred years ago, and hopefully it will remain in our family for another hundred years. As you see, it is a working ranch. We raise horses and bulls for the corrida."

Señora Santiago looked at Will to see his reactions. "Have you been to the corrida, Señor Archer?" she asked.

"Please call me Will. I have been a few times in Mexico; I find it fascinating. I have never seen the top matadors, but I intend to one of these days."

"Then you must be our guest," she said. "On Saturday there will be some good up-and-coming matadors to see."

"These are busy men, they may not be able to come, and we cannot take them away from their business," her husband interjected.

"I won't be able to make it, but we'll be finished testing by Saturday, and Will may still be here," Ray replied.

"If I can escape, I'd like to accept your kind offer," said Will.

"Good. We will save a seat for you in our box. When you get to the ring, just ask for me, and you will be directed there. This motor racing is a bit like bullfighting, no?"

"Yes, I suppose it could be," Will said. "It's funny, the first thing I ever wanted to be as a child was a bullfighter."

"It is never too late, Señor Will."

They walked into the house together, instantly feeling the

difference in temperature. The walls must have been two feet thick; the floors were red clay tiles scattered about with oriental rugs; the furniture was heavy and old; and the white ceiling was supported by huge, dark adzed wooden beams, the white walls covered with paintings and tapestries. There were no other people in the house. Will had the feeling that he was being given the grand tour. He found himself very attracted to the Santiagos; despite the difference in their ages, he knew that they could become his friends. They were obviously very wealthy, living in magnificent surroundings, and were a striking couple, he tall and grey, she almost as tall, with grey-streaked black hair, combed back into a bun, in the Spanish style.

He was attracted to a photograph of a young matador. "One of the greats?" he asked.

"He would have been had he survived."

"Who was he?" asked Will, almost knowing the answer before he asked.

"Our son," she said.

Will turned away because he did not want them to see the tears come to his eyes. Why should he react this way to somebody he didn't know? He felt as though he had been brought into this room for a purpose, as if his seeing the photograph was no accident. "I am so very sorry," he said, the words catching in his throat.

6

THEY WERE AT the track early next morning. The new car didn't look a lot different from last season's, which had been a development of the previous season's car that had almost killed him. That car had been a radical departure from the norm, "a breakthrough", according to the designers. It had taken them most of last year to get it working. It had been very fast in a straight line, with tremendous brakes. It also had been very fast in the wet. But in the dry it would roll too much, and break the half-shafts. Will had never driven a single-seater that you could two-wheel. It was fantastic to drive, but you couldn't win races with it. It was incredible in fast corners; he could drift it in the most glorious slides. It was spectacular, especially when he was two-wheeling it, and it had fantastic brakes. So why couldn't it win races? Because it rolled too much. Will could drive up the inside under-braking, overtake, and then sit there with wheelspin, as the cars he had just passed took off and left him standing. It had taken them all year to make the changes that allowed him to win the last race of the season.

He hoped they had retained the strengths, and reduced the downside. In winter trials and in their wind tunnel they had improved the aerodynamics, so that now the car should be as fast in a straight line but, just as importantly, it would leave a smoother wake behind, making it more difficult for the car following to slipstream him, which had been a real problem at the last race. It was just as narrow; however, Ray reckoned it wouldn't roll as much. Last year's car was so narrow and the seating position was so far forward that Will could read Goodyear on the outside of the tyres. The seating position had been moved back, for which he was grateful, because having his legs out ahead of the front wheels, ready to be ripped off in an accident, didn't thrill him a bit. It had been a dramatically good-looking car. But it didn't work as it was far too radical.

Will had received his testing instructions from Ray. The car was set up fully soft with the wings on minimum downforce. He was to do one lap at low speed before coming back into the pits to check for leaks. The mechanics pushed the car forward as he engaged first gear with a graunch. He put his foot lightly on the accelerator. The car jerked, jerked, jerked forward, till he could get it into second, allowing the revs to build to 6000 rpm before changing to the next gear. He completed his lap never exceeding 6000, paying attention to the way the car felt. He watched the gauges for any sign of a problem. He was effectively cruising around, but he could tell a lot from this low-speed test. He could tell whether the car felt balanced, whether it felt as a whole unit rather than a front and a back. He returned to the pits where the mechanics looked for any obvious problems, checking the tyre pressures.

Ray plugged in the communication lead and asked, "How is it?"

"Good," answered Will. "But the old one felt good as well."

He went out again, this time to begin testing; he was to concentrate on the second-gear right-hander leading onto the main straight. This was the most important corner on the race track because it led out onto the longest straight. The speed out of this corner determined the speed at the end of the straight. Speed on the straight meant the highest speed for the longest time, which meant faster lap times, and made overtaking easier.

On the first lap he let the car roll through the corner, assessing the feel. Next lap he increased his approach speed. The car started to push the front, understeering, not turning into the apex as it had at a lower speed. He went straight back to the pits. While he talked to Ray, the mechanics checked the car again. Ray instructed them to tighten the rear roll bar one inch. This would reduce the rear roll, increasing the load on the outside front wheel, reducing understeer. Will went out again. The adjustment worked. Good: the car was responsive to change. That was an important sign; the old car had not been at all responsive. He increased his speed through the corner and began to apply more power on the exit. It now started to understeer as he left the apex. He returned to the pits where they increased the compression on the rear shock absorbers, reducing the weight transfer to the rear as the power came on, allowing the fronts to work better. Will was still suspicious, waiting for the old wheelspin problem to reappear. He went out again. The improvement was immediate. As the day went on, the car was gradually brought up to racing spec. Not all changes worked: only one change was ever made at a time, and if that didn't work, the car was put back to where it had been before another change was tried. Every change was recorded; nothing was left to guesswork; they always worked from a proven base. As Ray always said, "You can't build a house on poor foundations." By the end of the day they were at racing speed on that corner. Tomorrow they would be going onto two or three more, but now they were not starting from scratch. Will felt hopeful: the wheelspin problem had not shown up. Yet.

By Friday, they were nearly two-and-a-half seconds faster than their best qualifying time last year. Everybody was pleased, especially as the times were achieved on old engines. Will was weary, but he had enjoyed it, not just the lack of the frustrations of last year, but also the camaraderie of the team, all working together, without any outside distractions. He liked the team members and they liked him. Word had got out about the newspaperman, and they thought it was the greatest thing, only *their* driver would pull a stunt like that.

7

On Saturday, Will went to the bullring, where he found a huge crowd with a very festive atmosphere. He was immediately escorted to the Santiagos' box after identifying himself, and was received most graciously by his hosts, saying they were glad that he could come and that they hoped he would enjoy himself. They asked Will how the testing had gone, and as he explained, he realised that they understood the basic concept of what he was talking about, without any prior knowledge of racing cars. He had surprised himself by explaining, something which he would never normally bother to do, as most people didn't understand. He was glad he had; they understood risk, and the need to reduce it by practice and preparation. They also understood balance, smoothness, and the moment to turn your back on the bull, or the moment not to overtake when it couldn't be done.

This was far and away the best bullfight he had ever been to; however, it was made much better by having the commentary of people who lived the sport. The bulls were like racehorses with horns, most of them coming from the Santiagos: their speed and agility was mind-boggling. He figured that if the picadors on the horses hadn't slowed up the bulls, there was no way that the matadors would last more than a couple of fights. He knew what the do-gooders had to say about bullfighting, but wondered whether any of them had been to a meat works. If he was a bull, he'd much rather live the good life, and go down fighting, than be lined up and slaughtered.

He sensed a presence and turned. Walking towards the box was a woman of about his age dressed in a white cotton material, wearing a broad-brimmed white hat. The dress swished around, outlining long, golden-tanned legs that went on forever, ending in flared hips. Will dared not look at where the two legs met. It wasn't the dress or the walk or the body so much that struck him; it was the eyes. He felt himself involuntarily rising from his seat. As she drew closer, he could see an amused look on her face. She knew that she had struck him dumb. Her eyes had not left his, and he could now see that they were green, not just green but emerald, and that her hair beneath the hat was either dark brown or black. He immediately sensed that this was his hosts' daughter. But there was somebody with her, an older man, a powerful man, both physically and in status.

After introductions, Señor Santiago told Will that the man was a politician of some note and that their daughter, Isobel, was being groomed for a political career. This did not make the situation any clearer, because Will wasn't sure of the daughter's relationship with this man. He could sense that there was less warmth towards the man than towards himself, and he was reasonably sure that he had been invited to the bullfight to meet the daughter. She wasn't making it any easier for him to figure out the situation, because the minute she turned those eyes on him his brain malfunctioned.

The Santiagos compensated by trying to include him in all the goings-on, but, as the man couldn't speak English and Will couldn't speak Spanish; the flow of conversation was awkward. After the bullfight, his hosts invited Will to a nearby restaurant. Will tried to avoid going by making excuses. The daughter pooh-poohed his attempt to get away, knowing full well what he was doing. They all walked to the restaurant, which was jam-packed with a noisy after-bullfight crowd. Walking behind her only made it worse. She had the most fabulous backside he had ever laid his eyes on. And the white dress was no help, making it almost more than he could stand.

As they were shown to a large beautiful old marble dining table, they passed other patrons who either clapped or stood up, shaking Señor Santiago's hand, with much back-slapping and congratulations. Will looked around at the old white walls covered in bullfighting photos and posters as the daughter arranged the seating, placing him directly opposite her. Will supposed that she wanted him in a position where she could burn him up with those eyes. He thought, "The politico knows exactly what is going on." Will decided that Isobel wasn't going to turn him into a mug. Concentrating on the parents gave him the breathing space to get himself under some sort of control. Her father had ordered for them all, lamb shanks in a huge earthenware pot with black beans, and a good Tempranillo in large goblets, followed by the best flan he had ever tasted. Over great espresso, her father asked Will when he was leaving, and was told that he would depart the following morning. When

Isobel asked him where he was going, Will told her that he was going to England for a day, and then to his boat for a week.

"What sort of boat is it?" asked Isobel.

"It's a sail boat, in the Bahamas," replied Will.

"So, what will you be doing in the Bahamas?"

"Not much; I will be leaving for Central America."

"Oh," she said. "A big boat, then. How big, and where are you going exactly?"

"A hundred feet, and to an island called Isla de Piña."

As they left the restaurant, Isobel asked him where his car was. When he told her he had come by taxi, and that he would get one back to the hotel, she offered to run him back to the hotel, as they had all come in their own cars. The politician said goodnight and left, and the parents, after extracting promises that Will would come and see them again, left also.

Will and Isobel got into her car. As she started the engine she said, "You have made quite an impression on my parents."

"They are wonderful people," said Will. "I don't find people that I relate to so easily very often."

"You remind them of my brother."

"I thought it might be something like that."

"I think they see you as a way of continuing the dynasty."

"What do you mean?" he replied, already knowing the answer.

"Use your head," Isobel replied irritably. "I am the only child, and none of my suitors have been to my parents' satisfaction. While my brother was alive, it did not matter, but now it makes a big difference."

"What about the politico?"

"What about him?"

"Is he a suitor?"

"What do you think?"

"I think he would like to be."

"Perhaps, but it is not that way. I am determined to represent the people of this area, and he helps. Like my parents I am, how you say, taken by you, but it is not to be. You see, my parents like you because you remind them of my brother, their son. I like you for other reasons," she said, turning those eyes on him again. "But it would end up in tragedy, and that neither my parents nor I could bear."

Will was not sure that he had grasped all this, although he had an inkling. "Why would it end up in tragedy?"

"Because you would end up like my brother, and my parents could not stand it a second time, and I would be a widow."

Will was speechless; he had no intention of dying, or of marrying anyone, and here his marriage and news of his death, as the man said, was greatly exaggerated. As she drove, she had a half-amused expression on her face. "You are having me on, aren't you?" he asked.

"Having me on?" she questioned.

"Teasing me."

"What do you think?" She swung into the hotel and parked the car. He expected her to say a breezy goodbye then, but she didn't. She got out of the car and walked with him through the lobby to the elevator. He expected her to say goodbye there, but she didn't. When they reached the door of his suite he expected her to say goodbye there, but she didn't.

He opened the door and walked in after her. She turned around and faced him. His mind was racing; he wasn't going to push this, let her set the pace. She put her arms around him. He felt the full length of her body against him. She fitted perfectly as if they had been designed for each other. Will had never encountered anything like this before. He knew she could feel him hardening up against her, but she neither pulled away nor responded, she just held onto him. His cheeks felt damp, and with a shock he realised that she was crying.

Isobel pulled away, blinked, and said, "Ciao, Will."

She turned and walked out the door. He wasn't sure whether he should go after her, but felt that she was better left alone. She knew her own mind. If she wanted him, she would find him. Will knew that this woman had changed his life forever; that she would be the benchmark against which all other women would be compared. He did not know if anything would come of it, but believed that they were kindred spirits, and that she knew it too.

•

The next morning, before Will checked out of the hotel he phoned Señor Santiago, thanking him for his hospitality. He replied that he was very glad that Will had called, and how much of a pleasure it had been getting to know him. Then he said a very odd thing: "We are very selective with our friends. If ever you need a place to rest up, or get away to, come to us." Will left him all his contact numbers and promised to keep in touch.

8

WILL LANDED BACK in England under marginal conditions. He'd had to abort his first approach because at three hundred feet he still couldn't see the runway. He liked instrument flying; there was a certain precision to it that appealed to him, but he didn't like that sinking feeling as the plane settled down towards the runway and all he could see was white; no matter what the instruments were telling him, it frankly gave him the shits.

The season was going to start in three weeks' time, and there were several agreements still to be completed. He spent the next morning with his lawyer, who told him what had happened at the brunch and how surprised everybody was that old Freddy had turned out to be a paedophile. But, he said, some people were saying that it could be that he had stepped on the wrong toes once too often. "That was just after your problem, wasn't it?"

Will looked him dead in the eye and said, "It might have been."

His accountant joined them, and after an extensive

discussion of his financial position they both tried to talk him out of what they called his "pet project". Will had been trying to buy an island, not just any island, but a big island. Buying the island wasn't that difficult, the hard part was turning it into a free port, not controlled by the whims of the mainland government which currently owned it.

The government wanted the money for the island and wanted the employment that would be created. However, it still wanted control of the island, which Will knew would lead to its failure, if not in the short term, then certainly in the long term. He knew that he was not making progress: there was a missing link somewhere, but he couldn't put his finger on it. The lawyer and accountant had done their jobs well, but it was up to him to sell his concept to the mainland. He also knew that he couldn't take on this project and motor race as well: it was one or the other. He had to clinch this deal before the start of the season, or leave it till the end. If he tried to do both, he would fail at both. Logically, it was a good deal for everybody, but there was a missing ingredient, and he sensed it was lack of trust. They simply didn't trust each other. It needed something to make it gel, but he didn't know what that was. He had done all the good things — wined and dined, free trips to the motor races, the whole bit — but there was an element missing. He was pretty sure it wasn't money, because if it was, they would have at least hinted at it by now.

It was a big island. In fact, it was several islands: a main island, some smaller ones, and a number of sand bars. The total area was about a thousand square miles. It went from mangrove swamps, which were used as hurricane holes in the old days, to white, sandy beaches protected by coral reefs, to rolling scrub country, to forest that had been logged of most of its valuable timber. Will had a plan for this place that would take him the rest of his life to complete; nevertheless he didn't want to have to worry every time there was an election that the rules could be changed. He had to have control. As much as he wanted the island, he wouldn't touch it without that control. To pay for it would mean selling off most of his other assets. To develop it at the speed he intended he would have to borrow money, and he would need better than clear title to achieve that. He had no intention of burying himself in some tropical backwater, stymied by inefficiency, bureaucracy and graft. He had two weeks to do the deal, or forget it till the next season.

•

Two days later, Will caught a 747 out of Gatwick for Miami. He was in first class, with the usual bunch of well-dressed men and a sprinkling of women. He often wondered how many of these guys were actually businessmen who ran their own businesses, or were corporate and government bureaucrats. He suspected that most of them were bureaucrats.

"You *are* that racing driver, aren't you?" she said accusingly. It was the same stewardess as last time. He opened his hands and shrugged.

"What would you like to drink?" she asked.

"Bloody Mary mix," he replied.

"No vodka?"

"No vodka."

"You *are* that racing driver, aren't you?"

"What do you think?"

"I think you are the type to abandon his girlfriend the minute she fell pregnant."

9

WILL REALISED THAT he wasn't getting anywhere with the politicians. It was all very pleasant; they were quite happy for this gringo to sink his money into another Central American pit, but they weren't willing to give him the long-term security of tenure that he required. Time was his worst enemy: if he didn't have control, in the end mañana would get him. It was too big a project for him without borrowing money or bringing in investors, but who would invest or lend money to this loco gringo with the big ideas?

He had been in the office of the high-rise building with the air conditioning going full blast all morning. It was an impressive office with marble floors, white walls, and Mayan artefacts scattered about. They were reasonable men, well-educated, all speaking good English. They understood the deal, nevertheless they wanted strings attached. Will wanted the island designated a free-trade zone, with no duty or income tax, so that he could maintain control. He knew that as soon as the island started to prosper, the politicians would start pointing their fingers at it, using it as a lever for political advantage. He couldn't stop that. But he wanted to make sure that they couldn't impose price controls, duties, or any other regulation that might win them an election and destroy the island. He had offered to pay an annual fee in lieu of taxes and duties, which they had not agreed to; they had offered fixed rates of taxes and duties. However, Will knew that so long as the politicos were involved in revenue collecting on the island, some day somebody would see it as a cash cow to be milked.

They were not making any real progress. Will thought it better to break rather than allow the situation to deteriorate. "If you will excuse me," he said, "I have some guests arriving from Spain on this afternoon's flight. I have to pick them up. Tomorrow we are going for a sail — perhaps you would care to join us?"

Will could see that they were curious about his guests, and did not expect them to accept, as they were more into sports fishermen and gin palaces. He told them that his guests were in the bullfighting business. To his surprise, one asked if their name was Santiago. They turned to each other and spoke in rapid Spanish. Finally, one said to Will, "We know of your friends. Their name is held in great respect in this country. We would like you to be our guests on Isla de Piña. We will have a small fiesta in their honour, and we would consider it a privilege if you would allow us to have them cleared through immigration, and delivered to your ship. We will hold a barbecue on the beach near where you usually anchor your yacht. Do not worry, we will organise it all." Will knew there was an opportunity here, that this could be the turning point, and that his Spanish friends might hold the key.

●

Imperialist was up against an old wooden wharf, her sails all furled, her brass and varnished woodwork gleaming. "Where are your guests?" Graham asked, as Will hopped on board.

"They are being given the VIP treatment for some reason. I'm not quite sure what the position is."

Will went below into the cool dark hull, and into the navigator's cabin. He lay down on the single bunk and opened the round brass porthole beside the bunk, feeling the cool breeze blowing through. He looked up at the laminated timber beams over his head and at the white grooved deck-head. He followed the beams with his eyes, from where they connected to the polished kauri knees, to where they in turn connected to the laminated ring frames, wrapping around the hull from the deck-head, and back up to the knees on the other side.

He never tired of looking at the golden timberwork, set off by the brass portholes and lamps. Will pulled the shade under the deck hatch above his head, closing out the sunlight, scrunched up the pillow, and lay back. He was not sure what all this meant, but what was the point in second-guessing? Still, he couldn't stop wondering what the implications were.

"Will, I think they are here," called Peter. Will hopped out of the bunk and got up on deck as a black Mercedes rolled up to the wharf. The Santiagos had arrived with a full escort. Two army officers leaped from the front and rushed around opening doors and offloading baggage. Will climbed up on the dock to greet his guests. "Señor, Señora, I am so glad that you could make it."

"We could not resist your invitation. We wanted to see your

yacht, and of course to see you, and your island, before you got too busy with your racing."

They climbed down onto the deck, Will showing them to the double cabin up forward. He could see the look on their faces: they might not have been sailors, but they appreciated quality when they saw it. He did not invite many people aboard *Imperialist*, because he had come to realise that it was wasted on them, although he had known that these people would understand what they were looking at, he was genuinely glad that they had come.

It was dark, and the land breeze had started to fill in by the time they were ready to leave for the island. They dropped all the mooring lines, except the bow line, and *Imperialist* slowly swung stern-first away from the dock until she was held head-to-wind by the line. The main and mizzen were hoisted, flapping lazily in the light breeze as they cast off. Will wound the wheel over to port. With the wind pushing *Imperialist* back from the wharf, the bow slowly fell away as they unrolled the jib. Will wound the huge wheel over to starboard; *Imperialist* heeled to the gentle breeze, slowly gathering way.

They sat on the deck watching the harbour lights fall slowly astern. Peter was on the helm with Graham, navigating, as they followed the ships' channel out to sea. The orange moon was peeping over the horizon, the wind was in the quarter, blowing away the day's heat with the balmy evening breeze. Daiquiris and ceviche were the order of the day as *Imperialist* slipped through the water, leaving a glowing, phosphorescent wake. Conversation trailed off, leaving everybody drinking in the beauty of it all.

By midnight they were anchored in the island's main bay

that Will had renamed Half Moon Bay after one of his favourite places. They all sat on deck for a while, watching the stars, so bright away from the cities and pollution; there was no sound, not even the lapping of the water on the hull. It was completely still, with the reflection of the hull shimmering in the moonlight.

"I now understand what you were speaking about, when you told us about your life on this yacht. This is a life worth living," Señora Santiago said.

"It is always different," replied Will. "You don't know what you are going to get, but it is almost always good."

The last thing Will did before bed was to set the proximity sensors, an alarm sounding if anything came within a hundred feet of the yacht. Will and the boys usually took turns wearing the alarm sensor on their wrists like a watch, as it would vibrate if activated. There were many false alarms, so nobody wanted to wear it, but it allowed them to leave the boat open for ventilation, without fear of thieves boarding while they slept. Along with the alarm went the stainless-steel shotgun, which was the only weapon on board. Will felt that a whole arsenal of weapons would be more trouble than it was worth. If they had a problem it would almost certainly be close up, and for that there was nothing better than a shotgun. The navigator's cabin, or naviguessor's cabin, as it was sometimes called, was a single berth on the starboard side, amidships aft of the navigation table, opposite the galley, and therefore close to the fridge. It was his favourite cabin, and he used it at sea and in port, except when he had female company, in which case he used the double up forward.

•

They all awoke to a perfect day with a light sea breeze. The boys had rigged the awning, a white canvas cover, which extended from the main mast to the stern, keeping most of the deck in shade, and creating a cool refuge both below and above decks with the hatches open.

A light breakfast was served in the forward cockpit under the awning with the gentle breeze barely ruffling the water. They knew that a day of eating and drinking lay ahead. Everyone sat around the big dining table on white cushions, drinking strong Guatemalan coffee. Will had baked bread overnight, serving it still warm with a wheel of goat camembert and English marmalade.

"This is the life," said Señora Santiago. "What more could you ask for?"

"It sure is," said Graham. "He even pays us, as well."

"What about me?" asked Señor Santiago. "I will stay forever, and you don't need to pay me, Will."

"Mi casa es su casa," replied Will with a grin.

Their hosts certainly knew how to entertain in the grand manner. They had awoken to the high-pitched whine of outboard-powered canoes ferrying out the first of the servants, who had begun setting up the barbecue by digging a pit for the logs on which they were going to roast the pig. By midday, the first of the sports fishermen and gin palaces started to arrive with their hosts. Will and his guests had been having a discussion on their hosts' reaction to their visit. It turned out that back in the thirties, as a result of the frequent revolutions that had swept the country, the grandfather of the present president had been sent into exile in Spain, and had spent a considerable time as the guest of Señor Santiago's father at the rancho. He told Will that he had a long-standing invitation to visit, but had never taken them up on it. Will realised that this could be a golden opportunity to break the deadlock with the government, but that he couldn't ask his new friend to help him. If it was going to happen, it would evolve, starting today.

A twenty-foot Boston Whaler with twin outboards and a centre steering console swung neatly alongside *Imperialist*. At the helm was one of their hosts in a bathing suit, baseball cap and deck shoes, wearing a gold Rolex Presidential, chain, and diamond ring. "Buenos días, Señores y Señora. Welcome, welcome. I am here to ferry you to the beach." They clambered aboard after much hand-shaking, swung the boat around, and headed in.

The sand was so white that it glared in the noon sun like snow on a ski run. The multi-coloured water lapped lazily on the semicircular arc of sand, while a fringe of coconut trees waved in the wind. This was Will's idea of paradise, and why he was prepared to risk all for it.

Their host cut the power, pushing the button to tilt the engine out of the water, as the boat coasted up onto the snow-white beach. The party was in full progress. There must have been fifty people there. The pig was on the spit, and people were already standing around with sharp knives slicing bits off, as it was slowly being turned by the cooks. There were five-gallon water coolers filled with frozen lime daiquiris floating beside the guests, who stood waist-deep in the sea drinking from plastic cups, and getting slowly drunk without realising it.

The sea had hardly a ripple; the water was crystal-clear, the white coral sand was hard, the sky was blue, with the odd fluffy white cloud drifting by. The leaves in the trees bordering the beach were rustling; birds were singing. "You can keep everything else," thought Will, "this was for him."

There were three sports fishermen anchored stern to the beach, in very shallow water, and another two anchored out. The ones close in could be boarded by walking out, with continuous traffic back and forth. This was a barbecue in the grand style, no burning of hamburgers and sausages in the backyard. The mouth-watering aroma of roast pork wafted on the light breeze. Guests were of all ages, from young children running around to grandparents lounging in deck chairs, with broad-brimmed straw hats warding off the worst of the sun. Some were water-skiing off the beach; some were tanning themselves; some were standing around drinking, and eating pork titbits; others were in the sea with the daiquiris.

Will was drawn into a group around the pig, which included their hosts and his guests. Somebody had brought him a coconut with a hole cut in it. Will loved coconut water. He put it to his mouth, tilted back his head, and drained the contents down his throat. He had the husk split. With a spoon he scooped out the white, soft coconut jelly. Some people were pouring rum into the hole, mixing it with the coconut water before drinking it. Much, much better than rum and Coke, Will thought, but not for him. He liked it straight.

Will kept an eye on his crew because he had warned them to stay clear of the women. The last thing he wanted was to end up with jealous husbands, or protective fathers souring the deal. Still, Will well knew the old saying that a standing cock had no conscience. Will realised from what he could pick up of the rapid-fire Spanish and the attitude of their hosts that the whole atmosphere towards him had changed since the arrival of his guests. This family do was definitely a big step forward. Will was always impressed by how close these families were, how central the mothers were to the whole unit. It still came as a surprise how close the teenage boys remained to their mothers, laughing and joking like compatriots, unlike their northern neighbours' surly teenage counterparts.

Will thought it a good idea to leave his hosts and his guests on their own, so he wandered off down the beach to watch the water-skiers. Most of them knew who he was, but were too polite to intrude. Eventually the questions started. They were a knowledgeable lot, with an affinity for fast cars and an understanding of car control. They may not have understood the formalities of motor racing, but because of bad roads and high speed they certainly understood the sport, and the skill behind it. The conversation drifted to what was the hot time between various cities, and who had done it, and whether Will thought he could do it quicker. Will amused them with some of his more hair-raising experiences both on and off the track, making light of his many accidents. One man asked about the availability of women at the races, and Will replied that the mechanics got them all, because the drivers had to go to bed early, which nobody believed. He told them the story of when he was driving Formula Three, and his mechanic had shown up hours late with the excuse that he had been sprayed with dairy whip and he couldn't leave until it had all been licked off.

•

After they had been shuttled back to *Imperialist*, they had a cup of coffee and talked about the day, although Will was more interested in what had transpired between his hosts and his friends. "Will," said Señor Santiago, "may I speak frankly?"

"Of course."

"You know that in any relationship, whether business or personal, it is the relationship between individuals that makes or breaks it. These people want you, but they are nervous. They are afraid of being pushed aside in their own country. Much has happened in the past caused by the norteamericanos. They like you but don't totally understand you. If you were a big corporation they wouldn't even be talking to you. They want the prosperity that the development could bring, but they don't want their lifestyle damaged. They saw how you reacted with their friends at their party, and how you enjoyed what they enjoy. That means a lot to them. They understand what you want, and they don't disagree with it, they just want to be sure."

"I understand what you are saying, but how can I reassure them?"

"Think of it this way. You said that you are going to have to borrow money. Why not bring some of them in as minority shareholders? Let them put up some money, at least offer this opportunity to them. Give them the option to refuse."

"I don't have any problem with that. But will that do it?"

"It may," said Señor Santiago, "but I know what will. They want a corrida."

"A what?"

"A corrida with my bulls."

"What do you mean? Bullfighting is illegal in this country."

"That is the whole point. The island will be a free port, and you could operate a casino if you wanted."

"I hadn't thought it through that far, but I guess they had. So they see the big buck."

"No," said Señor Santiago, "they would not get away with

it. The Church would never allow it, but maybe it would allow the corrida."

"It is going to take too much money," said Will. "The whole concept would be changed."

"Not so much. There is a market for my bulls in this area. The corrida need be no bigger than the one on my rancho."

"Who is going to run it? Who is going to finance it?"

"If you permit," replied the Señor, "I would be prepared to do both, but that depends on you."

Will felt himself tense up in the way he always did when he thought he was being hustled. "What do you mean?" he asked.

"Permit me to explain. Do not fear my motives. The corrida will be private as at the rancho; there will be no entrance fee. It will be a place to show the bulls and the horses. It will be a place that the matadors will be glad to come to during the off-season. Our friends in the government would very much like a private corrida, which nobody could argue against, especially as it would be seen as a new export industry. As for the money, it would be my pleasure to buy as many shares as you wished to sell, which I would agree to sell back to you at any time you wished."

Will felt tears come to his eyes. How could he ever have doubted this man? "Thank you, Señor, but I can't have you risking your money in a venture like this. There is absolutely no guarantee of success; the likely chance is less than fifty-fifty. It's a hair-brained dream that I have, and I can't let you risk your money on it. If you are interested, as I realise that your involvement could be crucial to the deal, I will give you the land for the rancho and corrida."

Señor Santiago laughed, "You are a generous man, Will, and

I am not as foolish as you think. First, the tax advantages to me are very important, and if it all failed the advantage would be even better. Secondly, I need some excitement in my life. Last of all, this is a beautiful place with wonderful people, and I hear it has one of the best pigeon shoots in the world. In fact, we are invited for a shoot on Wednesday morning."

Will shook his head. "You can never tell what motivates some people. This whole deal now swings on a bullfight and a pigeon shoot."

The Señor was shaking with laughter. "Funnier things have happened, Will. Have you shot pigeons?"

"Not for years, and I wasn't that great then."

They got up laughing and headed for their cabins. Will found that he couldn't wait for Wednesday morning.

10

THE SHOOT WAS in a cornfield that was breakfast, lunch, and dinner for the thousands of birds who flew in from the offshore islands to feed. Without the shooting, the cornfield would have been decimated by the pigeons. Their hosts, as at the barbecue, had provided everything: guns, ammunition, bird boys, cold drinks, the lot.

They were spread out at the edge of the cornfield with two bird boys each. They had no camouflage gear as the birds were colour-blind, and frightened by movement rather than colour. Will had been given a five-shot Remington 1100 automatic shotgun, a type that he had used before, and five boxes of number-six Remington Express birdshot. He put one box in a pouch on a belt they had lent him, tore the top off the box, turned the shotgun over and put four shells in the magazine, fed one up into the chamber, and put one more into the magazine.

They had explained to Will and Señor Santiago that the flight didn't start till six-thirty, and the bulk of it would be over in half an hour. The gun had a skeet barrel, and when Will asked why, he was told that it was close and fast, and that a longer barrel would be useless, as there wouldn't be enough shot spread.

At six o'clock it was just light. Will tried to hold a conversation with the bird boys, but their Spanish was too much for him. One of them suddenly squatted down and pointed excitedly.

"Señor, Señor, aqui, aqui!"

Will looked, but he couldn't see anything.

"Las palomas, hay mucho mucho."

Now he could see them. There was a flight of about twenty birds coming straight for them. Will held the shotgun across himself and pushed off the safety, keeping his finger out of the trigger guard. The pigeons were going to pass directly overhead, low and fast. The idea was to drop them in the old cornfield where they could easily be found, rather than let them fall in the thick bush behind them. The bush served a purpose because the shooters blended into it, and did not present a silhouette which the birds could see. The pigeons were on them and everybody opened up.

Will was talking to himself, "Start from behind, swing through, squeeze, don't jerk, focus on one, forget the rest. Left foot forward, knees bent, gun cupped up into your shoulder, cheek on stock, both eyes open, lean into it, pick the bird, look along the barrel, from behind swing through fast, well before you pass squeeze, bang, wings stop, fold, down, on to another one, follow through, squeeze, bang, miss. Swing through, bang, miss, bang again, miss. Calm down, clean swing. If you miss, start the swing again."

The excitement was infectious, with everybody yelling and

firing, bird boys diving in and out picking up downed birds. "Gun getting hot, gun jams, won't clear. Put the gun on the ground, grab the ice pick, punch out the locking pins, remove the trigger mechanism, and put in the spare, knock the pins back in, ready to go."

Between flights the bird boys were plucking, gutting, and packing the birds in igloos filled with ice. Will was not an expert like some of these guys, but he didn't embarrass himself too much. He finally settled down and got about one bird for every five shots; not bad for a novice.

•

The relationship with his hosts had improved dramatically since the arrival of the Santiagos. They were much more comfortable with Will now that they realised they had common interests. He wasn't the usual gringo. That evening they were invited to the home of one of their hosts to eat the birds they had shot. It was a big, beautiful cut-stone house with a red clay-tile roof and terrazzo floors, on a hill overlooking the city and the sea. The roof was supported by massive rough-cut wooden beams. The furniture was heavy, dark mahogany; the floors white marble. The white-louvered windows and doors were all folded back, leading out onto a large flagstone terrace by the swimming pool, with a monstrous brick barbecue at one end. Some of the birds were cooking in an enormous casserole; others were being cooked on the barbecue. Servants were circulating with cocktails and canapés.

One of their hosts explained that, although there was a bird-shooting season, there was no bag limit, because if they could not keep the population down by shooting, they would have to resort to poisoning. Damage to the grain crops was enormous;

were it not for the resistance from the shooters, poisoning would have been implemented years ago.

Will felt exceedingly comfortable in these surroundings: this was a lifestyle that he appreciated. He had forgotten all about the coming season, and even the deal on the island. He was totally relaxed. His hosts and their guests seemed to realise that he didn't want to become involved in motor-sport discussions, and didn't push the subject. There were a few good-looking women floating around, but he was careful not to get himself in a situation that would compromise his position. At the same time, he knew that he couldn't afford to give offence by ignoring them. He felt amused at himself because he was also influenced by the presence of the Señora. He didn't want any bad reports going back to her daughter. But the real truth was that he wished that Isobel had come with her parents; at the same time he knew that playing with her was playing for keeps, and he wasn't ready for that. That was church work. Then he thought to himself: the smart bitch knew all that, and was probably turning up the heat on him.

•

"Hello, Señor Will. What are you doing standing here all alone?"

Will turned around. He couldn't quite place her. One of the wives, he supposed, but which one he couldn't tell. She was not young, but elegant, and somewhat voluptuous in a long, low-cut evening dress. Shit, here comes trouble, he thought.

"Just enjoying the view, Señora."

"I would have thought that one of the señoritas would have captured you by now."

"As you can see, I am here all alone."

"Did you enjoy the shoot today?"

"Very much. I am not that good at it, but it was heaps of fun."

"I used to shoot, but I got too good for my husband's ego, so I stay home and play the little wife."

"I can't see you as the little wife, somehow."

"Are you alone on your beautiful yacht, or do you have some beautiful woman hidden away from view?"

"You should come and visit sometime."

"And who should I tell your crew I am?"

"Tell them you are my analyst."

"Maybe I should say I am an ornithologist."

"Birds?"

"Swallows."

A full moon was rising out of the sea, and the cool land breeze was coming down off the mountains behind. As it became cooler, the party drifted inside to the living room. The big ceiling fans were going whop-whop-whop while the evening breeze blew through the living room, maintaining the perfect temperature. They all sat down at a huge dining table seating twenty people. Servants shuttled back and forth to the kitchen, bringing out bowls of food. The pigeons were absolutely delicious, eaten whole, bones and all, served simply with wild rice and salad.

After dinner, the children were brought out by their nannies, to say goodnight to their parents before being put to bed. It was a comfortable scene, in an olde-worlde way. Maybe some of the customs would not be quite acceptable to the modern liberal northerner, but, Will thought, this was not half bad.

The evening ended with excellent coffee and flan. Will commented that they kept the best coffee for themselves and exported what they didn't want.

"But of course," was the response from Pablo Hernandez, his host and government contact. "Why would you do it any other way? Besides, norteamericanos wouldn't know the difference anyway."

Will had to agree that, with most people, serving them good coffee was casting pearls before swine.

11

It was the first race of the season, and it was sweltering hot. The Nomex suit and underwear he was wearing only made it worse. Will, in his own terminology, had absolutely blitzed them; he was half a second faster than anybody else in the first official practice session, and even faster in the second.

Ray and the rest of the team were in seventh heaven: all the work in the off-season was paying off. The car was working really well, and they were getting more and more out of it as the pressure increased. It was like music, driving this car; it flowed, it bowed under braking, and rolled into the corners; it was fluid and smooth. It asked to be driven smoothly; you wouldn't think of pitching it into a corner; it was too sophisticated for that, it made going quickly so easy.

Will came off the kerb, leading onto the short pit straight up through the gears; second, third, fourth, into the downhill right-hander. This time he didn't lift off, he kept his foot on it. It felt so easy he could hardly believe it. He used all the road and the kerbs, and knew that with this car he could do so consistently. The next corner was a much faster downhill left-hander. He thought he could take it flat as well, but this one was really dangerous; it had killed more than one person in the past. He tried to hold his foot down into the corner, but his right foot had a mind of its own, lifting off the accelerator and stepping on the brake, slowing the car more than he wanted. As he went past the pits, he could see people leaning over the pit wall. He knew what they were doing; they were listening for him to do it again, because they couldn't believe that he had taken the corner flat. He did it again, but he understeered hard into the kerbs hard this time, and his heart leapt as he thought that he might jump the kerb and slam front first into the Armco.

He concentrated his entire being on the next corner, right out to the very edge on the approach: using the brakes gently, gently, just rub the pedal, don't slow it too much, roll it in to the apex, careful with the kerbs, they could flick you; at this speed you could be killed. He glanced at the rev counter on the exit and knew that this was the fastest he had been around that corner, and that he wasn't going to take it flat, not this year anyway.

Up the hill and into the hairpin, heel in the rest; squeeze down on the brake pedal, the nose dips. As it slows, flick down through the gears: fourth, third, second. Wind on the steering into the apex, ease off the brakes, up to the kerb, feed on the power, wind off the steering, as the arse came around out to the exit. Down the long, undulating straight, check the instruments, cars ahead, get a draught off them and hope that nobody gets in the way before the end of this lap. This, he knew, was the pole time. As he blasted past the pits, his team hung out the "come in" sign. Will backed off and slowed down, cruising back. This was a good time to gather his thoughts for the grilling that he knew was coming from Ray. As he turned into the pit lane, people were clapping and giving him the thumbs up. His team was ecstatic.

"There are some demoralised people out there," said Ray. "You should have heard it. You came off the kerb onto the straight with the engine howling and echoing off the buildings. There were no other cars nearby so you could hear it plain as day. Then you went up through the gears, into fourth, and into turn one without a pause, without a break in the engine note. They couldn't believe it. Then you did it again! Talk about demoralised."

They were in the motor home, Will sitting on the couch with his Nomex vest off and his overall arms tied around his waist. Sweat ran off his chest even though the air conditioning was going full blast. Ray and some of the engineers surrounded him. "How was it?" Ray asked.

"Don't touch a thing. You really got it right this time. It's perfect, good turn in, stable under brakes and puts the power down. Fantastic balance. There isn't much more that you could ask for."

"That's wonderful news, Will. Now let's get down to the nitty-gritty, because as you well know perfect today can just as easily turn to hopeless tomorrow, if you need to go faster."

Qualifying was a disaster. Nothing worked. Will had gone from top dog to nothing in forty-five minutes. He was tenth on the grid. Will felt that the car was out of alignment and suspected he had bent the front suspension on the outside of the first corner. He knew he had slid hard into the kerb with the left-hand front wheel, but did not think anything of it. Now it had lost its edge and they were tenth.

The morning warm-up was damp, and Will set the fastest time again. Everybody now knew that something was moving when the car came under load in the dry, but in the wet there wasn't enough load to cause the problem. And now there wasn't enough time to find it, and fix it.

Will was antsy. He had nobody to blame but himself, showing off by taking turn one flat may have cost him the race. Tenth on the grid meant he was going to have to fight his way through the pack, assuming that the track stayed wet.

Will tried to jump the start, and that didn't work. The car in front didn't move. He darted right and clipped the right rear wheel with his front wing. "Shit," he thought. "I have to head for the pits."

By the time he left the pits with a new nose he was dead last, with a huge job to get into the points. Fighting his way through the field in a defective car was never going to pay a big dividend. Will ended up sixth, with one point to show for his efforts.

12

"THERE'S A CANOE over there with somebody waving," yelled Graham.

"Where?"

"At eleven o'clock. See? Wait as the swell rises."

"I'll get the binoculars," said Will.

Will reached into the deckhouse, and pulled the Zeiss binoculars out of their teak holder, scanning the horizon. It was dusk, and the sun was setting. They were running in light airs with all sail up: spinnaker, spinnaker staysail, main and mizzen. They had set the spinnakers that morning and had run with them all day. It couldn't have been a better sail. The big masthead spinnaker, in the Martini colours of blues and red, filled and rippled as it pulled them along in the light south-easterly breeze. They had been considering whether to leave the sails up overnight, as it looked a beautiful evening, but you never knew; one squall they wouldn't see approaching in the dark, and it would be a disaster. Three crew weren't much for a hundred-foot boat, with a huge masthead spinnaker. Sure they had it on a snuffer, but if anything stuffed up, they would be in big trouble.

But here was another kind of trouble. Who were these men? They were in the hundred-mile passage between Jamaica and Cuba. North were the communists, and south were all kinds of unknown problems.

"They aren't motoring. Maybe they are broken down. What should we do?" asked Peter. "Maybe they're pirates, or Cubans trying to suck us in. We'd better be bloody careful."

"Let's see what they want," said Will. "Pete, get the shotgun, make sure it's loaded, and bring up a box of shells but don't let them see it. In fact, you stay out of sight."

"Maybe they are armed," said Graham. "I don't like this one bit."

"Maybe they are, maybe they aren't, and if they're in trouble we can't leave them to die out here, so let's get rid of the spinnakers and the mizzen for a start. Pete, forget the gun till we get the sails down. Graham and I will douse the kite. You start the engine. Graham, run the brace, and come give me a hand with the snuffer."

Graham set the autopilot to run almost dead downwind and eased the mainsail out flat, slowly easing the brace so that the spinnaker pole rested on the forestay, then flicked the brace off the winch so that the spinnaker swung behind the main. He ran forward to help Will pull down the snuffer. As soon as it was fully down he ran back, opened the hatch and went to the foot of the mast where the spinnaker halyard was on its winch. He quickly eased it off as Will fed the snuffed kite down the hatch into the sail locker. They then did the same with the spinnaker staysail. In the meantime they were heading away from the canoe, whose occupants seemed to be getting more and more frantic. Once the spinnakers were dropped, they could start the engine, turn head to wind and dump the mizzen, followed by the main.

Finally, with the motor at slow speed, they gradually approached the canoe. There were three bearded old black men in what looked like a thirty-foot fibreglass canoe with an outboard motor in pieces. There were no sign of weapons, but of course there wouldn't be until the last second. "You ready with the gun, Pete?"

"What happens if I have to shoot them?"

"Just shoot them, and worry about it later."

At about fifty yards Will yelled out, "What's your problem?"

"Hingine bruck down," said one of the men.

"When?"

"Friday."

"You been drifting for seven days?"

"Yes baas, gi we a tow."

"What the hell's going on?" asked Pete

"Looks like three old Rastafarian fishermen, with a dead engine and no oars, typical. They now want us to tow them home."

"We can't tow that thing. It would do more damage to us than it's worth," said Graham.

"We don't want them on board, either," said Peter.

"So what the hell do we do? We can't just leave them here," said Will.

"You know what? The cheapest and safest thing to do is to give them our fifteen-horse motor with enough fuel and send them on their way," suggested Graham.

"I agree, it would be, but you can see the condition they are in. They are skin and bone. They could make it, but I wouldn't feel good about it. Here's what I reckon, but you guys need to agree. I won't push the issue. Let's take them aboard but keep them on deck, and not let them go below. Keep them together, one person stands guard, and we drop them off in Jamaica somewhere."

"What about the canoe?"

"We leave it."

"They won't be happy about that."

"Tough shit," said Will. He called to the men, "Where are you from?"

"Mo Bay, baas."

"What's he saying?" asked Peter.

"They are from Montego Bay." To the men: "We're going to take you aboard and drop you off on Montego Bay, but we can't tow the canoe."

By this time the men were right alongside *Imperialist* and it was obvious that they were no threat, just three skinny old Rastafarian fishermen. Will felt sorry for them.

"No baas we can't leave de cunu, jus gi we a tow."

"No," replied Will, "we can't tow it, but I tell you what, I will buy it from you and you can buy another one when you get back."

"Yu buy me boat an leff it ere?"

"Yes."

"US dollar?"

"Yes."

"Cash?"

"Yes."

"Ow much?"

"You tell me."

"Five tousen dolla."

"Two thousand."

One said to the other, "De man mad, dis a good cunu, wa im want it fa anyway, him mus wan to haul ganja."

"Yes breda Jasu, dat's wat dem want, to tief me boat so dem can haul ganja den dem blame me, and me go a jail."

"Dat right."

Will was getting fed up with this. "Listen, the only reason we stopped was to save your miserable lives. We can leave you where we found you and forget about it. We can leave you with food and water and call Jamaica. Maybe somebody will come looking for you, but I wouldn't bet on it. We could give you food, water, a motor and you would probably find your way home. But I'm not going to tow your miserable boat because it would eventually run into my boat and cause more damage than you frigging 'cunu' is worth. That's why I'm offering to pay for it so that we can leave it behind, and you can buy another one when you get back. If you can't get that through your miserable heads, then see you later."

"Hold on baas, now me understan, gi me tree tousan and drop us in Mo Bay."

"Okay, three thousand cash," said Will. "We'll toss you a line and pull you up to the stern. Leave everything behind. No knife, no club, no weed, nothing. Understood?"

"When a go get de money, baas?"

"When we reach Mo Bay."

Jesus, Will thought, now I'm speaking patois. They hauled

the canoe to the stern and the three old Rastas climbed on board. They were in sad shape. Will put them to sit in the cockpit and got them some water. "Drink slowly, and we will get you a little food. Don't take too much or it will make you sick."

They sat there in the shade drinking water and eating some buttered bread with ham and cheese. "What have you had to eat and drink since Friday?" asked Will.

"Wi have some bread, and bully beef and a likkle wata, but it finish by Saturday, so we eat some fish."

"When did your water run out?"

"'Bout Sunday."

"Sunday!"

"We drink a likkle rain wata, some piss and when that done, sea wata."

"You drank seawater and piss?"

"Yes, baas."

"But seawater will kill you."

"Seawata only kill white man, Rasta caan ded from seawata."

"They are telling us that they have survived nearly a week on seawater and beer, in this heat in an open boat. I don't believe it," said Peter.

"Believe it, guys, and no beer, piss means piss, not beer. I have heard of it before. They don't know that they can't drink it, so they do and survive. Whitey thinks he can't, and dies of thirst without trying."

The Rastas watched with interest as the sails were set and they altered course for Montego Bay. "Me used to have a sail cunu, long time ago. It never bruck down. Hingin notin but trouble."

"Why didn't you bring oars?"

"Dis hingin cunu, not pullin cunu, ship no carry oar."

"What's he saying?" asked Graham.

"Basically he said that the canoe is now a motor boat, not a row boat."

"For God's sake."

Before morning they were off Montego Bay, trying to raise customs on the VHF with no luck.

"What the hell happens now?" said Will. "I don't want to get caught up in some bullshit." Finally he got an answer, but from a charter boat, who promised to call customs on the land line.

Customs told them to tie up at the yacht club, but when Will told them that *Imperialist* drew fifteen feet they were directed to the cruise-ship dock. Customs were very suspicious of the relationship between themselves and the Rastas. Several hours later, after a long and incompetent search, in which they didn't even find the shotgun, they were allowed to go ashore.

Will and the Rastas headed for the bank, where their troubles started all over again. The bank was happy to give him cash on his credit card but only in Jamaican dollars and at the official exchange rate. Which meant that he had to pay the Rastas more. But that was not the worst of it — before he could leave he had to have receipts for the cash. Jamaica had draconian foreign-exchange controls to prevent their citizens shipping out their cash. Will knew he had a problem that wasn't going to go away. If he showed exchange control a receipt, from a bunch of Rastas he was going to end up in jail as a drug trafficker. So he decided the hell with it, just leave, or find an alternative. But what? Worry about it tomorrow, get some sleep.

•

What was that tapping noise? It wasn't a halyard: there was no wind. Will rolled over and looked at his watch. Six-thirty. Who would be tapping on the hull at six-thirty? The next thing that flashed through his mind was cops. But, no, they would be banging, not respectfully tapping. Will climbed through the hatch and looked over the side. There was a canoe with three grinning old Rastas. "Mornin, baas."

"Good morning, chief. What can I do for you this time?"

"Cum show you de new hingin cunu."

"That's good. Going fishing?"

"No, baas, we going look fo de odder one."

"Think you can find it?"

"Perhaps, Lord willin, good luck. A have somtin fe yu."

"What?"

"Tek dis," he said, and handed Will a scruffy envelope. Will opened it and inside he found several receipts from hotels, in-bond stores and a fuel station. A quick add-up told him that the receipts totalled more than the money he had given them. But what was intriguing was that they all looked official.

"Thank you," said Will.

"No problem, you is a good white man." And they pushed off, pulled the starter cord and motored off. Will started laughing and laughing.

"What's so funny at this time of morning?" asked Peter.

"Look at this."

"Receipts. So?"

"Where would those old Rastas get proper receipts from? How would they understand that we had a problem?"

"There have been more funny goings-on," said Graham. "Yesterday when we fuelled up, the tanker driver said that somebody would bring the bill today, which seemed unusual.

Take a look at the fuel delivery docket. It is the same as the receipt."

"You think that they paid for the fuel?"

"I wouldn't bet that they didn't."

"Poor dumb old Rastas, eh? Well, I'll be damned."

They had to get going. They had lost four days in the rescue. *Imperialist* was due to be hauled in Fort Lauderdale in five days, and they had hoped to stop off in Key West for a couple, but that was out of the question now, and Will had a race the weekend after *Imperialist* was hauled.

13

SHORT STRAIGHT, WITH a flat-out left-hander coming up, into
fourth early, rather than have to change up in the middle of
the corner, back moving around a bit on the uneven surface.
Another hundred-and-eighty-degree corner coming up, much
bigger and faster this one: third gear, don't try to push it too
hard, it won't work. Carry the brakes into the corner, trailing
throttle through the next. Then, gradually feed in the throttle
for the next quarter. Short straight with a very fast fourth-gear
left-hander, Jesus this thing felt good; he knew that he was going
to put it on the pole, and with any sort of luck he would win this.

Back in the pits, he sat on the pit wall swinging his legs,
singing, "Oh, it's so hard to be humble, when you are perfect
in every way," just to piss off the pits next door, laughing at
them every chance he could. He knew what it was like to beat
his brains out, trying to catch somebody who made it look so
easy. But they had rubbed it in when they had the chance, and
now it was his turn.

Will ended up on pole with nearly a second clear. Race day could not have been better. He led from start to finish. He virtually coasted the last ten laps, allowing the second car to whittle down his earlier thirty-second lead to ten seconds.

●

When Will arrived back in England, he found an invitation to stay at the hacienda during race week. He immediately rang Señor Santiago and explained that he would come and see them after the race, as he couldn't afford the distraction before it. He told them where he was staying, and sent them some pit passes. They understood the need for him to focus his attention on the job at hand, but he wondered whether they also realised what the main distraction would be.

He decided to drive to the race for a change. Will had no real interest in street cars, not when he was racing, anyway. Racing drained him; it sucked him dry. But he had an old Porsche which had been given to him for something or the other, he couldn't quite remember what. He hadn't driven it in a long time, and thought it could do with an airing. But as usual he left late; the traffic was bad; he missed the ferry, and by the time the crossing was over he was well and truly late. It rained soon after he left the terminal; the traffic was still bad, and he wasn't making up the lost time. Finally he got into open country, and gradually turned the wick up.

The old Porsche used to be in GT races years before, so it was pretty spartan and light. It had fantastic night-racing lights and proper seats, was very raucous, and hopeless around town, but fun on a trip like this.

The windshield wipers were on full blast, and the lights were being reflected back by the rain, but he was boring on. Will was enjoying himself, although he was tenser than in a race. He found himself leaning forward in the seat to try to see better. Every time he hit a puddle with a bang, the car would skitter and his heart would miss a beat.

He was coming down a straight with poplars on both sides of the two-lane road, overtaking the minimal traffic. He guessed all they would know of his passing would be the super-bright night-racing lights rushing up behind them, the boom of the exhaust, and the spray as he disappeared. This was fun. He approached a left-hander with a bridge following, braked, downshifted to fourth, had a quick glance to see that nothing was coming, and floored it. He had to work the steering a bit to keep it straight, as it bucked and kicked in his hands, the rear end sliding around in the puddles. He was nowhere near his limit — if another car had been coming he could have scrubbed off a lot of speed on the entry, and coasted out of the corner leaving room for the other car, but as nothing was coming he used most of the road.

He had to turn off at the next intersection, which led into winding secondary roads; he was in open country now, pastures with cattle, barbed-wire fences, and the odd house. The road surface was good and the rain had eased. He knew he was making good time. He was really working the old car, not using high revs, but driving it hard, while leaving himself enough room to manoeuvre if he had a problem. There was standing water at the apex of some of the corners. As he hit the water with a bang it would pitch the car. Will would flick in some opposite lock, stand on the throttle and come storming out of the corner. He was really enjoying himself, feeling every movement through the wheel; pitch it in here, a dab of opposite lock there, twirling away at the wheel as he stormed through the darkness. Will came over the crest of the hill with the right-hand corner flat in fifth. As the car became light, and before it could snap into oversteer, he flicked in some opposite lock and kept his foot buried. You had to catch the old girl early: she would bite if you gave her half a chance. He thought a bit about speed cops, but in reality they couldn't catch him, and with all the spray they couldn't pick up the licence plate anyway.

He remembered as a kid in Europe driving a racing Lotus Elite on the way to the Nürburgring in Germany. In the predawn, at a hundred and thirty miles per hour, a block house with the rails up popped up in the middle of the road, with customs and immigration officials leaping to their feet. A few seconds later another block house with officials jumping up. Will kept his foot on it till he got to the German border and waited for the trailer. He didn't know how he had survived those years. People were dying like flies. Formula One was still bloody dangerous, but back then it had been so much worse.

•

Will slowly drove into the pit area, easing the car through the crowd, sinking the clutch and blipping the throttle, partly to keep the plugs from fouling, and partly to get the people out of the way. The old Porsche was streaked with dirt from his trip through the rain. He had made it with plenty of time. Will climbed out of the car and stretched. He had driven until midnight, then checked into a hotel, had a good night's sleep, got up late and finished his journey. He was primed for practice today: after his ride through the night, he felt on top of the world, ready to deal to them again.

Ray walked over and shook his hand. "Everything is ready,

Will. We'll start with the same settings we used during testing and go from there."

"Good. I'm looking forward to it."

A couple of journalists they both knew hurried up to them. "That your Porsche, Will?"

"Yes."

"Did you come through the forest road last night?"

"Maybe. Why?"

"I told you so," one said to the other.

"We were changing a tyre in the rain, when we saw the lights and thought it was an aircraft, you were going so fast, and you drenched us with spray. We were pretty upset, and the only way we recognised that it was a Porsche was by the sound. How fast were you going?"

"I dunno," said Will. "The speedo doesn't work."

"How many revs were you doing then?"

"Oh, maybe six or seven. I didn't pay much attention."

"That must be at least a hundred and fifty miles per hour."

"Naw, it can't be. That old car won't go that fast."

Ray and Will walked off, hoping the journalists wouldn't write about it, and create more hassles. They walked into the motor home and discussed strategy for the day. After the last race they were considered the pace-setters, especially as they had been testing here last. They had two options open to them: go out and do a repeat of the last race, and blitz everybody, or hold back till the last qualifying session on Saturday. The competition was expecting an attempt at blitzing them, so there was every reason to do the exact opposite; however, it was risky. Suppose when the speed was required there wasn't any. What then?

The decision was made for them in the first practice session. The car wasn't working; they were in and out of the pits, and they weren't getting anywhere. It wouldn't come off the tight corners, and it was twitchy in the fast stuff. At the end of the session they were fifth fastest, and the rest thought they were sandbagging. The car's settings were exactly the same, but the track was different, the tyres were different, the surface was different, and the air temperature was cooler. But the difference wasn't showing up in the tyre temperatures, and that was their clue.

The next session they went to softer-compound rear tyres, and the car immediately stabilised, but it wouldn't turn in now. They knew they were on the right track, and went to softer fronts as well. They were immediately turning quick times, but now tyre wear was unacceptably high. They had set the third-fastest time, which wasn't too bad, but they couldn't race this way. The other teams knew that they had soft tyres, but most of them thought it was all part of the scam. The team was in trouble, but nobody else knew it. They were pretty sure that the tyre company had changed the compound, without changing the numbers.

They had a round-table with all the mechanics in the motor home. At the end of the discussion, they appointed one person to find out whether they were on a level playing field. It didn't take rocket science to come to the conclusion that if everybody was on the same tyres, they would have to work around the problem, as the softs would not last the race.

The logic then was to soften the car to try to make the tyres work. To do this properly, they would do one thing at a time, or run the risk of losing their way. They would treat the third practice as a test session, and if they used the second-to-last one for testing, then the last one was it, one shot. They were third on the grid at the moment, but that wouldn't last. By the end of the third practice, they would be back to tenth at least.

•

Will began to think about Isobel. It was a distraction that he didn't need, but he couldn't get her out of his mind. He called the hacienda and Señora Santiago answered. She insisted that he come for an early, very casual dinner. He knew he shouldn't go. He needed to be absolutely focused on the tyre problem, but he couldn't help himself. The magnet was pulling him and he couldn't resist.

They had dinner on a terrace under a large tree by the pool. "It is going well?" asked Señor Santiago.

"No, it is not," said Will.

"But the TV thinks it is going well."

"Yes, we let them think that."

"What can you do?"

"Tomorrow we have to sacrifice half the day to try to correct the problem, which doesn't give us much time to qualify."

Isobel sat there with her green eyes and dark curly hair falling to her shoulders, listening, and both pretending that there was no tension between them.

"Suppose it rains, what happens then?" she asked.

"Everything changes."

The green eyes flashed. "I understand that," she said, "but is it to your advantage?"

Jesus what a smart-arse bitch, he thought, and said slowly through half-clenched teeth, "It is only an advantage to those who have nothing to lose."

"Do you consider yourself in that position?"

He looked into those mocking eyes. "Yes," he said, "I do."

Señor Santiago said, with an amused grin, "Don't let her take — how do you say? — the mickey out of you."

Señora Santiago responded, "Will does not need this, Isobel, and you know it."

"It is time for me to go," said Will. "Tomorrow is going to be a heavy day."

"It will not be a heavy day for you. It is going to rain all weekend," said Isobel.

Will was startled. "Why do you say that?"

She looked back at him with those eyes, and said nothing. Will was going to push the point but decided to let it drop. He would bear it in mind.

"Will," said Señor Santiago, "do you realise that your political friends from the island are here to watch the race? And that they have brought TV crews with them as well?"

"No, I had no idea. I didn't think they were even interested."

"Yes, you are their man now. They will be broadcasting it live back to the capital."

"Where are they staying, Señor Santiago? I should get in touch with them."

"That is not necessary. They know that you will not have time to entertain them. They don't want to distract you, and asked me not to let you know that they were here. But I thought you should know. And another thing, don't you think it's time to stop calling me by my surname?"

"As I can't call you papa just yet, will Don Alphonso do?" And they all burst out laughing.

14

It rained after lunch on Saturday. They had been in and out of the pits in the morning qualifying session, making one change after another. This meant sitting in the car, talking to Ray through the headphones, while the changes were being made, hurtling out of the pits, establishing a time and coming back in. If there was an improvement, they would discuss it and decide on the next move. If there was no improvement, the car was immediately changed back to the way it had been. They had to be ruthless about it; you could not build on a weak foundation. They knew they had a problem: as they tried to run the car softer to get the tyres to work, other control problems appeared. The car was now bottoming under braking, lurching and twitching in the fast sections. They were going faster, but they were boxing themselves into a corner.

At the end of the first session, they were down to tenth on the grid. They were going nowhere. Then, out of nowhere the rain bucketed down, and the final qualifying session was cancelled. The rain had not been forecast; it caught everybody, most of all Will, by surprise. How the hell had Isobel known? It was spooky.

At the debriefing, it was all doom and gloom. It couldn't be the tyres, so what turned a race-winning car into a non-competitive one, from one race to the next? Will became fed up because they weren't getting anywhere. He jumped up and said, "Don't worry, it is going to rain tomorrow and we are going to win."

Everybody laughed and the meeting broke up. But Will couldn't get his mind off the rain prediction. How had she known? She could be right about race day.

•

Race day dawned overcast and drizzly, just like an English summer's day, thought Will. They were in the motor home discussing the weather, when one of the officials came bearing an envelope for Will. Inside he found a terse note from Isobel: "Today it drizzles all day."

He handed it to Ray, who asked, "What does this mean?"

"She told me it was going to rain yesterday and it did. Today she tells me it is going to drizzle, and since nobody has come up with anything better I reckon we should go with that. We should set up to run with intermediates, full soft on the suspension, and full wing. We don't have anything to lose; everybody else is running around trying to figure what to do."

"You mean to tell me that you want us to set the car up for conditions that have been forecast by some woman contrary to the weather report, which claims that it will clear this afternoon."

"She was right yesterday."

"Well, what the hell," said Ray. "We don't have a chance if it's dry, so let's set up for rain."

The race started in a light, intermittent drizzle. Will was tenth on the grid, and on the warm-up lap discovered that the outside of the first corner had more grip than the racing line. Maybe something good would come out of all this balls-up after all. He got a good start, and as they reached the first corner they all lined up on the racing line nose to tail, and Will drove around the outside. His heart was in his mouth as he was doing it, but it was easy; he just sort of tiptoed around, and was third. On the approach to the next corner he was second, and he picked off the leader at the end of the straight. Will couldn't believe his luck: here he was leading a race that he had already written off in his mind. But he had to be careful: it was still very slippery, but at the same time the soft tyres would not last, unless he looked after them. If it rained a bit harder, he would have to go in for wets, but if it stopped drizzling, he would burn out the intermediates he was using.

They were coming after him. He knew that they thought that he had conned them into believing he was having problems. Will was driving the race of his life. Some of the time he was off the racing line because of too much water, or too little. He was working the throttle and the brakes as gently as he could, no wheelspin, no locking of brakes. The hounds were after him; sometimes they would catch right up, then they would have to go into the pits for more tyres, repeating the process all over again. He hung in there like a bulldog; he wasn't going to let go, no matter what. A couple of them caught up, but the only way past was over the top, as far as Will was concerned. He would give them room where the track was wet off the racing line, and let them try to out-brake him, which ended up with them flying past with their wheels locked, spinning off. Others would try and try until their tyres went off; then had to pit.

When he crossed the finish line, Will threw both hands up into the air, yelling, "Got you, you bastards!" He was leaping up and down in the cockpit, as much as his belts would allow, shaking his fists in the air. As he drove back into the pits, the mechanics went mad, throwing their caps in the air; one was even stamping on his, and whooping. When Will climbed out of the car Ray grabbed him in a bear hug, almost squeezing the breath out of him. People were slapping him on the back, shaking him by the hand, more hugs; he just hoped no males would try to kiss him. The way they were carrying on, anything was possible.

He saw Isobel standing in the corner, watching him with a mysterious smile. "Thank you," he said. "How did you know?"

"Did you not know that I was a witch?"

"One day you will tell me."

"Perhaps."

Will looked over her shoulder and saw Carlos Menendez, the Argentinian Ferrari driver, shaking his head. Will responded by energetically giving him the fingers. The presentation was a real circus. The second-place finisher accused him of doing a con job on everybody else, and Will just laughed and laughed, and sprayed Moët left, right, and centre. At the press conference the media was convinced that the team's non-competitiveness in practice was to lull the rest into a sense of security, and Will only confirmed this to them by denying it.

In the motor home during the debriefing, they kept being interrupted. Ray was growing annoyed especially as Will kept telling him that it was all a big waste of time because this set of circumstances would never happen again.

"How the hell did she know?" asked Ray.

"She says she's a witch."

"It never rains here; plus the weather forecast was for hot and dry."

"I don't know any more than you do, but what I do know is that if she is going to play this witch-bitch game for a while, I don't want any part of it."

"Will, let's get on with it. We have to finish the debriefing; we need to record this. As you say, it is highly unlikely that this set of circumstances will ever repeat itself. I must say that it was tactically the most brilliant race that I have ever seen. It's a pity they all believed they were conned."

The whole team, including hangers-on, were invited to the hacienda for another of the Santiagos' famous barbecues. Will did not feel like facing scores of race fans, and there was no way that they could have gone out for dinner in peace and quiet anyway. Besides, he wanted to see the Witch again and his Latin American friends were going to be there.

•

The barbecue was a great success in every way: they were fascinated with Isobel, who displayed her considerable abilities as a hostess. The mechanics were their usual rambunctious selves, encouraged to no small extent by Señor Santiago, who brought out some calves for them to play bullfighter with.

Will was relieved to be forbidden by Ray to have a go, as he knew he would have had his ribs stoved in. He could feel the pain already. Most of his Latin friends acquitted themselves well among much laughter, as they had a fair idea of what the sport was about. They raved about the race; he was now their man for sure. The rest of the season was going to be televised live back home. The deal with the island was as good as done. Will and Señor Santiago agreed that it was better that he finalise the arrangements so that Will could concentrate on the rest of the season. Their Central American friends didn't want him distracted either, and were going to make sure that the deal went through with the minimum of fuss.

The team could not afford to hang around socialising. They had to get moving, as they had not traced the source of their problems, and there was another race in two weeks. Thanks to the Santiagos' influence, they were going to be allowed to use the track exclusively for testing over the next three days.

As they were saying their goodbyes, one of their friends from the island suggested, with an amused expression, that the next time Will went to the island he should bring Isobel with him. Neither of them said a word in response, but Isobel gave both men a "sweet little girl" look. Bitch, thought Will, there you go again. One day I'm going to catch up with you.

He did not really know what he wanted to do with her. He had never been as attracted to anyone before, but it was so complicated. He had to concentrate on winning the championship; he had thrown away the opportunity more than once before, and he was determined not to do it again. Even if he got involved with her, there was her career: she wouldn't give that up to follow him around. But then he didn't want her to follow him around; he enjoyed his freedom. But he had his freedom and he wasn't using it, so what was the point in that? Then there was her family, which he was rapidly becoming involved with in business, and he didn't want to jeopardise that either.

"Will," she said, "when you have finished your work, where do you go?"

"Back to London."

"I have to write an address and I can't do it here or at the office. So I am going to the beach house for a few days. Why don't you join me?"

Will looked in the eyes and saw nothing of the amusement or impishness that had been there before. She wasn't playing games, and she knew the consequences.

"I should be there by Wednesday night at the latest. Give me the directions."

Will knew that she had thought this through, and he didn't need to ask a bunch of dumb questions. One thing he did need to do was get it out of his mind until after testing was over.

15

It was dry on Monday, so they reset the car the way they had it in the first practice. They knew it would be different because of the rain, but they had to start somewhere. They were slower than in practice; the car didn't seem to have any stick. Will had to control himself and not push too hard, as he would only be defeating the purpose of the exercise. The car had to do its job; he couldn't do the job for the car.

By the end of the second day, they were no further ahead. The car was responding to change in the normal manner. It was working on the soft tyres, but not on the harder compound, and the soft tyres would not last a race. Will suggested a halt.

"We aren't getting anywhere. We may just have a tyre problem. We've done everything that we can, so let's be realistic. We have won two of the first three races; we can afford to throw away the fourth and still be in the lead. We can't find a problem with the car; let's take the bull by the horns, and accuse the tyre company of switching tyres on us, and see how they react. Don't just accuse them, do it through the media, and make a big fuss over it. Maybe then we'll get to the bottom of it."

Ray laughed. "I agree that we are getting nowhere and should pack up, but we can't go after the tyre company with the media; nobody's going to believe us — we conned them, remember? But I do believe that the tyres are different, regardless of the numbers."

•

Will left that afternoon in the old Porsche. Now that he was on his way to the beach he felt a tightness in his stomach, much as he felt before the start of a race. It was a great drive, narrow, twisting roads along the cliff-side, and the blue rolling sea; white-washed houses with flowers cascading from the balconies; the exhaust note of the old Porsche rasping and echoing as he worked up and down through the gearbox. He was enjoying this. He had enough in reserve to avoid the unexpected, but the old car was getting a workout just the same.

He arrived at the white villa on the cliffs overlooking the sea, its red clay-tile roof about level with the road. There was a large, open wrought-iron gate between white gate posts. The driveway fell away steeply from the road, and he had to ease the old car over the hump, as the bottom graunched on the ground. He parked behind a big, black Mercedes and switched off. The old Porsche crackled as it cooled down. The yard was of cobblestone; the steep, rocky hillside was covered in bougainvillea of every colour. An old man with a hose, sprinkling the garden, said something to Will in rapid Spanish which he didn't catch, and walked towards the house.

Will got out and stretched, looking along the side of the house out to sea. It was a beautiful day; the sea was deep blue with the colour changing to lighter blue as it grew shallower closer to shore. There was just enough wind for a few white caps. Will's mind went immediately to what it would be like being out there in his boat.

He tried to see whether there was an anchorage for *Imperialist*, but there was nothing that he could see. It was too exposed, the sea travelling for miles before it hit the cliffs with a dull boom. It was hot, and the sweat was trickling down his back. He was only wearing a light, long-sleeved cotton shirt turned halfway up at the sleeves, brown cotton pants, Bally loafers and no socks, but he was uncomfortable. The leather strap on his watch was irritating him.

The old man showed up again and beckoned Will to follow him. They walked around the side of the house towards a patio, with a large kidney-shaped swimming pool surrounded by clay tiles, on the cliff overlooking the sea. Behind the patio were French doors, folded back, leaving the house wide open. There were huge pot plants with flowers cascading everywhere, and what looked like a grape arbour stood at one end of the patio.

She walked out of the house with that long-legged flowing stride of hers, in white Bermuda shorts, bra-less, in a multi-coloured silk shirt knotted at the waist. Will felt his stomach tighten. Jesus, he thought, this was everything he had ever dreamed about.

She smiled and took his arm to walk alongside him. When their hips touched, he almost jumped, it was like fire.

"Welcome, welcome Will, did you have a good trip? Was the testing successful?"

"Yes and no. The trip was good, the testing was unsuccessful."

"Why is that?"

"We don't know for sure, but enough of that. I am so glad to be here. This is really beautiful."

"What would you like to drink?"

"Whatever," said Will.

"Sangria?"

"Sounds good."

"Had difficulty finding the house?"

"Not really."

"So, what is the problem with the car?"

"I think it's me."

"What do you mean?"

"I suspect I am driving the car too hard and killing the tyres. I may have to slow up a bit, on the entry into the corners. I'm braking too hard, and the car is sliding around too much as I get into the corners; and these new tyres won't handle it."

"When did you find that out?"

"On the way down here."

"On the road?" Isobel inquired with eyebrows raised.

"Yes. I guess I have always pushed too hard, and on the way down here, that old car really shows you up if you arrive in a corner going too fast, especially downhill; not knowing the road emphasised that. Because you are going so much slower than in a race car, and the loadings are so much less, it is easier to analyse what is happening."

"How fast were you going?"

"Fast enough."

"Be careful. I don't want you killing yourself."

They sat by the pool, sipping their drinks in silence. The sun was starting to set and Will wondered whether he would see the green flash, but then realised he was too far up. He needed to be at sea level for that. He wondered what he was letting himself in for. This wasn't a hit and run; this was church work, and he needed that like a hole in the head. It wasn't as if he was a loner, or objected to living with women, it was just that he wasn't in the nest-building business. His conscience always bothered him when he had to call it quits. He wished women would leave him for a change; he could pretend he was hurt and devastated, and go off whistling down the road. This one was different; there was no doubt about that, but he didn't want to get too involved. He didn't want a home to return to; he didn't mind having no fixed abode. What was he doing here anyway? They should have been in the sack by now of instead of sitting here like some old married couple.

"Feel like a walk on the beach?" Isobel asked.

"Sure," he replied. "Well, well, skinny-dip time," he thought.

They walked down the long, steep stone stairs to the beach. There would be no doing it in the water here, he thought, too much swell. Suddenly her clothes were coming off and she was diving into the sea. He thought of his wallet for a fraction of a second before tearing off his clothes. She was a better swimmer than he, and he couldn't catch up. She rolled over and started swimming on her back. He felt like a dachshund after an Alsatian. Her feet were just out of reach. He thought he could just see the furry thing, but he wasn't sure if he was imagining it. She headed for the beach and scrambled out of the water, shaking her long hair and laughing at him. Will climbed out of the water gasping for breath and sat down on the sand. She walked up and stood over him. I'm going to go blind if I see any more of this, he thought.

She reached down and pushed him over on his back and sat

astride him, eased herself up, helped herself to his organ and slowly started to work herself down on it. She held his shoulders with both hands pinning him down, and then slowly rotated her hips round and round and up and down. Jesus Christ, he thought, I am being screwed! I don't believe this, I am being screwed! Better hang in here until she tells me to stop, this is totally out of control.

Isobel watched him with the same amused expression that he had seen before. I can't let her get away with this, he thought, she is going to screw me then get up and laugh at me, and this can't work. Will grabbed her by the arms, rolled her over and set to work on her. She tried to keep the amused expression, she really did, but it soon disappeared. Will was putting on the show of his life. Isobel was thrashing around and moaning. He was getting in control of this, if he could stay on top. She was really bucking now, hollering out instructions of the most specific kind. Will thought of everything other than what he was doing to distract himself, until she had reached her peak, and as she let go, he did as well, ending with a shuddering rush together, both of them gasping for breath. The amused look was gone, replaced by something else. He rested on his hands looking into those emerald eyes; he knew it had been a near thing, but what now?

She had a slight smile on her lips. It wasn't the usual look — it was something else. He got up and pulled her to her feet, hugged her and they walked into the sea together. "I do not want what most women want," she said.

"Could have fooled me," said Will.

"No, that is not what I meant," she said, smiling. "I have no interest in tying you down."

"What happened there? What were you trying to prove?"

"I knew what was going through your macho mind, and I was going to teach you a lesson. I may not have exactly taught you a lesson, but I gave you a good fright."

"You sure did. I have never been raped before."

"Well, do you think you have earned dinner?"

"You are damned right I have; you half-killed me."

Dinner was on the terrace overlooking the sea; the moon was up, with its yellow beams reflecting off the water. The table was set with candles in glass holders on a wrought-iron, glass-topped table. They sipped dark red Tempranillo from outsized goblets, as course after course of tapas were brought out. The aroma of flowers surrounded them, while the light sea breeze pushed the small waves up the beach, reflecting the gentle glow of the moonlight.

They ended up in a huge, white bedroom, the floor white marble with several Persian rugs scattered around. The doors were heavy varnished timber, and a louvered door led into what Will assumed was a walk-in wardrobe, dressing room and bathroom.

The night breeze off the land blew in one side through the open white wooden louvers, and out the open French doors, while the ceiling fan whopped, whopped, whopped away, cooling the room, better than air conditioning ever could. The sea rolled up the beach below, ending under the cliffs with a regular dull boom, lulling them to sleep. The bed was a large, old mahogany four-poster.

They were no longer competing with each other. They lay in bed and talked for hours. Finally, Will said, "Why did you rape me?"

'Because,' Isobel said, "you were too confident, too arrogant, and I decided to teach you a lesson. Besides it was fun. You should have seen the look on your face."

●

Will woke with the sunlight streaming through the open doorway. He eased himself slowly out of bed so he wouldn't wake her. He had to be careful; if he woke her, maybe she would rape him again. He let himself out, and went for a run. He had to keep fit: it was lucky he enjoyed running as it made life a lot easier. As he ran through the village, his immediate impression was that the residents all knew who he was, and what he was doing there. The sweat was soon pouring down his face, and the shirt was sticking to his back. It was not yet hot, but it certainly was humid. He ran for an hour, and then headed for the beach. He threw off his top; pulled off his shoes, and dived into the clear, blue water. Instantly re-energised, he swam parallel to the beach, up and down, up and down until he couldn't go any more. He staggered out of the sea and collapsed on the beach. As he lay there with his chest heaving, he looked at the beautiful setting, and relived the night before. This, he thought, was more than any man could want.

Breakfast was rock melon and Parma ham, followed by poached salmon. The orange juice was fresh and thick with pulp, the bread crusty, and the Cuban coffee strong and sweet.

Will said, "You certainly make sure that a man will want to come back for seconds."

Isobel looked at him with those deep emerald eyes. "I grew up among men like you. My brother was one. Call me if you feel like it. Don't call me unless you want to, and if I do not feel like talking to you, I will not. I will call you if I feel like it, but you do not have to talk to me if you do not want to."

"You mean this is a one-night stand?"

"That is exactly what it is, and that is all it will ever be."

Will had never heard this one before. "Why?" he asked.

"I have my life to lead and you have yours, and there is no chance of that changing."

Will had never been given the message before, and he wasn't sure how to handle it. He wished he had heard it at some time from every other woman he had ever had. It would have saved him a lot of heartache. He couldn't argue with what she had said. It all made sense. But he was properly hooked, this was no ordinary woman. There was never going to be another like her, he was absolutely sure of that. He didn't want to be involved, he didn't want to have to tell her he didn't want to be involved, yet when she did the dirty work, and did it for him, he wasn't sure that he liked that either.

"Don't look so stunned, Will," she said. "Have you never been rejected before?"

"No, not after you worked me half to death all night, then tell me to buzz off and give me the 'don't call me, I'll call you' routine."

She laughed. "You will recover. We are both too busy, and talking about busy, I am already late for a meeting in town."

Will couldn't stop shaking his head as he walked to the car. This woman wasn't letting him get away with anything. As he was throwing his bag in the car, the old gardener sidled up to him. "Señor, you be Señorita's husband?"

"No," said Will. As he fired up the Porsche, and eased it out of the driveway, he thought about the old man's question. Why would he think that he was going to be her husband? Then it dawned on him. She wasn't half as big and bad as she made out. She didn't bring men here, so the gardener assumed he was her fiancé. Will laughed and laughed, as he drove through the village heading for France and the ferry to England.

16

WILL SAT WITH Ray and the tyre people in the office at the factory. They went over and over the information that they had from the testing. Will had voiced his theory, that the tyres had the wrong serial numbers stamped on them. At first the tyre people pooh-poohed the idea, but in the end it was agreed that, as there was no other reason that they could see, they might as well go down that track. After the tyre people left, Ray and Will did what they had done so many times in the past when they had had a major problem: they went back to basics.

"I believe," said Will, "that I make up time on the entry into corners, because I brake into, and sometimes round, corners. I think these new tyres are not handling it. What if the tyre walls are softer, flexing and generating more heat? If we went to the harder compounds, there wouldn't be a problem. But we can't, because we would be at a disadvantage with everybody else on the softs. So therefore I either have to change my style, which may make me uncompetitive, or change the set-up on the car so that I am forced to change my style, which may still make me uncompetitive."

"Will," said Ray, "the only realistic thing to do is to dial in some understeer, so that you are forced to slow up to get the car to point into the apex. You may compensate by being more comfortable on the faster corners and pick up some of the speed lost on the entry. You'll lose your ability to overtake so easily, which has always been your advantage. But we have to try something. The trouble is that we have no test time between now and the next race."

●

Unofficial practice started on Thursday. Will was first out on the track, rasping up through the gears using low revs and throttle settings, getting a feel for the car and the track, smoothly rolling the car through the corners. Into the pits for a quick check. Out again, more power, more revs, and still feeling good. Keep increasing speed; start to use the brakes harder. Still smooth as silk, rolling in and out of the corners, flowing smoothly, building up the speed, gradually feeling out the new set-up. Concentrate on the exit speed, less emphasis on the entry. Faster and faster, watch the pit board as the lap times come tumbling down lap after lap.

By lap fourteen progress had stabilised; there was no more improvement. Ray signalled him to pit. Will got out of the car, had a stretch and then went into the motor home. "Well?" asked Ray.

"It feels good, but I'm not pushing it. What are the tyre temperatures and pressures like?"

"Both good. You are currently over a second off the pace, so we'll see when you go back out."

Will put on the pressure. He started using full revs, and was braking later and later. The lap times were gradually coming down, but so were those of the other front-runners. Will was concentrating on keeping it smooth, trying not to kill the tyres. He was using the brakes harder and harder, while not allowing the rear to come loose. The times were coming down, no question, but he was still a second off the pace and he didn't like that. The temptation to stop pussyfooting around and go for it was almost overpowering.

Will dove into the pits again for another tyre temperature check. The tyres were getting hot but weren't going off. He charged out again, just as one of the front-runners came past. He set out after him, really pushing it now. He was braking later and later, and his entry speed was higher and higher. He was getting the hang of this new set-up: he had to change his line a bit on the slower corners, but on the fast stuff it was more stable. Maybe he could run less wing, get rid of some drag, get some more straight-line speed. He headed back to the pits for wing adjustment and stormed out again a couple of minutes later. He instantly noticed the difference; a bit more skittish on the fast stuff, but 500 rpm more on the straight. The times came down again.

Back into the pits for new tyres; worn tyres can lead you astray. Out again: instant improvement, a quarter second off the pace. Turn up the wick and go for it while the tyres are still fresh. Flat out through the long, fast left-hander, really humping now, 175 mph, feel the back squirming around, back out! Sideways, opposite lock, too late. Lost it, lock brakes on, opposite lock, back on full lock, try to localise the crash. Master switch off, wham, into the Armco, right corners off, over the barrier upside down. I am dead.

Will saw individual blades of grass as the car rolled, knowing exactly where his head would be planted. I'm dead. Bang, upside down, roll, crash right side up. Alive! Fire! No fire.

He flicked the release lever for the seat belts off and tried to bail out. He was stuck, his left leg caught. Starting to panic, he reached for the fire extinguisher button, and then remembered the golden rule: don't start the extinguisher until there is a fire. He twisted around in the seat looking for the fire, and for help. People were running towards him, good, but he still had to free himself. If it goes on fire, they would not help him. Other cars were stopping; drivers running towards him. Good, they wouldn't let him burn if they could help it.

Finally, after a long while, they extracted him from the car. His ankle didn't look broken; maybe it was just sprained. But it hurt like hell and as he couldn't walk they wouldn't let him go back to the pits; and he was carted off to hospital in an ambulance.

●

Will was released that afternoon into Ray's care, with instructions to keep the foot elevated for at least a week. "What happened?" asked Ray on the way back from the hospital.

"It just spun, too little wing, going too fast, I guess. How is the car?"

"We should recover the engine, the gearbox, and some bits and pieces. You were lucky, the roll bar was clipped off by the Armco, so you must have pulled your head in pretty well, but then you have a lot of experience crashing," Ray laughed. "I see you didn't fire the extinguisher this time. You aren't much use to us this weekend; we're going to pack up and head for home, but what do you want to do? Bearing in mind that you are supposed to keep your feet elevated. We have a race in three weeks and I hope that you will be fit enough for that."

"Yes, I understand that. I need to thank the guys that pulled me out, and then I'll figure out what to do."

"Just make sure that you are ready for work in three weeks' time. We were lucky that we just about got all the information that we needed. The crash put us out of one race, but with a lot of luck we may not have lost that much."

With an innocent expression, Ray suggested, "Why don't you go down to Spain? That should keep you quiet for a while. You'd be really well looked after. Don't go down to that bloody boat, you'll be leaping all over the place and in three weeks' time you'll be worse off."

"Just because *you* get seasick and spew all over the place doesn't mean that I have to hurt my ankle."

"Does that mean that you are going on the boat?"

"No, I'm not sure. The most important thing is to do well in the next race. To do that I need everything going for me, so I need to stay near the best help I can get."

17

WILL WOKE UP, not exactly sure where he was. He opened his eyes to the feeble light filtering through the curtains, and realised that he was in his London townhouse. Oh Jesus, he thought, as he felt the throbbing pain in his ankle. He remembered now that he was here because the doctors and physiotherapists were here, and he was supposed to stay in bed for a week, to give the torn ligaments a chance to mend. He tried to put together the cause of the crash. He knew that they were running too little wing, but that shouldn't have caused the car to snap around so suddenly on him. It felt as though he had hit the bump stops, and that had pitched the car. He didn't believe anything had broken, or if anything had, it wasn't a major component, it could be something secondary, like a roll-bar fitting. He had spoken to Ray several times, but the car was such a wreck that it was going to take days before they found anything, if ever.

The phone hadn't stopped ringing, but the housekeeper

fielded all calls. He would return some, but the bulk of them he would let pass. There were many offers of solace from past, present, and would-be female acquaintances. He had returned a few calls, including one from Isobel. She asked him how he was, not in the usual sort of way, but in a way he understood. She knew danger and death: although she did not understand the details of the risks, she certainly understood the concept. She invited him down, but understood without argument why he had to stay in London. The ankle ached and ached, but over the days the swelling started going down.

He spent the days and well into the nights on the phone. The deal on the island was finalised; detailed aerial photos were taken, and from the photos a model of the island was being produced. Will was determined not to get carried away about the island: he didn't want to over-commercialise it, but he sure as hell didn't want it to drive him broke either. He needed to find a good architect, with the vision to put the concept together. But before he could do this, he needed an absolutely clear vision of what he wanted to achieve, so he could impart his ideas efficiently to the professionals.

They worked on his ankle every day. Between phone calls and meetings he got as much exercise as possible without hurting it. At the end of the first week the swelling was gone, and so was most of the pain. The clock was ticking: there was a week and a half to unofficial practice for the next race. He had made up his mind that if he wasn't satisfied that he was close to a hundred per cent he was not going to play hero and risk setting himself back another race. He had to feel good, or he wasn't going to go.

•

Race day arrived bright and clear. Will still limped a bit, and knew it was going to be painful. He was nowhere near the hundred per cent fitness he had promised himself he would need before he raced again. He was there because he couldn't bear to let the side down. He was lucky it was the left ankle, because he could always drive without the clutch. He had tried it in practice, to get his hand back in, but the most difficult part wasn't changing gear without the clutch, it was convincing his left foot not to move. He had driven most of a twelve-hour sports-car race, years before, without the clutch, because his co-driver couldn't, and destroyed the gearbox in the few laps that he did. It wasn't that hard with a close-ratio gearbox with equal spacing between the gears.

Will had his gaze riveted on the starter, trying to jump the start without being caught. But this time he was not on the pole — he was fifth. He was holding down the clutch with his bad foot, waiting for the flag to drop. His foot was trembling and the pain was making his vision blurry. The starter's left shoulder lifted, and Will dropped the clutch. He darted right for the pit counter; nobody else seemed to be moving. He was going up through the gears heading for the long, fast right-hander. He had forgotten not to use the clutch, and he had forgotten the pain.

He was up to third, and closing fast on the two leaders. Will had the bit between his teeth — he was going for it, His momentum took him past the Lotus going into the first corner, but he knew he couldn't pass the Ferrari. He lectured himself again, "Settle down, settle down." He couldn't pass going into the esses, it was way too risky; however, he could let the other driver think that he was so he would screw up the entry onto the main straight. The exit from the right-hander onto the main straight governed the straight-away speed. If he could rattle Menendez in the Ferrari a bit, putting him offline into the corner without screwing himself up, he would get by on the straight. He glanced into his mirrors, realising that discretion was the better part of valour, because if he made the slightest mistake, he would be nobbled by a train of cars behind.

The train roared out of the esses down into the right-hander and out onto the back straight, with the Lotus nose stuck under his wing. This was tricky; the Ferrari in front was dead meat. Will could pass him at any time, but the Lotus behind him could do the same to him, as could the other Ferrari behind him. If Will moved first, the Lotus behind him would go with him, slingshot past Will, and probably take the number-four car in the line with him as well. If Will waited, he could easily be bottled in and be back to third or worse in a flash. But they would probably wait for the braking area to make the move, so he would move now. Will popped out of the slipstream, overtook, and popped back in front of the Ferrari, hoping to break the tow of the car behind.

He was in the lead. He wasn't in the clear, but he was in the lead, and the only way they were going to take it off him was to fight him for it. Will knew that one of them was going to try to out-brake him into the right-hand first-gear hairpin, but he was going to see them in hell first. Will was the last of the late brakers, leaving the braking impossibly late, but still one of them tried. Will watched him come roaring up the inside, hell-bent on destruction. Will moved over on him, not allowing him enough room to get a proper entry to the corner. He watched him lock the brakes, smoking the tyres, and go straight off the end of the track, onto the grass, and out of the race. A quick glance in the mirrors told Will that he was clear to turn in for the hairpin; he was down to first by this time. He held the brake pedal down till he was halfway round the corner, and the right-hand front wheel was halfway up the sloping, candy-striped kerbing. Opening up the throttle in one glorious surge of power, he swung the tail around in a smooth arc, unwinding the steering, and blasting over the kerb at the exit. As he straightened up he eased it into second, then third, and grabbed an early fourth, setting it up for the bumpy left-hander. He went through the corner in a long, flowing, twitching drift at full power. The trick was getting back to the left, in time to line up the right-hander. It was never easy; the speed was high, the bank was unforgiving, and once committed to a blind corner, it was hard to lift off. It was always a good idea to have a look at the flag marshals, or even the crowd, to get a feel for what was happening out of sight.

Will got over to the left and rolled the car into the long fast uphill right-hander, with the apex at the crest. The car was moving around a lot: he had to work the steering to keep on line. The tyres were still not up to temperature, and were not yet delivering their full grip. He knew he was working it too hard, and the tyres wouldn't last long at this rate. He was still using the clutch; he hadn't settled down enough, and the adrenalin was probably blanking out the pain. His ankle would start to hurt sooner or later, and he hadn't taken any painkillers for days, because he felt that that would dull his reflexes.

He went by the pits in the lead, just. He wasn't about to give it up, tyres or no tyres, pain or no pain. Turn one again, but this time at full speed with the length of the pit straight behind him. It was always scary getting into this one, flat on the first lap; you needed to work up to it, but there was no time for that. The big trick was the exit, which was immediately followed by high-speed esses; he had to be extremely smooth, just gently rubbing the brakes, and slipping directly into third on the entry, maintaining speed with a half throttle, slipping through the esses, keeping off the kerbs, until you ended up on the extreme left-hand side of the track in second gear. Turn in, under brakes, let the inside front wheels ride up on the kerbing, load up the outside front, the rear coming around, on the power, slide out over the rumble strip onto the dirt on the outside. Look in the mirror, a cloud of red dust. Eat that, you bastards. Will was onto the straight with about a half-second jump on the crowd. They wouldn't get into his slipstream from that distance, so he could start cleaning up his act. He went through the gears up the straight without using the clutch, which was not too bad, but now that he had time to worry about his ankle, it started to hurt.

Will concentrated on keeping it smooth, nursing the tyres; he was gradually pulling ahead by about a quarter of a second per lap. He wasn't used to this set-up, but as the race progressed he wondered why he hadn't tried it before. It was easier in the fast sections, no quicker, but easier, more stable. It was in the slow sections that he lost out; it was definitely slower there. But this was a high-speed track and it was magic.

He wasn't using the clutch at all now, but the more comfortable he got with the car, the more his ankle hurt. He would have liked to have taped it up with foam in case he bumped it, but there wasn't enough space in the foot-well, so he had to put up with it beating itself to death on the side of the chassis. He was concentrating more on the pain than on going quickly. He was losing ground. He forced himself to ignore the pain, which was like a knife being pushed into the bone. He started to sweat. He felt as though he was going to vomit with the pain, but he was in the lead and wasn't going to give that away.

He still wasn't using the clutch, but if he didn't press down hard on the footrest, his ankle would bang on the side of the foot-well. And if he pressed down on the footrest, that hurt as well. He was starting to worry that if he blacked out from the pain he would crash, and he didn't want to crash on a high-speed circuit like this one. Three laps to go. All he had to do was forget the pain for eight minutes. He was driving tactically now, keeping it smooth out of the slow corners, slowing up the approach, defending the overtaking areas, making sure the exits were smooth and fast, keeping the high-speed corners fast. But they were closing on him; all he could do was hold them up as best he could.

Last lap; Menendez was on his gearbox now. Will had to shake him off or he would tow past him on the straight, and win. Past the start-finish line for the start of the last lap, Will lectured himself, "Stay in tight for the flat-out right-hander; don't let him up the inside. Concentrate, one corner at a time, he can't stay on your tail through the fast corner or he'll lose front downforce and run wide; just rub the brakes for the esses, don't screw it up. Into third, keep the speed up. Good. Wait; wait, hard on the brakes out to the edge, good, good. Second, pitch it in, stand on it." He drove the inside front wheel up the sloping kerb. The further up the slope, the more load on the outside wheel, turning the car into the corner faster. Out to the edge, over the judder bars, onto the dirt. "Got the jump on him.

He won't be able to get a tow now. Concentrate on the hairpin, forget the pain, watch the mirrors. Not close enough for a tow, hairpin coming up hold it; hold it, on the brakes hard. Roll it in, roll it in. Don't screw it up."

He turned into the hairpin under brakes with smoke pouring off the inside front tyre. "Careful, careful, ease off the brakes. Don't flat-spot the tyres." On the throttle, get over to the right for the left-hander. "Good. Get into third early. Jesus, it's vibrating. Dickhead, the right front is flat-spotted. Doesn't matter; only have to get to the finish line." Over to the right for the left-hander. Car vibrating bad enough to rattle your eyeballs, tyres flat-spotted. "Please God; just get me through the last two corners."

Big drift through the left-hander, going too wide to get back for the right-hander. Glance back. "He's on the right line going faster, he's got the line for the right-hander, the last corner of the race; he's going to win, if he slows down now, and lets me into the corner first; he will easily pass on the exit. No, he's going to drive around the outside, idiot, he won't make it, because I'll be on the apex going sideways, and there'll be nowhere to pass, then it will be a drag race to the finish."

Menendez came up alongside, as Will pitched his car into the apex; he was in a huge opposite-lock slide at 150 mph. He kept his foot buried. He had the back hanging out like a dirt-track car. There was no room for the other one to pass; it was a drag race to the finish, and Will made it by inches.

The crowd went mad with delight, and Will almost went mad with the pain. He had to force himself to wave to the fans. He was scared he was going to vomit; it was only the thought of arriving back at the pits stinking that stopped him. People were all over the track. He popped it out of gear, and killed the engine, in too much pain to use the clutch to ease it through the crowd, coasting till the crowd got too thick, then stopped. He was surrounded; he released the belts and unplugged the oxygen. He tried pulling his left foot up to ease the pressure off his heel, but that only made the pain worse. People were trying to help him out of the car, but he waved them off.

He undid the chin strap and removing his helmet and put it on his lap. People were pushing bits of paper with pens under his nose. Somebody shouted, "He's sick, stand back." Another stuck a microphone in his face. Will shouted, "Move it, or I'll spew on it." It was hastily withdrawn. Suddenly there was a parting of the crowd, and Ray was there with some of the mechanics. Will said, "It's my ankle."

"Okay, we'll push the car back to the pits and lift you out there."

Will sat in the car while Ray steered and the boys pushed. TV camera crews walked backwards, asking questions. Ray finally exploded, "Can't you see he's hurt? Give him a break. He can't talk to you, he's in pain."

Ray shouted to one of the mechanics, "Find an official to approve going to the pits first to get Will out before the car goes to the parc fermé. If he agrees, get it in writing. If not, tell him we want an ambulance at the parc fermé. Bring his painkillers on the way back."

But the official wouldn't give the authority to go to the pits first, so an ambulance was forcing its way through the crowd, siren blaring.

"Bloody nonsense," said Ray. "There's no need for all this bullshit. We could have lifted you out at the pits. Now they're going to make you go to the hospital."

"Oh, for Christ's sake," said Will. "Help me out of here, and I'll walk."

"We'll carry you," said one of the spectators.

"You get him out, and we will carry him."

So Will was carried through the crowd by spectators to the rostrum. The media had a field day.

18

WILL TAXIED THE Baron up to the hangar where customs and immigration were waiting. Isobel was standing with a small group, which included the officials and her father. He carefully stepped down from the aeroplane and limped across to them. A huge smile forced its way across his face as he saw her. She was as beautiful as the last time he had seen her. She gave him a huge over-exaggerated wink, which thrilled him even more, and made him laugh.

One of the officials took the paperwork and told him that they would take care of it, returning it to him at the rancho. They drove off in Isobel's big black Mercedes. Her father sat in the back leaning over between the seats. "That must have been very hard," he said. "We watched the race on television. We saw you slowing down and knew that your foot was troubling you."

"It was the pain, it takes over the mind," said Will. "It made it very difficult to concentrate on the job."

"How is it now?" asked Isobel.

"It's not bad. It's back to where it was before the race. It didn't bother me at all flying the plane, so it should be okay by the next race."

"You are leading the championship and should win it according to the magazines, but one of them said that you were tired of racing," said Señor Santiago, "and if you won you would retire. Is that so?"

"That's probably the first time that they have ever got it right. Right now I would give it up if I won, and I would probably give it up if I didn't win, but it's not that easy — I have the team to consider. We are smaller than most; we have only one driver. We haven't had another driver for two years now. I have never discussed this with Ray; it's something we need to work out between us. I can't just walk off; it's not like a big team. If it were, I would give them notice right now."

"What happened to the other driver?" Isobel asked.

"He was killed at Monza year before last."

"Sorry, I shouldn't have asked. Halfway through I knew the answer anyway."

"Arne was a good guy; the car was very hard to drive. It put me in hospital for three months as well."

As they drove up the driveway to the big house, Will wondered what the sleeping arrangements would be like. Señora Santiago was standing on the front steps waiting to greet them. "Welcome. It is so good to see you, Will."

"It's great to be back here. It feels as if I've come home."

"You *are* home. How are you feeling? Are you in much pain?"

"No," said Will. "It wouldn't be a problem if I could rest it for a while, but I keep banging it on things, and charging around in racing cars doesn't help."

"Come in and relax. Rest is what you need. Would you like a drink? How about some sangria?"

"Perfect."

They sat under the huge veranda in the cool of the evening, and talked about motor racing, politics, business, the island, bulls, bullfighting, the ranch and back again. Will couldn't keep his mind off the sleeping arrangements; and he knew Isobel knew what he was thinking. Every now and then she would look at him with that amused expression. He wasn't at all sure that her parents were not aware of what was going on between them. Dinner was just fabulous as usual, they had the best tapas he had ever eaten, all the little dishes coming out one after the other, with big frosty jugs of sangria. Frogs croaked and the crickets chirped. It was just what the doctor ordered. Time for bed, Will thought, wondering how this was going to work.

He and Isobel were in adjoining rooms connected by folding doors, which turned it into one huge bedroom. Will laughed and laughed, as she looked at him with that amused smile and those green eyes. For the first time in his life Will believed he might be prepared to roam no more, to pass up the thrill of the chase. But then, when last did he chase? Usually it was like shooting fish in a barrel. He could see himself arriving at a cocktail party somewhere with her, circulating around after a while on his own. Would he be tempted? Would he regret having to pass up an opportunity; would he wish that he was not tied down? The answer was of course he would be tempted, but the excitement never lasted. With her, he suspected that the excitement *would* last. It had lasted well beyond the norm already; it would be an all-encompassing thing with family involvement. It would be a merger. If it didn't work, it would create havoc.

When they arrived for breakfast, the Señor and Señora were already at the table. He had been out early on the rancho. "Buenos días, Will. Did you sleep well?" he asked.

"As well as can be expected," answered Will. Then he realised what he had said, and could have kicked himself. "Oh, I'm sorry. I didn't mean it to sound that way."

"Do not trouble yourself. It was probably the right answer anyway." Señor Santiago smiled. "Will," he said, "you are one of us, and you have been for a while. If you marry our daughter, that will be very good. If not, you will still remain one of us."

"I feel like one of you, and Isobel is a dream come true to me."

"There is no need to say any more. It is not necessary. You have much to do and the time is not right. We knew from the beginning that you could be the son that we lost."

Will felt himself go cold, goose-bumps appearing on his arms. If he were superstitious, he would have said that somebody had walked over his grave.

•

The next morning they left for the house on the cliff on a beautiful, clear day with a few clouds scudding by. Will watched Isobel as she drove; she was a natural, with an easy, flowing way of handling the big car. He showed her how to use the road, improving her line through the corners, how to use the camber, how to use the brakes. Soon the stink of burnt brakes filled the cabin as she hustled the big Merc into the corners, hand-shifting the automatic. The smell of burning transmission fluid joined the smell of the brakes as they began to fade, and the fluids started to boil. "You'd better back off a bit," said Will, "or we'll have to walk home. The car won't take too much more of this."

"Okay," she said. "That was fun, and I also understand much more now about your job."

"You are a natural," he said, "but you can't overdrive it like that — it won't last. It's a street car; it wasn't set up to be hammered that way. I tell you what I am going to do. I'll send you my old Porsche and you can have some fun with that. You won't be able to overdrive it on the street." She gave him that amused look, but said nothing.

They arrived at the house on the cliff with the gauges in the red and the brakes dead. The old retainer opened the gate, and didn't appear surprised to see him. "Buenos días, Señor. Cómo está usted?"

"Bien, gracias," responded Will. "Y usted?"

"Bien, Señor."

Will couldn't wait to go for a swim; the water was crystal-clear, cool and calm. They swam out to rocks off the beach, side by side, and climbed onto the rocks which had emerged as the tide went out. They lay back on the big smooth black rock soaking up the sun. Isobel was wearing a white one-piece bathing suit, contrasting with her deep tan, which made her look even better than in a bikini. Her smooth tanned legs were starting to set Will off again, sending him back to the night before, and the way the sleeping arrangements had been handled.

They had gone to bed early, made an absolute mess of one bed, and then moved into the other. In the morning they had woken up early, with the sun streaming in the windows. Will had propped himself up on one elbow and looked at her, curly dark hair everywhere.

She smiled at him. "What are you looking at?" she asked.

"You," he replied.

"How long have you been looking?"

"All my life."

"What do you mean?"

"All my life I have been looking for you, but now that I have found you, I am afraid that I may have found you too soon."

"I know," she said. "There is too much pressure on us, the pressure of time, the pressure of the past, and of the future. I do not want pressure."

The next day she dropped him off at the airport. For the first time, he did not want to go back; he didn't want to drive any more. No, it wasn't that, he didn't want to push himself to the limit again; he didn't want to have to extract from himself the last ounce of reserve. He didn't want to suck himself dry any more; he had done it for too long, and he was tired, very tired. He was walking towards the terminal when he swung around. She was still parked in the same spot. He dropped his bag and ran back to her, reached into the car, put his hand behind her head and pulled her to him. "I'll miss you," he said, and ran back to recover his bag. He turned back and waved, as he dashed through the door.

•

Race day was bright and sunny; the forecast was for a hot day. Practice and qualifying had gone well. He should have been on the pole but he wasn't; he was third. The car was very good, he could have got it on the pole, but the will wasn't there. Some people would say he had matured and was now more sensible, that he was playing the odds. They were right, but he wasn't playing the odds for the odds' sake; he just didn't have the desire to fight for it any more. He was sure Ray knew exactly what was going on, but so far nothing had been mentioned, and nothing would, so long as he continued to win races. And that would only continue as long as he had the best car. He no longer had the stomach for fighting with an uncompetitive vehicle.

Will got off to a good start: he didn't try to win the race on the first corner as he usually did. Instead, he sat back and watched the two in front fight for the lead. This was a new experience: he had never waited for an outcome in his life before; he had always been in there going for it. Will knew both drivers in front well. He had been racing them for years. One was an odds man, and the other was a balls-to-the-wall, do-or-die merchant. They had been in Formula Ford together, and later in Formula Three. One was a Scotsman and the other an Argentinian. Jackie Flint, the Scotsman, was cautious and calculating: his nickname was The Professor. He was small, tidy, and realistic. He took as few chances as he could. His argument was that he had seen too many of his friends die, and he planned to stay alive if he could. He was silky smooth, very quick, never driving the car beyond its limits. He made the car work for him, spending hours in the workshop with the engineers, going over and over the issues till he got it right. He never spun, and he almost never crashed. He didn't womanise, didn't booze, leading what Will thought was a boring life. But he was a very good driver, and had already won the World Championship twice.

Carlos Menendez was the maniac, tall, blond, good-looking and a lady-killer. He collected women in droves. He would arrive at the track in a Ferrari convertible, in jeans, a jeans jacket and a cowboy hat, with a couple of hot babes sitting up on the back of the seat. He was very quick. Quicker than Jackie if the cars were not perfect. But Jackie would usually win when it worked for him. And Carlos crashed often. He had walked away from some horrendous accidents. Carlos would always fight for the win, which made the mechanics love him, while Jackie would take what he could get. Carlos would probably not live till he retired.

Will tried to convince himself that he was stalking them, but in fact he was waiting for one or both of them to fall off. Jackie was leading and Carlos was right up his backside trying to pass. Will had a feeling that Carlos would take him off, as Jackie was blocking him. It was early in the season and no team orders had been established yet. And so it came to pass, late in the race, that Carlos pulled off one of his do-or-die moves. Jackie closed the door on him, and they took each other off. Will was left with an easy win. The media said he had matured, that he was now a strategist in the mould of previous champions. Will felt a certain satisfaction from the win, but not the exhilaration he got from a hard-fought race, even one he hadn't finished. Right after the race, Will phoned Isobel and asked her to meet him on the boat. She asked a lot of questions about the race, but Will didn't want to talk about it.

19

Isobel walked up the concourse, bag slung over her shoulder, with that long-legged, hip-swinging stride that left men gaping. Long, curly, dark hair bouncing as she swung towards him with a huge smile, emerald eyes sparkling. He couldn't help grinning as he took her bag, and put his arm around her waist, hips rubbing against each other, heading for their connecting flight to the boat.

Graham and Peter were lolling around on the dock waiting for them. As they looked up and saw Isobel, they leapt to their feet. "Calm down guys, stick your eyes back in," said Will. They climbed gingerly down the slippery mossy stone steps of the old dock to the big canoe that they had hired to take them out to the island, and carefully eased aboard. "Okay?" asked Will. Isobel nodded as they seated themselves.

Will watched as the canoe captain wrapped the starter cord around the flywheel of the old outboard motor. "Shit," he thought, "I hope this thing doesn't break down and we end up drifting till we die of thirst somewhere. Eventually they started for the ride out to the island. Will had forgotten how well these canoes rode at sea. They just sliced through the waves, not slamming from one wave to the next like the usual power boat. Will remembered fishing one night in a big launch and beside them was a canoe with a Tilley lantern, absolutely comfortable, while the launch was rolling its guts out, making everybody sick.

As they came alongside *Imperialist*, Will stood up and grabbed the gunnel, and handed Isobel onto the boarding ladder. The other two grabbed the bags and climbed aboard after them, while Will paid off the canoe. Isobel stood on the acres of teak deck and looked around. "This is classical," she said, "a thing of great beauty."

"There is nothing like her anywhere," said Peter. "We helped build her, but we couldn't bear to let her out of our sight, plus we didn't want to leave her to Will's tender mercies."

"Come on down," Will said, "and I'll show you where to stow your gear." They walked through the white deckhouse, framed with glowing varnished laminated beams, down the companionway steps, with the teak grating at the bottom. "What does that do?" she asked, pointing at the grating.

Will told her it was to let water brought down the companionway by wet-weather gear drain into the bilge. That all wet gear was stowed here in heated lockers, and that wet gear was not allowed forward of the galley and the navigation area, or to the aft cabins. Salt water attracted moisture; and the upholstery, once wet, would stay wet.

As they walked past the nav area with all its dimly lit instruments, Isabel looked at the galley with its deep fiddles and aft-facing four-burner stainless-steel stove, complete with pot holders. "Why three, I would believe one would be enough?" she asked, as she looked at the three deep, narrow sinks.

"One to stack, one to wash, and one to drain," replied Will.

"But boats this size usually have dishwashers."

"I know, but this is a real sea boat and we don't want to bother with things like that. They use too much power and they don't like the environment."

They walked into the saloon, where light was pouring in from the deck hatch, above the twelve-place, polished teak dining table. On the portside forward bulkhead was an oil painting of a yacht race in a brass frame, in impressionist style, all blues and greens, lit by a brass lamp bolted to the bulkhead above.

They went forward into the only double cabin on the boat. "What a wonderful place, such atmosphere. It is a beautiful cabin," said Isobel, looking around and taking in the queen-size bed, the woodwork glowing in the light, and the white ceiling, with the cooling breeze drifting through. "But it does not look lived in. Do you use it only to entertain women?"

Not for the first time, she had succeeded in making Will feel uncomfortable. He was about to deny it, but realised that it would only make it worse. He couldn't come up with a smart reply: the best he could do was a lame, "I usually sleep in the navigator's berth."

"Why?"

"Because I prefer it."

"So who sleeps in here?"

"Guests, usually."

"Guests on their own, or guests with you?"

"A bit of both," was all he could manage.

"So, which sort of guest am I?"

"The sort that sleeps alone, if she doesn't stop asking so many damn questions."

"Well," she said, reaching out for him, "I had better, how do you say, shape up or ship out."

That evening as the enormous golden moon slowly rose from behind the hills, *Imperialist* swung slowly this way and that in the cool breeze. They spent the evening sitting on cushions in the centre cockpit in light cotton shirts and shorts, having dinner by lamplight from an oil lamp hanging off the main boom, throwing its yellow glow over the table. They could just hear the coconut trees on the island rustling in the gentle land breeze that had started after dark, when the trade winds had dropped.

Peter and Graham knew this woman was different, and were on their best behaviour. They offered to go into town in order to leave them alone, but Will would not hear of it. If he was going to chain himself to one woman, he sure as hell wasn't going to change his life as well. If they could both adapt to each other's lifestyles, then there was a chance of a one-woman life working. He wasn't at all sure it would, but if it was to work, this was the one.

•

The sun rose with an orange glow over the eastern sky. High-altitude mare's-tails spelt wind for later on, as they prepared to leave. Isobel had spent summers on a yacht as a teenager, and it was soon obvious that she had not forgotten all that she had learned, but Will warned her to be careful about the gear, as there were huge loads on blocks and lines, and she must not put herself in the position where she could get hurt if something let go.

The wind was light and warm, with a long low swell as *Imperialist* slid down the back of the waves with a gentle whoosh, and waited for the next one to pick her up and slide her forward again. As soon as they cleared the reef, Will had set the lines, hoping for a tuna or a dorado for breakfast, and maybe sashimi for lunch. The sea was dark blues, winds were light and warm, and calypso was pouring out of the cockpit speakers. Isobel was sitting up by the main shrouds, in a skimpy black bikini, catching the sun and looking out to sea. When Will sat down beside her, she said, "You brought me here to see whether I would appreciate this, did you not?"

"No, I knew you would like it, but when it gets tough, I hope that you will still like it."

"I hope so too. This is heaven on earth; how could I not like it?"

20

By early afternoon, they started to pick up signs of their destination. The colour of the water started to change from the deep ocean blue to the lighter colours of the shallows. The dark strip on the horizon slowly turned into a low-lying island with coconut trees waving a welcome.

As they got closer, they dropped the spinnaker and spinnaker staysail, followed by the mizzen, continuing on with the main and self-tacking staysail. Will started the engine while Graham was up the mast sitting on a spreader with his polaroids giving hand signals, conning them through the narrow pass into the lagoon and around the coral heads and into the horseshoe-shaped lagoon. Will headed her up into wind as they rolled up the staysail and dropped the main. Peter ran up forward and waited for Will to signal him to start paying out the anchor chain. Will could see the white, sandy bottom clear as crystal, even though it was five fathoms deep, as he signalled Peter to let her go. The chain rattled out and *Imperialist* drifted back, finally settling on the anchor. Peter watched it for a while then walked back.

"Swim time," yelled Will, as he grabbed Isobel and jumped over the side. They rose to the surface laughing and spluttering. "What a wonderful day it has been." She looked at him with those eyes, serious for once. "I don't want to marry you, but I will be your mistress. I will be devastated when you have other women, but of course I will forgive you. I do not want you any different than you are now. I don't want you to have to stay with me." But," she said with that look again, "you must not ask me where I have been when you do not know where I have been."

Will laughed a little nervously. "Is this reverse psychology?"

"No, I am just making it easier for you. I don't want anything to change. You are like a wild thing; you would not survive in a cage. It is better this way. You are involved in a dangerous game. I could not stand to lose you after losing my brother, and neither could my parents." Will had nothing to say. He couldn't argue with her logic. He wished other women thought like this. What a wonderful world that would be. But he wasn't at all sure he liked this plan.

They climbed up the boarding ladder. Isobel went off to lie in the sun while Will organised himself to go spearfishing for lunch. He and the guys dragged the big inflatable dinghy out of the sail locker and pumped it up. They mounted the 25 horsepower motor on the back, lowering it over the side. Will primed the motor, started up, and slowly headed for the reef. He couldn't help looking back at *Imperialist*, he just loved that boat. He scouted along slowly, looking for a likely spot. It was absolutely clear, and he could see the white, sandy bottom with clumps of coral rising. The main reef was almost up to the surface, while the bottom was five to six fathoms deep. There was a bit of swell on the lee side of the reef as the sea broke over it. It would be a hundred fathoms deep on the ocean side, which was far more than he was interested in today. He was on his own, and had brought only snorkelling gear, anyway.

All was peace and quiet inside the half-moon shaped reef, with the water calm and light green. On the outside, the deep blue sea came rolling in, breaking over the top with a hiss and a roar, withdrawing with a sigh. The breeze rippled the surface of the lagoon, giving the effect of a nineteenth-century impressionist painting.

Will motored the dinghy as close as he could to the reef, dropping the little anchor over the side onto the sandy bottom, before cutting the motor. He pulled on his flippers, spat in his goggles, wiping the saliva around with his fingers to demist them, washed them out with seawater, and put them on. Pushing the snorkel into his mouth, he clamped down with his teeth, and eased himself over the side. He reached back into the dinghy and picked up his spear gun. He positioned its handle into his stomach, pulled the rubber band with both hands onto the slot in the spear. He didn't bother to set the second rubber, as he didn't think there would be anything big enough to need it. He kicked his flippers slowly, as he worked along the reef, getting accustomed to his surroundings. There were many small striped fish about, and some reasonable blue parrot fish, but he was not interested in any of these. He was after a big snapper, or a few small ones, for lunch.

Will was always a bit apprehensive by himself in the sea. He didn't like the odds if some shark decided he was dinner. He felt much better when there were others about; it gave the old shark a better selection, and Will better odds that he wouldn't become dinner. Despite his slight nervousness, he decided to get on with it. Any worthwhile fish would be hiding under the reef, not wandering about in the open. He took a deep breath, arched his back, kicked his feet, and swam down to the bottom. His ears started to hurt, but he kept going. The goggles, squashed against his nose by the increased pressure, began to leak.

He swam along the bottom, looking up under the little caves, nooks and crannies, to see what was there. Will finally ran out of breath, stopped swimming, and floated back up to the surface. There were plenty of good-sized fish about; the reef did not seem to have been spearfished much. The visibility was amazing, the white, wavy, sandy bottom, with walls of coral. He could see way off into the distance, looking down canyons in the reef, almost like city streets between high rises. If he dived and looked up, he could see the surface shimmering in the sunlight. The reef itself almost came up to the surface, but the sandy bottom was deep. On top of the reef he could stand on brain coral, and be chest deep, while he emptied the water from his goggles.

Will swam straight down to the sandy bottom again, his chest skimming the sand, his legs working the flippers hard, his ears hurting, the pressure squashing the mask tightly onto his face. Right up under the reef he could see something bigger among all the smaller fish. Supergun fully extended, at about six feet from the red snapper, he fired. Bam! Got him. The fish was thrashing about with a spear through the gill. Will picked up the spear, and, holding it away from himself, swam back to the dinghy. He threw the gun into the boat, unscrewed the head of the spear, reached into the boat and let the snapper slide off into the boat. He reloaded and went looking for more fish.

As he swam past the entrance, he saw a large, dark blue body with a dorsal fin glide by. "Shit, shark," he thought. He didn't like this one bit. He was accustomed to seeing grey reef sharks, but this one was dark blue with a deep body. Could it be a mako? Should he just head back to the boat? But there was quite a bit of open water between the reef and the boat. Did he just wait here? Although it could be a reef shark that lived in the reef. What then?

After a while he started spearfishing again, although his heart wasn't in it. Whether or not it was sixth sense he looked around, and there was the shark coming down the canyon between the reefs, straight for him. Will's heart went into high speed. What to do? Get up on the reef. Will swam up over the shallowest part of the reef as the shark glided past. What now? He couldn't stay there forever. He suddenly realised that in his panic he had forgotten the dinghy, and didn't have to swim back to the boat. His heart was pounding so hard he thought it would jump out of his chest. But even the dinghy was a problem. He should have gone to it when he first saw the shark. Now it was too late. "Think, damn it. What could the shark do? Eat me, of course. But I have a supergun and with water this clear, he couldn't sneak up on me, plus I have the reef to climb on." So he disconnected the rubber from the spear so he could use it like a lance, and let the shark run into it if it attacked. With the supergun disarmed, he would not be able to fire it and lose the spear.

Will decided that his best course was to work his way along the reef at the shallowest part, so the shark couldn't follow till he got close to the dinghy. But at some point he would have to cross in deep water. He inched himself along the top of the reef, being careful not to cut himself. Blood in the water would not improve his day. By this time the shark was growing very agitated, and was rushing up and down the canyon alongside the reef.

Will finally got to the end of the reef. There was the dinghy, and there was the shark. Will jumped into the water on the other side of the reef and the shark went shooting down the channel, roaring up the other side. Will swam on his back as fast as he could, with the supergun pointing at the oncoming shark. He swam straight into the dinghy, bumping his head into it, flipping himself over into the boat. The shark circled the dinghy; Will's next fear was that it would bite the tube and sink the dinghy. In total panic he threw his catch as far as he could into the sea, and yanked the starter cord. Once the motor was running, he hauled up the anchor and left at full throttle.

•

Will sat with Isobel in the Air France 747, en route to Paris. He was trying to adjust his head back to racing mode. It was extremely difficult at best, switching from one mode to another. It was worse now that he didn't really want to go back. He had to lock his mind into racing mode; he must turn everything else off. Switching his head from one mode to the other was the hardest part. It was like grabbing his head with both hands and yanking it around. If he didn't do it, he was stuffed; he would just not be competitive; he had to be focused, lean, mean and hungry. He forced himself to visualise the track, the approach to the corners, the entry, the exit, every camber change, the kerbs, every single detail gleaned from his years of racing there. He knew how essential it was to get into this frame of mind.

Isobel reached over and squeezed his hand. "Qué te pasa?"

"Nada." They sat silent for a while; "Tell me, how did you pull that witch trick with the weather?"

"Simple. Carlos, the gardener at the beach, told me one of his plants bloomed, which meant rain."

"He sure as hell got that right; he won me that race."

"Will," she said, "do not push yourself if you do not have the desire any more. My brother continued after he should have stopped, and the bulls got him."

"Did your father know?"

"No, but I did. It became a matter of pride. Then there was this woman."

"What woman?"

"A famous actress, a married woman. Her husband owned one of the television stations. She was very bad for him. He became, how do you say, obsessed."

"What happened?"

"Her husband knew, everybody knew. There was another bullfighter; there is always another. The news media built up a rivalry between them, which had not existed before. It grew worse and worse, and he took bigger and bigger risks. I tried to get him to stop, but he would not listen. I knew that her husband was trying to get him killed. I spoke to him, tried to reason with him, but it was no use. My father refused to supply the bulls, but that did not stop him; he wanted to defeat her husband. He did not care about the bulls any more; he became cruel, as he pushed himself to the edge. Finally, one day, she arrived with her entourage in the middle of a fight. She entered her box with the cameras flashing, and all the dramatics that went with it. He was distracted at the wrong moment, and he was gored."

"What happened then?"

"They tried to get the bull off him, but it was too late. He bled to death before they got him to hospital."

"What did she do?"

"She collapsed in front of the television cameras. But of course she could not make it too obvious, or she would have thrown herself on top of his body. Think what that would have done for her ratings? The strange part was that I do not believe he really loved her; he was obsessed with her, and he wanted to beat her husband. Without her husband I do not think the affair would have lasted. It was an obsession, that is all."

Will didn't say anything — what was he to say? That he was sorry? Of course he was sorry. He squeezed her hand. He understood what had happened with her brother. It was competition, pure and simple; the challenge had been thrown down, the duel had been accepted; and even though it was one-sided, it had to be fought. The good guys did not always win.

21

THEY WALKED INTO the motor home together. Ray looked up, trying to keep the surprise out of his face, and failing miserably. "Don't stand there with your mouth open," said Will. "Say hello or welcome, or please leave, or something."

"It's just that I never expected to see you two together. Where have you come from?"

"The boat," said Will.

Ray's eyebrows shot up. "Did you have a good time?" he asked Isobel.

"Yes," she said, "I had a *wonderful* time," and gave Ray one of her looks.

Ray's eyes darted between them. He cleared his throat. "Well, yes," was all he could manage. Then, "We are all ready. We have a bit more horsepower and a new wing, a glider wing. You know, the same profile as a glider. The wing is the one we have been testing in the wind tunnel. It has less drag at high speed, with no loss of downforce, except at low speed."

"Loses how?" asked Will

"It is short on downforce at low speed, which means you may have an oversteer problem in the tight stuff."

"That is going to be peachy with soft tyres. How am I going to keep the rear tyres alive, if the arse end is sliding all over the place?"

"If it doesn't work, we'll go back to the old set-up, but it should be worth at least five miles per hour on the main straight by itself, plus the engine should be worth another two or three."

"OK," said Will, "we can but try. What's the story on the tyres?"

"They have a new intermediate, which they hope will fill the gap between the softs and the hards, so that may solve your problems."

"*My* problems?"

"The problem of you is tearing up the tyres by overdriving the car."

"Bullshit," responded Will, "the goddam tyres were too soft, and you knew it."

Ray had got the last laugh, and was happy again.

●

Race day was hot, stinking hot. There wasn't a cloud in the sky. It was going to be bloody awful in the car, 100-plus degrees. Heat exhaustion was going to be a problem, especially for those who were not accustomed to a hot climate. You could lose ten pounds in a race like this; cramp could be a problem as the salt sweated out of your system. They had tried to ventilate the car as best they could, but without the ability to test they couldn't take the risk of some modification causing an unforeseen problem.

The crowd was not as large as normal; the beach seemed to have been the preferred option for many people. The cars were out on the grid, their battery boxes plugged in. Some drivers were already in the cars with mechanics holding umbrellas over their heads; others hovered around doing last-minute adjustments; some just kept their drivers company. Will waited till the last possible minute, in the air-conditioned motor home, before he ventured out. He wanted to stay cool for as long as he could.

The warm-up lap was a lot less energetic than normal, with less weaving and braking to warm up the tyres and brakes. They rolled back into their start positions. An official was running around with the one-minute board, the starter on the rostrum, a different little fat man this time, engines being rasped up and down.

Will was third on the grid, behind the pole-sitter, beside the fourth car. He was already sweating. There was no umbrella over them now; the heat was beating down, and the engine temperatures were rising. "Hurry up, you little bastard," Will shouted, but it was the man's moment of glory, and he wasn't going to be hurried. The start-finish straight was narrow. It was going to be difficult to jump the start; there was nowhere to go. He needed to grab the lead early and get away. He didn't want to have to fight for it; he needed to conserve himself, and his car. He couldn't afford to do too much slipstreaming, as it would make his car overheat. Close behind another car, he would have less air going into the radiators, and would also be sucking in hot air straight out of the exhaust pipes. He needed to grab the front as soon as possible and stay there.

The flag was up. Watch his left shoulder raise, go, don't, wait for the flag. Damn — the pole car, Menendez hadn't moved. On the brake; on the gas again. Early into second, looking for a hole, turn one coming up, sandwiched on the inside, wheels everywhere, stuck, no room, traffic jam. Through turn one, on to the main straight, nose still stuck up the backside of Menendez; can't go to the outside, boxed in, Jesus Christ. Three abreast going into turn two; go up the inside or let them go? To hell with this — let them go. Will had to talk to himself: slow down and win, slow down and win, don't go at it like a bull at a gate; use your head.

Still, at the end of the first lap he was fourth. Into turn one again, a high-G 180-degree banked oval track-type corner. It was one of those almost flat-out fourth or fifth-gear jobs that could leap up and bite you if you got it the slightest bit wrong; but it could put 5 mph onto the straight-away speed if you got it right. Will concentrated on getting the approach right, hoping to get the exit speed, which would allow him to draught pass, under-braking at the end of the straight.

In his peripheral vision, he caught a glimpse of a Lotus coming in over the top of him. The stupid bastard, what do you think you're going to gain by that, except stuff both of us up? Will had two choices: fight him for it and possibly let him take both of them out; or let him go, and hope to pick him up again on the straight. Will let him go, and concentrated on getting out of the corner and onto his tail with more speed. They ended up on the straight with Will's nose right up under his wing. Will popped out of his slipstream halfway down the straight, grabbing a tow off the third car sooner than he had expected.

As the slipstream took effect, he could start backing off the throttle. Just before the braking area he popped out of the tow and went by with his last of the late-braker's trick. He could feel the front dip and bite under the brakes. As he wound on the steering into the corner, the unweighted rear started to come around. He modulated the brake pedal with his foot. With his heel locked into the heel rest he could increase or decrease brake pressure, loading the front wheels, and lightening the rear just enough to increase or decrease the rate of turn into the corner.

Now he was third, but Menendez in the lead Ferrari had got away while all the kerfuffle was going on. Time to take stock: temperatures were hot, but the oil pressure was still good. Will wanted to open the visor to let in some air, but the last time he tried that, the visor had blown off, leaving him to drive the rest of the race with crap coming off the cars in front getting into his eyes… He didn't want to try that again. Will started to talk to himself again: "Keep it smooth, save the tyres, save yourself, but don't let him slip away; put pressure on him, up closer, but keep it smooth, creep up on him, let him sweat, a tenth of a second per lap."

Will put the car ahead out of his mind, concentrating totally on each corner as it came up, working on his line to make sure that the maximum speed was extracted, at the minimum cost in wear and tear. He was inching closer, some laps a quarter of a second, some none, nevertheless he was closing, closing. It was hot in the car. He was tired; the temperatures were going up, and the oil pressure was starting to come down. His lack of fitness was telling on him. He didn't spend his life in the gym, as some did. He ran, he swam, he rowed, but he hated gyms. Now he was getting tired, and the dickhead in front wasn't. But Will used less energy than the others. He didn't climb out of the car at the end of a race drowned in sweat like most of them. He cut the revs back by five hundred. The temperatures didn't drop, but the climb slowed, and the pressure stabilised; the problem was, he wasn't gaining ground any more.

Will now had a choice. He could wait and see, and maybe finish second. If nobody fell out, he could ease off a bit more and at worst finish third. The chance of both the others finishing wasn't that good, so a second was likely. Or he could go back to full revs and pressure the car in front, or half a dozen variations on that theme. He couldn't make up his mind; he didn't realise that the heat was affecting him as well. He checked the pit board. He wasn't losing ground, but the fourth car was closing. What did that tell him?

Will put that in his mental computer and made a decision. The guy behind, Menendez in the Ferrari, was desperate for a win and was willing to gamble. The others knew him as well as he knew them, but he had an advantage — they would be working on the old Will, who would have gone for it regardless. The new Will talked to himself and had become an odds man. The odds were that he could finish second and with six points towards the World Championship, but if he could persuade these guys to break down, and have no points, whatever he got would be much more valuable in the final analysis. Will decided to maintain his rev reduction for ten more laps and check the temperatures then. Ten laps later, Menendez had picked up a second and a half, and Flint was still three and a half seconds ahead. The temperatures had stabilised, so Will went back to full revs. He couldn't believe it; he immediately picked up half a second per lap. Not only himself, but the engine, and especially the tyres, had benefited from the rest. Flint did not respond, probably couldn't, and Will was closing rapidly. The temperatures were rising again, risking engine problems. If he could knock off the lead quickly, he could ease off again. There were fewer than twenty laps left.

The fatigue was getting to him; he could no longer hold his head up through turn one. His neck muscles were shot. The G force was forcing his head over, bouncing off his shoulder as he went through the corner. The lower edge of the helmet felt as if it was digging a hole in the skin. He was looking out the corner of his eyes like a peeping Tom, as his head bounced around.

He could no longer change gear on the entry to the corners — the G forces on his upper arm were too painful. He knew he was falling apart, and promised himself that as soon as his vision started to blur, he would slow down. But he was still gaining on the lead car.

Will was now leaning his head over onto his inside shoulder, trying to hold it there as he entered turn one, but the G forces would still push it over onto his outside shoulder, no matter how hard he tried. With his head bouncing off his shoulder he had to look out of the corner of his eyes — that was screwing up his perspective. Menendez was smoking! Smoke was coming out of the engine of the lead car. He was finished. But the car behind Will was closing on him again, and there was nothing he could do about it.

Will was talking to himself again. "Stop worrying, the lead Ferrari is all but dead, yours is dying, and you have no idea what the position is with the one behind. If you do nothing stupid you will finish second. If you try to fight off the third car you won't finish. Use your head.

"Concentrate on one corner at a time, forget about the other two." The lead car was smoking badly now. Will's oil pressure was dropping; he stopped looking at the water temperature, because it was well into the red, and there was nothing he could do about it.

As he went past the pits, the pit board showed five laps left, the second car half a second ahead; Menendez less than a second behind, and Will running a second a lap slower than he had been.

He didn't want to close up too much; he was sure Flint was going to blow up any second, and dump oil all over the track. He didn't want to be caught in that, but he couldn't wait forever. If he could get close enough on the exit out of turn one and slipstream him up the straight, and Flint blew up in front of them, at least it wouldn't be on a corner, and with a lot of luck the guy behind could end up in the oil.

Will used all his remaining energy to stop his head from flopping over, closed right up. His visor rapidly clouded over; it was blowing oil, but it was still fast. Will couldn't see. He had only one tear-off left, and he couldn't use it till he was past, and he couldn't pass till he could see. Will had no choice. He couldn't slingshot past till the braking area, and he couldn't go into the braking area blind. He didn't know where the third car was; it was a big risk to pull out of the slipstream, and not know where it was. Suppose it pulled out of his slipstream at the same time?

"Fuck it, go," Will jinked left, and ripped off the tearaway, sight at last. He had passed too early, he wouldn't pass cleanly, they were side by side going into turn one, with the third car behind, getting a face-full of oil.

Will was talking to himself again, "Use your head, don't try to get clean away, just get into the lead at the last moment; don't let Menendez follow you through. Let him suck the oily smoke for a while, maybe it will give you time to get away." With the last drop of his energy, he barged his way into the lead. It wasn't a pretty sight, but he made it, just, hanging on to the finish. The chequered flag was the most welcome sight he had ever seen. As he crossed the finish line, he felt like a balloon that had lost all its air. All deflated, not a scrap of energy left, just an empty sack.

He had to be helped from the car; he didn't have the strength to get out by himself. They had to stop him guzzling drinks, but they poured a bucket of water over his head. Boy, that felt good. Isobel stood there with a huge smile on her face, giving him an enormous, exaggerated wink, which made him laugh. She was a good winker, and he winked at her in return. This was getting too tough; he wasn't made for this type of shit. Still he was pleased with himself, not so much for winning, which was always good, but for using his head.

22

WILL WOKE UP next morning to the sound of the surf pounding on the cliff below the beach house. The sun was streaming in through the open French doors. Isobel wasn't in the bed, but he could smell the rich aroma of good coffee. He reached over to the heavy mahogany side table for his watch. It was nearly eleven. He was not surprised; he couldn't remember when he had been so exhausted. He hadn't thought that either the car or he could have lasted more than a few more laps. By the time he had stopped, all the gauges were in the red. They had been lent a private jet, which had brought them directly to the local airport, no customs or immigration. I know who pulled that one, Will thought.

Isobel walked in, emerald eyes, barefoot, long, dark, wet hair hanging down, khaki shorts, deliciously flared hips, small perky boobs, T-shirt, big smile, perfect white teeth. "Buenos días, Lazarus."

"What do you mean, Lazarus?"

"You slept the sleep of the dead. You slept all the way on the plane, and when we arrived, you stumbled in here and slept again. How do you feel?"

"I think I feel okay. When I get up I'll tell you. Who rigged customs?"

She laughed. "We have ways. By the way, Mamá and Papá are here. Mamá is cooking you breakfast. I have had several calls from the TV people asking for interviews. I hope you don't mind — I told them that you were in England. I don't think that they believed me."

Will got up. Jesus, he felt weak. That kind of thing really took it out of you. He went and stood under a cold shower, and just let it beat on him, feeling as if he were absorbing the water like a sponge. The shower was all marble, with a heavy glass door on big brass hinges. Quality. It was like his boat, something you could be proud of. It made you feel good.

They all had breakfast on the marble terrace overlooking the cliff and out to sea. It was a beautiful day, blue sky with a few cirrus clouds scudding by; the sea deep blue with a long, low swell, bursting under the cliff, like cannon fire in the distance. It wasn't hot yet, for which Will thanked God. He needed the heat like he needed a hole in the head.

He was very comfortable with the Santiagos. They had become part of his everyday life and his family. They were his kind of people. He loved their lifestyle, and their way of doing things. There was no pissing about with them — look how they had got him here, straight in, no customs, no record, nothing. And best of all, no way the media could track him, unless they got in a car and drove down to find him, and no way they were going to do that. "Thank you for your help last night. It sure made things a lot easier," Will said to Señor Santiago.

"But it is nothing. I saw you get out of the car on TV. It was better you woke up here, than in some hotel room. How do you feel now?"

"Weak, but I will get over it. I have to be testing in England on Wednesday, so I had better be okay by then."

"It is going well for you? They say that you have never won the championship, but it looks as if you will win this one. They say you have almost always driven for the same team, and now there is no other driver on the team, only you. Why is that?"

"It's a small team like a family; Arne, the other driver, was killed a few years ago. It is very difficult to introduce an outsider without creating difficulties. We have had other drivers since, but ego is always a problem. We have a very flexible structure; everybody knows his job and gets on with it. We are merciless on non-performance — we expect the best, and if we don't get it you are out, end of story. That goes for drivers, mechanics, secretaries, everybody. There is no hierarchy, and most people find that difficult. People in industry talk about excellence, but they don't know what excellence is. This is a tough game in so many ways. Competition is fierce, not only on the track but also at the technical end."

"Plus," said Señor Santiago, "there is always the danger, like the corrida. How long will you keep going?"

"Don Alphonso, I am getting tired. Maybe a rest is all I need, but I think it may be time soon. I am also afraid that if I stop, I may want to start again, and it will be too late."

Will left on Tuesday evening for England and more testing. Wednesday morning started out dull and grey with intermittent drizzle.

He had left London that morning in bumper-to-bumper traffic. The old Porsche hated it almost as much as he did. People looked at him as if he was some kind of hoon, because he had to keep blipping the throttle to stop the plugs from fouling, with the raucous exhaust echoing off the buildings, receiving many a disapproving glance. Will couldn't have cared less what people thought; he was going to make damn sure that he didn't have to change spark plugs on the side of the road. It would probably have been easier to change the engine than to change the plugs on the old twin-ignition engine.

•

Will was sitting in the motor home finishing off his fifth coffee when Ray walked in.

"Pour me a coffee," he said.

"It's finished."

"You drank the whole lot?"

"That I did."

"You'll end up with the shakes if you keep drinking that stuff at the rate you do. Jesus Christ, I can't believe you finished the whole lot. Here you are, sitting on your arse while I'm outside working my fingers to the bone, and you didn't even leave me a drop."

"Don't panic," said Will. "I'll make some more. Besides, the only thing that you have been working is your mouth."

"Oh gee thanks, that's mighty big of you. And when you have finished, would you mind dragging your backside out of here and placing it in the damned car so that we can do what we came here for?"

"Yas suh, baas, whatever yuh seh, baas."

By the time they were ready to go out, the track was pretty

near dry. The sky was still solidly overcast, but at least there was not much wind, and the rain had stopped some time before. One of the mechanics leaned over and did the final pull on the seat belts, while another plugged in the battery box. Will turned on the master switch, pumped the accelerator a couple of times and pushed the starter button. The engine came to life with a raucous howl, settling down to a high-speed idle as they allowed it to warm up. Without his helmet the noise was deafening. The exhaust was one thing, but all the gears and belts thrashing around without any form of insulation went straight into his body and ears. Everybody else had ear protectors except him. He just had to put up with it till he put his helmet on.

Will pushed in the clutch, let it out, pushed it in again, hauled the gear over towards him and back with a graunch into first gear, blipped the throttle, and eased out the clutch. They were here to test the new suspension set-up, which was fitted to one of the cars so as to give them an accurate comparison. They would do back-to-back tests till they arrived at a conclusion. The trade-off was between handling and stick, or balance and adhesion to the road. A car that handled well was not necessarily fast, if it did not have enough stick. At the same time, a car with lots of stick but no handling was not much good either, but could be quicker. They had to find the balance between the two.

Will was not happy. They had started out with a brilliant car. Then there had been a change in the tyres supplied, and it had all turned to shit. As there was only one tyre supplier this season, there was not a damn thing that they could do about the situation. Will was a good test driver in a non-technical sense. He could feel what the car was doing, and relay the information back to Ray fairly accurately, although he couldn't translate that into the more sophisticated parts of chassis design. He could use the adjustments that were available to all drivers, such as tyre pressure, ride height, spring rates, shock-absorber settings, roll bars, and camber. But beyond that he had to rely on Ray and the engineers to understand what he was telling them.

Sometimes he became frustrated, and sometimes he got lost, and didn't know where he was going. When Ray tried to get it out of him he became difficult, and wouldn't tell him anyway. When it got to this point, they both knew it was time to pack up for the day. This was one of those days. The car was handling well but the lap times were down, a second and a half slower than with the original car. However, it felt good, and the tyre temperatures were okay. It was more stable in the fast sections, and turned in better in the tight stuff. Will liked the new car, but he knew that if he showed up for qualifying in it, and it wasn't fast enough, he would soon start to hate it. So they called it quits for the day, after deciding to change the engine to see whether that made any difference; although they didn't really believe that was the problem.

•

They were staying in an old pub, in a village near the track. Will had been using this pub almost as long as he had been racing. It looked the same as it always had, but the patrons were different. He first used to stay there when he was driving Formula Three. The patrons then were local farmers; now they were yuppies from the new stockbroker belt nearby. Will was realistic enough to know that he couldn't be expected not to be recognised, and he also expected to be approached. If he was honest with himself, if he wasn't recognised he would have wondered why.

But he wasn't in the frame of mind to socialise with people he didn't know, and didn't want to know. He was still exhausted from the last race. He supposed he was more dehydrated than anything else, and was still drinking gallons of water.

It was a beautiful old pub, with low dark ceilings supported by huge beams, and slate floors, with a gigantic fireplace. The speciality of this old pub had always been duck for as long as Will had been going there. He had looked forward to an early dinner and early to bed, but then he had been dragged into the bar by the mechanics. He didn't want to offend the boys; besides, he enjoyed their company. They were good fun, but he wasn't up to it tonight.

A few of the stockbroker types had spoken to him, some to impart their great knowledge of motor sport, others trying to engineer him into investing in this or that. Will put them all on to his accountant, which he knew pissed them off, because they were being dead-ended, and couldn't do anything about it.

Tonight, however, had an added component. The yuppies had bored wives and girlfriends with them, and here was a racing team with a bunch of raunchy mechanics and a famous racing driver. The famous racing driver wanted to go to bed, but the mechanics wanted to get into the wives and girlfriends.

This was an explosive situation, particularly as the yuppies seemed to be part of the local rugby club and were already full before they got there. One long, skinny blonde was giving him the eye. Why he winked at her he didn't know, but the husband or boyfriend saw. He was big, drunk, and aggressive. Oh shit, thought Will, do I need this? The man came up to Will, who was still leaning up against the bar, and pushed him in the chest with both his hands, pushing him back over the counter. Will knew he had a fraction of a second to make up his mind what he was going to do, or he was going to get mauled by this macho idiot.

He slapped his hands to his chest, pinning the guy's fingers, and bent forward. As the guy's finger bent backward, he sank to his knees. Will let him go, stepped back and dropkicked him between the legs. Will felt the satisfying impact of instep on soft testicles; just like a penalty kick in a football game the guy flew backwards and rolled around on the ground howling. His mates leapt up and it was all on. Will felt a hand grab his collar and he was dragged backwards at high speed out of the bar. He thought he had had it. He twisted around to defend himself and with relief saw Ray's red face. "That's enough for you tonight, sport. Go to bed and stay there. And while you are there, ponder on how much that arsehole is going to sue you for."

23

Needless to say, the engine didn't get changed that night, and it was not till after lunch that they managed to get the car out on the track again. By that time the local bobbies had arrived, which held up the testing for another hour; however, it was all in a good cause. By the time the police left, they were confirmed motor racing fans, with pit passes for the big race. Such great guys couldn't have been responsible for the brawl in the local, and they didn't like the yuppies either.

It had started to drizzle again when they finally got going. By God, the car was quick! Not in the dry, but in the wet. It was flying on the damp track. Will had experienced this before. Cars that were fast in the wet were seldom fast in the dry. But this one was exceptionally quick, and it was not really wet, only damp. The car had a lot of feel to it; he could feel it working under him. He could feel it hunker down under braking, roll, and set on the entry to the corners, transferring the weight to the rear, and squatting down under acceleration. It felt good, really great.

Will pulled back into the pits. Ray stuck in the intercom jack and said, "Well?"

"Let's stop now, do nothing. It's fantastic in the wet. Tomorrow, if it's dry we go out again, set a time, and then up the spring rates front and rear, then set another time. I suspect it's good, but too soft. That's why it works in the wet but not in the dry — it's too soft for the new set-up. It all goes back to the beginning. The car is good, very good. It's the blasted tyres. We've been trying to work around them, confusing ourselves in the process."

The next morning was dry and clear. Everybody had had an early night, trying to stay out of trouble. They were the first out on the track. Will trundled around using low revs, slowly increasing his speed as he played the car and himself in. Even though he was cruising, he was still getting pit signals every lap: the times were coming down at a steady half a second per lap, which was the way Ray and Will liked it. There was no hurry; they had all day, and all week if necessary. They were confident they were on to it, and they weren't going to rush.

Eventually the times stabilised. They were not going to go much faster — it was time to make the change. They changed the springs and went out again. This time Will went at it within a couple of laps. They got to the original time very quickly, but no quicker than before.

Will shot into the pits. "It's pushing the front in the tight stuff. We could go tighter on the rear roll bar or increase the compression on the rear shocks, but I think we should go with the springs."

"Okay," said Ray, "but before we harden the rear springs, how is it on the fast sections?"

"Good, it's very stable. If we go up on the rear springs, we may lose some of that stability. I think we're on the right track. I have a gut feel that we're onto a winner. We haven't even considered the wings, and I don't think we should touch them yet."

"All right, we'll raise the rear springs by ten per cent and see what happens."

It was all to do with weight transfer and the rate of transfer. The car remained the same weight, but it had pitch and roll, just like an aeroplane. When the brakes were applied, the car pitched forward, making the front heavier and the back lighter. When it turned into a corner, the weight transferred to the outside wheels. When it turned into a corner under brakes, the weight transferred to the outside front wheel. Under acceleration, the weight transferred to the rear. It was the balance of all these forces that affected the handling of any car. But on a racing car, it was all adjustable and there were optional springs, shock absorbers, roll bars, tyres, and gear ratios, to name just some of the variations available. Not to mention the wings, front and rear, which increased weight by increasing aerodynamic downforce. All these possible permutations had to be tried one at a time.

Will went back out. He knew it was better at the end of the first lap, turning in crisply, which was what he was after. But, best of all, the change had given him a solid gain in the slow sections without costing him anything in the quick ones, picking up nearly a second. By the end of the day, they had made many more changes. Some worked, some didn't, but there was steady progress. They weren't at the hot times yet, but they were moving steadily forward. Some of the early sweet feel of the car had been lost, but they had gained a heap of stick.

Back at the pub that night, Will had a quiet dinner and went to bed early. This was unusual for him. Normally he would either have found some female company or imported some by now. Instead, he phoned Isobel and spent nearly an hour talking. He told her how the new car was going, something he had never done before. It would never have occurred to him to discuss his motor racing with anybody not directly involved, except on the most peripheral level. He had never talked about it with any of his previous women, even the long-term ones.

He could sense that Isobel was in a quandary over her political career; whether to push on with it and see Will as and when, or to slow down and spend more time travelling with him. She never said so, but Will could feel what was going through her mind. She wasn't trying to engineer a commitment or anything like that; she was trying to trade off in her own mind what she would prefer to do. Will tried to imagine life with her after motor racing; the upside was definitely pushing back the downside. The downside was lack of freedom to womanise, but he had the freedom now, and he wasn't using it, so what good was it?

By the end of the next day's testing, they were right on the button. The car was as perfectly balanced as he could get it, for the day's conditions. It ended up a whole second faster than the old car, with more to go. They had done enough. Time to go back to the workshops and consolidate what they had. There were engines, gearboxes, and a spare car to be rebuilt. They had less than a week to have two cars, two spare engines, and spares ready to roll, and Will had contractual commitments with sponsors, and media interviews.

•

Race day dawned bright and clear. Practice and qualifying went well: they were the quickest all weekend. It looked as though all they had to do was to hold it together on race day and the championship would be one step closer. The car was working well. It was quick everywhere, allowing Will to drive it smoothly, and let the car do the work; he didn't have to go mad squeezing the last ounce out of it, to put it on the pole. He had concentrated on fine-tuning the chassis, rather than trying to wring the last bit out of a reluctant car. It had been a dream few days, speed gradually increasing a tenth here, a tenth there.

Their pole time had ended up over two seconds quicker than during practice, although some of that had to be attributed to the rubber being laid down by all the other cars. For the first time this season, Will did not try to jump the start. He knew they were watching him; also, he didn't need to jump it anyway. For once in his life, he didn't need to take any risks. He had a distinct speed advantage everywhere; and the car handled so well they had gradually backed off on the wings. Now they were running less wing than anyone else, which translated into less drag on the straights, which meant more speed. The wing settings had not gone unnoticed; they all knew what that meant. The handling was so good, they could afford to trade off a bit of handling for straight-line speed. There was a simple logic in the trade. It was easier to pass down the straight, so the loss of speed in the corners meant that another car trying to overtake would have to do it in the corners, which was never easy, especially with Will's attitude of "If you want to pass, drive over the roof."

•

All the best-laid plans of mice and men. Will was lucky to walk away from the crash. But George Lucas wasn't. A first-corner crash, car coming up the inside, wheels riding up over Will's, car launched into space, shadow passing over, barely clearing Will's head, flying through the air, slamming into the Armco, other cars spinning off, dust, Will's right rear corner gone. Master switch off, out of the car, flag marshals, fire extinguishers.

"Oh Jesus, another one." George Lucas had hit the Armco head on and gone underneath. Will did not look — he knew he was dead. "Stupid, stupid, stupid bastards." The Armco was installed to highway specs to stop a road car and trucks. Racing cars were much lower.

The marshals were running around like headless chooks. And the ambulance hadn't arrived. "Cover him up for fuck's sake. Don't you see the condition he is in?"

"Wait for the ambulance."

"Don't need one."

Helmet off, trudge back to the pits, media and more media. "Whose fault?"

"His fault. Bloody stupid to try to overtake there; it wasn't a one-lap race. Now he has paid for it with his life, because some arsehole didn't have the brains to figure out that the barriers were too high. It's not a fucking highway, with Armco, to stop trucks running off the road, for Christ's sake, it's a race track, and race cars are low, not like a frigging truck. Jesus Christ Almighty, where do they find these frigging people who can't see that the cars will go straight under the barrier? And rip the poor bastard's head off? Who is going to tell his girlfriend that his head is lying on the ground yards from the car? And his body is in the seat, headless. Jesus Christ."

More questions, talk to Ray, sinking feeling, repeat of previous years? Crashes and more crashes? Death. Not my goddam fault, stupid bastard tried to go up the inside with wheels locked. New chicane, dumb, was bound to have caused an accident. Now another one is dead. Careful, don't shoot your mouth off to the media too much, they'll twist it. Nine points lost, and George dead, what a waste.

Into the helicopter, directly to the airport, gone.

24

THE FORECAST WAS for fifteen knots out of the north, which was where they were going. But the actual wind seemed to be out of the north-west, which meant that they should just be able to lay their course. The wind was beam on in the marina from the starboard side. Because *Imperialist* kicked to port in reverse from the torque of the propeller, backing out of the berth was going to be tricky. She was over a hundred feet long including the bow sprit, with a ketch rig and plenty of windage. *Imperialist* had no bow-thrusters as most boats of her size would normally have had, so they would have to handle her the old way.

"Okay," said Will, "we'd better use a spring line from the midships cleat, looped through the ring bolt on the dock back to the primary winch. As we back down on that, we feed out the line; you control the amount of drift."

The boys rigged the spring line, and came astern at low idle. *Imperialist* drifted off a bit, but soon took up on the spring line, which pulled her up against the windward dock. As she continued to slowly back out, the guys eased out on the heavy spring line triple wrapped around the primary winch, which was bar taut, keeping her to the windward side of the marina. There was no discussion, no shouting or running about. As they cleared the marina, they flicked the end of the line off the cleat, and recovered it from the ring bolt in the dock. "Just like a bought one," said Graham. "You should have seen what happened last week, the turkey next door with the gin palace. Twin engines, bow thrusters and all, tried to back out, rammed the pile, took out the lifelines on his port side and half-wrecked the boat in the next marina. You should have seen the excitement."

"Yeah," said Will, "when in doubt, scream, run about, and shout."

It was hard on the wind. Will was sitting down to leeward on the side deck, steering with his left hand holding one of the spokes. He could watch the "wools" on the staysail lifting and falling, as he worked the yacht to windward in the rising sea. These were little strips of plastic along the windward and leeward side of the sail, which showed the wind flow over the sail. When they were both flowing smoothly, the sail was correctly set.

"She feels sluggish," he said. "She feels over-canvassed and she's not going. Maybe we should pump up some more backstay."

"I know what it is," said Graham. "The leeward water tanks are full, and the windward are empty. Tack, and we'll transfer the water."

They tacked, and *Imperialist* took off. "Yes, that's the problem. Open the valves and transfer the water." On the other tack they opened the now-windward transfer valve and drained the water into the new leeward tank. As two tons of water ran down to leeward, they could feel the effect on the boat. As soon as the transfer had been completed, they tacked back onto their old course.

They hadn't hoisted the jib or the mizzen because the forecast was for fifteen knots. *Imperialist* would do over twelve to windward, which meant that their apparent wind was going to be twelve knots of boat speed plus fifteen knots of wind speed, a total of twenty-seven over the decks. With the staysail and full main up, they were not yet overpowered, although the weather fax was spitting out some funny stuff, which was not coming through in the forecasts. The wind was increasing; there was no doubt about that. Will was using the puffs to climb to windward. He leaned out on his right arm, steered with his left, letting the boat point up to windward as she climbed over a wave, and pulling down on the spoke as she peeled off the top. He enjoyed the precision, needed to work her up the wave and over the top, avoiding dropping off with a crash. As she rose up each wave, he would give the spoke a tug to leeward, and she would run along the back of the wave and slide down the other side, coming down with a huge whoosh as the sea came boiling down the lee deck. Will felt as one with the rhythm as she rose and fell to the sea. The apparent wind was now gusting thirty knots, and she was becoming overpowered. It was time to put in the first reef. "What do you reckon guys, reef time?"

"It looks like it," said Graham.

Will tossed off the mainsheet and eased the vang with the hydraulic dump valve. The boom ran out and kicked up, the sail flogging and shaking the rig. With the pressure off, *Imperialist* stood up, no longer overpowered. The guys were up at the mast working quickly. Peter let the main halyard go, and Graham pulled the sail down over the first reefing eye. They tensioned the main halyard, and ground the reefing lines in. Will pumped the boom vang back on. The sail was now quiet, no longer flogging; the only thing left to do was to retrim the main and they would be back in business. A two minute operation if done in sequence. One thing at a time. A balls up if it got out of sequence.

The boat was no longer heeling as much and was going faster. Will was suspicious of the forecast showing a confused scenario to the west. It was hurricane season, early, but still the season. Which was why they were moving the boat. They wanted it to be closer to a hurricane hole, in case of anything. He wasn't worried about an immediate hurricane, because this wasn't how they started but, still, he wasn't exactly comfortable.

By dark the wind had dropped, and they were motoring. It was flat calm with a dull grey sky and an oily sea. The weather maps weren't showing anything new, and they weren't picking up any shipping forecasts on the radio. It felt spooky. They all sensed it; there was something ominous about it. Everybody was sneaking peeks at the barometer, but so far it was still holding up. Nobody was talking about a big blow, but without any discussion they had started to pack away loose gear and prepare themselves for it. *Imperialist* was built for heavy weather; all her fittings were installed to remain in place even if she ever went upside down. The main worry was the rowing skiff, which was on deck under the main boom. If it got really bad, it couldn't stay there, the decks had to be kept clear. Big seas could rip it off, tearing a hole in the deck if the ring bolts were pulled out. They might have to dump it if the worst came to the worst. That would be a real shame; it was a work of art. Will's friend had built it from laminated timber, all beautifully varnished with polished brass fittings. In anchorages on quiet evenings, Will would sometimes go rowing in the skiff. It had a sliding seat and spoon oars. The long, slow strokes and the whoosh of the hull as it glided through the water was peaceful and satisfying. He sometimes went for miles, from one bay to the next. The skiff had a wicker seat in the stern, which was a great chick thriller. He could see them imagining themselves in long, white Victorian dresses and big floppy sun hats, lounging on the seat as he rowed them along in some secluded bay.

By morning it was raining; still no wind, but now they were motoring flat out for their hurricane hole, although they knew it was hopeless. Even if they got there before the hurricane which was now forecast, it would be full. Still, they had to try. As the autopilot steered, they huddled around the weather fax and radio, trying to get a feel for the position they were in. They couldn't outrun it; they could only hope that it would swing north, which would mean they would get only a flick of its tail.

It was a new hurricane; it had only just achieved that status, but the dangerous part about it was the speed at which it was travelling. It was apparently the product of two lows, which was the reason for its rapid growth and speed. At the moment it was blowing seventy knots and moving at twenty, which meant ninety on the front side and fifty on the back side. But yesterday, as far as they knew, there was nothing, so the day after tomorrow when it should hit them, how strong would it be, and which quadrant could they position themselves in? In the meantime, all they could do was track it and get ready. So they motored on, with all sails furled, in a leaden sea with a long oily swell. Everything was battened down; the rowing skiff was being left for the last minute because, if they had to jettison it they would, but only if that was unavoidable. There wasn't much for them to do now, as most of it had already been done. They didn't even have to cook food in advance, because there were plenty of frozen precooked meals on board. So they just motored on and hoped that the hurricane would change course.

By the next morning the forecast indicated it had, but not enough. And it had increased speed: it was now over a hundred knots. The eye was forecast to pass thirty nautical miles north of them that evening. Typical, thought Will. Why do hurricanes always come at night? During the day the size of the swells gradually increased, becoming bigger and more ominous by the hour. The barometer started to fall slowly at first, but with gathering momentum.

25

By AFTERNOON IT had started to blow, at first only light puffs followed by lulls and light rain. Soon the puffs turned into gusts, the rain grew heavier, and the gusts turned into sustained, heavy wind. They got the sails up, trying to put as much distance as possible between them and the hurricane. There was now no question of making the hurricane hole, or outrunning it: they could only try to avoid being caught in the front quadrant, which meant the speed of the hurricane, plus its travel speed, plus the boat speed.

Imperialist was storming along. It was rapidly growing dark, with lightning crackling everywhere, followed by huge claps of thunder. The barometer was plummeting at a rate they had never seen before. They could almost watch it fall. They had to start reducing sail again, and soon were down to the storm jib and three reefs. Still she was bowling along; the seas were huge, and becoming bigger by the minute. They were surfing at incredible speed, with a minimum of sail up. Will was standing up behind the wheel in his wet-weather gear, keeping her running, keeping her upright, picking his way through the worst of it, but knowing this wasn't going to last. The seas were too big, and they were going too fast. The wind was up to fifty knots now, and it was going to get a lot worse. It was better to quit now, and prepare for the worst.

As *Imperialist* got to the top of a wave, exposed to the full force of the wind, she accelerated like a car and took off down the other side. As she got to the bottom out of the wind she would run into the back of the next wave, bury her bows, burst through the top of the wave, and take off again down the next one. Talk about excitement — this was the ride of a lifetime. They were whooping and hollering as the speedo burst through the twenties. At this speed, the steering had become finger-light, and *Imperialist* was tracking perfectly. But Will knew that if he timed a wave wrong they could get rolled, big as she was, or even pitch-poled end over end if the bows dug in. They had run as far as they could. Running any more was only going to land them into big trouble. They were achieving bursts of unbelievable speed. The true wind speed was over seventy by now, but they were seeing only low fifties on the speedometer as they were going that fast downwind. Graham looked worried. "We're going to pay the piper real soon. We'd better quit while we are ahead."

"Agreed," said Will. "This is insanity."

"Way too much fun," agreed Peter.

"Chicken merry, hawk is near", as they say. "That's for sure; we can run but we can't hide. Let's set the cargo chute."

They had an ex-military cargo parachute they had carried for thousands of miles for just this eventuality. The plan was to use it as a sea anchor with a thousand feet of nylon line, which would be like hanging off a mooring on a length of shock cord, or so the theory went. But first they had to deploy it, and that would be a trick on its own. They had already run a line from around the base of the mast out through the bow rollers, outside lifelines and back into the cockpit, where the parachute and the spool containing the thousand feet of nylon line were stowed, ready to be heaved over the side.

Will had slowed *Imperialist* down by bringing her up into the wind, and she now slowly reached forward in seventy-five knots of wind, howling through the rigging. He didn't want anybody hurt, so instead of putting the parachute into the water and feeding out the line, they elected to drop the parachute and the spool with the line over the side, hoping that it wouldn't tangle. They continued to reach slowly along, after the parachute and spool had been dropped into the sea, waiting with bated breath.

Suddenly *Imperialist* slowed, swung around, and went head to wind. So far so good.

The guys crawled up the foredeck against the wind, wrestling the thrashing storm jib down. It was no easy task; the sail was like a mad thing trying to beat them to death. They unclipped the sail, flapping and shuddering, dragged it back to the cockpit, and stuffed it down the hatch. Now that they were no longer running with the wind and sea, they were feeling the full effect of both. The parachute was holding *Imperialist*'s head to the wind and sea, as they hoped it would, but she was taking green water across the deck, threatening the rowing skiff.

The wind was howling and spray was being driven horizontally across the decks. It had become difficult to move around. They had waited too long to get rid of the skiff, but it had to be done. It was usually launched by using the boom as a derrick, but in this wind they wouldn't be able to push the boom out. So they had to rig a line to the end of the boom and winch it out until the skiff was over the water and then lower it in the normal fashion, with one exception: Will wanted to sink it, and let it drift back on a line in the hope that it might survive the hurricane. They let go the stern line of the skiff, the wind blowing it almost horizontal as it hung from the bow line, twisting round and round. They let the bow line go before it self-destructed. It fell stern first into the sea and turned over, filling up with water.

So far, so good. At least it couldn't injure them now. It rapidly drifted to the end of its tether. They had already rigged a line with shock cord, which they hoped would stop the line from pulling out the bow fitting which had never been designed for hurricanes. They now had to get the furled sails off and down below. Will was not sure that this was a good idea; the sails could easily be destroyed or could hurt one of them before they could be wrestled to the deck. They hauled them down in the end, but it was a job that should have been done much earlier. The sails were heavy and never intended for use in this wind. Dragging them down was hard enough, but getting them through the cockpit hatch as greenies swept the foredeck was almost as bad.

The crew retired to the deckhouse and watched the seas build as the wind increased. The deckhouse was an island of peace and quiet after the foredeck. They were out of the wind and rain, dry and relatively comfortable. Will made coffee in an old-fashioned stainless-steel bubble-top percolator, heated on the gimballed gas stove. On most boats, it would never have crossed anybody's mind to design a galley in which you could heat coffee on the stove during a hurricane. But to be able to produce, in relative comfort, hot apple pie and ice cream to go with coffee after lasagne would have been totally beyond most people's imagination.

The seas were high mountains of grey water, going off into the distance, hills and valleys marching past with white spume blowing horizontally from the tops, a canvas of white parallel streaks. As each mountain advanced on them, *Imperialist* would rise till she reached the wind-driven tops, when water would rush through the anchor slot in the bow like a fire hose, gushing down the deck, breaking over the winches and around the mast like rapids in a river, before running up the sloped face of the deckhouse, to be blown away in the wind. They knew that life jackets were virtually useless, but they wore them anyway. The life raft was equally useless — it would simply blow away in wind like this. They resorted to gallows humour, laughing that when their bodies were found; at least the authorities would be happy that they were wearing life jackets.

The noise from the wind had reached an oppressive level, gusting over a hundred knots and rising, although the sea wasn't as huge as they had expected. It was not much bigger than they had seen before, but the spume flying off the tops of the seas had blown into a fine mist, and was nothing like they had ever imagined. It was as though the top of the sea, much less the waves themselves, was being lifted off by the wind. There was constant green water coming across the decks, and sometimes over the deckhouse. They weren't worried about that, because *Imperialist* was flush-decked: the only thing to stop the water was the deckhouse, and if that carried away, so what? Access to the interior was through a hatch, which was already closed. *Imperialist* was like a submarine. The water could pass right over her, and not do any damage, as long as she didn't go beam on to the sea and get rolled.

They had checked all the hatches, locked off some dorades and turned others around facing backwards to allow for some ventilation. There wasn't a leak in any of them, although there was a fair amount of water coming down the masts, but that was to be expected. Each mast was in a head, which had its own bilge anyway, so that wasn't a problem. The barometer had dropped till the needle was almost vertical; they were fascinated by it, the needle fluctuating in the gusts. They couldn't decide whether this was caused by changes in barometric pressure, or in altitude, as the boat rose and fell to the huge seas.

They had seen seas this high before, but not accompanied by the violence they were witnessing. As the seas hit *Imperialist*, she would rear back on the thousand feet of nylon line that they had deployed, and then surge forward when the wave had passed, just as though on an outsized elastic band. They kept the engine running, in case the parachute or the line failed, so that they had a chance of keeping her head up into the sea. But there was another eventuality that they had not thought of.

If the system failed and the line broke in the middle, they couldn't use the engine until somebody went on deck and dumped the rest of the line over the side, because the trailing bits would tangle in the propeller.

The radio was alive with distress calls. Some were sending out Maydays by this time, not the usual rubbish that is heard in a bit of a blow, but calls for assistance from merchant shipping.

There was nothing they could do to help anybody. They could only track the path of the hurricane on the weather fax and, using their barometer, plot their position in relation to the storm's path. It looked as though the eye would pass directly over them in about two hours, then the wind would shift and come from the opposite direction; with the shift the cross-seas would start. Waves on top of waves, and some waves on top of waves on top of waves. What they called rogue waves, which weren't really rogue at all, but a simple statistic.

The boat would be held head to wind by the new wind, and the new seas, but the old seas would still be very much alive. But first the eye would pass over, leaving dead calm with a huge leftover sea. Then it would blow from dead opposite. How big was the eye? How long would the wind take to come from the opposite direction? What to do? Stick with what had served them well, or cut it loose? They couldn't hope to recover the parachute in these conditions. Go for it, or wait and see? They couldn't make up their minds.

The first problem was cutting the line loose. You couldn't just walk up on the foredeck and cast off. If that was accomplished without serious problems, they would have to motor up into these seas, picking their way as best they could, without making a single mistake for hour after hour. What about fatigue? They were only three of them and they would only be able to concentrate for maybe half an hour at a time, with not much chance of sleep for any of them.

The eye was a disappointment. It was dead still, no wind, overcast; and lasted the better part of two hours. It wasn't the clear eye they had heard about that you could look straight up into. It was just a still, grey day, but it was nerve-racking just the same. They had to keep *Imperialist's* head into the sea, but what was going to happen when the wind reversed direction?

They decided that discretion was the better part of valour, went below and closed the hatch. They were now more apprehensive than at any time since the start of the hurricane. *Imperialist* was rolling quite heavily; the odd cross-sea was slamming into the sides with massive explosions. They fully expected to be knocked down with the masts in the water. That was not the problem; the problem was being rolled over and losing the rig, and then having to go on deck and cut the rig free. Once the rig had gone, the chance of another roll was greatly increased. Will fully believed that they were going to be rolled; however, he didn't expect much damage: they would survive it. There wasn't real fear, more apprehension than anything else.

It wasn't the size of the sea, but the breakers, when the new wind-driven sea slammed into the old. With the wind shift the waves started to come from the opposite direction, and were soon climbing on top of the old sea, which meant that some of the breaking waves were far bigger than anything they had yet seen. The old sea was piling into the stern, and the new sea was coming over the bow. The old sea would hit the stern and explode with a huge bang shaking the whole boat, while the new sea was sweeping across the bow. They were looking out at grey mountains of water separated by huge valleys, with hissing white frothy spume being blown off the peaks, and white streaks down the valleys. Sometimes they would ride up on each other, fall off, and come cascading down the face of the wave. It was like a wind against tide situation, multiplied by hundreds. If they survived this, Will thought, they could survive anything. Why in all the information he had ever seen on hurricanes had they not talked about the collision of waves coming from opposite directions? He had heard about freak waves, but to him that was just hype. If two wave trains collided and doubled in size or height, what was freakish about that? He tried measuring the height of the big ones with a sextant, but *Imperialist* was being tossed around so much by the confused, breaking sea that he couldn't take a good reading.

By afternoon, the barometer was rising steadily, and the wind speed was starting to drop. They were going to survive, but they had to start planning for the next danger. The seas would still be large and confused after the wind dropped. Many boats had survived major storms only to be rolled by big seas after the wind had abated. They had to get her moving soon. With no wind to hold her head up into the seas, the parachute would no longer be an asset. To recover it was going to be a major activity. Recovering the skiff was not going to be easy either. They didn't want to dump her, but they might well have to.

Then Graham came up with an idea. They would tie the skiff warp and the parachute line together, note the exact position, and pick them both up when the sea had dropped. It was easier said than done. In the end they tied the two together with a third line, making sure that it didn't tangle with the prop, motored up on the parachute line and tossed it overboard. To help find them again was going to be a serious problem, so they left a Danbuoy emitting a radio signal, much as fishermen used to relocate nets. It had been a dangerous job going forward in the huge seas, as the decks were still being swept by breaking waves.

Will and Graham crawled along the deck, with their harnesses attached to the jack line as seas broke over the bow and came roaring down the deck towards them. They had had to lie flat on the deck as the sea broke over them, intent on taking them over the side. Once *Imperialist* was free of her tether, they motored up into the seas at slow speed for the next eighteen hours, maintaining a two-man rotating watch as the seas gradually subsided. They could have picked up the equipment that evening, but decided to leave it till morning. They were all absolutely exhausted from lack of sleep, nervous tension, and the sheer physical effort of hanging on as the yacht rolled and pitched in the mountainous seas.

•

Next morning dawned a beautiful clear day, with a long, deep blue swell, and not a breath of wind. There was no evidence of the hurricane of just two days before. The recovery of their gear was so simple they could hardly believe it. They had no trouble finding the beacon; the parachute recovery line was visible on the surface so they launched the inflatable, picked up the line and brought it back to *Imperialist*. They ran the recovery line through the bow roller to the anchor windlass, grinding the line in until the parachute was within reach, then pulling it in by hand. When they got to the parachute warp, they disconnected the parachute and wound in the thousand feet of line with the powered windlass. When they reached the end they disconnected the intermediate line, brought that in by hand, and then recovered the skiff in the usual manner, using the main boom as a derrick.

They couldn't believe their luck. There was no damage: the skiff was unmarked, and so was *Imperialist*. They were exhausted; they could all have slept for twenty-four hours; however, they had a boat to run, and Will had schedules to keep.

Two days later they pulled into the half-moon bay on the island. They set the anchor and slept like the dead. They had come back to the island because the hurricane hole was now full of wrecked boats, and there was nowhere else to go.

26

WILL THOUGHT HE was dreaming. Tap tap, tap tap. "Señor." Tap tap, tap tap. As he slowly surfaced out of the fog of exhausted sleep, he realised that somebody was tapping on the hull.

"Jesus Christ," he groaned, "who the hell could that be?"

Will dragged himself out of his bunk, pulled on a pair of baggy shorts and staggered up the companionway.

A middle-aged man with a droopy moustache stood there in a shabby uniform, obviously an official of some kind. "Señor, Señor, El Jefe, por favor?" he said pointing to the city.

"Okay, okay," said Will.

"Okay, Señor, I wait."

Will had a cold shower and got dressed. He hated to wake the guys but he had no choice. "Pete, wake up."

"What? What's going on? Why are you up? Where are you going?"

"Calm down," says Will. "Sorry to wake you, but I have to go into town. I may be back tonight or I may not. I'll see if I can short-circuit customs so they come out to the boat and do the clearances."

"Okay Will."

"Go back to sleep.

Will hopped on board the Boston Whaler that they had sent to fetch him. He wished that they had waited till tomorrow. Now that he was up, he was growing excited by the day's upcoming events. Señor Santiago, who had his power of attorney, had done the deal two weeks before. Will was there to start work on the island; he had brought the overall master plan with him. The tricky part was working within the system without wrecking all the goodwill that had been created. He knew he could be his own worst enemy when it came to things like this. He had no patience, no tolerance for what he called the "mañana business". He got to "el Jefe's" office a bit after eleven, where he was greeted like royalty. There would be no problem with customs and immigration, and yes, the officials would go out to *Imperialist* to do the paperwork.

"So now," said Pablo Hernandez, "not only are you a race-car master, but a hurricane master as well. We were worried about you. How was it?"

"I would hate to have missed it, but I wouldn't do it deliberately," replied Will. "It passed right over us. It was not as intense as we thought it was going to be, but still quite an experience."

"Good Capitan, eh? Did you see the eye?

"No, no. Good crew, good boat, the boys are still sleeping it off. And no, the eye was a disappointment, not like the photos you will have seen, nothing like that. It was huge, two hours wide, just no wind, that's all."

"Now," said Pablo, "if it meets with your approval we will have an early lunch with the people who have been involved in this project from the start, a kind of celebration. After lunch, we have invited some contractors and some engineers to meet you."

"After lunch" turned out to be a media event. Will realised that he should have known this anyway. It had to be done sooner or later, so sooner was probably better. Pablo asked him to explain to all present what he was going to do with the island.

Will started slowly and carefully, knowing that he was going to be misquoted either deliberately or accidentally. He was not planning an industrial development, and he was not promising massive employment. He intended to develop the island into a free port and tax haven, which, without the restrictions and the overhead costs of a normal country, would generate employment and industry, without the huge set-up costs usually associated with such a venture.

The first question was, "What about a casino?"

"No casino," answered Will. "And no big hotels either. The initial buildings will be limited to two storeys."

"What about a cruise-ship dock?"

"You already have docks. What do you need another one for?"

"What industry do you intend to attract first?"

"Rice production."

"Do you mean rice production or rice farming?"

"Rice production, farming and packaging, ready for the supermarket. At present this country farms rice, but the bulk of the rice consumed is still imported."

"But that will mean that the import duties on rice will go up to protect your industry."

"You miss the point," said Will. "The rice produced is not destined for the mainland; it is destined for the world market. Any rice exported to the mainland will pay duty like everybody else. We should be competitive against your traditional suppliers because we have a transport advantage, but in the case of countries with subsidised rice production, we will not be."

"What about tourism, no casino, no hotels? Surely an opportunity is being missed."

"Tourism in the accepted sense of the word will be minimal, but what will evolve are the free port and the tax haven, which will attract individuals who see the other benefits of the island and invest or spend time here. For this clientele we will establish a small country-style hotel and villas, with which you are all familiar. We are not going off chasing the same rainbow as everybody else. You already have a lifestyle which most people would envy. Our tourism will make that lifestyle available to people who would appreciate it."

"What you mean, Señor, is tourism for the rich. Is that not so?"

"Tourism can be quantified in two ways, numbers of people or numbers of dollars, take your pick. At the end of the day it boils down to one thing, dollars. So why not increase the number of dollars and decrease the number of people? This way, we don't have to build those huge hotels and port facilities for cruise ships, if you can attract the dollars without the people."

"Are you going to be logging?"

Will knew this question was going to come up, and was ready for it. "The answer is yes and no. Yes, we will be logging in the future. No, we will not be logging in the short to medium term, because the island was logged years ago and was never replanted. There is no economical logging left. We will start replanting native trees, but as you know they are slow-growing. They may be logged by the next generation; however, we believe there is an opportunity for faster-growing varieties, which we are investigating now. If this is practical, a logging industry will evolve over time."

Will could now see that he was getting them on his side: the doubting Thomases were beginning to nod their heads. Will glanced at Pablo to see whether he was getting it right. Pablo had a slight smile on his face, and gave Will a barely perceptible wink.

"Señor Archer, why do you want to do this? You talk about lifestyle — you already have a lifestyle that we can only dream about. It can't be money, so what is it?"

"That, my friend, is a question I have asked myself many times. I guess the only answer is that I want to build something. I suppose the pioneering aspect, starting from scratch, appeals to me. But there is more than that. This is a beautiful place and I would like to live here, but I would have to have something to do, or I would get bored. If I wasn't going at it flat out with everything laid on the line, it wouldn't be any fun."

Somebody started to clap, and they all took it up. Will stood there dumbfounded, and then started to laugh. "Does this mean that the racing is finished — that you have exchanged one high-risk game for another?" Pablo whispered in his ear.

"What do you think?" Will replied.

27

When Will walked out of the terminal it was cold and wet. He looked up at the dull, depressing, leaden sky. "Christ Almighty," he thought, "who needs this?" He felt like hopping back on the plane and heading back to the island, but work beckoned. He had a race in five days.

When he walked into the office Ray said, "Well, well, the wanderer has returned. We heard that you had been blown away. Isn't there something in your contract that expressly forbids riding around in hurricanes?"

"You should have been there, Ray. You would really have enjoyed it."

"Yeah, I bet. Okay, down to business: all the equipment will be at the track tomorrow afternoon. Be there before lunch. We have a new fuel system to test. The dyno results have been outstanding: a healthy increase in mid-range torque, and another forty-five horsepower. We also have the new tyres, which I hope will overcome the recent problems. Don't forget, be there before lunch."

"Yes suh, baas. Can I borrow your car?"

"No, you have no respect for other people's property."

"Oh, come on, just because the last one got wrecked. It was old, anyway."

"It didn't just get wrecked, you wrecked it. And it wasn't old. Drive your own."

"I don't have one any more."

"How do you mean you don't have one any more? Where's the Porsche?"

"I gave it away."

"People just don't give cars away, not cars like that anyway. Who did you give it to?"

"Isobel."

"Oh, shit. What about that Jeep thing that you had?"

"Sent it to the island."

"Why don't you rent a car, then you can always wreck theirs?"

"Can't afford it. I just bought the island."

Ray knew that this was Will's way of telling him that this was his last season. Ray had not really believed it, but now he had heard it from the horse's mouth. He slowed down and became serious. "Are you sure you are doing the right thing?"

"I hope so. I am not nearly as committed to this as I used to be. Not nearly as hungry, which is not fair to you."

Ray held up his hand. "No, let me finish," said Will. "We have the best chance we've ever had to win the championship. Win or lose, I've had a fair go. In a couple of years I will be a has-been, and I don't want that. There are a few young ones coming up that are going to push the current top-liners aside.

It is better for both of us if I bow out now. I know the island is a huge gamble: all the professionals tell me not to do it, but I am going to do it anyway. Ray, you know me, it wouldn't be any fun if it weren't risky."

"All right," said Ray. "I knew this was going to happen. I hate to see you go. You are probably right, but I think you have a few years in you yet. As you know, I have had several offers for the team, but I have always turned them down. As long as you were around I wouldn't sell, but the reality is that it's in my blood, I can't give it up. But I must find the right driver, or drivers. Without that I wouldn't want to continue."

"What can I do?" asked Will. "We should start looking for a replacement now, arrange test sessions with prospects."

"Wrong. We are going to do no such thing. We are going to win the World Championship first and worry about the rest later. In the meantime we have work to do. The boys are at the track getting set up, so let's go."

Will drove into the paddock area past all the big trailer rigs, the huge motor homes, the hospitality tents, flags flying, all the excitement of many circuses wrapped into one. Formula One had become big business; it now cost millions a year to run a racing team. Their team cost over one million *per race* to run; some cost twice that. But then most of them ran two cars. He parked Ray's car carefully; it would be just his luck for some fool to back a trailer into it.

Will was first out in the pit lane, and first out on the track. He wanted to see what the increase in power was going to do for them. Or if, as had happened in the past, the engine just blew up because they had tried to crank too much power out of it. But most of all, now that he had made up his mind that he was going to retire; he was in a big hurry to finish the job off right.

A couple of laps of build-up, and Will got right into it. Down the main straight past the pits into the 120 degree right-hander. On the brakes, feel the front dip, fourth, third, second, turning in, winding on the lock. Back coming out, easing off the brakes, right-hand front wheel on the apex, throttle, gradually open it, tail should swing. Damn it, pushing the front, head for the pits.

Ray plugged in the intercom. "Too much weight transfer to the rear."

"Where?"

"Exit turn one."

"What about two clicks on the rebound of the front shocks?"

"Try that."

Will stormed out of the pits twenty seconds later. After one lap he was back in the pits. "Well?"

"Little better, but not enough."

"Put the shocks back and try springs?"

"Yep."

The springs took a little longer to change; Will was back out in fifteen minutes. They had put heavier springs on the rear to stop the car squatting and transferring too much weight to the rear under acceleration and lifting the front, causing it to get light, lose adhesion, and run wide on the exit. Two laps later he was back in the pits. "Much better, put the shocks back."

"Okay."

Seconds later he was out again. They had tightened up the rebound on the front shocks to the previous settings, which slowed the rate at which the front would lift under acceleration. Will was back again in a couple of laps. "Well?"

"Better, but we need to reduce understeer."

"Where?"

"Everywhere except when under brakes."

"Roll bars?"

"Fronts. Softer."

"Okay."

Seconds later he was out of the pits and on his way. They had softened the front roll bars, allowing the front of the car to roll more, enabling the outside front wheel to bite better, which caused the car to turn in crisply. Five laps later Will was back in the pits. "Bit unstable on entry to the fast right-hander at the end of the straight."

"Bars?"

"No. What about more rear wing?"

"What about less front?"

"Try it."

Will was out again. His lap times were no quicker and the car was harder to drive, being less stable. Back into the pits. "Too skittish, put it back."

"Okay. We'll try more rear wing, but watch your revs at the end of the straight, but get out now and have a rest. The session's about over anyway and the tyres are going off."

Will climbed out of the car and sat on the pit wall with the top of his overalls down around his waist, the sleeves tied in front. "How did it go?" asked Ray.

"Pretty well. The changes came together quickly."

"Okay, let's go through it corner by corner."

28

As Isobel came bouncing out of customs, with that long-legged walk, Will couldn't help smiling. She threw her arms around his neck, "Why are you smiling? Do I look funny?"

"You make me smile."

"Why?"

"Because."

"Why because?"

"Just because."

They walked out of the airport arm in arm and climbed into Ray's car. "New car?"

"No, Ray's."

"Did you not have an accident in his last one, and he wouldn't let you drive his new cars any more?"

"Yes, but I haven't had an accident in this one yet."

"How did you manage that?"

"Rolled it."

"You mean you turned it over."

"Yep."

"Tell me — it's like pulling blood out of a stone."

"Well, you know Carlos Menendez."

"The Ferrari driver."

"Yes, he caused it."

"Go on tell me, what did he have to do with it?"

"He bet me I couldn't take a round-about flat."

"Oh no, you didn't. Not in Ray's new car."

"I did."

"And what happened?"

"It rolled."

"What do you mean it rolled? Something must have caused it to roll."

"It couldn't go around it flat."

"So it just rolled."

"No, it started sliding and when it hit the kerb it rolled."

"And what happened then?"

"It rolled through this lady's garden."

"I bet she wasn't happy."

"No, she wasn't."

But she was happy after, thought Will, as he had spent the rest of the night in her bed.

•

By the start of the first official practice session on Friday, Will was raring to go. He had come to terms with Isobel in his mind, and wanted to finish with this part of his life and get on with the rest of it... By the second lap out, he started to push the car, it certainly felt nervous, and there was nothing smooth about it any more. But Will was adaptable — he could drive anything, and he quickly got the feel for the new settings.

The result of their after-testing analysis was that they were not making enough progress. He had been in and out of the pits all session, and although they were a lot faster than when they started, so was everyone else. At Will's instigation they decided on a radical change: they would up the spring rates by twenty-five per cent, to see what happened. They had never gone this route before because Will had always liked a soft car, but as he said, he had been effective in stiff cars in his pre-Formula One days. Within a couple of laps he realised that it was much faster out of tight, right-angle corners and slower in fast corners, because it was so twitchy. But out of the tight stuff he could flick it and boot it, and it would just go.

Will stormed into the pits.

"Change them back, right?"

"Wrong, it's really quick in the tight bits, but we need to get a bit more stability in the quick stuff."

"What about going to heavier bars front and rear, twenty-five per cent again?"

"Sounds good."

Five minutes later, Will was out on the track. It was years since he had driven anything like this. He would approach a corner, brake, flick the steering; the car would go sideways, opposite lock on the steering, on the throttle, and it would rocket away. No finesse, just a brutal display of aggressive power.

He was in and out of the pits fine-tuning the chassis, but he was in control. He had adapted his style of driving to the new settings: smooth Will had disappeared and aggressive Will had reappeared. Past the pits, exhaust echoing off the walls. End of the straight, hard on the brakes. Flick in; wham, full on the throttle, opposite lock, on, off, on, off, the throttle. Balance it, engine howling, up through the gears, fast, awkward left-hander coming up, used to need gentle braking and a trailing throttle. A quick stab on the brakes. Flick the steering, bam, on the throttle, away. Will was blitzing them; he was a second faster than the next-fastest car.

•

"We should sit out the first part of the next qualifying session and see how the rest do," said Ray. "How do you feel about that?"

Will was standing with his arm around Isobel's waist. "We'll see you tomorrow then," he said with a big smile.

"Hang on, hang on a minute mate," Ray spluttered. "Just you wait, there's plenty of time for that. You be ready to go in a minute's notice."

As it turned out they could have gone home, they were still a half-second clear, solidly on pole.

Will was surrounded by journalists. "Congratulations, Will, that race was a demonstration of supremacy. It looks as though you'll be the next World Champion."

"Thank you. We took a big gamble and it paid off."

"Are you going to be the new champion, Will?"

"Guys, I gotta go, I really do. And no, I won't be. You know I always stuff it up."

"Yes, but you're older and smarter now. We think you'll do it."

"Wish me luck, guys, but I really have to run."

29

THEY WERE IN the London office of Will's lawyer, with his accountant in attendance. "Talking about gambles," said the accountant, "you have bought this island at the other end of the world; you are going to retire at the end of this season with no income, and you are planning on spending huge sums of money with very little prospect of a return."

"Hear, hear," said the lawyer.

"You will be entering into an indefinite period of negative cash flow. How are you going to fund it? The banks won't, I assure you. I truly fear for the outcome."

"All right," said Will. "Let me tell you what I have done since we last had a meeting. As you know we bought the island."

"Who is we?

"I had a little help from Señor Santiago. As you know, the banks would only help with mortgages on property and other assets in this country, which was a drop in the bucket. As you also know, I have had a master plan drawn up for the island."

"Yes, but these grandiose plans are going to take a huge amount of capital and will not show a return for years."

"If you will let me finish, you will understand what I am about. I am setting up a number of agricultural projects. One is a rice production facility. Farming and processing to retail. I have a heads of agreement on the sale of twenty-five thousand acres for this purpose with one of the world's largest rice production companies. The agreement is that they will pay cash upfront for the land, upon signing the final agreement, and they will pay a two-and-a-half per cent royalty on the gross returns from their entire production, plus they will start paying the minimum royalty from year one."

"That is amazing. Why would they want to enter into an agreement like that when they can produce rice in other places without paying royalties?"

"Simple," said Will. "First of all, two-and-a-half per cent royalty is a lot cheaper than paying taxes. Second, their investment will be made from pre-tax profits from their base, and they can take their profits here without paying taxes. In the scheme of things, two-and-a-half per cent royalties is nothing. Third, I am going to build a world which they will enjoy."

"Yes, yes, we can see that, but what about this world you are talking about?"

"Let me finish," said Will, "I am about to sign up a huge US-based cattle operation, which is going to buy and develop 100,000 acres, including growing grain and building an abattoir, on a similar arrangement. These two deals will almost pay off the banks, and I am working on another five."

"But who is going to provide the infrastructure, roads, water and so on?"

"They will provide their own. Each will build their own roads, provide their own water and electricity."

"So are you going to play the part of the gentleman farmer?"

"You remember that I said that there was more to this than tax advantages? The owners of these companies have one thing in common: they are all outdoors types. We have some of the best game fishing in the world right on our doorstep. In the 1920s, before it was logged to destruction, the island was full of wildlife. Pigs, jaguars, deer, fish in the lakes, and one of the world's best bird shoots. We're going to rejuvenate all that and turn it back into the paradise it once was, without all the political bullshit. That's what I mean."

"That is very interesting, and are you planning on living down there?" asked the accountant.

Will knew what was coming next. The accountant had always liked his house; in fact he had persuaded Will to buy it, although Will could not have cared less about it. Will knew he was after a deal.

"Of course," he replied

'Then you won't be needing your London house any more."

"No."

"Would you be interested in selling it?"

"Of course."

"How much do you want for it?"

"Make me an offer."

"Oh, I couldn't do that."

"Well," said Will, "everybody else is going to, right after the end of the season."

"How do you mean?"

"Just think how much it could be worth if I win the

championship." Will looked him right in the eye. "The social climbers will be chasing each other, just to be able to say that they own the Formula One World Champion's house."

30

THE RAIN WAS drumming on the deck; the wind was moaning through the rigging, and *Imperialist* was heeling over and swinging in one direction, then the anchor chain would pop and bang in the fairlead before heeling over and swinging back in the other direction. Will and Isobel had arrived two days before at their anchorage in Half Moon Bay, and it had rained ever since. At first, with the best intentions, they had gone ashore to prepare for the arrival of the first barge-load of equipment, and then gave up when the barge didn't show up, because it was holed up somewhere, hiding from the weather.

They started off by having a major discussion on the way the island was going to be operated, which soon deteriorated into playing blackjack, baking bread, and reading books. Isobel rapidly adjusted to the lolling-about lifestyle of swinging around the anchor. It was also time well spent, for Will was able to involve Peter and Graham hoping to get them enthusiastic about the project. "We realise that some big changes are being made, boss," Peter said, "but we don't see how we fit in."

"First of all," said Will, "I am going to keep the boat. There is no way that I am going to be without her. Second, this is my last season of motor racing, I think. Third, the development of the island. You guys have been involved from day one and know some of the traumas that we went through to get it. You also understand what we intend to do with it. The opportunity is there for you to get involved in any way that suits you."

"How do you mean?" asked Graham

"You guys are both top boat-builders, right? We are going to have to put in telephones, an airstrip, roads, water, a sewerage system, and houses for a start. Somebody is going to have to look after all this, why not you? It will be a lot easier than building *Imperialist*."

For the first time, Will had all the priorities in sequence in his mind. He had always had a rough idea, but there had been no time to put it into order. He knew with the establishment of the rice and beef operation, and with others to start, his priority should be communication. Telephone first, followed by an airstrip, then roads. Water, sewerage, and houses would come later.

•

The rain finally stopped that afternoon. The sun came out and birds filled the bay with their songs; swarms of multi-coloured parakeets in their reds and greens flew from tree to tree with raucous noise; seabirds dived into the flat, calm water with enormous splashes, looking for fish.

Later that evening, the moon was rising out of the sea, as the slight wind ruffled the reflection in the water. The boom tent was up, covering the deck from the main mast to the mizzen.

They sat around the dining table in *Imperialist*'s cockpit, with a lantern hanging off the boom. Isobel had spread a white tablecloth with white serviettes, and the best dinner service. They had just dined on fresh charcoal-grilled crayfish speared by Peter that afternoon, cooked on the barbecue hanging off the stern. They had finished their third bottle of Pinot Grigio kept chilled in an ice bucket, and were now into sticky wine, espresso and cheese. All was well with the world. The offshore breeze was wafting the scent of the island to them and with it the fresh perfume of flowers. "Could be worse, couldn't it?" Commented Will to Isobel.

"It is beautiful, but can you develop it and keep the beauty, all at the same time?"

"I think so. This island has been logged heavily for a couple of centuries without any replanting. As soon as cash flow permits we'll start replanting native hardwood trees. But before that we'll plant fast-growing varieties as soon as I can arrange the contracts. Once the rice and grain are planted, there will be a lot more feed, which will attract more bird life. The tree replanting will also bring more. I have done a deal with the local conservation society, and they will start releasing native wildlife next week."

31

WILL WAS IN the operator's seat of a brand-new Caterpillar D8 bulldozer. The surveyor's pegs, with their bright red plastic ribbons on wooden stakes, spaced every hundred feet, showed the way for the first proper road to be built on the island. The pegs wound their way from the beach along the side of a hill covered in scrub and rocks. It was a beautiful sunny day, with a light sea breeze rippling the water. Woolly cumulus clouds were sliding by overhead. The barge had come in the previous day loaded with brand new earthmoving equipment, which they had unloaded that afternoon. Will could not wait to get his hands on the gear. He had not operated a bulldozer in years, and was a bit anxious about making a fool of himself, but then nobody there knew that he had ever sat in a dozer operator's seat before. Will pulled back the throttle lever, pushed down the decelerator pedal and turned the starter switch. The big diesel rumbled into life. Will let it warm up for a while, then lifted the ripper and the blade, and pulled the power shift lever into first, before easing off the decelerator. The thirty-five ton dozer clanked off.

Will pulled out the left steering clutch and pushed the left brake. The dozer turned left. Using the steering clutches and brakes to steer, left hand going from right clutch to left clutch controlling direction, he raised and lowered the blade with his right hand, his elbow resting on the armrest. By moving the lever side to side, the hydraulic rams tilted the blade. As he got to the first peg he lined up the dozer, lowered the blade and started his first cut. While cutting on the left, the earth piled up in front of the blade, the load started to swing the machine to the left. He pulled out the right clutch with his left hand and used the load on the blade to steer the dozer.

Will was cutting on the high side against the survey pegs with the hydraulic tilt blade angled into the hill. He would make a cut, casting the earth to the side away from the hill, which made a platform on which the dozer could sit. He would then back up, go forward, and level off the fill, so that he was eventually working on a flat surface, side-casting the cut from the hillside, building the road bed. He was really enjoying himself; the work was not that technical, but he wouldn't attempt to trim the banks or do much grading.

He was getting thirsty. He had pushed over a few coconut trees and was hanging out for some coconut water and the soft jelly. He was also looking forward to the hearts of palm from the centre of the tree that they would have with dinner that night. But right now he was just plain thirsty. He jumped down onto the blade arm and down to the ground, thoroughly pleased with himself.

"Where did you learn to operate a bully?" inquired Peter

suspiciously.

"Oh, I read the manual last night."

"Bullshit. Pull the other leg."

"Seriously, when did you learn?" asked Graham.

"When I was a kid my family was in the construction business. I used to spend the holidays out on the jobs. That's where I learned to drive, tearing around in pickups."

"So what else can you operate?"

"All of it, except cranes. We didn't have any cranes."

Isobel had that amused look again. She didn't say anything, but tucked her arm through his proprietarily, as they walked over to the shady spot under the trees, where the Mayans had set up a cookhouse. It was going full blast. There was a wood fire inside an old bulldozer fuel tank, with four holes cut in the top. Tortillas were on the metal, and over the holes were pots, one with mince and chillies, one with black beans, another with sweet-smelling Guatemalan coffee.

One of the Mayans brought over a coconut, holding it in his left hand, a machete in his right. With a back-handed flick of his wrist he cut the top off the coconut. Will offered it to Isobel, who shook her head and suggested that he try it first. Will did not need any more encouragement. He picked it up in both hands, put his mouth over the hole and tilted back his head. The delicious cooling liquid poured down his throat, spilled down his chin, down his shirt, staining it forever. But he loved every bit of it. When he was finished he handed back the empty shell to the Mayan, who put it on a stump and with one swipe split it in half. He gave half to Will with a spoon, cut from the outer shell of the second half, which he also handed to him. Will used the spoon to scoop out the soft jelly from inside the shell. Delicious.

"Todo está bien, Señor?" asked the Mayan.

"Está bien, gracias."

Life was coming to the island, and the Mayans sensed it. With the machines had come operators, servicemen, surveyors, and engineers. The first Mayan service industry was the cook shop; others would follow. Some would be hired as labourers; some of these would in time become servicemen and operators. Others would become part of the survey crew. Will knew that this was now his life's work. He couldn't wait to get into it full-time; however, he had a World Championship to win, and a plane to catch that night.

32

WILL WAS NOW well clear in the championship, but not far enough ahead not to lose it. He had been this far ahead before and not won more than once. The biggest difficulty he had now was concentrating on the job in hand. He had to force himself to concentrate on racing, to erase any thoughts of the island from his mind. He had to focus. If he didn't have absolute concentration all the time, he was going to blow it, no question. Total commitment was the only way he was going to get the job done; which meant no phone calls, no distractions, nothing. Even having Isobel around could be a distraction; however, without being told she seemed to know. She had her own affairs to run; she could not spend much time with him anyway.

They had brought three cars to the race this time. The new one, which went against all the conventional wisdom and their own experience, was a short-chassis version of the car they had raced the last time. The theory was that if stiffer was better, then shorter and stiffer was better still. The argument was logical but risky, because if something went wrong, they had no identical backup. Even more likely was that Will would spend so much time hopping from car to car that he wouldn't have time to do any one car justice. The decision was a dollar each way, but no commitment. He would start practice with the car he had raced last, and set a time. They would then start on the new car. If it was immediately quick they would keep going; if not, they would park it.

It was not immediately quick, although it was close. By the end of the session they were fifth-fastest, but there wasn't much in it. It was mind-blowingly quick on certain sections of the track, and diabolical on others. In the tight stuff it was magic, but in some fast corners it was dangerous. Twitchy and unstable. As they say when it was good, it was very very good, but when it was bad, it was very very bad. Ordinarily, they would have parked it, but everybody had a good feeling about the car. They all hoped that they could keep the good bits while eliminating the not so good.

•

Will had come up behind one of the quicker cars on the downhill entry to a third-gear left-hander. As the other car braked hard on the downhill approach, Will went up the inside, dabbed the brakes, pitched it sideways and booted it. It seemed to leap off the corner. By the time Will looked in the mirrors he was fifty feet ahead. The next corner was a second-gear right-hander leading onto the main straight. Same thing again, another fifty feet.

The next corner followed a dip at the end of the main straight, rose up under a bridge, and at the apex fell away as it dived right. The entry was uphill, the apex was the crown, and also blind under the bridge, and the exit was alongside the pit lane. This was where Will was going to show the other driver something to go back to his pits with. He braked hard, into fourth, pitched it in, up over the crown, brushed the kerb on the apex, foot to the floor, engine howling, wheel straight ahead, sliding across the pit lane entrance onto the straight, away, fifty yards, fantastic.

But here comes the bad part, uphill very fast right-hander, a lot of finesse needed for this one, high-speed entry, need to trail the brakes into the apex. This is where it all turns into the brown stuff. This is where a soft, long chassis car excels: it is smooth and flexible. But this one is short, stiff and jumpy. All Will's gains are lost and the other car is back on his tail.

Back in the motor home, Ray analysed the problem. "If we could trade off some of the low-speed performance for better high-speed control we would still be ahead, but I am damned if I can think of anything beyond softening it or using more wing. Maybe we should park it."

"We could try more wing," said Will, "but maybe it's me. Maybe it's quick in the pitch and boot mode, but slow in the smooth mode. Maybe I should pitch and boot it everywhere."

"That's absurd. You wouldn't last two laps. You can't pitch it into turn one, it's not that kind of corner, plus its way too fast for that kind of thing."

"No, no, no, that's not what I mean. I've done it before. Instead of coming into the corner on a trailing brake because the corner tightens up, square it off. Keep going straight for the last possible moment, hard on the brakes, turn for the apex, pitch it, and boot it. It's not a new idea — that's how it used to be done before cars became so stable that you could brake them around corners. You couldn't do that in the old wingless cars; you had to brake in a straight line. You remember when your father taught you to drive, "Brake on the straight, boy. Don't step on the brakes in the corner or the car will skid. Come down hills in the same gear you went up, boy, or you'll burn out the brakes."

"That was then; this is now, and you are not skidding around on some dirt road in an old Ford."

"Yeah," said Will, "but if I can reduce some of the loss on the fast stuff, and still keep the advantage on the tighter corners, we'll be in a good position. I'd like to try it, but I'd like to try more wing first and if that works, then give it a go."

"Okay, we'll try the wing first."

Will went rasping up the gears out of the pits, weaving the car back and forth, impatient to get the tyres warm so that he could get into it. Halfway round the course he was flat out. It certainly felt more stable, but the question was how much speed would he lose on the straight by the increased drag of the wings. In the end the benefit was zero; it was faster in the corners but slower on the straight, and the lap times were virtually identical.

Will dived into the pits. There was no gain from the increased wing so put it back where it was, even if it felt better. You had to be merciless in this game. Leaving the wings as they were would only confuse the issue at the next change when they wouldn't know whether or not the wing had anything to do with it.

Will went out again, not quite as enthusiastically this time. He was on his own; he had to make it work. Will approached the problem corner flat out in fifth. Instead of braking in an arc towards the apex he would brake straight to a point on the outside of the corner and make his entry from that spot.

The disadvantage was that the others would be able to come up his inside, out-braking him into the corner and preventing him from turning in; however, on the upside he would be accelerating earlier and have an advantage on the exit.

Will got on the brakes hard to the outside of the corner. Big right flick of the steering, boot it, bang, power on, opposite lock, up the kerb, away. Fantastic!

A few laps later, back to the pits to see what the tyre wear was like. It hadn't been any faster than the others in the fast sections, but it was a whole heap faster in the tight stuff. This wasn't the smooth, flowing style Will had cultivated throughout his career, but it was effective, fun and bloody dangerous. They were on the pole by over half a second, a big margin in Formula One terms. They were the talk of the pits.

•

The next day dawned bright and clear. As was his habit on race day, Will tried to sleep in late and have a big breakfast because when he got to the track he wouldn't eat again. He had found out years before that food made you feel comfortable, dulled your edge. You needed to be hungry, he would say: a hungry man is an angry man. He had breakfast sent up to his room. He expected a lousy breakfast, and he wasn't disappointed. It was typical hotel food, overdone, overloaded omelette, rubbish bread and weak coffee. Great start to the day for a man who appreciated a good breakfast.

The race started with a bang, and ended with a bang. Will had had a good start; however, going into the first corner, as he had feared, three others went up the inside, so he was now fourth. They were nose to tail at the end of the main straight. Will popped out of the slipstream as they got into the braking area three abreast, jostling for position, banging wheels. Boot it, nothing, out of gear? Back into gear, boot it, no drive, others overtaking. Whose wheel is that? He could see a rear wheel complete with the suspension rolling down the hill towards the pit lane. "Oh shit, it's mine," It dawned on him that he had lost the inside rear suspension and wheel. That was why he had no drive. The outside front wheel started to lift off the ground as he lost centrifugal force. He pulled over on the grass, flipped off the master switch, unplugged his oxygen, turned the quick release for the six-point harness and got out. The whole right-hand rear suspension was gone.

•

By six o'clock all the work was done. The cars were locked away, and the entire team was on its way into town in the motor home. Will was driving because nobody else would, and the rest of the team were down the back drinking beer. They were travelling on a six-lane highway with little traffic.

Will waited for a level straight section, set the speed control, and had a few practices letting the steering wheel go, before sauntering down the back. All of a sudden everybody wanted to drive. They were diving over the seats in their keenness to get their hands on the wheel. Will shook his head in perplexity. "If you were all just waiting to have a turn, why didn't you ask? I wouldn't have minded."

33

WILL SAT ON the teak deck leaning against the cabin top. The sun was a large, yellow-gold orb, rising above the dark-blue sea. Its silvery path crossed the rippling water in a dead straight line, ending between Will's bare feet.

The wind was just disturbing the water, making the reflection of the sun shimmer. He was eating from a jumbo-sized coffee cup with a spoon. Earlier he had cooked himself his favourite breakfast of chopped-up soft-boiled eggs, grilled bacon and toast, all mixed up together. He had had two eggs, remembering as a child watching his father eat eggs. The difference was that his father had had six in his. Cholesterol had not yet been heard of. As he sipped the rich Guatemalan coffee, he remembered seeing somewhere a cartoon of an old sailor on a boat with the caption, "Sometimes I sits and thinks, and sometimes I jest sits."

He heard the whine of an outboard motor. Over to his left was a fisherman in a dugout canoe, a large, multi-sided wire-mesh fish pot balanced on the gunnels, heading out to sea.

The canoe crossed the sun's reflection, the wake disturbing the silver path. Will waved, and the man returned the greeting. He wondered what the man thought about this huge yacht anchored off the island. Did he resent it? Did he hate the rich gringo who came with the yacht, or did he see it as an opportunity?

Will thought about the flight he had just been on. It was one of the worst he had known. Quite often he could get away without being recognised; sometimes he could deny who he was. He had even tried disguises a few times. They worked quite well; at least nobody had yet confronted him. But this time he was besieged by autograph hunters and motor-sport enthusiasts. He didn't mind enthusiasts; what he couldn't stand were earnest ones, especially earnest female ones. He had tried to sleep, but it was hopeless — they just kept coming. One woman kept trying to drag him into an in-depth discussion of his motives for racing. Fed up, Will finally beckoned her closer until she got her ear close to his mouth, then whispered the most obscene suggestion he could come up with. For a moment she hesitated, and he thought, "Oh no, I may have to go through with this." Then she shot off back to her seat, where she entered into an animated discussion with the man she was with.

The man's head kept flipping back and forth like a spectator at a tennis match with his mouth agape, looking at her then at Will in rapid succession. Will finally caught his eye and gave him an exaggerated wink. That stopped the tennis-match action. Finally, the woman called the stewardess and lodged a complaint.

"Did you really make that suggestion to her?" said the stewardess.

"Sure did."

"That was very original. What if she took you up on it?"

"For a moment I was scared she would."

•

Now the canoe was returning, its wake crossing the sun's path, leaving it shimmering behind. He was an old, black man with a grey beard and almost-white hair. He sat in the stern in front of a beat-up outboard with the cover off and the flywheel exposed. As he let the boat idle up to *Imperialist*, he reached into a burlap bag at his feet and dragged out two lobsters which he held up by their feelers, while they energetically flapped away. He started gabbling away in Spanish. Will held up his hands and said, "No comprende, no comprende, la cuenta?"

The man held up his right hand with thumb and four fingers extended and said, "Cinco."

Will nodded and mimed that he was going downstairs to get the money. He slid down the companionway to the smell of the boys cooking bacon and eggs. He took some money out of his pants pocket, and as he passed the galley he grabbed Peter's breakfast, including the coffee and the cutlery.

"Hey! Where you going with that?" yelled Peter.

"Swapping it for lobsters."

"Oh. Okay."

Will went up on deck, put down the breakfast, and held up the money. He walked to the stern, stood on the open transom and beckoned the man to back up to the transom so that the fish pot wouldn't graunch the topsides. The old man dug out a paddle and skilfully backed up the canoe. Will gave him the money, and took the two lobsters, being careful not to drop them, or break off the feelers, which would amount to the same thing. The old man nodded his thanks, and Will held up his hand indicating that he should wait. He fetched the breakfast and offered it to him.

A huge smile of delight crossed the man's face, as he took the food and settled back down on the seat. Will sat on the transom with his feet in the water, watching him. These canoes hadn't changed in centuries, or the fish pots. The only thing modern was the motor. The motor gave greater range, allowing him to fish alone. In the old days, he would have needed two oarsmen, and would not have gone nearly as far. But then the outboard motor couldn't have broken down, possibly leaving them to die of thirst miles from land either.

The man handed back the plate and cutlery and said gravely, "Muchos gracias, Señor, muchos gracias." He wrapped the starting cord around the groove at the top of the fly wheel and, after a half-a-dozen attempts, the old motor roared into life, belching a cloud of oily black smoke. As he moved off he waved, and Will half-saluted. Here he was, a rich gringo, part of the high-tech western world, and there was this old man with his ancient canoe and a clapped-out motor, eking out an existence in paradise. Who was better off, the fisherman with nothing, or the salaried man fighting the traffic to and from his big house in suburbia?

•

He felt fingers running through his hair. "Why did you not wake me?"

"You needed your sleep."

She sat down beside him, dangling her feet in the water.

"Want some coffee?"

"In a while."

They watched the sun continuing to rise. The path of light across the water slowly disappeared, replaced by a light wind rippling the water. In the background the blue-green hills slowly emerged. There was not a sound to be heard since the old fisherman had gone.

Will got up. "I'll get you some coffee." As he made it, he thought about Isobel. Their relationship had settled from the early turbulence to an easy-going, yet exciting, independent relationship. That she was the best woman he had ever been involved with was not in doubt; that he was not going to find anybody better was a certainty. They were friends and lovers; he was like a son to her family. What else did he want? The answer was: nothing. The problem wasn't her, it was him. He had never been faithful to a woman in his life, and he wasn't sure that he could be now.

He had not had another woman since he had started seeing Isobel, and he just wasn't interested. That was not the problem. He had never been in the habit of turning it down if it was offered. It wasn't as though he went looking — he hadn't gone looking for years. He didn't have to, it just sort of arrived. It wasn't polite to turn it down; besides he didn't know how. Anyhow it was fun, a heap of fun. The bad part was getting rid of them after. But if you didn't get involved, it wasn't a problem. Will knew the signs when they were closing in and it was the time to skip. He knew if he didn't get out right then, he would be on a conscience trip, and he hated conscience trips.

Isobel was different; there were none of the usual signs, underwear left in the bathroom, none of those little markers. Will thought that women must have all gone on the same course: they all did the same thing. Sometimes Isobel wouldn't get in touch with him for days, she was so independent; she either didn't want a commitment from him, or was much smarter than the average bear. One thing Will did know, he did not want to lose her. But the old question always surfaced: if a woman made a move, how could he turn it down? It was just plain rude. With the other long-term relationships, it had varied between not caring if he got caught, to hoping that he didn't, to hoping that he did. But this was different. He didn't want to, but what if he did? What if he couldn't resist? What if he got caught? Even though she was Spanish and supposedly used to infidelity, he knew that if he strayed, that would be it.

Will went back up on deck with two cups of Cuban-style coffee, freshly ground from the best Guatemalan beans. He sat down beside her while they drank the rich, sweet coffee. "Feel like a swim?" he asked.

"No."

"Well, what *would* you like to do?" She just gazed at him with those emerald eyes.

"Why didn't I think of that?"

They picked up their coffees and dropped them off in the galley on their way back to bed. It was always different with her, not contrived — different, not like some women who had read about it in a women's magazine. Sometimes she was aggressive, sometimes compliant and passive, other times almost feline. Sometimes she was so noisy that he had to put a pillow over her mouth.

Later, they went ashore in the rubber dinghy, tied up to the new dock, and climbed into one of the new Chevy 4WD pickups Will had bought in Miami. Since he was last here, a great deal of road had been cut; they couldn't even hear the equipment. Will and Isobel drove up the newly cut and graded road, as it followed the contour around the side of the hill on its way inland. They had not brought any gravel in to surface the road yet, but that would begin as soon as they opened the quarry, which Will wanted to see. He was tempted to go blasting up the road, although he knew that would be setting a bad example, digging up the new road before it had been surfaced. It soon started to get rocky; one section had been left for the dynamite crew. Will was glad of the 4WD, and the high ground clearance, as he eased over the rocks, the pickup rolling and skidding.

They could hear the equipment now as they came around the corner. They came upon a Cat D9 with the ripper down trying to tear its way through rock with its single ripper tooth. The huge bulldozer, all fifty tons of it, concentrating its power and weight on the ripper, trying to break through the rock surface. The tracks were squealing and skidding on the rock with white stone dust coming off the grouser cleats, as the ripper skidded along the top. Will watched for a while, realising that it was hopeless. Will caught the eye of the operator, who pushed the throttle lever forward and lowered the blade.

He climbed out of the pickup and walked over to the huge bulldozer. Will hopped up on the blade arm and stepped on to the track. He leaned under the cab, held out his hand, smiled and said, "Buenos días. Como esta usted?"

"Buenos días. Estoy muy bueno, Señor."

Will pointed to the rocks and shook his head. "Los son muy malo,"

"Si, Señor, son muy malo."

Will had run out of Spanish, but they understood each other.

There was no point in wrecking the equipment; it was cheaper to use dynamite. He mimed that he was to clean off the rock as best he could, so that the drill rig would be able to access the rock. "Comprendo, Señor Will."

They crossed several other sections of rock as the ground grew steeper, eventually finding two drill rigs operating. Looking like huge tracked mosquitoes, with their probes stuck in the ground, the operators standing beside the drill, the bits clattering away and a stream of white dust blowing back out through the hole and over the operators. They hadn't done the first blast yet; however, they had drilled a large area. The surface earth and loose rock had been cleaned off by a dozer. The rock surface looked white from the drill dust. Bush stuffed in the holes to plug them, appearing like a pineapple field planted in snow. The blasting crew had already started. Parked on the site were a 4WD truck and a pickup. The truck had half a dozen drums of ammonium nitrate, and a drum of diesel, and the pickup had boxes of 2.5-inch dynamite on board.

A couple of men were mixing the diesel with the nitrate. They had removed the top of a 45-gallon drum of nitrate, and poured a five-gallon pail of diesel into it, mixing it in with an old paddle. The simple act of mixing the ammonium nitrate or fertiliser with diesel turned it into cheap explosive. All they needed was dynamite as a detonator. Will climbed out of the pickup and wandered over to the crew, immediately running into language difficulties. He turned and looked back at the pickup; Isobel came over immediately. The drillers' faces were a picture, awestruck. La Señora had arrived. She translated back and forth for a while, got the gist of what was needed, and took over. In no time she had them eating out of her hand.

They continued up the partly constructed road, most of the time in low range, creeping over the worst parts, the pickup lurching back and forth as Will eased it through the roughest sections. The road followed the contours of the hills, gradually climbing. The vegetation was thick, tropical bush, mostly secondary growth, as it had been logged for years for its mahogany and other hardwoods. The road ended at a river — more of a stream than a river he supposed, but a beautiful spot. The water was crystal clear, with deep, rocky pools among huge, dark boulders. Some parts were quite shallow with a gravel bottom. The vegetation had completely changed since they had neared the river. It had been replaced by scrub pine, in a golden sandy soil Will had never seen before. The pine trees were swaying and moaning in the wind, drowning out the sound of the river, and if they looked down the river between the trees, they could just get a glimpse of the sea. Carefully stepping from boulder to boulder, they followed the river downstream. Another noise was now dominating the scene, and they were no longer aware of the wind in the trees. It was a dull roar; growing louder the further they went down. They realised that it must be the sound of a waterfall. Soon they could see the wind-driven spray being blown back from the face of the falls. Will and Isobel worked their way around until they came upon their own waterfall. Only a few feet wide, and about five hundred feet high, the river had been squeezed between two boulders, shooting out as through a high pressure hose.

The waterfall dropped for about a hundred feet, hit a ledge, bounced off, and then fell straight down to be swallowed up by the huge trees below. It was real tropical jungle. The old-timers would not have been able to haul the trees out when they were logging early in the century.

They stood there at the top of the falls with their arms around each other. "You are so lucky," Isobel said.

"Why?"

"To be able to preserve this, to look after this beautiful place."

"*We* are so lucky," said Will.

"Maybe."

Will knew he was now on the slippery slope, but he was not unhappy. It needed to be said, and he meant it. He had never known anybody he would rather have shared this with. It was a dream come true, a huge gamble. Then again, everything he had ever done had been a huge gamble. She would be another gamble, but far less risky.

By the time they had returned to the dynamite crew, the men were ready to blast; however, there was a problem: the sky had darkened, and it was beginning to rain. Forked lightning had started to slash across the sky, followed by large claps of thunder. The problem was that they hadn't finished connecting up the charges, and as they were electronic, they could be detonated by an electrical charge. Static electricity from the atmospheric conditions could set off an explosion at any time. They couldn't drive through it, and there was no other way down. The blasting foreman kept looking at Will, then back at the blast area. Will knew what was on his mind. Should he finish tying up the blast in this weather, or risk the ire of the Patron? Will leaned out the window and signalled him, no, forget it. There was instant relief on the foreman's face.

The squall finally went through an hour later, but it was still overcast with the odd distant flash of lightning as the squall moved away, with reduced static electricity. Will still didn't like it, but they couldn't stay up there all day. "Oh shit, I hate this," thought Will as he climbed out of the pickup, and walked into the blast area carefully, so that he wouldn't damage any of the connectors. He couldn't let them do this on their own as they were pushing it so that he could get down. The blast area was covered with a maze of fine wires in different colours connecting each row of blast holes. Each colour denoted the millisecond delay, so it did not all go off at once, controlling the timing of the blast.

Every time lightning flashed, the hair stood up on the back of his neck, as he waited for the whole thing to go off. The smell of dynamite gave him a nauseating headache, making him feel like vomiting, but he helped as best he could, concealing the headache, and trying not to jump every time the lightning struck way off in the distance. The men were surprised that he knew how to tie up the connecting wires, and even more amazed that he was willing to take the risk with them. Will knew that to make this thing work, he needed every advantage he could get, and their respect was a definite advantage.

They backed the vehicles away from the blast area to protect them from the rain of rocks that would result. The charge went off with an earthshaking whomp! Earth and rock flying skywards and outwards, which was expected. The unexpected was a mushroom cloud all pinks and greys.

Isobel was surprised. "Why all those colours? Where did they come from?"

"It must be from the red earth between the rocks. I've seen it once before."

"It was beautiful. I never expected that; it must be your

rainbow, your good-luck sign."

"I hope so," said Will. "We need all the luck we can get."

The dozer quickly cleared them an access road through the blast, and they were on their way down the hill, with the pickup slipping and sliding on the wet dirt, with Will trying to keep as far away from the edge as he could. He found himself modulating the brakes as he did in a racing car, to prevent the wheels locking and losing control.

Eventually they reached the beach. *Imperialist* was still there, beautiful as ever. Will never got used to the sight of his boat. Whatever else happened, he hoped to keep her for the rest of his life. She was an expensive mistress; some people would say, "a hole in the water surrounded by wood, into which you poured money". There was no doubt about that, but she was beautiful.

34

It was grey, grey, grey. There was not a trace of sunshine, not a trace of cloud, just a grey, blanket-like covering. It was all grey: the sky was grey, the buildings were grey, and the spray off the cars was grey. The traffic was solid and slow, the trucks were nose to tail on the inside lane, the cars were nose to tail on the other two lanes. Will wondered when these people had last seen the sun. How could they live like this? His feet were freezing; there was no heater in the old Porsche, never had been. Will wondered why he had bothered to bring it back from Spain. He never drove it in winter, so it shouldn't be a problem; in fact he hardly ever drove it. Will had no real interest in street cars. He probably would have if he weren't racing, but street cars were pathetic things after a Formula One car. He only wanted transport, and in London the best from of transport was a taxi.

The old Porsche wasn't a street car, and it was a pain in the backside to drive in traffic. It cooked you in summer, and froze you in winter. It was noisy inside and out. It was like being inside a drum; every sound was magnified: every thump of the tyres, the whining gearbox, the whirring of the gears in the engine, not to speak of the exhaust resonating through the uninsulated body. It was meant to be driven by somebody with a helmet on. He should buy some earplugs, but he never could remember.

The traffic would speed up, and then slow down again to a crawl. The clutch was heavy; there was no radio, no demister, so he had to open the window, but the windshield still fogged up. People kept looking at him as if he was some sort of delinquent, because he had to keep sinking the clutch and revving the engine. The old car did not like traffic, and Will did not want the plugs to foul. The old girl was loud, worse than loud — raucous was more the word.

"Why did I drive? Why didn't I fly? What am I doing here? People actually do this day in, day out, for years and years. Why would anybody subject themselves to this? Wouldn't the old fisherman with the canoe be better off?" Will thought, watching the spray off the cars in front as they accelerated up to a reasonable speed for a change. They finally cleared the city, travelling through the countryside. This was better; there were some green fields at last, some beautiful country houses, and grey stone farm buildings.

Will thought, "It's still raining; it's still grey, my feet are still freezing." The rain was now running down the partly open driver's window, and he was getting wet. But he couldn't close the window, because he wouldn't be able to see when the windshield fogged up. "The traffic is getting worse; it's slowing again, so I will have to open the window even more, and get even wetter, but the wind chill is less. Thank God for small mercies. I am going to die of pneumonia in this goddam car, in this goddam traffic, on this goddam road, in this goddam country."

Will was on his way to a tyre-testing session, and he also wanted to look at his potential replacement. After a totally painful trip, he finally arrived and parked behind the pits. It was still raining, that awful misty, sticky, horrible, non-stop, drizzly English rain. He trotted across to the motor home. Ray and the new guy were sitting at the dining table. The new guy leapt up, shaking his hand enthusiastically.

"Sit down, sit down," said Ray. "Where have you been? We've been waiting all morning for you."

"I've been freezing in the bloody traffic, that's where I've been, freezing in the bloody traffic."

"It's your own fault. Why don't you buy yourself a proper car?"

"I should have a company car, and then I wouldn't need to drive this thing."

"You wrecked the last company car."

"No, that one was yours."

"Even worse, you are not a fit person to have a company car. You have no respect for other people's property."

"It was only a car. Besides, the insurance gave you a new one."

"It was my brand-new Mercedes-Benz — how can you say it was just a car?"

The new driver's head was swivelling back and forth. He didn't know how to take the exchange, not knowing whether or not it was serious. Will laughed. "Borrow his car before he signs you up, because once he does, he goes all cheap and mean, and won't do anything for you."

The driver being tested was Jean-Claude Clemond, the European Formula Three Championship leader, considered by the media to be an up-and-coming man. He was young, French, and supposed to be very good. Well, they would see.

"Will," said Ray, "I want you to go and set a benchmark time, and then we'll let Jean-Claude have a go."

"You are going to let him go out in this shit?"

"He has to start somewhere."

"But he's never sat in a GP car before."

"Just do it, Will."

"Okay, you're the boss."

Will suited up and climbed into the car. It had already been warmed up in a new set of wet tyres. The rain had stopped, but the track was still soaking wet, although they'd had the helicopter flying around trying to blow some of the water off. Will had no intention of trying to set a time. If the new guy was any good, there was no point trying to break his spirit, or having him kill himself trying to beat a quick time. The track was slippery but not too bad; the car was set on full soft with full wing. He came back in after three laps for a ride-height adjustment, went back out and set a comfortable time. He came back in, and after a seat change and pedal adjustment, the little Frenchman went out. In ten laps he was within two seconds of Will's time.

Ray looked at Will and raised his eyebrows. "Not bad, eh?"

"Not bad."

"It's drying out. Let's bring him in and have a chat."

They sat around the table in the motor home, Jean-Claude bubbling over with enthusiasm. "Such power, such grip, fantastique. How close was I to the time?"

"Pretty close, but don't worry about that now. Tell me how the car felt. Tell me every detail."

Will groaned and got up.

"Where are you going?"

"I don't want to listen to you torturing him, asking him endless questions. I'm going to the pub."

"No you don't, you stay right here. In fact, it's drier now. Go out on dry tyres and set another time."

Will went out again, this time on an intermediate suspension setting with full wings and slicks. In a few laps he had knocked nearly five seconds off his previous best. When he came back in, Jean-Claude was waiting, ready to go. He had definitely gained confidence; he was pushing hard, perhaps too hard, and he eventually spun coming onto the pit straight and stalled. They sent the truck out and towed him in, but he had equalled Will's time.

"The boy's good," said Ray. "Go out and lower the time."

"Do you really think it's a good idea?"

"Yes. I want to see how he reacts to pressure. He's feeling pretty cocky right now."

"You're the boss."

Will went out again, came back in for some fine-tuning and got right into it. Blasting around two seconds quicker. Came back in, took some rear wing off and knocked another half a second off.

Jean-Claude went out, did two laps, came back in, took some more rear wing off and was still two seconds off Will's best time. "Shit," thought Will, "this little bastard's good."

"Can you go faster, Will?" said Ray.

"Maybe another half a second if the track stays the same,

faster if it is drier."

"Go out and set a hot one, see how he reacts."

The track was a little drier, and Will let it all hang out. He came back in five laps later a second quicker. "Now let's see what you do about that," he thought. Jean-Claude went out and damn near did it — he was a second off when he crashed. He tore both left-hand corners off against the Armco at the fastest section of the track.

"Don't say I didn't tell you. You pushed him too hard and now you've lost a car."

"It's all in a good cause. It's better to know now than find out we have been backing the wrong horse later. The kid's good, he's got fire in his belly, plus he's smart. The feedback I was getting from him was excellent; he's no dummy. I was going to try a couple of others, but I have a good feeling about this one. What do you think?"

"Well, you could be right. The boys seem impressed, and they are pretty difficult to please. When do you want to start him?"

"I'd like to start him now, but of course we can't — he has to finish the F3 season. I want to get him into as much testing as possible for the rest of the year. I'll need your help."

"Only if you lend me your new car."

35

WILL'S GUTS WERE tied in a knot, the tension rising throughout his whole body. He was angry, to the point of being beyond anger. He had just received a letter from the Department of Mines requiring him to produce the licences granting him permission to operate a quarry on the island. The worst part was that they required him to cease work on the quarry until he produced the licence, which he didn't have. They had caught him in a typical squeeze play. He had invested millions of dollars and now they were trying to hold him over a barrel. The lawyers had screwed up. The laws on mines took precedence over any other agreement, so that the state could claim rights to any precious metals found. The lawyers had not foreseen that the mining law could be applied to a quarry, and used for blackmail, graft, and political advantage.

Will couldn't sleep. He had spent nights tossing about, the whole thing revolving around in his head, over and over again. It wasn't until he figured what was griping him so much. It wasn't the stunt that had been pulled on him; it was that he couldn't get even. That was the main problem. He couldn't get even without hurting himself as well. It wasn't just frustrating; it was eating up his guts.

Now he was marching up and down the ornate offices of his lawyers, ranting and raving. "How the hell are we going to build any roads without road-building materials? We were set up. This is no accident. It's plain blackmail. What do the other government ministers say? Never mind, I know the answer. The law is the law and they can't make a special case. I wonder how many of them are involved."

"Señor, we will appeal to the Minister. This is not correct, it is not proper."

"Appeal to the Minister, don't make me laugh. The son of a bitch set it up."

"Señor, Señor, calm down. This will not get us anywhere, we must keep calm."

"Keep calm shit. I have millions tied up in this crap and the bastard knows it."

Will knew it was pointless. These people had been fleecing gringos for generations, the same way they were fleecing him now. Suck you into the mire, then spring the trap for whatever they could gain. Just like the old-timers setting a lantern in a tree to lure ships onto a reef. It didn't matter the damage, just so they could skim a little off the top.

He would have to get back to Isobel's father; he might be able to sort it out. It had been all going too well: he should have been watching for something like this. "Chicken merry, hawk is near." How was he going to deal with all this and try to win the championship as well? He should have left it alone till after the season before looking at it. That's what the odds men would have done, but no, he had to rush at it like a bull at a gate. Typical — he was always biting off more than he could chew. Jesus, he was pissed off. But who was he pissed off with? Himself, mostly, for allowing himself to fall into this trap. He was in too deep; they had him just where they wanted him.

•

Will was on the radio to Miami. "Send back the barge, pick up all the gear and put it up for auction. Yes, all of it. I am not getting sucked down this rat hole."

Will had put a Radphone call through to the barge operators from *Imperialist*. Because it was a radio call to a telephone it was broadcast. It would soon be common knowledge that he was pulling out. They would think he was bluffing, but when he cancelled all the contracts and laid off all the staff, and they saw the barge leave with the equipment, they wouldn't be so sure.

Next, he wrote letters cancelling all contracts with the engineers and architects, explaining the position and leaving them in no doubt why he was pulling out. He had hoped for a more aggressive response from them, at least some support or some ideas to tackle the situation. But no, nothing, nada. They were fatalistic, accepting their lot in life.

He gave his employees a month's pay and closed down the operation, leaving a skeleton crew to prepare the equipment for loading on the barge. *Imperialist* left the following morning for the Bahamas, and Will flew back to Spain. As Will walked up to customs, an official approached, asking Will to accompany him.

"What now?" he thought. They walked down a corridor and through a door, and there was Señor Santiago.

He threw his arms wide. "Will, welcome, welcome," banging

him on his back.

"I thought I was under arrest."

"No, Señor," said the customs officer," but we can't make it look like, ah, special treatment."

As they walked out of the airport, Don Alphonso Santiago was full of questions about the island. How was it going, were the roads on time? What was it like inland? Will explained what had happened, and how he had reacted. Señor Santiago laughed. "They will be running around like, how do you say?"

"Headless chickens,"

"Si, headless chickens."

They were picked up outside arrivals by a new chauffeur-driven Mercedes-Benz. "New car and chauffeur?" said Will.

"As you say, keeping up with the Joneses."

"Yeah, sure," thought Will. "Pull the other one."

"He is the son of one of my oldest employees; I could not find anything else for him to do. You are his hero. He drives very fast. No accidents, yet!"

He did drive very fast, but he was good, a natural. They swung through the gates of the rancho some time later, into the tree-lined driveway Will had entered when he first visited. It seemed like a long time ago, yet it was less than a year back. So much had happened since then. So much would not have happened had he not met these people.

Just before dinner Isobel arrived, walking into the living room with her dancer's toe-out gait. Her long, curly dark hair and emerald eyes stood out against the white linen pants and top. Jeez she looked good — there was nobody like her, she was a knockout, Will thought, and she knew it. He started to get out of the deep leather armchair, but he never quite made it. She pushed him back into it, and slid over the arms into his lap, ruffled his hair and looked at him with her half-amused smile without saying a word. "Well," he said.

"Well," she replied, and they both laughed.

Dinner was the type of affair he had become accustomed to at the Rancho. French venison rack, so rare it was all red with a burnt border, smothered in green peppercorns, crisp on the outside, and virtually raw in the middle. Coffee was served out on the veranda with a very ripe goat's cheese. The four of them sat in their easy chairs, sipping the fine coffee, and tasting the strong billy-goat-smelling cheese.

The light evening breeze wafted through the veranda, bringing the scent of the flowers from the garden. "What happens now?" asked Señora Santiago.

"I finish the season. If nothing is sorted out by then, I keep racing and try to recover the loss."

"But that is very risky."

"It is more risky not to do anything, because if they get away with it once, they will do it again. The contract has got to be rewritten to cover any repeats of this type of thing, or we should forget it."

"Do you not think," asked Señor Santiago, "that you should go back down there and talk to them? It may be a problem that our friends can get around."

"I am too much of a gringo to put up with this foolishness. They know what's going on; why have they not contacted me?"

"Maybe they are not in the position to fix the problem, but with your help they could overcome the people who are causing it."

"I believe," said Will, "that if I don't make a stand now it is lost anyway."

Nobody said anything for a while, all pondering the situation. Suddenly Isobel got up. "Well, Señor Macho Man, you are so full of talk, leading me to believe that we had a life together on the island, then at the first problem you walk away. What are you? I thought it was your dream, yet the first difficulty from some politico arsehole you give up. Well, I am not prepared to give up. I will find out who is behind this."

"I am not giving up, but I can't fight this from a position of weakness. I am no longer vulnerable, I have closed it down; the overheads are gone, and I have accepted the loss. They can't hurt me any more than they have. But you will be able to get to the bottom of this much more easily than I, so if you think you can help I can only be grateful."

"Okay," she said. "I will start on the phone tomorrow, to find out what is behind this."

"What I can't understand," said Will, "is that I thought we were among friends, and that these friends had clout; yet at the first sign of trouble you can't find them. Sure, I understand that there are political considerations that I don't comprehend, but that is no excuse to go to ground and not return calls."

"These people have embarrassed me," said Señor Santiago. "I am sure that they must be having problems, but surely they could have given us a sign that they were trying to fix the problems. I will make contact with somebody tomorrow who will know, but I am not sure that I will be told the answer."

"Okay, let's leave it at that. I'll concentrate on winning the championship. In a way, this may be a godsend. I have to focus on the championship or I'll lose it. If I don't win this year, I never will."

"But surely," said Señor Santiago, "there is next year? You are still young."

"Maybe," said Will, "but the combination of driver, car and team has to be right. Even more important, there is no hotshot among the other teams with the right combination. So it has to be this year. I should have won the championship before, but I threw it away by trying to win races, when I should have settled for a good finish."

"But that is you," laughed Señor Santiago. "That is who you are, the matador who turns his back on the bull. The conquistador who goes into battle knowing he cannot win, yet wins anyway because his opponent does not understand, and thinks there is something else. You cannot change. That is why you closed down the island, and that is why you will win. But a little help will not do any harm. Isobel will spy out the land and report back."

36

RACE DAY DAWNED grey and drizzly. Will was third on the grid. Practice had gone well until the engine blew with an almighty bang on the main straight at over 180 mph, spreading a trail of oil and smoke almost its entire length. More power, more unreliability. Nothing new; it was the old story, nothing for free. It was a struggle playing catch-up after that, and he was lucky to grab third. He was seventh-fastest until three minutes before the end of qualifying. One desperate lap got him up to third.

Now it was going to be a wet start, the drizzle having turned into solid rain. Unless he could jump the start, he would be driving into a wall of spray left by the leaders. Will did not hate driving in the rain as such; he hated not being able to see for the spray from the cars in front. Sometimes it was like following hydroplanes. The spray from the wheels went fifty feet into the air, leaving the following cars driving into a wall of water with no visibility. Some seemed to manage it better than he did, but it scared Will witless, and he didn't mind admitting it.

It was insane racing in zero visibility; anything could be just sitting there waiting to be hit. Then there was the aquaplaning, when the tyres rode on a film of water and the car went where it wanted, under no control whatsoever. He had once come onto the straight in the rain and seen five cars spinning down the track. They had all hit a puddle and aquaplaned together, pirouetting down the track in tight circles like some kind of high-speed, eighteenth-century waltz. Will could do nothing about it but hold the wheel straight, the clutch down, trying to roll through it. He rolled through the middle of the waltzing, spinning cars, waiting for the crash. He didn't expect an enormous crash, because they were all travelling at nearly the same speed. When he was clear of the water, but still spinning, he collected second gear and waited till the car was pointed across the track, revved the engine, and dropped the clutch. By the time the wheels bit and the car took off, he was pointing straight up the track, blasting away in the lead. Sixth to first, just like that.

•

The flag dropped. Will went for the gap between the two front-row cars as they went into the gentle right-hander after the start. He had had to let them go. He just couldn't see. The spray was bad, but it would get worse as the speed increased. The next corner was a third-gear right-hander. Will didn't like this a bit. He couldn't see the apex; all he could see was spray. Then out of the corner of his right eye, a car was coming through. He almost swerved in surprise as it went by. Down to fourth, shit. On to the straight; as expected, it was worse. There was almost zero visibility. He was at less than half throttle; two more cars went by. His heart was racing, not from fear, but from what he knew was in store for him if he pulled out. He could try to bluff it out, but he knew he wouldn't. It wasn't that he was afraid of crashing; it was that he couldn't see what he was doing. He couldn't will himself to hold his foot down when he didn't even know where the end of the straight was. A couple more passed him. None were going particularly fast, but fast enough to overtake him. As he turned into the hairpin at the end of the straight, there was enough visibility to see the yellow flags being waved.

The thought flashed through Will's mind, "Thank God, at least nobody will be able to overtake under the yellow." That at least put off the awful decision to drive into the pits, park the car and face the world's media. He would do another lap and see what happened. The next lap was no better, but now there were yellow flags everywhere and some white ones as well, indicating an official car, probably an ambulance or a wrecker on the course. "Great," thought Will, "all I need is to drive into the back of a frigging wrecker."

He was no longer even trying to go fast; he sensed rather than saw cars behind him. He knew there were wrecks out there, but he hadn't seen one. As far as he could tell there were yellows on all the corners. There must be a long line of cars behind him, and the leaders must have gone, probably caught up with the tail-enders by now. He hated this; he would rather stop than continue with this charade. On the other hand, they might stop the race and restart later. If he stopped he was out, and that would be that. He could easily lose his lead in the championship if the right one won. But he could crash now, and spend the rest of the season in the hospital, or worse.

Blinded by the spray, he didn't see the car until he hit it at over 100 mph just behind the back wheels. It tore off his left front wheel and suspension, flipping the car up. As he passed underneath it, he could feel the heat from the engine; the end of the gearbox took off the roll bar and fell back, ripping the left rear suspension off. But it didn't end there. Will's car spun and hit the wall, tearing the two right corners off. Without wheels, it slid on its belly for another hundred yards before coming to a stop.

Will couldn't believe his luck. When he saw the other car across the track, he knew he was dead. When it hit the wall the first time, he knew he was dead. When it hit the wall the second time he knew he was dead. The relief after each near-death experience was overwhelming. When the car was sliding on its belly with sparks pouring from it, he knew it was going to catch fire and cook him.

Before the car stopped, Will turned off the master switch and undid his seat belts. He remembered not to hit the fire extinguisher button this time. He was terrified of fire after watching Lorenzo Bandini burn in a Ferrari at Monaco live on TV, the flag marshals standing by and watching as he struggled to extricate himself. Will climbed the wall, hitched a ride with a cop back to the pits, and told Ray what had happened. Got a ride to the airport, heading for the boat.

37

WILL WATCHED THE thin, silvery wake fade off into the distance. There wasn't a breath of wind or a ripple on the surface as Will reached forward for his next stroke, feathering the spoon oars and sliding forward in the seat. It was stroke and stroke and stroke, a steady, smooth, powerful rhythm as the beautiful wooden rowing skiff was propelled rapidly across the dead-flat bay in the moonlight. He loved rowing. Of all the forms of exercise that he was forced to endure to maintain his fitness, this was by far the most palatable. Even though it was a relatively cool evening and he was only wearing a pair of shorts, the sweat was rolling down his chest and back. The skiff was strip-planked over laminated beams, a work of art. It was varnished with brass fittings and had had wicker seats, but Will had fitted a sliding seat to make it more efficient to row, so he could use it as an exercise machine.

It was a beautiful evening and he was forcing himself not to think about it, but he couldn't stop cursing himself. He was lucky not to have been killed; he should have parked the damned car and faced the music, rather than let fate decide the outcome. So he came out looking like a hero for soldiering on under impossible conditions. It was all nonsense. They had no business racing in rain like that. The organisers faced a big problem with sponsors, spectators, and TV rights. So what? It was people's lives they were playing with. He had wrecked half a million dollars' worth of car, and nearly succeeded in killing himself, for what? Ray should have called him in. The car should have been parked long before the crash.

As it was now, he had lost his lead in the championship. He was now third, with two thirds of the season gone. There were only five races left and it was beginning to look like other seasons when he was leading in the beginning, only to blow it by crashes or mechanical failure. At least this time he wasn't in the hospital. The motor racing could go wrong, the island deal could stuff up, but there was always *Imperialist* to come back to. She had never let him down; she was always the refuge to come home to. The only trouble with her was that she cost a fortune to maintain, so to keep her he had to earn, and keep on earning.

As he rowed, he thought of Isobel. She had seen the crash on television, and he had talked to her soon after. Although she didn't say much, he could sense what she was thinking. This was a repeat of her brother's death. Will was still not sure what to do about her. He had been over it, over and over again. What should he do? He didn't want to lose her; he would never find another woman like her. But he didn't trust himself. He knew what he was like, but then since they had become involved he hadn't looked at another woman. Why not? He couldn't answer that.

The sweat poured down his chest as he rowed his beautiful skiff, deep in thought. His mind jumped from the championship to the island; to the huge investment that he had made that looked as though it was going down the gurgler. He was prepared to leave it until the season was finished: he couldn't do both. This was his last chance to win the World Championship. If he stuffed this up, there might not be another opportunity. He had to go back and single-mindedly concentrate on winning. If he did not totally focus, he was going to lose, simple as that.

There was an 80-foot charter motor yacht anchored in close to the beach. For all its length it looked dumpy, too much accommodation for its length. It reminded him of a chicken without its tail feathers. There was a noisy party going full blast on the afterdeck. "Hey Will, Will, Will, come on over," someone was yelling, and waving a glass. Will changed his stroke, turned the skiff and headed over to the yacht; not quite knowing what he was getting himself involved in, wondering who they were and why they knew who he was.

"Come aboard, join us!" Will still didn't see anybody he knew, and really didn't want to get involved. "Come and have a drink — we're all motor-racing buffs. Come and join us, we're having a great party!"

Oh shit, thought Will. There was nothing worse, or more boring than a bunch of motor-racing buffs, particularly drunken ones. But he was stuck now; he would have to be deliberately rude to escape, and he didn't want that. But he also knew that by the time he left, he would wish that he had been impolite. He tied up the skiff and climbed on to the boarding platform.

"What's your poison?" asked a big blowsy blonde.

"Hang on a minute. Let me cool off, and then I'll have a drink."

Will took a deep breath and dived over the side. The water was crystal-clear and so refreshing. He took great pride in how far he could swim underwater, and this time he really put some effort in. They would be wondering where he had got to. When he surfaced, there was a row of people looking over the side. Will slowly swam back to the boat and climbed back on board.

"We thought you had drowned," said one.

"I never thought anybody could swim that far underwater," said another.

"Would you like a towel?" said a perky little redhead.

"Thank you," said Will.

"What would you like to drink," asked the blowsy blonde.

"What have you got?"

"Whatever your little heart desires," giving him the goo-goo eyes routine.

The little redhead came back with the towel. "Thanks," said Will.

"What sort of engines you use, buddy?"

"Engines for what?"

"Your race cars."

"All sorts."

"Yeah, but V8s?"

"Some are."

"Chevy or Ford?"

"Neither."

"Not Chevy or Ford?"

"Nope."

"Then what kind of engines do you use?"

"Specialised ones"

"Want a daiquiri?"

"Yep, sounds good."

"You going to win the championship?"

"Hope so."

This was worse than he had expected. Hairy chests, big bellies, gold chains, broads with big teeth, big tits falling out of bikinis.

"Yeah, we're in the car business too, and we move more iron than anybody in the south-east."

"Have another drink."

"No, thanks."

"You are like an athlete, aren't you?" the one with the biggest boobs asked.

"Kinda."

"You don't drink?"

"No."

"Or smoke?"

"Nope."

She looked him dead in the eye. "What about sex?"

"That neither."

"No sex?"

"No sex."

"Really?"

"Really."

"That's terrible."

"It is."

"But why?"

"My contract says I'm not allowed to touch women."

"Not allowed to touch women?"

"Not allowed to touch women."

She came up really close till her oversized mammaries were against him and whispered, "But what if you did it without touching?"

"How would you manage that?"

She got really coy at that. "We should be able to figure out something."

"I'd have to call my lawyer first."

38

"WILL, YOU'RE LOSING it."

"Losing what?"

"It."

"What the hell do you mean? What does 'it' mean?"

Will was in Ray's office. He had just flown in, and had gone directly to see Ray and was totally stunned by Ray's comment.

"You've lost your focus. For five years you have been a contender for the championship; for five years the championship has been lost for one reason or the other. We are a one-car team now, so we don't know how competitive you are any more. We lost the championship at least three times, thanks to mechanical failure or accident. We had no way of knowing whether somebody else would have won. There is no cross-check. There is no way to quantify your or our performance. This season looks as if it is turning out the same as the others. We are three-quarters through and now we have lost the lead. In fact, we are now third."

"What is this all about, Ray? Have the bean counters been getting at you again?"

"You are not focused. You are more interested in your island and the boat. You are being distracted by that woman."

"She has a name Ray."

"Sorry, Isobel. We are going to take on another driver."

Will jumped up. "Good luck to you, Ray," he said and walked towards the door.

"No, no, not instead of you, as well as you."

"That is your prerogative. But I put you on notice right now, if there is any detrimental effect emanating from your decision, you will be hearing from my lawyers."

"I had hoped that you would take this decision in the spirit that it was given, that it was best for the team."

"You heard me. If this move is detrimental to me in any way, you will hear from my lawyers."

Will stormed out of the office, slammed the door, marching out past the startled secretaries.

●

Test day was Wednesday. Will was still angry, partly because some of what Ray had said was true. He *was* distracted, he wasn't focused. There was nobody quicker; however, natural talent wasn't enough. He also knew that Ray, his friend for years, was letting him down. He would never trust him again. When he arrived, Ray started the briefing as if nothing had happened. They were in the conference room in the motor home. The new driver, Jean-Claude, was there along with Will's engineer, and a new one he had never seen before. The interesting addition was three men in Savile Row suits from a cigarette company.

Sponsors had never been involved in briefings before, and these characters looked more like money men. Throughout the entire briefing, Will said nothing. He was still stewing. He didn't really care that there was a second driver; he *did* care how it was done.

Ray wanted him to lead out with Jean-Claude behind so that the newcomer could follow Will, learn the circuit and get comfortable with the car. "Sure, you can follow," thought Will, "if you can." Jean-Claude stayed behind while Will was warming up the car, but as his speed built up by the third lap Jean-Claude had dropped back. Will watched the pit board with his lap times. The times were dropping by about a half a second per lap. By the fifth lap, he got the "come in" signal. Will ignored it and kept going. He stayed out until the times stabilised, then came in.

Ray was busy with Jean-Claude. As his engineer leaned over him, Will said, "Lower the front right height two turns."

"We should wait for Ray."

"Ray's busy. It's understeering."

"Okay."

As he rolled out of the pits he could see Ray standing in the pit lane with his hands on his hips, furious. Will almost laughed. The understeer was gone but so was the stability in the fast stuff. He was determined to go faster, even though the change had not really made an improvement. Five laps later he was back in the pits half a second faster than before, but not happy.

Ray walked up to the car with that stiff-legged walk of the really angry. "Why did you leave the pits without seeing me first?"

"You were busy."

"Why didn't you wait for the second car? Why did you leave him behind? I asked you to show him the ropes."

"I did show him. He couldn't keep up."

"Why didn't you come in when you saw the board?"

"I was focusing on going quicker each lap. There was no need to come in."

After a tyre change, more fuel and a bit more rear wing Will went out again. In two laps he was quicker than before; in five laps he was well below the official lap record. He was really hanging it out, going faster each lap. He knew that this was not the way to test, but he was pissed off and he was going to show them. The "come in" sign was up on the pit board, but Will was still going faster on almost every lap. He was not going in till the speed peaked. The engine spluttered and died, out of gas on the backside of the track. Will coasted to a stop. Bastard, he thought. Ray deliberately reduced the fuel so that he couldn't stay out. Well, stuff you.

Will hopped out of the car, and some spectators came running over.

"Would you like a ride back to the pits?"

"No," said Will, "but if you could drop me somewhere so I could call a cab I would appreciate it." The spectators were a couple of local farmers, taking the opportunity of a test day to watch the cars without the crowds. They were happy to drive Will back to his hotel. Will enjoyed their company. They were sensible men, knowledgeable about motor sport, but not pushy. Will asked them about their farms and farming and told them about the drama down at the Island. In the end they waited for him and drove him to London. No sooner had Will got back to London than he phoned his manager and brought him up to date. "It's a bit extreme, isn't it, walking off in the middle of testing, just because the car ran out of fuel?"

"Maybe, but listen carefully. I want you to write a letter to Ray saying that we are concerned that the team doesn't have the ability in its present form to run two cars, as evidenced today when my car ran out of fuel, cutting short the testing."

"Will, that's only going to make the situation worse."

"So what? I couldn't give a rat's arse. Let the son of a bitch figure out the next step."

39

AFTER A NIGHT of tossing and turning, Will woke to a steady banging noise. It was daylight; he looked at his watch. Seven-thirty. He staggered out in his underpants, and opened the door.

"What the hell are you playing at?" demanded Ray.

"Playing? I've been sleeping, as you can clearly see."

"What the hell do you mean by walking off in the middle of testing?"

"The car had no fuel. It wouldn't go, so there was no point in staying."

"We would have put more fuel in it."

"Why didn't you do that in the first place?"

"Because you wouldn't come in when we wanted you to in the first place."

"So you short-supplied the car with fuel so I would have to come in early."

"Something like that."

"Well, you chose to interfere with my testing rhythm, and I

chose not to be stuffed around."

"We will be testing tomorrow."

"Fine."

"What does that mean? Will you be at testing tomorrow?"

"No."

"Your contract requires you to do testing."

"Not if there is a second driver, and you have another driver. Up to this time I have done all the testing. Now that you have a second driver he can do some of the testing."

"I may not have a car available for you for the next race."

"Please inform my manager in writing," said Will calmly.

Ray spun around on his heel, slamming the door behind him. "Good job," thought Will. "That really pissed him off." He knew he was playing a high-stakes game. He needed the money. He had just walked away from millions invested in the island already, and he just might have walked away from the source of the finance. But stuff it, if the worst came to the worst, some other team would hire him. Maybe this whole thing started because he lost his lead in the championship, and that came about because of the crash in zero visibility. What would have happened if he had come in as he had wanted to, and parked the car?

•

Will booted it coming off the hairpin; the rear end swung, the steering wound itself into opposite lock; the left rear wheel was up the kerbing as Will slammed it into second. He was ill-treating the car, but he didn't care. A week and a half had passed, and he was just as pissed off as he had been on day one. In fact, more so. He was so continually angry that he hardly slept. He would stay awake, fuming. He was brutalising the car, braking late, with tyre smoke trailing off the inside fronts as he drove up the inside overtaking backmarkers.

He was twenty seconds in the lead and opening the gap at over a second per lap. He had received several "take it easy" signs but had ignored them. He had broken the lap record four times so far and was still going quicker as the fuel load lightened. He was taking out his anger on the car, revving it past the red line, slamming it from gear to gear, tearing up the dog rings, and smoking the tyres, under-braking into the corners. He was going through the fast corners in huge drifts, flicking it in and just standing on it. The crowd was loving it; he could see them leaping up and down and waving. He supposed it was the crowd that eventually made him slow down.

His anger was abating; he didn't feel like fighting any more. He just felt worn out; it was as if he had fought and fought and now he was just exhausted. He was glad when the chequered flag came out. He just didn't have any more energy. The crowd were running out onto the track, but he didn't have the interest in doing anything except give a half-hearted wave. He was worn out, and just wanted to go home. There was a huge crowd at the presentation chanting his name, Will, Will, Will. But he didn't feel part of it; he felt bad for the spectators. He wanted to respond to their enthusiasm but couldn't. He didn't want them to think that he was stand-offish or a snob, but he couldn't help himself. He was burned out; he needed to get away.

Ray came up to him and said, "Well done, Will."

"Thanks," said Will, turned his back on him and walked off. He knew Ray was trying to make amends but he didn't care. The damage was done: he would never trust Ray again.

•

Isobel met him as he cleared customs. She threw her arms around him, holding him for a long time. "Do you feel like going to the beach house, or do you want to stay in town?"

"The beach house."

"Bueno."

She drove the big black Mercedes in her usual aggressive way, hard on the throttle, hard on the brakes; hand on the horn, manually changing the automatic to get the most out of it. Will reclined the leather bucket seat right back, and closed his eyes. Most of the tension was gone. For the first time in a week and a half, he wasn't thinking of Ray and the injustice of it all.

The next morning dawned bright and clear. The sea gently breathed in and out. He could hear it sigh with each breath, as the waves ran up the beach at the foot of the cliff. The French doors were open, and the gentle morning breeze wafted into the bedroom. It was after ten and Isobel wasn't there. She would be down in her study working, waiting for him to get up when he was ready. He had slept like a log. He was totally fatigued. Will didn't believe in stress, it was all bullshit, as far as he was concerned, but what was this? Worry? Lack of sleep? Or was there something to all the psychiatrist crap?

The bedroom opened and Isobel stuck her head round the corner. "So, Lazarus has arisen."

"I slept really well."

"So I noticed. I tried to assault you in the night, but you just rolled over and snored like somebody's fat old husband. Ray called and wanted to talk to you, but I said you were asleep."

"Stuff him."

"I told him to call back on Tuesday. I do not think that he was very happy. Do you feel like some breakfast?"

"What do you think? I could eat a horse."

The morning was lazed away breakfasting, and generally lolling about. They talked about the island, but did not get too deep into the issues. Isobel did not want him worrying about it. "Win the championship first," she said, "and fix the island after."

But winning the championship was no longer straightforward. He had Ray to contend with. Ray did not like to be crossed. He was an autocrat in his own right, and if he felt threatened as he did now, he would react violently, even if it caused him short-term damage. Will acted as though he didn't care, but he did. He had thought of Ray as his friend. Friends didn't just turn on you.

•

"Will?" It was Ken, his manager.

"Who else do you think it could be?"

"Good race, congratulations."

"I want another drive."

"Do you mean sports cars?"

"No, F1."

"What are you getting at? Come clean, I'm your manager, not your mind-reader."

"Okay, I'll come clean. Ray is stuffing me around and I want another drive."

"At the end of the season?"

"No, this season."

"That's impossible. Besides, you have a contract with Ray, an ironclad one."

"I don't give a shit. Ray is screwing me around. Look, Ken, I know it's the end of the season, I know about the contract. The fact is that Ray is destabilising me and I want to push him back.

What I need you to do is get something in the press, start the rumours, set up a test drive, stir the pot, create a little havoc."

"Okay, I see where you are coming from. You want to push back."

"Yes."

"Well, why didn't you say so in the first place? Just give me a couple of days. I'll have rumours flying in every different direction."

"Good."

•

When Ray called on Wednesday, he didn't waste time on preliminaries. "We're testing Friday. Are you available?"

"Yes, send me the details."

"Okay, I will have that done. What are these rumours I'm hearing?"

"Rumours?"

"Rumours that you are looking for another drive."

"I am quite entitled to look for another drive."

"You are contracted to me, you understand." Ray was getting hot under the collar.

Will grinned. "You don't want me, yet nobody else can have me, is that it? I'm not your wife, Ray."

"Who said I didn't want you?"

"You did."

"I did not."

"What was all that bullshit in the trailer then? Did I just imagine it?"

"I was trying to get you to focus on winning the championship, not frittering it away as in previous seasons."

"I frittered away the championship in previous seasons? As

I am frittering it away this season? Well, why bother? If I am going to fritter away the championship, you might as well let me off the hook right now."

"There you go, flying off the handle again. All I am trying to do is getting you to focus on the job in hand. If you'd listen to reason, you'd understand where I'm coming from. You virtually destroyed the car! The gearbox is a wreck, the engine is nearly a write-off, the chassis is damaged from grounding, the rivets are all loose, and the chassis will have to be rebuilt. What were you trying to do, demolish the car? I tried to get you to focus, and you responded by trying to destroy the tool you need to win. I don't understand you."

Will took a deep breath. He could see some of Ray's point of view, but he would be damned in hell before he was going to back down. He never started this. "Why don't you try some of the others and see how they treat your cars? How is Jean-Claude going? He didn't just tear up the gearbox, did he? He tore up the entire car. At least I, the incompetent, didn't crash it."

"He's new. How many cars have you crashed? You wouldn't help him when I asked you to; you drove off and left him to fend for himself. Then you proceeded to systematically destroy the car."

"Your benchmark crashed the car and I won the race. Put that through your calculator."

Ray sounded out of breath, he was so angry. "This is not getting us anywhere."

"So why did you phone?" said Will. "You knew it wasn't going to get anywhere; you knew it was going to be a waste of time. You have told me what your position is. You want a benchmark? I want one as well. I don't need to drive your car to win the championship; there is no law that says that I have to drive one make of car all season. Maybe I didn't fritter away previous championships; maybe your cars weren't good enough. Maybe I had to overdrive them to be able to do any good. Maybe that's what happened at the last race. I had to drive it so hard I just plain wore it out. Maybe Jean-Claude had to drive it so hard he crashed. And just maybe that's why Arne got killed, trying to go fast in a slow car."

Ray was furious now. "I'm not going to put up with any more of this," he shouted and slammed down the phone.

"I have the son of a bitch now," Will thought. Blaming Ray for Arne's death was a low blow, but so what? I'm going to give him something to worry about. He picked up the phone and dialled. "Ken, I just heard from Ray. He's spitting tacks. Has he heard rumours?"

"Yeah, I've spread the word about. But if you were serious, there are a couple of people that would be interested. Right now they believe that you wouldn't switch, but if you give me the green light it could be interesting."

"Make it interesting."

"You serious?"

"Why not?"

"Remember who told me to go ahead."

"I'll remember." Will walked out onto the patio. The wind had started to come in; there were small waves on top of the main swell. It was starting to get warm, time for a swim. Will walked up behind Isobel, reclining in an antique wooden slatted chaise longue contoured to fit your body and be far more comfortable than most of the padded ones.

"Feel like a swim?"

"Who have you been talking to?"

"Ken, you know, my manager."

"I have never met him, anything interesting?"

"I have turned up the wick on Ray."

"Turned up the what?"

"The wick, like turning up the light on a lamp."

"Increase the pressure, is that what you mean?"

"That is exactly what I mean. He is putting the word around that I am available, which will of course get back to Ray. It may just make him back off a bit."

40

WILL COULD FEEL the tension as he walked into the pit. They all knew who he was, but nobody acknowledged him until the Ferrari team manager came up and shook his hand. "Mauro Fillipetti. The car is ready. We hope that the seat is correct, but it only arrived late last night. You have missed testing, and the first practice was closed an hour ago. The next session is at two. Have you driven sports cars before?"

"No," said Will.

"It is different from Formula One. Formula One drivers do not often make good sports-car drivers."

"Yes," said Will.

"We were instructed to make this car available for you. Our regular driver now has no drive; testing is finished; practice has almost finished; there is not enough time for you to become accustomed to a sports car."

"Yes," said Will.

"Would you like to try the seat?"

"Yes."

Will was not about to get involved in the internal politics of Ferrari. They had been directed from on high to make a car available to him, so one driver had to be sidelined halfway through practice. They had not been told the reason why: just make space for this hotshot who had just walked up. The resentment was total.

Will walked up to the pit counter and looked over the wall at the crimson Ferrari sports cars. There were three parked nose to tail, mechanics in brown overalls swarming all over them, getting them ready for the next practice session.

"Are you not going to put on overalls to fit the seat?"

"This will do."

Will stepped over the side and stood in the seat, then slid down into it. He pushed himself back into the seat with the steering wheel, wriggled from side to side and tested the pedals with his feet. They had done a good job; as best he could tell without driving, the fit was fine. He climbed out.

"What adjustments do you require?"

"None; its fine." Will could sense them looking surreptitiously at each other. Nobody got into an unfamiliar car and did not want the seat changed. Especially not a hotshot Formula One driver, who had been leading the points for the World Championship.

Ken, Will's manager, had set up this drive as part of the plan to turn the pressure up on Ray. Will knew that Ray would be absolutely pissed off, when he found out Will had driven in a sports-car race, but he would be twice as pissed off when he discovered he was driving for Ferrari.

The International Championship for Sports Racing Cars

was well under way, and for Will to arrive to take the drive off a team driver in the middle of the season, by directive of the Commendatore Enzo Ferrari himself, was not well received.

Very few Grand Prix drivers drove anything but Formula One cars any more. In the old days they had, but no more. There were too many races, and too much at stake. Will could feel the animosity, the uncertainty, the curiosity, as he walked out to the car — the beautiful crimson, ultra-aerodynamic, twelve-cylinder, three-litre car. He stepped over the side into the left-hand seat. As a mechanic tightened the belts, he looked over the long, drooping bonnet, bulging fenders, steeply raked windscreen, Nardi steering wheel, and the big aluminium gear-lever knob in the polished gate.

They plugged in the battery cart and gave Will the thumbs up. He turned on the master switch, pumped the accelerator twice and pushed the starter button. Two or three turns and the engine burst into life with a low-pitched howl, then settled down to a high idle. Will banged the gear lever over towards himself and, pumping the clutch a couple of times, graunched the lever into first. A blip on the throttle, and he eased out the clutch.

He rolled out of the pits, gradually accelerating up through the gears as he headed for the South Curve. He rolled into the corner in no hurry, accelerating away up the straight towards the North Curve, through the corner and down the hill, accelerating all the time.

The Nürburgring was the longest racetrack in the world, fourteen miles per lap, and 180 corners through the Adenau forest. Too many to learn. There was no way that you could learn it well enough to go flat out as you would on a two-and-a-half-mile racetrack.

Will had long since learned to concentrate on driving the car and forget about trying to get the last ounce out of it. The best advice he had ever received was from the great Juan Manuel Fangio when he was a kid driving 1000cc GT cars at the Nürburgring: leave it in high gear, forget about trying to get the absolute limit out of it; 180 corners per lap is too much to learn; be smooth and flowing, and end up going faster without wearing the car out.

He had expected to feel awkward, not looking straight down the middle, dead centre between the two front wheels. He had thought sitting offset to one side would feel unbalanced, but it didn't. Even the gear lever felt good; the big alloy knob in the polished aluminium gate was familiar. The black crackle-finished dashboard with the mid-mounted chronometric tachometer was a lot like an old road Ferrari he had had a few years before.

Will was really enjoying this; the car was softer and slower than a Grand Prix car, so he was operating well within his limits. He had to restrain himself from overdriving the sports car. True, it wasn't as precise, but it was more forgiving. It had more top speed because of its aerodynamics. A Grand Prix car had a smaller frontal area; however, it was not as aerodynamic because of the exposed wheels and suspension. It also had heaps of torque or pulling power, unlike a GP car, which was all high-revving horsepower in a narrow band. This thing could pull from four thousand revs all the way to ten.

He reckoned he would make less than a dozen gear changes per lap and go faster that way than trying to go for the optimum. He felt comfortable as he rolled the big car through the pine forest, the sweet Ferrari engine note howling, as he swooped through the long, flowing bends. His main concern was slow traffic as the closing speed between himself and the smaller cars could be as much as a hundred miles per hour. If he got caught in the three downhill corners leading to the Adenau Bridge, each one falling away steeper, and steeper, it would be difficult to back off without losing it. Piling into a concrete bridge abutment at full speed could ruin your whole day.

Will was enjoying himself. He almost felt as though he was in his old Porsche, except there was no traffic coming the other way. The car was understeering a bit, pushing the front on the tighter stuff, but it responded quickly when he wound off on the front roll bar a little, using the cockpit control knob, making the front softer, allowing the weight to transfer to the front outside wheel, causing it to bite more, giving more grip.

Up to this point, he had paid no attention to his pit signals. He had had difficulty seeing them anyway, so he had not bothered after the first two laps. He started to grow concerned about fuel. He didn't know how much was in the car, and as he suspected that they would have put a light load in, he decided to return to the pits. As he pulled up, the mechanics rushed up to the car, taking note of the water, oil, and tyre temperatures. They were all over the car like a rash, yet nobody asked him any questions. He was accustomed to Ray's immediate interrogation, but here there was nothing. Strange.

Will took off his helmet and Nomex balaclava, zipped down his overalls and pulled off his Nomex vest. He tied the sleeves around his waist and fetched himself a glass of water. They were looking at him curiously, some of them sort of hovering. "What's the problem?" he asked the team manager.

"No problem."

"Well, if you don't need me for anything, I'm off."

"What do you mean, off?"

"Leaving, going to the Sport Hotel. I'm hungry."

"Oh, okay. Will you be coming to final practice tomorrow?"

"If you don't want me to come, just say so."

"No, no, it is just that you are so much faster than the regular drivers that you may not want to, or need to."

"Is that why you were all over the car checking it to see if I was wrecking it?"

The team manager looked embarrassed. "We could not believe you could go so quickly without over-stressing the car, plus you were out for one more lap than the amount of fuel we provided. We couldn't believe that the tyre temperatures were low, as well as the oil and water temperatures; which means that you were not stressing the car at all. And look at you."

"What's wrong with me?"

"No sweat. You are not sweating, I have never seen a driver go fast and not sweat."

"Maybe my pores are blocked."

"No, it means to me that you are not pushing the car or yourself, that there is a lot more speed left. How was the car? What do you need adjusted?"

"Nothing, really, I backed off the front bar two turns, and it seems okay, but I don't know what it will be like on full fuel load."

"Good. I am sorry we did not welcome you as we should. We have had Formula One drivers before, and it seldom works. Also, this is in the middle of the season with no warning. We only heard yesterday. Are you going to be driving Formula One for us next season?"

"I don't think so," said Will. "It is very unlikely."

"That is a disappointment. I will report back tonight and my recommendation is that they do their best to entice you. You would enjoy living in Italy much better than England. The lifestyle is so much better; you would be treated like a prince, and the women, beautiful, the best in the world."

"I am convinced," laughed Will.

•

Will was talking on the phone with Ken, who asked, "How did it go?"

"They're fizzing. They want me for their Formula One team."

"Ray will have a haemorrhage."

"How is he going to find out?"

"The team manager will be interviewed, and the specific question asked. It will be in tomorrow's press."

"Does he know I am here?"

"He will certainly know by tomorrow, and he will hear of a Ferrari offer as well."

"What offer?"

"The offer that will appear in tomorrow's news."

41

THE LONG PAIR of skin-tight jeans-clad legs swayed closer and closer. Will was sitting in the car after coming back in from final practice, so where the legs met was at about nose level. That the jeans were skin-tight was something of an understatement; there was no imagination required. Talk about camel toes. Camels had nothing on this one. If this was their method of persuading him to move to Italy, they were doing a hell of a job. He yanked at the oxygen connection to his helmet; he wanted to get the helmet off so that he could get a better look at the bait. He finally got it off, and threw it onto the seat beside him. He flipped the quick release handle on the harness, shrugged out of the shoulder straps and started to climb out. She was a knockout but not his type, too skinny, with tits too big, and not enough arse, plus she was blonde and a bit brassy. Well, guys, you got that wrong, but nice try. He had to laugh. A couple of years ago he would have nailed it. He must be getting old, picky, or Isobel had done something to him.

Practice was over and he had put the Ferrari firmly on the pole. He was nearly half a minute faster than the rest. The team was ecstatic. A drivers' meeting set up to discuss tactics turned out to be an attempt to find out Will's secret. He almost told them, but decided against it. Why the hell should he? The great Juan Manuel Fangio used the same method years and years before. It was no secret; let them figure it out for themselves.

•

Ray was unhappy. "What are you doing driving for Ferrari?" he yelled over the phone.

"For fun."

"What the hell do you mean, for fun?"

"Driving for you is no fun any more. I have to find some fun somewhere."

"This is in breach of your contract."

"So sue me."

"For Christ's sake, Will, what are you up to? Is this your idea of getting even?"

"Yes."

"Are you planning to drive for them next year?"

"Drive for who?"

"Their Formula One team, that's who."

"They haven't asked me."

"What if they do?"

"There are some nice-looking women in Italy."

"For God's sake, be serious for once in your life. Are you going to drive for them next year?"

"Ray, they have not asked me to."

"Yes but if they do?"

"*When* they ask me, I'll think about it."

"Just remember we have a contract."

"Till the end of this season."

"I have an option if you continue."

"You've already hired another driver for next season."

"Is that what all this is about?"

"Ray, I'm busy."

"Busy doing what?"

"You know."

"I don't know. That's why I am calling."

"I am being taught Italian."

"Who is teaching you Italian?"

"These two young ladies are teaching me. I thought basta meant faster, but it turns out it means stop, so they are straightening me out."

"Crash," went the phone. That will really piss him off, thought Will, as he rolled over and went back to sleep, thoroughly pleased with himself. He had opened up the game. He was no longer under pressure — Ray was.

●

Race day dawned overcast, cold and drizzly. Will wandered down for a late breakfast, which would be all he would eat till after the race. The dining room at the Sport Hotel was full, but they had a table waiting for him at the window overlooking the main straight, and across from the pits. At most races, he ran the gauntlet of fans seeking autographs, but here it was different. In this old hotel the fans were more discreet. Everybody was here for the race, but they weren't pushy. As he entered the dining room somebody started clapping, and the rest of the guests and staff took it up. There were a few other drivers about, and some of them nodded recognition.

Will smiled and bowed. He was no longer embarrassed by this sort of thing. You could run, but you couldn't hide, so he made the best of it by taking the recognition in good style. He had hoped Isobel could join him this weekend, but she had her career, and it wasn't always possible for her to take time off. Will sometimes wondered whether she was deliberately making herself unavailable. He was not by nature monogamous; one woman was not for him, but more by default than anything else, he just wasn't interested in anybody else. That she was beautiful was certain; that she was a challenge was beyond question. Maybe she had also figured him out better than he had figured himself out.

He had a huge breakfast as was his habit on race day. It was laid out smorgasbord-style in the grand German tradition, with hams, sausages, salamis, cheeses, fruit, and breads of every description. The table was set with a crisp, white, linen table cloth, and huge matching napkins. The silver was heavy and old. Will had no sooner helped himself than a journalist who had flown down to Spain with him early in the season came over, and asked to join him. Will could hardly have refused, but it would serve a good purpose to wind up Ray some more, even though the man's breath would ruin his breakfast.

He asked all the expected questions: Why was he driving sports cars? Was this a tryout for Ferrari? How did he like driving for them? What did Ray think of it?

Will told him it was a one-off, but that he really enjoyed driving for them. It was refreshing, like a breath of fresh air. He said it slowly and carefully, making sure that the journalist got every word right. He knew it would piss Ray off big time.

•

Will had never seen more cars lined up for a motor race. In the mirror, as far as he could see were race cars. He was on the pole, with another Ferrari lined up beside him. It had stopped raining, but it was still overcast and the track was still wet. It had been a big decision in tyre choice: he had gone for intermediates, his teammates for wets, and some optimists had even gone for dries. The mechanics were still hovering around the cars. Some had their engines running; some waited till the last minute. Most had battery carts behind waiting to start them, or restart them, in case they had to shut down. There were many people looking skywards, hoping to get a sign from above to tell them what the weather was going to do. Will wasn't certain that his tyre choice was right, but it was too late to change now anyhow; he was stuck with what he had.

It had started to drizzle again, but the Ring was fourteen miles long, so it could be raining in one spot and dry in another. Will needed to get through the South Curve first; he didn't want to be caught up in the spray from the cars in front, although it would be nowhere near as bad as in an open-wheel car race, where the spray from the tyres would not be restricted by fenders or bodywork.

Will watched the starter climb onto his stand; the horn had already sounded to clear the grid. He didn't know the starter; and the preliminary races had all been started by somebody else, so he'd had no chance to check him out. He had asked some of the other drivers, but most of them had never thought of studying the starter. Up went the flag in his left hand; his right hand held the rail around the starter's box. No sign there: he must counter the drop of the flag with a shoulder movement. Revs up, twelve cylinders howling, Will's eyes searching the starter's upper body for any sign of a balancing movement before he dropped the flag. Down went the flag with no early warning, just a limp drop of the flag. Will was caught by surprise. He had been watching the man rather than the flag, his tried and trusted method. He had lost the initiative; there were two cars in front, his teammate and one other. He was going to have to suck the spray after all.

Glancing in the mirror, all he could see was cars and spray. Cars were coming up on the inside and the outside. Gentle left into the South Curve, followed by a sharper 180-degree right. Spray not half as bad as in open-wheelers. Turning right into the South Curve. Squeeze on the power, back, jump sideways as it loses traction, slippery, off the power, on again, careful, really slippery, not good. Onto the straight up behind the pits, up through the gears, wheelspin, almost like on ice, should have gone for wets, intermediates not grooved deeply enough.

Will was trying to settle down, but it was slippery. He held the steering wheel as lightly as he could, letting it buck and twitch between his fingers as the back slipped and slid, trying to get grip. Gee but the steering was sweet, excellent feedback as he squeezed the throttle down, the rear breaking loose. He backed off to get some grip, on again, off again, into the North Curve, a 90-degree left-hander. Will had a flashback to the first time he had been to the Nürburgring years before, as a young kid driving a 1000cc GT car. A bug-eyed Austin Healey Sprite, a little alloy-bodied thing that handled like a dream. He used to two-wheel it everywhere. If the corner had enough grip it would pick up the inside wheels. He could lift them over the kerb so that the outside wheel was up against the kerb and the rest of the car hung over the footpath like a motorcycle sidecar.

That wasn't what jogged his memory; it was the girl who had been sitting topless by herself in the stand on the inside of the corner. Goggle-eyed, drivers locked on their brakes, leaving long black tyre marks and skidding straight off over the bank. They had to move her, as she would have killed somebody for sure. Topless women were a big thing then, not like nowadays when it was no big deal.

The track wasn't getting any drier, but the spray wasn't too bad. He could see reasonably well if he didn't get too close. He had settled down; another car had passed him, but there was no point in trying to fight them off with a thousand kilometres to go. In the past he would have fought to the death rather than lose one place, but he was getting older, smarter, less aggressive or what, he couldn't be sure.

They were in the forest now, huge, dark pine trees bordering the track. At least nowadays there was Armco, to keep you out of the trees. In the old days the trees were right up to the edge of the track. If you went off, you hit one, kaput, end of story. Nowadays, you bounced off the Armco back into the middle of the track, and the following car T-boned you. Kaput, same story.

Will was feeling comfortable now; he was lying fifth at the end of the first lap. There was nobody threatening him from behind, and he was far enough from the car in front that he could see. This was so unlike Formula One where it was almost always ten-tenths the whole time. Will had time to plot and plan; it was much more tactical. Of the four in front, at least one was going to drop out for one reason or another, so he was effectively fourth at the moment.

If the rain eased off a bit he would be on the right tyres and the ones in front would become easy prey, so in the meantime he would hang around fifth and see what happened. The wind was really blowing; he could feel it as he pulled over 230 mph up the straight. The huge hedges that ran alongside had gaps in them, and the wind shoved the car sideways as he passed the gaps in the hedge. He remembered complaining about this to some old German, who wasn't at all sympathetic, retorting that in the 1930s the old Mercedes and Auto Unions used to pull 200 mph up the straight in the pouring rain, on tyres with the tread cut by a hacksaw, with the drivers wearing cloth helmets.

The track was drying in parts, but seemed to be wetter in others. This was not making life any easier. He would catch up in the dry sections, and then fall back in the wet, and in the wettest parts the cars behind would close up. He thought about this for a bit, and then decided that maybe this wasn't a bad situation after all. He would overtake in the dry, and hold up the cars behind in the wet because the spray would make overtaking difficult. So then he was third, and by the first pit stop he was in the lead.

He had won the 1000 kilos by a huge margin, virtually by himself; the co-driver was only allowed one short stint. He was tired at the end, but not exhausted. It was the longest race he had ever driven, but he was sure he could have done the whole distance by himself. The after-race party was something else, heaps of booze and good food. Pussy was everywhere; Will almost had to be batting them off. Isobel had screwed up his life, turned into some monogamous whatever. He couldn't believe it himself, here he was in a world of eager women, just winning the big race and fighting them off. He must be sick or something. Formula One was too serious; this is how it must have been in the old days. Nowadays it was jump in the jet, and home to Mummy. There were few parties, and everybody took off immediately after the race.

Will had a great time, and could have got himself laid half a dozen times, but somehow he couldn't bring himself to do it. Stuffed.

The team thought he was the greatest thing since sliced bread; some were convinced that he would be driving their Formula One cars the following season.

42

WILL WAS HIT by a blast of hot air as they walked off the aircraft and down the steps. It was so hot it almost took his breath away. It had just finished raining, and there was steam rising from the puddles. There was a band playing, and the coconut trees in the background swayed in the trade winds. The white airport building's waving gallery was like a big veranda running around the second storey, with people hanging over the rail waving.

Will thanked God there was no visible reception committee. He and Isobel walked across the tarmac; inside, the expected relief of air conditioning was missing. It wasn't the same as outside, though. The heat was less direct but more muggy. Will looked at the customs line balefully. This looked like at least an hour to him. Then: "Señor, Señorita, por favor, follow me."

"Thank God," said Will. They followed their saviour, who took their passports to an official who immediately stamped them without even checking. "Welcome," said their benefactor. "El Jefe said to bring you to the casa grande."

They pulled out of the airport, onto a four-lane road into heavy traffic, full of minivans. Horns were blowing; the vans ducking and diving from lane to lane, swerving to avoid the worst of the potholes and each other. The median strip planted in hibiscus was in full bloom; the dark mountains in the background formed a dramatic dark green backdrop to the dusty dry plain below. When Will wound the windows down, the car was filled with the stench of the urban tropics: diesel fumes, BO, and rotting vegetation. Their driver tried to make progress through the traffic, hand on horn, in and out, changing from lane to lane, accelerate, brake, accelerate again. This boy knew what he was doing; he wasn't just showing off, he was getting on with the job hustling through the traffic. Among the minibuses, weaving about, were motorcyclists on small 125cc bikes, all with a death wish, darting in and out of the traffic. It was a mobile seething mass, survival of the fittest being the order of the day. The traffic started to ease, and as the speed increased, they started to overtake. There was no patience, no waiting for somebody to move over. It was rush up behind, on the horn, kick it down, and away. Nobody seemed to take offence; there was no aggression despite all the horn blowing; nobody tried to block anybody overtaking. In a way, it was smooth.

They arrived at the big house, swinging in under the porte-cochère. Servants rushed out, opening the doors and taking their bags inside. Pablo Hernandez was there to greet them. "Welcome to you both. I am so glad that you could come. I know how difficult it must have been to get away. My apologies for not picking you up personally, but I hope your stay will be worth it."

"Thank you, Pablo; it is our pleasure," replied Will.

"It is so good that you could bring Isobel with you."

"We see so little of each other that we must grab every opportunity," said Isobel.

"Of course, with her understanding of our culture you have an inbuilt adviser."

"Yes," said Will, "without Isobel and her father I would be lost. I would be just another dumb gringo."

"Hardly that, Will, we treat you as one of our own. You have become something of a local hero, and some people, including myself, have been watching your races on TV. Before you, there was no coverage, but we have even sent TV crews to cover some of the races. Everybody likes it when you drive Ferrari, very Latino, not so Anglo. Next year you go to Ferrari full-time?"

"No," said Will. "Not much chance of that."

"The people used to have only football, but now they watch you as well."

After coffee they got down to the nitty-gritty. "The problem on the island has become an embarrassment to the government, and they want to fix the problem," said Pablo.

"The problem, as you put it, was created by one individual. It shouldn't be hard to fix."

"Yes, but by closing down as you did, it gave him power. He closed you down, therefore he was powerful. You thought that by shutting down, *you* were demonstrating power. You were right, but you also gave him power which he never had before, and that is the problem. The leftists see him as defeating the capitalist. If you had ignored him he would have gone away, but you gave him authority. You gave him respect, which he never had before."

Will felt his blood beginning to boil. He was in this man's house but he wasn't going to put up with this crap — then he felt a hand on his arm. "We really should not be discussing all this now," said Isobel. "There is plenty of time tomorrow, and Carla has a special dinner for us."

"Oh yes," said Pablo. "She would never forgive us if we did not enjoy the dinner."

Things lightened up over dinner and Will was willing to concede that he could have been wrong. But Jesus, what was he supposed to do, just lie down and put up with all the bullshit? He was glad Isobel was with him — he would have blown it by now, for sure. Isobel tried to get him to understand what had come out of the discussions after dinner. "Will, they need a face-saving gesture, something that will defuse the situation. What they will agree to is that the mining licence will be issued, but that it does not cover minerals."

"I suppose that could be all right but I still don't like it. Why should we give in to some bloody grafter? All he wants is a pay-off."

"I agree, we should not give in that easily. We must *appear* to give in, but strengthen our position at the same time. What I think is this: we should agree to their proposition, but we pay royalties on specific items such as gold, silver or oil, and nothing else. We agree those royalties now as a percentage of the going price at the time of discovery, less development costs."

"Which could be anything," said Will.

"Exactly. They have saved face and your position is strengthened. But at the same time he has struck a bad bargain. If he had left it alone and minerals were discovered, he would have had an opportunity to negotiate then. But now he has blown it, and his enemies will crucify him."

"So what happens next?"

"If it all goes to plan, you start up again."

"It's too late. I don't have the time. I have Ray screwing me around, a championship to try to win, plus I have lost interest."

"Will, it's me you are talking to, not Ray or the government. This is your dream. You can start up again, but more slowly. The boys can run it while you concentrate on the championship. I will look after the people here and my father will help. He has already helped, more than you know."

"I suspected that he'd been working behind the scenes. Yes, this could be a better deal than the original. But I'm still pissed off. I don't like being jerked around by them, by Ray, by anybody. What happens next?"

"If they agree, and I believe they will, then you are in a better position than before, and it's less likely that anybody will try to, how do you say?"

"Pull the same stunt again?"

"Si, that's it."

43

WILL WOKE WITH a start. He had dreamt that he was back in hospital, the result of the accident that had nearly cost him his life the year before last. If it hadn't been for Freddy Jamison he would have been burnt alive; trapped in the wreck that had burst into flames seconds after Freddy had dragged him out of it. He later asked Freddy why he had stopped when nobody else had. Freddy said he didn't know. He just did.

He didn't know Freddy very well. He was one of those who only lasted one season. An English aristocrat playboy, with the good looks, money, and enough success in Formula Three to buy himself a ride. None of the others had stopped, only Freddy, which probably explained why Freddy only lasted one season. He wasn't selfish enough. He didn't have the killer instinct. Some of the others would have stopped had there been a fire, but by then it would have been all too late for Will.

He was unconscious with a shattered lower right leg in an upside-down racing car about to catch fire. How Freddy managed to roll it over by himself was a mystery. The crash of the car as it fell back on its wheels must have jerked Will awake, to be met with the excruciating pain.

The seating position in the car had been way forward, with the steering rack under his knees, and his legs in front of the front wheels. It was so narrow; he could read Goodyear on the outside of the front tyres. It was aerodynamic, very fast in a straight line, very quick in fast corners, with tremendous brakes, great in the wet, and hopeless in the tight stuff. It was too narrow and too soft. No matter what they did they couldn't correct it. It would roll and spin the wheels with no traction as he tried to accelerate out of a tight corner, which meant that on most race tracks he lost out on the corner leading onto the straight, sitting there spinning his wheels, while everybody else took off, leaving him behind. They did not finish a single race with it. It would roll so much that it would break the half-shafts.

Before the accident, Will had been pushing hard. If he was going to do any good with this thing, this was the place to do it. He was in the German Grand Prix at the Nürburgring. Fourteen miles per lap, with a hundred and eighty corners. He was running third, the best he had done all year. The car felt good, really good. But then it always had. The trouble was that it was hopeless coming off a tight corner. The difference with the Ring was that there were not that many tight corners. If he was going to put it on the podium, this was the place to do it.

The half-shaft broke in the middle of the carousel, the famous very steeply banked concrete one hundred-and-eighty-degree corner, if you could call it that, which was only wide enough for a car to fit in it. It was like driving the wall of death, or like an aircraft in a high G turn. To enter the carousel fast was like banking a fighter into a dive. Turn the wheel hard left and drop into the slot. When you were in, you couldn't see out, and had to keep going till you lined up the tree near the end, so that you would pop out, and be ready for the right-hander following. When the half-shaft broke partway through, it spat him out over the top, and into the Armco, tearing off the nose, leaving his feet dangling out the front, flipping upside down.

After Freddy had dragged him out, and lain him on the ground, Will remained conscious and could hear what was going on, but as most of it was in German, understanding very little. Spectators and Freddy were trying to make him comfortable while they waited for help. Finally doctors arrived with a helicopter. As they were putting him on a stretcher he could hear a doctor talking to Freddy in English, telling him that Will would be very lucky if he didn't lose his foot.

Will was taken to Guys Hospital in London, where Ray had hired the best orthopaedic surgeons available. After a six-hour operation, they put him in a soft cast to prevent infection, and in traction to deter movement. Six weeks later they removed the soft cast, replacing it with a hard one. He was in hospital three months, with post-surgery and rehabilitation. The bone damage had been bad, but it had not shattered, nor had it broken the skin, resulting in infection.

They hadn't amputated his foot, probably because he wouldn't let them. He told the doctors in no uncertain terms that they might as well kill him on the spot if that was what they were planning to do. So they persevered with it and he started to recover. His heel was the worst part, but it eventually started to mend. The boredom set in after a month in rehab. The exercises were excruciating, but he knew that he had to do them if he was to prevent muscle atrophy. Ray visited regularly with stories of the new car they were building to replace the extremely narrow forward-seating one. Ray would arrive with drawings, and they would discuss features that were worth keeping and those to get rid of, including the extreme forward-seating. Angela was there most days, but Will found it uncomfortable after a while, and tried to convince her it wasn't necessary, but she dutifully spent hours with him, although he was convinced she would much rather have been off with her society friends. Freddy came with his gorgeous sister several times. But Angela put the frighteners on her. Freddy would have liked to have driven Ray's car for the rest of the season, but Will talked him out of it. The car was dangerous. It was better to leave it alone. There had been lots of people trying to see him in the beginning. Journalists, other drivers, mechanics, his manager, but as time went by the visits became fewer and fewer.

In the beginning he felt so bad that he didn't care about anything. As the foot healed he became anxious. Was this the end? Would he be able to drive again? Would he have full ankle flexibility? If not, what would he do with himself? Would he have a limp for the rest of his life? He knew of people with the Lola limp, where the front suspension wishbone had broken the leg above the ankle, after knocking a wheel off. But this was much worse. He had known people who had had similar injuries. Even if they staged a comeback they were never as effective again,

Just the simplest bodily function was a chore. However, as he improved, his other bodily needs started to raise their ugly head. As his right leg was up in traction the nurses had to attend to his personal hygiene. This meant that they had to work around his private parts, washing them. One nurse took particularly good care of them, washing them diligently. Another one apparently took offence at them, hitting Will's organ with a pencil when it started to stir, instantly killing it.

One night the nurse with the pencil showed up. "Now," she said, "we won't be having any more of that silly business like last time will we?"

"Of course not, Sister," said Will. "I am way too scared for that."

Will watched her going about her business, preparing him for his ablutions. She was a bit older than the rest and very businesslike in her manner. Unlike most of the nurses she did not seem to be impressed that she was looking after the jewels of a famous racing driver. She wore no make-up, had a severe hair-cut, and loose uniform as though she was trying to hide her looks.

She went about her business industriously, tight lipped, without saying a word. Will really did try. He really did, thinking about anything that would make his organ behave itself, trying hard not to let it happen again. The more he tried, the more he realised he was losing the battle. He waited for the pencil blow, but it never came. She just kept on scrubbing the same area, over and over again. "What the hell was she doing?" thought Will.

Suddenly she stopped scrubbing, said, "Oh dear God, forgive me," hauled up her uniform, dragging off her underwear, swung her leg over, and sat on his erect organ; and immediately started thrashing about, digging her nails into his shoulders, with her head rolled back and her mouth wide open, moaning and groaning. Will had a couple of months' juice stored up and couldn't hold on, coming with a rush. She immediately got off, grabbed her panties, and without a word rushed out of the room.

"Jesus," thought Will, "what was that all about? She was certainly no dyke, as he had first suspected, but what was her problem?" He didn't see her for another couple of days, and she didn't say a word to him, trying not to make eye contact. Eventually Will said, "Don't worry; I am not going to tell anybody."

"Yes you are. You are going to boast about it."

"Boast about what? Coming in two seconds; what's there to boast about?"

"I am so sorry," she said, "I don't know what overcame me. I just don't know. Anyway it won't happen again. I won't be attending to your hygiene any more. I have asked to be taken off that duty."

"Why," said Will, "was it that bad?"

"No, but I requested a transfer. I told the head nurse that I couldn't deal with you any more."

"I feel bad about that," said Will

"Why? It wasn't your fault. I did it, I caused it."

"No, I feel bad because I didn't do a proper job."

"Never mind," she said, "I won't sully your reputation. In any case the young nurses are all lining up to take care of your every need. Goodbye Will, I wish it had been different." Will was all confused, did she have crush on him or something? He would never understand women. They were an absolute mystery to him. Half the time he had no idea where they were coming from.

The other nurses must have found out about it, because

after that, it became a big free-for-all until the matron found out. One young nurse was working her show on him when the matron walked in. She nearly broke his leg bailing off. Funny, the matron didn't say much, except that some men were put on earth to disrupt women's lives.

Will had a feeling she was talking about the nurse with the pencil.

44

He arrived back in England to all kinds of press speculation. "Are you going to drive for Ferrari next season?"

"No."

"Then why did you drive for them at the Nürburgring?"

"I was bored."

"What did Ray have to say about it?"

"Ask Ray."

Ray was not happy. Will arrived at the workshop to find a very uptight team owner. "What's it going to be, Will, are you going to honour your contract?"

"Why would I not honour my contract, Ray?"

"What about all this press speculation about you going to Ferrari?"

"The press are always speculating — that's their business."

"Are you going to Ferrari or not?"

"I have no contract with Ferrari."

"That's not the question. Are you going to Ferrari or not?"

"I have no contract, letter of intent, or any correspondence with Ferrari."

"Then why did you drive for them at the Nürburgring?"

"To piss you off."

"Jesus Christ, why can't I get a straight answer out of you? Is that it, just to piss me off? Why?"

"Because you pissed me off."

"Is that it — is that what all this is about, just your weird way of getting even?

"You got it, Ray."

•

The media were starting to get to him. He used to be able to avoid them. It had never been this bad. They were speculating about next season and Ferrari. The women's magazines were asking questions about Isobel; the baby business had come up again. Strange people were chasing him: PR agents, advertising people, people he'd never had to deal with in the past. One offered to make him rich. "I'm rich already. How much richer do you want me to be?"

Now that the business with the island was settled, he had to force himself to concentrate on winning the championship. Not just on a race-by-race basis, but tactically. There were three potential winners, all with similar points and five races to go. Aside from the satisfaction of the championship itself, it was worth millions to him, money that he was going to need if he was going to make his dream work. But he had to concentrate on acquiring as many points as were available, as opposed to winning each race. He had to play the odds. A win was nine points, second was six, third was four, fourth was three, fifth was two, and sixth was one. One was better than zero; he had to change his head. He could have won more than one championship in the past if he had played the odds; lesser men had done it, going on to fame and fortune. The odds men would also have left Ray, and gone on to one of the bigger teams a long time before. But he had persevered because Ray was his friend. Besides, he thought, chuckling to himself, who else would have put up with me?

This was his last chance. He needed to clear the decks, be ruthless. No women, well, he had virtually done that already. No boat. No island. Just concentrate on earning enough points from each race to keep him in the lead till the end of the season. The problem was the other driver. He had to be ruthless: if Ray ran two cars his chances were reduced, no question. So what were his options? Go to another team or get rid of the driver. Ray was not going to get rid of his new driver, because he wanted him for next season, so what about another team? Ferrari would probably run a third car for him if they thought they could have him for next season, as might a couple of others. But what chance would that give him? Probably less than he had with the present set-up. If he agreed to another season, Ray would probably park the new guy, but he had it in his head that he wanted to run two cars next season anyway. How to get Ray to run one car and get rid of the new driver? The answer, it seemed to Will, was that Ray must believe that he was going to lose him now. Not next season, but this season. So he rang Ken.

"I want to set up a test drive with Ferrari."

"You've already won one race for them. You don't need a test drive."

"I mean Formula One."

"What about Ray?"

"What about Ray?"

"You can't just wander off in the middle of the season and start testing for somebody else."

"It's the last quarter of the season."

"Even worse."

The whole situation was fraught with risk. Here he was trying to play conservative, yet there was no base from which to play conservative, so the whole thing could backfire on him. With two drivers in the team Will believed the chances of success had been reduced. Going to another team who already had drivers vying for the World Championship would be worse; in addition he now had new cars and new people to deal with. New engineers, new mechanics, new personalities, new egos, new methods. The other wild card was the media, who had been harassing him non-stop, and his only real experience in dealing with them over the last few years had been avoiding them. But how to use them? He was not sure. There were people who specialised in that sort of thing, and he was certain the odds men had used them.

He went out to the team base the day before the race. Jean-Claude was there. Will didn't feel the odd man out, but he definitely wasn't kingpin any more. Even the girls in the office didn't react the same to him; it was no longer Bond and Moneypenny. There was a young lion in the pack and the old lion's days were numbered. Ray's attitude was very professional, but the old camaraderie had gone. What would the odds man do? Resort to the contract? Too late; when he could have insisted on no second driver he hadn't, he had only realities left.

Ray needed him, he needed to win the championship, and if

he won, Ray could have his two-car team next year. He wanted to keep Jean-Claude because he was good, and came with a heap of sponsorship money. Was there any point in discussion? Will didn't think so. Maybe Ray was right. Maybe he *could* run a two-car team. He'd hired more people; he had enough cars. Was this just emotion on his part or would it jeopardise his chances of winning? Of course it would. The simple fact of losing the personal contact with Ray would be enough.

●

The phone rang. "Will here."

"I've set it up."

"Set what up?"

"The test."

"With Ferrari?"

"Yes. This Thursday."

"Jesus, now you've thrown the cat among the pigeons."

"Hey, wait a minute, Will. You asked me to set it up."

"Yeah I know, it's just that—."

"Just what?"

"It's so risky. We could blow the whole thing."

"It was your idea, not mine. And there'll be a lot of Italian media there. You know what they're like."

45

WILL RECOGNISED A couple of the people from the Ferrari sports-car team at the Nürburgring. He already knew some of the Formula One personnel, and of course he knew the drivers, one of whom was three points ahead of him. There were the same questioning looks as at the Nürburgring: what are *you* doing here?

This was not going to be as easy as at the Nürburgring. It would be a lot tougher. The media were out in force, not just Italian, but also French and British. They expected fireworks, which the old Will would have given them, but the new Will was here to play the odds, to turn up the wick on Ray, but not to take risks. How could he not take risks? It was a risk being here in the first place.

They had done a great job with the seating position and the seat fitting. The car felt comfortable. It was beautifully built: the flat 12 engine sounded even better than the sports car. Sharper, sweeter, harsher, louder. Just stupendous, that unique Ferrari sound was so different from any other. Will eased the car out of the pits, weaving it back and forth to get a feel for it. Jesus, the steering was heavy, and so was the gearbox. It felt solid and stable as Will gradually increased speed.

Up through the gears, the wonderful howling sound of the flat 12, the gearbox and the heavy, solid brakes made it feel like a car from another era. It was fast, had heaps of power, and was very stable in the quick sections. In the tight stuff, it was a handful. It wouldn't turn in. It didn't have that crisp feel of Ray's cars. It was slow it up; feed in the steering slowly, open the throttle carefully, or the front would push, and the car would run wide.

Will did ten laps and came in. His lap times were progressively faster, but he was nowhere near as fast as the other drivers. He didn't expect to be at this stage; had he been, it would only have meant that he was pushing all out without trying to learn anything, making it a pointless exercise. As he rolled up the pit lane with the ignition off, he wondered what the approach would be: how would they handle the feedback.

As he rolled to a stop the chief engineer plugged in the phone jack and in almost accentless English asked him how the car felt. "Too much understeer in the low speed corners," Will said. "Very stable in the quick stuff, engine magnificent."

"We have a problem with the understeer. We have never been able to correct it without upsetting the handling in the high-speed area. Your lap times have been consistently dropping, which is impressive. If you would persevere with the current set-up for the next few laps, we may make a change."

Will went out again. This car was different from what he was accustomed to, but he would try to use its advantages. It had plenty of horsepower throughout the range. So it understeered, and he hated understeer; in fact, he was terrified of it. Hitting a solid object head on was what killed people. Spinning or turning over wasn't so much of a problem; the sudden stop was. He concentrated on carefully turning it into the tight corners, and getting the power down as soon as possible, using that wonderful engine to propel him to the next corner, and the rock-solid understeer stability in the fast stuff to bring his times down to fractions of a second off the faster of the two works drivers, and quicker than the other.

He was not entirely certain what the response was in the pits. There were smiles, some enthusiasm, but a lot of caution. After all, what was he doing here? Presumably, he was being tested for next season, or was it this season? The engineer was pleased with the feedback, but Will could see the caution. Would he be using what he learned from them, or was it for real? The sports-car people were enthusiastic. Will couldn't understand what they were saying, but he could see that he was their man. "Will, you have given us solid feedback on the handling of our car, you are as fast as our fastest driver, you now know where the strengths and weaknesses lie, yet you have made no recommendation."

"It's not that I can't make a suggestion, but if it does work and there is no deal between us, then I have put myself at a disadvantage."

"Yes, but if it worked and you went faster, then we would almost certainly run a third car for you. But my belief is that you drove for us at the Nürburgring, and you set up this test for other reasons, which you may have achieved without going any faster. The press is everywhere, tifosi are in the stands, our drivers are nervous, and our engineers are impressed. I suspect you may have the answer to our handling problems, but won't say."

Will laughed. "I wish life were as simple as that. I have an idea, which has a small chance of working, but could just as easily upset the high-speed stability that you don't want to lose."

•

"What about next season?"

Will had never seen Ray so angry. He was absolutely spitting tacks. "What's the game? What are you playing at?"

"It's very simple, Ray. I am, for the first time, seeking my best interests."

"What do you mean, seeking your best interests?"

'Giving myself the best chance of winning the World Championship."

"And you think that driving a third car for Ferrari will do that?"

"Who said anything about driving a third car for Ferrari?"

"Do you mean to tell me that they'll lay off one of their drivers for you, at this late stage in the season, with no guarantee for next season?"

"You are making all kinds of assumptions."

"Then what's the position?"

"I intend to do my level best to win this championship, come what may."

"You are already in line to win it, with a team that I would like to remind you, you are contracted to."

"Circumstances have changed within that team, which leaves me with grave doubts as to the ability of that team to furnish me with championship-winning equipment. You are trying to run a two-car team this late in the season, which will split the effort; that impinges on me."

"And you think that you can do better by jumping ship."

"I have already proven that I can do better."

"Proven? How do you mean proven?"

"Simple. I was as quick as their fastest driver, who is a contender for the championship, in a total of twenty laps of testing, and I know how to make the car go quicker. You tell me why I should be jerked around, when I can get into a championship-winning car without these hassles, and earn more while I am doing it."

"If you think you're better off that way, go right ahead and do it, but expect to hear from my lawyers." With that he stormed out of the office.

Will knew he was taking a big risk, but if he was going to win in Ray's car, he needed his undivided attention. He wasn't sure that Ferrari or anyone else would take him on, but Ray didn't know that. Still, the Italian media were convinced. Will had never had so much press attention. Normally he hated it, but now it suited his purpose and he used it to best advantage.

46

THE PRESS WERE having a field day. Will was approached on almost a daily basis for speaking engagements and other opportunities, offering unbelievable sums of money. Several of the other teams had made approaches, which he appeared to consider. Ferrari wanted to know about next season, talking about a three-year contract. No money was mentioned, but there could be a third car ready for him for the next race.

He had not heard from Ray or his lawyers, and there were ten days to the next race. Normally they would have been testing by now. Will was sweating, but he knew that Ray was sweating even more. The trouble was that Ray knew him too well; at the same time he also knew Ray. In two days, if he hadn't heard, he would commit to drive that Ferrari for at least one race, if they would have him.

The boys called every few days from the island. Some of the equipment had arrived back; most of the ex-employees had shown up. They had started to repair roads that had been washed out, and the blasting crews were opening up the quarry again. They assured him that *Imperialist* was fine. They had moved some Mayan women in as cooks, and were renting out the rest of the bunks by the hour. "Great," said Will. "I always suspected you guys were capitalists at heart."

Rather than worry, he headed to the island. The boys weren't doing too badly; they hadn't turned the boat into a whorehouse after all. The road as far as the waterfall had been reopened and had been surfaced with gravel from the quarry. It was good to be back: the weather was absolutely beautiful as usual. The sea was deep blue; inside the reef were all the greens; the surface gently rippled; the fluffy cumulus clouds drifted by. Coconut trees waved in the breeze. Why go back? The hell with it, if everything went right he had enough money. Maybe lower his sights a bit. What better life could anybody want?

He was jerked out of his reverie by a Radphone call from Ray. "Yes, Ray, fine. How are you?"

"Where are you?"

"At the island."

"I thought that was all over."

"No, it's all fixed now."

"Full speed ahead, then?"

"No, a bit more cautiously, but we are progressing."

"When are you coming back?"

"In a couple of days."

"We need to talk."

"I thought I was going to hear from your lawyers."

"Let's not get into that now. We need to talk, but the whole world is listening. We need to talk face to face, or at least over a proper phone."

"I'll be leaving tomorrow, so I could see you the next day."

•

Will could feel the tension when he walked into the office. The girls' smiles were over-bright; the banter forced, not funny. He was carrying a two-suiter over his shoulder.

"Just got in?" asked Ray.

"No, I got in last night."

"Where are you off to, then?"

"Modena."

Will could see the anger in Ray's face and in a way he felt sorry for him, but it was too late. You started it, he thought.

"I thought you had come to settle this."

"I have, but if it's not settled today, I'm going to Modena."

"What if they don't want you?"

"They want me all right."

"Okay, what do you want?"

"Nothing."

"Nothing! Then what is this all about?"

"It's all about winning the championship, that's all. Nothing more."

"If that's what this is all about, why don't we get on with it?"

"Under the present scenario, we are not likely to do that."

"What do you mean?"

"I mean that running a two-car team is too much. The effort is going to be fragmented, which means that my chances will be reduced. Therefore, my best option is to go to Ferrari, who has the capacity."

"You mean to tell me they are prepared to lay off their number-two driver in favour of you this late in the season."

"No, I didn't say that. I have no idea what they are going to do with him."

"You mean they are going to put him back to test driving sports cars or something?"

"I have no idea. It was never discussed."

"Well, that's what the Italian press are saying."

"I can't read Italian."

"What do you want, Will?"

"I want the chance to win the championship. I should have won it years ago. This is my last chance, and I'm not going to let it pass, for any reason, or for anyone. So I am going to take the best opportunity, and right now the best opportunity to win it is with Ferrari. Unless you can show me a better way, I have a plane to catch."

"Okay, okay," sighed Ray. "You win. We will run a one-car team, and Jean-Claude can do the testing, but next year it will be a two-car team."

"I don't care about next year. All I care about is this year." Will got up. "When do you need me?"

"Wednesday, but where are you going in such a rush?"

"Modena."

Will wished he had eyes in the back of his head to see Ray's expression as he walked out the door. He wasn't heading for Modena, but Madrid, where he had been invited by the Santiagos to watch some top bullfighters in action.

47

EVEN IN MADRID he wasn't able to avoid the media, instantly being recognised. Would he finish the season with Ferrari? Would he drive for them next season? If not, why did he do the 1000 kilometres at the Nürburgring? Why was he testing the Formula One car? What about Isobel — were they getting married? What about the poor pregnant lady he had ditched? Did he think that bullfighting was like motor racing? It went on and on. Will answered the questions as best he could, without being his usual flippant self. This was the new, professional Will. At least he was trying to be.

There had been more media interest over which team he was going to finish the season with than where he was in the race for the championship. Ken was running around trying to capitalise on this, signing more sponsors and trying to get Will to do personal appearances, a thing he had resisted in the past; now, however, it was becoming irresistible. The numbers they were talking about were too much to just leave sitting on the table.

•

Friday dawned frosty and cool. The crystal-clear sky overlooked a lush green valley with a black strip of asphalt following the contours of the sides of the valley. Grassy green meadows covered the valley floor, and dark brooding forests looked down from above. The peaceful scene would soon be shattered by the screams of multi-cylindered racing cars warming up. Spectators lined the slopes around the track, trying to be first to the prime viewing areas. Some just waking up from their tents scattered about in the pine forest. It certainly was one of the great tracks, but it wasn't going to last much longer. Too dangerous, they said, too costly to fix, too fast. People had been killed there. One the year before. To abandon it now seemed such a waste as a lot of work had been done to increase safety, Others had tried to get Will involved in safety committees, but he wasn't a committee person, shying away from all the personalities involved. He had felt bad about it because they were hoping to save lives, including his, and he was making no effort to help, often complaining about their efforts, particularly some of the chicanes they had produced, which he thought was increasing danger rather than reducing it.

They had done some good work, but some of it left a lot to be desired. He felt that some of the effort trying to reduce speed was counterproductive and caused more accidents than if they'd been left as they were. This was one track, from his experience testing the Ferrari, that there was no point in trying to win. Ferrari would be just too fast, with their high-speed stability and horsepower. He would have to play the odds and just try to get some points towards the championship.

Will was first out on the track for the first practice session.

He always tried to be first out. It might be psychological, but first was first, and he might as well start early. The car felt good after the Ferrari, light and nimble, super-crisp turn-in, zippy, a lightweight flier. He was back into the pits after three laps. There was no point staying out longer, the track was too dirty. There wasn't enough rubber down yet. He would wait till later in the session, and put in a couple of quick laps. The minute he got out of the car the media were onto him. It wasn't every day that a driver contending for the championship drove two Grand Prix cars, virtually back to back.

"How did it compare with the Ferrari?"

"It's different."

"Ferrari has more power? Does that mean the Ferrari is faster?"

"Not necessarily."

"Does your car handle better?"

"In some places, but not in others."

"What is the real difference between the two?"

"I can't answer that."

"Come on, you can tell us, we won't tell anybody." Laughter.

"Where is the Ferrari faster besides the straight?"

"On the fast corners."

"Let me see if I have got this right. The Ferrari is faster in a straight line, faster in the fast corners; you didn't go any faster than their quickest driver. Therefore, it must be very slow in the slow corners, or have poor brakes. Or it would be winning all the races, am I right?"

Will tried to count to ten before he answered but only got to five. "I only drove the Ferrari once, on one track. Racing cars often act differently from day to day, and from track to track. My impression is from one track; under one set of given circumstances, on a given day under specific weather and track conditions. It could be totally different here."

"Does this mean that you will be driving for Ferrari next year?"

"No offer has been made."

"If an offer was made?"

"Then I would have to consider it. They are a great team. I enjoyed the Nürburgring and I enjoyed the test day; also, I would rather live in Modena than London any day." Laughter. "I have to go, guys."

"What was that all about?" said Ray.

"Motorsport journos. They wanted to know which was better, yours or theirs."

"What did you tell them?"

"I told them yours was longer, but skinnier."

"Oh, for Christ's sake."

48

WILL WENT OUT ten minutes before the end of the session and set the fastest time. He caught it just right — it had started to get cool, and there was a reasonable amount of rubber down. The car felt really good, really pitchy; he was flicking it into the corners and it was just rocketing out of them. He was getting the same speed at the end of the straight as the Ferraris, because he was coming onto the straight a lot faster, and getting off quicker as well.

The media was on to him again. "Will, you told us that the Ferrari had more power, yet the speed traps at the end of the straight indicate that the terminal velocity is virtually identical. How do you explain that?"

"What's that big word again?" Laughter.

"Terminal velocity — it means speed." With a grin.

"I see. Well, I guess the Ferrari's velocity must have terminated at some point." More laughter. "It's as I said earlier, guys, every track is different, and every car and every team reacts differently to the changing circumstances. The next session tomorrow will be different, and the end result could be totally different as well. I gotta go, the boss is calling."

"Very diplomatic," said Ray. "I never knew you had it in you."

"You mean the bit about the boss?"

"No, the bit about changing circumstances. Well, how did it go?"

"The surface is still slippery; that new chicane is a pain in the arse, but it will be worse for the Ferrari than for us because we will be able to use the kerbs more easily than they will. I don't think we need to make any changes. I'd be inclined to wait until there is a bit more rubber down, and see what the additional loadings do."

"No adjustments at all? Not even ride height?"

"Ride height, maybe, it's not grounding anywhere, maybe — no better leave it. We should go out on full tanks sometime in the early session tomorrow. It will probably start grounding then."

At the end of the next session he was fifth fastest; there was more rubber down and everyone was seconds quicker, including Will. There wasn't anything specific; it just didn't seem to go that much quicker than the day before. Will suspected what the problem was, but he wasn't going to tell Ray or anybody else. When he left the track the day before he had gone back to the hotel and spent the rest of the day and into the night on the phone dealing with issues relating to the island, and he was due to do the same again tonight. His biggest problem was switching his head from race driver to businessman and back. He couldn't do it. He had to do one or the other, or he wouldn't be able to do either.

"Ray, I'm shifting hotels tonight."

"What's wrong with the one you've got? It's where you always stay."

"Too much distraction."

"See, you've wound up the bloody media, and now you can't turn them off."

"Something like that. If you don't mind, I'll use the helicopter and stay in the city."

"They'll still find you."

"Maybe."

Will wasn't concerned about the media; he wanted to get away from the business of the island till after the weekend. He needed to be unreachable. Switching his head from businessman to racing driver and back again wasn't going to happen naturally; he was going to have to consciously make the change back and forth as required, keeping the two separate, or he was not going to be any good at either. It was going to be difficult being inaccessible to one or the other for periods, but he had no choice. How he was going to explain that to business people was certainly going to be a problem. The issue was keeping his mind on one thing at a time, stopping it from wandering.

The result was that the afternoon session was much better. He had switched off all communication with the island, and anything to do with it. His lap times were just slightly slower than the two Ferraris. He had run with them for a while, and what he had learned from his test day was absolutely right. They were bog-slow in the tight stuff, very stable in the quick, and fast down the straight.

If he was driving the Ferrari he knew what he would do, but he now had a psychological advantage over these guys, particularly the number two. They thought that they were going to use their straight-line speed to hold him off. If he could break that confidence, their security blanket would disappear. He had one shot to do it, and it had to be some time in the final, qualifying session. He needed two consecutive slipstreams or tows up the straight by one or both of the Ferraris. He needed to blow past them on the straight, going directly into the pits. To do this, he needed to set the wings as flat as possible to reduce drag, which meant that he was going to be slow in the corners; however, the tow should cancel out the loss, dragging him up the straight. He must remember to get them to fit a higher top gear as well if he was going to capitalise on the increased speed. And if he was really lucky he might even end up on the pole.

Will didn't tell Ray what he was up to when he suggested they run the wings flat to see what would happen. It was something that occasionally worked. He left the pits when both Ferraris were out, cruising around waiting for the first tow. There were seven minutes to go before the end of the last qualifying session. He was already third on the grid and wasn't going to get any further up, unless he was prepared to risk all, as he would normally have done. This time he hoped to use his head, if not to get further up the grid, at least to shake their confidence. He wanted to blow by them on the straight just once.

They both overtook him just before the main straight. Will followed them to the corner onto the straight, and then made sure that he entered the straight as fast as possible, ending up under the second Ferrari's wing. As he tucked into their slipstream, he could hear the multi-engined sound you get from a piston-engine aircraft that hadn't been synchronised, a kind of a rur-rur-rur sound from the three engines running at different speeds, but in the same sound cone. Halfway up the straight he was well into the tow. He had to ease off the throttle or overtake, and was now at half-throttle. He waited another few moments, put his foot down and popped out of the slipstream of one, picked up the draught from the other, and slingshotted past him. He glanced at the rev counter, and was not surprised to see that the needle was well into the red.

"Will, you are on the pole. I thought you told us that the Ferrari was more powerful, but you passed them both on the main straight like they were standing still," said one of the journalists.

"Nothing stands still at Grand Prix level. We've been working on the engines for some time, and certain improvements have been made. You can never be certain what gains have resulted until they have been tested."

"It would seem as if enormous gains have been made."

"It would appear so, but tomorrow will tell."

"Would it be fair to say that your race at the Nürburgring and the Formula One test session was an intelligence-gathering exercise?"

"If you mean intelligence-gathering as in spying, no, but if you mean did I learn anything, of course I did. They are a wonderful team with great people and a long tradition. I would love to drive for them at some point if they wanted me, and the circumstances were right."

"Yes, but did you learn anything specific?"

"Of course I did — they had more horsepower."

"Which appears now to be no longer the case?"

"You said it, not me."

•

Sunday morning Will sat over his usual pre-race breakfast. German-style, with coarse multigrain bread, sausage, and cheeses. He had spoken to Isobel the night before to tell her where he was, and why he had moved. She laughed at his qualifying stunt and the reaction in the media. "Yes," she said, "they have been reporting that with your new power increase, you were now fastest on what is a power circuit, and that boded well for a win today."

"Well, by the end of the day, they will know it was all a big scam."

"Where are you going when you leave?"

"Back to London was the original intent, but if you will put up with me I could stay till Wednesday. I have to be testing by the weekend."

"I think I could put up with you. By the way, it looks as if your ex is not with child any more."

"When did you find that out?"

"They had her on television last night, and she did not look at all fat."

"What a disappointment."

"I didn't know that you wished to be a father."

The helicopter picked him up from the hotel roof at eleven, half an hour later depositing him behind the pits. Will thought, one day I must learn to fly one of these things. The trouble with them was that it was a bit like rubbing your head, and patting your belly at the same time.

The minute he disembarked from the helicopter it was all on again, media everywhere; the Ferrari thing had certainly created an uproar. Their number two was quoted as saying they had lost their power advantage, and their low-speed handling wasn't good enough. They wanted to know what Will thought of that. Will reckoned that they shouldn't complain; just get on with the job. The Ferrari was excellent.

"Do you mean that bad workmen blame their tools?"

"Did I say that?"

●

Will buried himself in the motor home deep in thought. He was on the pole, but he shouldn't have been. "I'm on the pole, but there is no way that I can hold them off on the straight. If I start better than them, maybe I can put some distance between us on the first couple of laps, but there is no guarantee there either." The only decision that he could come to was that he must finish; he must not take too many risks. Don't dive for the hole that may not be there when you arrive.

49

HE GOT AWAY to a beautiful start, read the starter perfectly, had the revs right. The wheelspin was perfect and he dragged them into the first corner. By the end of the first lap, he was over a second in the lead. He knew it wouldn't last, but he wasn't going to give it to them. Concentrate on each corner as it comes up, forget the rest, just concentrate, conserve the tyres, conserve the engine, make every corner a winner, glance in the mirror, closer, they are onto you; don't push any harder than you have to.

The first Ferrari went by on the fifth lap and the second went by three laps later. Will couldn't hold them, they were too fast. Don't give up, he kept talking to himself, all kinds of things could happen. Then Menendez the number two hit a backmarker, and that was him parked. Will ended up second, with six points and the number one Ferrari driver Flint got nine. They were now equal, with three races to go.

"What happened to your power advantage, Will? They just

ran you down?"

"It's as I said, guys. One day it's one thing and the next day it's another."

"Did you have a problem? You seemed to be going away at the start, and then they started closing on you."

"Yes, I did have a problem. I didn't have the speed we had yesterday."

"Will it be fixed by next race?"

"We will be looking at it, that's for sure."

●

"What's that crap you were telling the media about the engine?" demanded Ray. "There's nothing wrong with it."

"I know that, you know that, but they don't. The Ferrari guys don't know either."

"So what's the point?"

"The point is we have a championship to win, and we need every advantage we can get. They half-believe we have a horsepower advantage. Don't let them think otherwise."

"What if they go and crank some more power out of that flat 12?"

"What if they blow it up trying? You've done it before. If they had more horsepower to get at this late stage, they'd have produced it by now."

"What the hell do you mean?"

"You know what I mean. Every time I hear about more horsepower, I worry that it's a fire-cracker not an engine."

"Yeah, yeah, I've heard all that shit before, bad workmen blame their tools. But you certainly rattled their number-two man."

"He was a cinch. It's the other bastard that's the problem."

They went through the usual after-race briefing. The car had worked well; their only problem was that they were at a power disadvantage. Sure, it wasn't as stable in the fast sections but they knew the reason for that. If they had more power they could run more wing, which would give them more downforce and thus more stability. They didn't make their own engines; these came from Cosworth, a brilliant engine-builder who made engines for most of the other teams. They had had many discussions with the engine people, but the little V8 was just about at the end of its life. All the horsepower they were going to get out of it had already been extracted. There was a new one on the drawing board, but it would be next season before it saw the light of day.

•

Will was at the beach house by dark. It was now his refuge. Tomorrow morning he would switch his head back to business mode, working on island issues until Wednesday. After that he would be back in motor-racing mode. They had dinner by candlelight out on the terrace overlooking the cliff. All the tension of the day had gone. The warm, heavily scented air and the steady breathing of the ocean soothed him; slowing him right down, calming him till he could feel himself going limp, sliding forward in his chair. He had to shake his head to wake himself up. He was falling asleep like some old fart over dinner. Isobel watched him, amused. She could see the tension leaking out of him. "Wake up old man, dinner is served."

She had been busy writing a major speech, but had also spent time working on the island with her father, making plans to shift a small part of their bull-breeding operation down there. The aerial photos had been turned into a twenty-foot-long model of the Isle of Pines. For the first time they had something they could really use for planning the future of the island. Now that they had one made, Will ordered six more. He realised that this was an excellent way of marketing the project; the punters could see exactly what they were letting themselves in for.

Over dinner they discussed the various possibilities: decisions had to be made, and a schedule drawn up with bar charts to keep them on track. He had to get the engineers going again. The development had to be phased: success would encourage other participants. There was no point in going at the whole thing like a bull at a gate. In a couple of months his income would be rapidly reduced, therefore the island had to be self-sustaining. Each phase had to pay for itself.

The access roads were an investment in phase one — without access there would be no development. He needed to sell the land for the cattle ranch and the rice farm. He needed the cash to finance the infrastructure, roads, water, lighting, telephone, and the equipment to build it. The guest house, which would later be a hunting lodge, had to be built right after the wharf was finished. He had the guest house firmly in his head. Two storeys, all solid, unfinished timber. No glass, no paint, louvered windows, marble bathrooms, terrazzo floors downstairs. Timber upstairs and big verandas on three sides. Ceiling fans, rough shingle roof, no ceiling. Will couldn't claim fame for it; it wasn't his idea. He had stayed at a hunting lodge exactly like that before, and had never forgotten it. It had been on a huge sugar estate in the Dominican Republic, a perk for the senior management of the parent company.

Will spent the morning on the phone with engineers, architects, agricultural experts, contractors, and potential investors. The only thing he didn't have to worry about was bureaucrats: there weren't any. He kept the people on the mainland up to date with repeated phone calls. They had been invited to invest; however, so far nobody had put up a cent, it was all mañana. The rice farm was going to be huge, twenty-five thousand acres. Looking at the plans, Will had not realised it would be like a small mid-western town, to house all the people and services required to operate and maintain the enterprise. They were setting up their own crop-dusting operation with three aircraft, which was a surprise to him, but what stunned him was that they had provided for thirteen drag lines to build and maintain the paddies. There weren't going to be thousands of labourers tending the rice. It was going to be highly automated: the rice would leave packaged, ready for the supermarket. The cattle ranch would be four times that size; there would be a feed lot and a small processing plant. Most of the product would be retail-ready, packed in branded packaging, aged and ready for the supermarket. Within those farms would be areas of woodland that would foster wildlife. There would be some problems with the jaguars and the wild pigs, but the investors in these operations saw this as an upside rather than a downside; they were drawn to the island much as Will had been, by lifestyle more than anything else. An opportunity to do business at the same time was a sweetener.

Will had to limit the time spent on the island. He had to separate his life and think of only one thing at a time. He couldn't be available to whoever wanted him. The media was now taking up more of his time; personal appearances were so lucrative that he couldn't turn them down. The next problem was that if he won the championship he would be made an outrageous offer to drive again next season, which would be difficult to refuse. In the meantime, he thought, "Here I am with this beautiful woman, in this beautiful house with this beautiful view waiting to see what culinary delights her cook will produce. What could be better than this? All I have to do is keep my head straight and it will all work out."

50

By Thursday morning he was at the factory. The media had been on the phone non-stop, as had Ken; Jean-Claude was hanging around like a bad smell, looking aggrieved. As Will passed him in the corridor he couldn't resist saying, "Don't fret sport, only three more to go, and you won't see me for dust."

Next, he rang Ken, who demanded, "Where have you been?"

"Spain."

"You must give me the number."

"Not on your nelly."

"Ferrari called."

"Yes?"

"Big bucks, Will, big bucks."

"What for?"

"Next season, three-year contract."

"Did they call you or did you call them?"

"They called me."

"I have a contract with Ray that says if I drive next season,

I drive for him."

"Contracts are meant to be broken. What do you think they have lawyers for?"

"It's only academic anyway. I am not driving next season. It's all over."

"Yes I know all that, but think of the bucks."

"Do I walk funny?"

"No. What do you mean?"

"I want to walk away from this thing; I don't want to be carried out on a stretcher. Do you know how many guys died in the last few years? I don't know anybody any more Ken — they are all dead. Do you see how many guys are walking around with gimpy legs? I don't need that. There are even a couple of guys in wheelchairs. That I certainly don't need. My eyes are going, I don't see every blade of grass any more, and my reflexes can't be what they once were. Sure, I could win on cunning for a couple more years if the desire was there, but it isn't. I'm tired; I've had enough. I should have started to play the odds years ago, instead of three-quarters through my last season. I wouldn't be worrying about having to find the money for this damned island."

"Okay, Will, we'll leave it for now. If you change your mind, call me."

Will felt exhausted after this speech, which he had never verbalised before, and he wasn't sure that he genuinely believed his feelings on retiring. He didn't often think about getting killed, but he should do. One or two Formula One driver drivers died every year, plus many others in Formula Three and sports cars. Was he immune? The bit about his eyes was probably right: sometimes the apexes of corners didn't seem quite as crystal clear as they used to appear. He had been to an eye specialist who couldn't find anything wrong, and had ventured to say that he saw very few people with eyesight as good as Will's. Nevertheless it was all relative — how good was good? He had no idea how good his eyes had been, as this was the first eye specialist he had consulted. Some of the other drivers had dieticians and masseurs and all sorts of specialist consultants. He had kept himself fit by running, swimming, rowing, and biking, but he had never spent any time in a gym. He could have done better, played the fool less, taken life a lot more seriously, but he'd had fun. If that was what life was all about, then he had done well. But now that the end of his chosen career was in sight, had that been enough? How much more could he have done?

•

Jean-Claude had done a good job testing; Will told him so. The car worked very well straight off, although it had been set up with too much understeer. Will soon dialled that out, and in ten laps he was quicker than Jean-Claude had been in two weeks of testing. "Don't be upset," said Will. "If I wasn't quicker I would be depressed. Better you depressed than me." That didn't console the younger man a whole heap; however, his attitude seemed to improve. Anyway, Will thought, when he drives the car again with less understeer it will go quicker, and he will be happy again.

•

Will left Friday night on the Jumbo for Miami. Lo and behold, the same stewardess again, the third time that he had flown with her. This time she was all smiles. "I watched your last race on television. It was very exciting, and you're going to be a father.

What are you hoping for, a boy or girl?"

"Neither."

"Neither?"

'I have no intention of being a father in the short term, thank you."

"But what about your lady?"

"Ex-lady."

"Well, what about the child?"

"What child?"

"The one that I read she was going to have."

"I don't know anything about it. If she was planning to have my child she should have given me notice."

"Women just don't have children on their own."

"She hasn't notified me that she is with child. In fact, I questioned her on the subject and she didn't answer. However, I will watch the media with interest if there is a birth, and then on our next meeting in space, I will be more up to date on the progress."

51

WILL DIDN'T KNOW what woke him, but he was wide awake. The proximity sensor was flashing, but the buzzer hadn't gone off. He listened for any strange sounds. Something had woken him, and it wasn't the light. Then he heard it again — whispers. He strained to hear where the sound was coming from, staring in the dark to see if he could see any movement. A creak, what was that? It wasn't the boat; it was a dead-still night.

He slowly lifted off his sheet, listened again and rolled slowly out of the bunk. The shotgun was in the cupboard at the foot of the bed. He felt around for the latch to release the door, hoping it wouldn't creak. He slowly eased it open and felt inside for the stainless-steel 12-gauge five-shot pump gun. He hoped it was loaded; there was no way that he could check it without making a noise. He slowly peered around the side of the cabin door. Could they be listening to him? There was more than one, if he wasn't imagining the whole thing. What to do? He couldn't see. They could be anywhere and he wasn't sure the damn gun was even loaded.

The hatch over his bunk was open, but not really wide enough to climb through. He slowly stuck his head up through the hatch. Nothing. Then he heard it again — whispers!

Will stuck the shotgun up through the hatch and pulled the trigger. BLAM, pandemonium, shouts, running feet, the boys yelling. He ran to the forward hatch and climbed through: an outboard being started, one, two, three, panic-stricken pulls. He was on deck; the motor had started, they were getting away, he could see the phosphorescence from the motor, up with the shotgun, aim for the motor, BLAM, BLAM, BLAM, click. Motor still going, the whole canoe lit up like daylight, with Peter holding a searchlight on them. Three of them all hunched over, willing the canoe to go faster.

"Pass me some more shells."

"They are out of range. Did you get any of them?"

"I don't think so, but I shot up the motor. Anything missing?"

"Not that I can see," said Graham." We'll have a better look in the morning. What happens now? Do we call the cops?"

"I'm not sure what we should do. We need an expediter."

"A what?"

"An expediter, a fix-it man, somebody we can call on day or night to sort out problems."

"Well, for once it's a good thing we don't have a telephone."

"Why is that?"

"We can go back to bed, and forget about it till morning."

In the morning, Will had ended up at this movie-set of a police station. The police chief was pure Hollywood Mexican, right down to the big cigar.

After Will had explained what had happened, he asked the

chief whether he had heard anything. "No, Señor, nothing. We will hear nothing official, but in a few days word will get out."

"Do you think they might come back?"

"No, Señor. If they were communistas or drug dealers, you would all be dead by now. They are just from the shanty town, looking for something to steal."

"Would they try to steal the boat?"

"No. What would they do with such a boat? The dinghy, yes, but the big boat, no."

"But the dinghy was just tied on at the back as always; they could easily have taken it. They were after more."

"Do you keep money on the boat?"

"No more than you would expect. We don't keep the payroll or anything like that. The bank sends it out on payday."

"If we hear anything we will inform you. In the meantime, it is not permissible to shoot our citizens for trespassing."

Will looked at him to see whether he was warning him, but behind the cloud of cigar smoke it was difficult to tell.

When he got back from town there was a small deputation waiting for him at the beach. "Que pasa?"

"Señor Will, we stop again?"

"No comprende."

"Hay una problema la noche pasada?"

"No, está bueno."

"They try steal the motor, Señor."

"No, I think they wanted the dinghy"

"No, no dinghy, motor only, Señor, to sell, dinghy es una problema."

"Okay, now I understand. They were trying to remove the motor from the dinghy. The Zodiac was too easy to identify."

"Si, Señor, only the motor, no Zodiac."

Will said very slowly, "Do you know who they are? Are they fishermen?"

"No, Señor, not fishermen." They started to pull at their pockets."

"Pickpockets?"

"Si, ellos son pickpockets. Bueno, bam, bam, bam, es muy bueno."

Will finally got the picture. They were first of all concerned about their jobs, and now they were pleased that he wasn't afraid to stand up to petty criminals.

•

Will sat on the new dock with Pablo Hernandez, looking out to sea. "Where are you going to build the house, Will?"

"What house?"

"Your house, the casa grande, your home."

"I don't need a house. I have the boat, better than any house."

"I agree, you now live the cowboy life, which believe me, I envy with every bone in my body, here today, gone tomorrow, not to mention the beautiful women. Here, there, everywhere, a life to be envied. But a man has to live somewhere. You can't continue like this forever. We would all die of jealousy."

"You can come and live on the boat with me. There's plenty of room."

"What would I do with my wife, and all my children?"

"Bring them, and then I could move into your house with some of your mistresses."

"Shh." Pablo looked around. "The walls have ears. But seriously, you know what people will say, that you are not permanent until you have a house. You should live somewhere.

It is important. Even a small house, a little casa."

"I see your point. It could become an issue, but right now I am not going to worry about it."

"It is not important today, but it could be used against you by someone in the future."

"Yes, I understand, and thank you for the advice."

•

Under the boom tent in the cockpit of *Imperialist*, Will went through the work in progress with Carlos De Souza, one of his contacts in the government. Will had rolls of drawings, which he occasionally produced to show how the development of the island was going. "What we need are like-minded people," he said, "people who like the idea, the lifestyle, and who are already in an industry compatible with the general development plan. For example, the rice farm: it will be huge, one of the biggest in the world, and the product that leaves here will be retail-ready. How will that benefit you? Your rice will be cheaper, and there will be employment. The technology developed here could be transferred back to the mainland, at little or no cost; all the help in the world right on your doorstep.

"Similarly with the ranch, the product that leaves will be mostly retail-ready or close to it. Same benefits. But we don't want to turn the whole island into a farm. The bulk of it will end up as it was before the arrival of Europeans, with reintroduced wildlife, sanctuaries for the animals, reforestation, alongside selective logging. Eco-tourism will evolve; tourists will come in and out of the mainland, which will be good for your tourism. Benefits without cost. We are going to restock the lakes with fish, and at the same time set up fish farms so that one finances the other."

"It sounds like an ecologist's dream."

"It's no dream if we can make it work. It could be an example of what could be done in other places."

"On the mainland?" asked Carlos.

Will looked at him; he had to be a bit careful here. "More difficult. This is a start from scratch; on the mainland there is too much already established, although it certainly could be done in places. But if you decided to do it, you have help right on you doorstep. And nobody could say it was impossible."

"True, there are always those that believe everything is impossible."

Will considered what he was going to say next very carefully. "You know we spoke about investment."

"Yes, I remember."

"So far nobody has come back to me about it." Will held up his hand. "Wait, let me finish. What I wanted to say was there is no hurry, no time limit, and no pressure. Come in when you like. You will never be closed out; you can pick selected projects or be part of the whole. You can set up a project of your own, but subject to the same criteria as everybody else. We have to be very strict here, you understand."

"That is very good, excellent. We are cautious people, and we have seen so many projects fail for one reason or another, which is probably why nobody has come forward at this time."

"That's fine, so long as you know the door is open."

"Do we get to buy in at the same price later on?"

"Go on, pull the other leg."

"Pull the other leg, what does that mean?"

"It means that you can't be serious."

"Pull the other leg, I must remember that. I am sure that I will get a chance to use it tomorrow when the House sits."

52

TIME WAS UP, back to Europe. Four races to go and tied for the championship. Will had never been this close to winning before; he had usually blown it by now. He had had so many accidents that he could barely remember them all. He couldn't remember how many times he had been convinced he was dead, as he slammed into a rail, or wall, or another car. There were seasons when he didn't finish a single race, not only from crashing, but just from plain mechanical problems. But here he was, four races to go, and in with a chance. Now that he wanted to quit, more money was being offered than ever before. He could more than double his earnings next year. He wouldn't mind a year with Ferrari, living in Italy. He would enjoy that.

The morning was cool and clear but windy, with the breeze blowing straight down the valley and into the bay. He had been awoken by the Zodiac chafing against the hull. It was unusual to have this much wind so early. It would moan in the rigging in gusts, and *Imperialist* would swing and heel over, not enough to risk spilling his first cup of coffee, but enough for him to pour it into one of the wide-based cups with the non-skid bottom and the narrow top.

Will tossed a pair of boots into the Zodiac and headed for shore. He wanted to check on the service crew, make sure they were doing their jobs. He had hired a local who had worked for the Caterpillar dealer as foreman, but he needed to check on him. See if he was at work on time; see if he could be trusted. Will tied the dinghy to the old dock, put his boots on and got into the pickup. The road was looking good: the limestone surface was down and rolled. The grader was already at work. Will looked at his watch: six forty-five. The operator stopped the grader and lowered the blade. "Que pasa?" He pointed to his watch and the operator gave a sheepish grin and a shrug, followed by rapid Spanish, which Will couldn't follow.

"He say that the machine so nice, that he want to work it night and day." Will turned around. It was one of the servicemen. He had not heard the truck with the service rig drive up behind him over the sound of the grader.

"Wouldn't he rather stay in bed a little longer, with his wife?"

A rapid exchange in colloquial Spanish followed by laughter. "He say wife old and fat, grader much better to operate." Will nearly choked laughing.

He looked back down the road. The operator had been doing a good job. Using a grader properly required skill, and this man was skilled. Will made a mental note: this was the kind of man he was going to need. He couldn't speak English, but then Will would have to learn Spanish. He'd done it in school, but for what he remembered he may as well not have bothered.

"Donde es Señor Ramos?" he asked, in his schoolboy Spanish.

"Señor Ramos not arrive yet."

"Okay, gracias."

Will climbed back into the pickup and drove up to the end of the graded section of the road. It was now seven and the blasting crew were getting set to start. "Buenos días, Señores."

"Good morning, sir." So much for that, thought Will; nobody believed he could speak the lingo.

"Everything okay?"

"Si, yes, we need more Primacord, but we have enough to last till lunchtime."

Will looked up at the slope of the side cut. It was a bit ragged. They were working in limestone, which made it difficult to get a nice clean break, but they could do better. "Can you do anything about the slope? It's ragged. Have you got enough delays?" They looked at each other, puzzled. "You know, pre-split, mark the slope."

"Ah, Señor, okay, we have no delays."

"Delays should have been ordered. In fact, I am sure they were delivered."

Shrugs. Will realised the problem: these men had been handling explosives for years but had no experience of the more sophisticated aspects. The problem was that Will understood the theory, but couldn't teach them, and he didn't have the time, anyway. He made a note to contact the supplier to send a rep out to show the men how to use the millisecond delays.

It was eight when Ramos arrived. "Good morning, Señor Will."

"Good morning, Señor Ramos. Do you know what time the

grader started? Seven o'clock?"

"Si, Señor."

"You have been signing them for seven?"

"Yes."

"How do you know that he has been starting at seven or six-thirty or seven-thirty for that matter, if you are not here?"

"You have to trust somebody sometime, Señor."

"That is exactly my point. I trust you, and you are trusting somebody else, so who am I actually trusting? The grader operator? Would it not be better for me to put my trust in the grader operator, whom I know I can trust?"

"Señor, if you do not have trust in me, then I should leave."

"I agree, Señor Ramos, you should leave."

"But Señor, just for being late?"

"Señor, if everybody was late it wouldn't be so bad, but on the one hand here is a man that you are responsible for, who works longer hours than he is being paid for, and the man who is supposed to be looking after him doesn't know. What about others who start late? You wouldn't know that either. The conscientious are not being recognised, and the slackers are getting away with it. You are signing timesheets paying some people too much and others not enough. What do I need you for?"

"Señor, my job is not only signing timesheets. I am running the job. I am responsible!"

"Okay, why are the slopes so ragged?"

"Slopes?"

"The banks in the side and centre cuts."

"I will get onto the bulldozer operators right away."

"No you won't. It's not their fault. The blast areas have

not been pre-split, and the banks have been shattered by the explosion. The dynamite crew know nothing of pre-splitting techniques."

"I will talk to the blasting crew. Maybe we should get another foreman."

"No again. They need training. They are good men, just short on modern techniques, and you are a poor officer leading good men. You have to lead by example."

"Yes sir, but—."

"No buts. There is no other way. You lead by example, that's it. If you find that too difficult, just let me know."

Will walked off and hopped into the pickup. He was angry with himself. He should have fired Ramos on the spot; he would never change. Perhaps he imagined that he was working for a rich playboy and the whole thing was pie in the sky anyway, but then Will supposed that was the way the guy had always worked. Next year he would sort them out. By that time the grader operator could be the boss. Wouldn't that throw the cat among the pigeons?

●

Will was rushing for the ticket counter late as usual, when he saw the chief of police.

"Señor Will, just a moment."

"Yes, Chief. Did you find them?"

"Si, we found them, or to be exact we found one dead, which led us to the other two."

"What?"

"Si, dead. You shot him, Señor, in the back, when he was running away."

Will had a sinking feeling. He was in deep trouble, and they could charge him with murder. Jesus, what happens now? Kiss the championship goodbye, for a start, and then some stinking Central American jail, but Will didn't really believe this. First of all, he didn't think that he had hit the guy, and even if he had, a shotgun wouldn't kill at that range, or would it? What if it had hit him in the head? Or was this all a big scam — fleece the gringo? If he was under arrest, where were the rest of the police? "Am I under arrest?"

"Oh no, Señor, not at this time."

"What about my flight?"

"You may go; you will be back, and we will continue our investigations. Please let me know when you return."

They have me now, thought Will. If they don't get you one way they get you another. Any way he looked at it, he had a problem. If he had actually killed the guy there was a big problem, but even if he hadn't, he still had a problem. Somebody could fix it, and he would owe them, still a problem. Of all the scenarios he could come up with, extortion was the most likely. He had played right into somebody's hands. How the hell was he going to concentrate on the rest of the season with this hanging over his head? He couldn't get it out of his mind. If the media got hold of this, they would have a field day. What could he do? If it was a set-up, who was involved? Just the police chief? What about the mining minister? Talk about getting even. Shit, they hanged people for murder there. Who do you talk to, what was his legal position, what if he never went back? What about *Imperialist*? She was Cayman-registered; he didn't think they could stop her leaving. What if he just called the boys and told them to leave? Could they extradite him? He didn't know the answer to any of these questions, and didn't want to ask anybody. If it was a set-up, and the mining minister was involved, they would just love him to run, because then they would seize all his assets. He would have played right into their hands. Even if a hint of this got out, he was finished.

53

"PABLO, DO YOU remember that burglary attempt that I told you about?"

"Yes."

"Have you heard anything about it?"

"No, as far as I know, they were never found."

"Well, I saw the chief of police at the airport as I was leaving, or I should say he was waiting for me. He said that one of the would-be burglars turned up dead, and that the police were carrying out investigations."

"Well, they could be and I would not know about that. This a serious matter. If it is true, what would you like me to do?"

"I don't know. If one of them is dead, it is highly unlikely that I killed him. We could see the man steering the outboard after I had fired the last shot, so he was alive when I last saw him."

Will was really sweating as he considered his predicament. He needed a serious expediter, a Mr Fix-it who knew his way around the murky world of Central American graft and politics. He didn't think that he had hit the guy. If he had, he couldn't have killed him; it was a shotgun, for Christ's sake, not a rifle. The range was too far. He could see the man steering the outboard after he had fired the last shot, so he was alive when those on *Imperialist* last saw him. And if Will *had* hit him, where had the man been all this time? So he was more than half-sure that the whole thing was some sort of set-up. But what sort? Was the police chief prospecting on his own? In the meantime Will had a race to run, and he needed to concentrate totally on it. If he wasn't panic-stricken he was close to it. He needed help. He needed an expert.

There was only one person who knew exactly what was going on — the police chief. The answer was simple: squeeze him. Question was: how? Answer: money. Question: how much? Answer: probably very little, and in the overall scheme of things, nothing. So the solution lay with the policeman. The hell with this, thought Will, I am going to fix this, win, lose, or draw.

Once in his hotel room, it took him less than half an hour to get hold of the chief of police in his office. Will was worried about the conversation being recorded, but on his visit, the station had seemed so low-tech that he thought there was no real risk. "Chief," he said, "I want to thank you for the way in which you handled that matter at the airport."

"No problem, Señor, what else could I have done?"

"Chief, there is a matter that I would like to discuss with you."

"Is it concerning the problem at the airport?"

"Not directly, you see, we have not provided for security on the island, and this matter has brought it to a head, so to speak."

"I see," responded the chief.

"We need to set up a security organisation of some sort, to prevent a recurrence of the event that took place on the boat. If it is going to develop in the manner in which we plan, we must protect against this sort of thing. We were considering consulting with a New York security organisation in the near future, who would advise us on how to set up our own security, because many important people will be visiting and even living there."

"That would be very expensive advice, Señor."

"Very," said Will, "but not only that, they have no understanding of local laws or customs. I was very impressed with the way you handled my situation, and was wondering whether you could recommend anybody who could advise us on security, and perhaps organise it."

"I cannot think of anybody at the moment. I am due for retirement in three years, but you would not want an old man like me."

Got the bastard, thought Will. "I was hoping that was exactly what you were going to say, but did not want to be presumptuous. If you would be willing to take over the security, it would be a big load off my mind."

"No, no, Señor, at this time I would only be able to give advice, but after my retirement I would be able spend more time on the project."

"That's fine. We can discuss it when I get back, but the conditions that we were discussing with the people from New York were performance-related, base fees, and another amount if they settled any problems that we had. Plus expenses, of course."

"Of course."

"You know how expensive these New Yorkers are. I might even be able to save a bit of money."

"It is possible, Señor, but as they say, do not count on it."

Will thought, I am either deeper in the poo, or in a better position than when I started. It's going to cost me a hundred grand, and it could all be for nothing, but if the minister of mines was behind the set-up, then it's worth every cent.

Now he could prepare himself for the next race in a better frame of mind.

54

THE NEXT CIRCUIT was a handling track. If he could get his head right, he was going to blow the Ferraris away. Jean-Claude had done a fine job testing. He was no longer setting up the cars with so much understeer, not because he was doing it for Will, but because he found that he was quicker himself. It took Will twenty laps before he was as quick, and then another five before he was a full second per lap faster. The boy was quick, and would eventually do a good job for Ray.

Will still couldn't keep his mind off his problems. He could be in a much worse position than he had been before: he could be up for attempted bribery as well, finishing up in jail the minute he stepped off the plane. There was no way that he could think of to protect himself. He needed to know the answer before he returned. He decided to brazen it out, and either extricate himself, or end up in deeper, so he phoned the chief again: "Chief, our insurance company would like to meet with you. They are concerned that you are not an established security company and would like a meeting. It is in both our interests if you agree to meet in Miami. Two first-class tickets will be at the airport waiting for you; a limousine will pick you up at the Miami airport to take you to your hotel. All expenses will be paid."

"I am very busy. It will be difficult. I will see if I can fit it in. Phone again this time tomorrow."

•

He rang the chief, who said he and his wife Clementina would be on the Friday flight to Miami, and would meet Will there on Monday morning. By then Will had set up the meeting with his insurance broker, who had no idea what this was all about, but nevertheless played along.

Will sent a limousine to pick up the chief, who arrived in a western suit and a Stetson. Will introduced the chief to his broker, whose palatial offices and patrician demeanour went a long way towards convincing the chief that he was finally in the big game. They next saw an affiliate of Will's lawyers, who went through the proposed security-service contract, including the clause for extraordinary payments.

"That," said Will, "is for when services are required outside the normal terms of the contract. This covers expenses, rewards, etc. etc. The contract allows for an upfront payment for setting up an office and relocation of personnel, which will be paid on signing. We had not seen the need for security at this early stage, but in view of that recent problem we have decided to bring it forward. However, the major problem now is to get to the bottom of the current situation. Therefore, upon signing, the mobilisation amount specified in the contract an allowance provided to cover expenses in your investigation will be paid.

As provided for in the contract, there is a success fee that will have to be negotiated on a case-by-case basis."

The contract was signed and duly notarised. The initial payment was made, and everybody shook hands. "Time for some lunch, chief?"

"Si Señor, as they say, what a great idea," with a passable imitation of an English accent.

"Señor, at the present time, I have to wear two hats, one as the Chief of Police, and the other as your head of security."

"I understand," said Will.

"The investigation is under way as to how this fellow met his death. There are two witnesses who claim that they were in the canoe with him, that you shot him, and that he died later. That part is clear-cut. The strange thing is we have found three different-sized shotgun pellets in his back. There is 00 buckshot which has just broken the skin, and a big hole full of number six and number eight birdshot. Which leaves the question: did you have number eight birdshot and number four loaded at the same time? It seems to me unlikely. If you were a peon, who got the odd cartridge wherever he could find it, or reloaded it with whatever he had, I would say it was probable. But you, no. So if it wasn't you, who was it? Why are his compadres saying it was you, and why are they spending so much money in bars? That is the question. If it wasn't you, then you have an enemy who has paid these men to perhaps kill their friend, and then claim it was you."

"It seems to me," said Will, "that this business should be handled in three phases. One, establish how the man died. Two, who killed him and why? Then, three, who ordered it?"

"That is logical, Señor. Do you know of anybody who would

wish this problem on you?"

"I can think of one possibility. I would rather not say at this time. But if it looks as if it could be, I will certainly tell you. As for the incentive, I believe it should be in four parts, with the first part receiving half the incentive. What do you think?"

"Si, Señor, that seems reasonable, but I should like a bonus if I get all four, and the person is who you think he is." He looked Will straight in the eye.

"Fair enough. I will write down the name of the person and put it in a safety-deposit box, giving you one of the keys. If it is him and you can prove it, and I don't mean in a court of law, but reasonably, I will double the bonus."

"As you say, Señor, fair enough."

Will now knew that he had set a thief to catch a thief.

55

THE NEW ENGINE blew up on the third lap of the first practice session, laying down a trail of smoke and oil that effectively ruined practice for everybody else.

"Good job," thought Will. "I can't practice, but neither can anybody else."

"Sorry about the oil, guys," trying to suppress a grin. They knew he was taking the piss out of them.

After the engine went, things never improved. At the end of qualifying, Will was eighth on the grid. He knew he was distracted, and so did Ray. He tried to force himself to concentrate, but his mind kept going back to the core problem. If the chief double-crossed him, he could be in worse trouble than ever. He should never have told them that he had fired at the motor. That was stupid. He should have told them that he had tried to frighten them off by firing shots into the air.

He became so frustrated in practice that he said to Ray, "Put Jean-Claude in the car. I'm not doing any good."

"Too late," said Ray. "You already put the kibosh on that."

Will grew so angry with himself during the race that he threw all his good intentions of accumulating points towards the championship out of the window. He was diving for holes in passing manoeuvres that didn't exist. He was banging wheels, overtaking on the outside of a 150 mph corner — a suicidal move, nevertheless he got away with it. He was worse than in his worst Formula Three days, taking monumental risks. The crowd were on their feet. He was coming off the corners with opposite lock, diving up the inside, turning in under brakes with smoke coming off the inside front. It was total madness, but it took his mind off the problem. He could see the two Ferraris ahead and he was going to get them, come hell or high water. Even in the fast sections he was closing in on them. At 170 mph, he was flicking the car into the long fast bends, and standing on it in one long glorious drift. Like they used to do in the fifties, except he was going twice as fast.

That arsehole Carlos, in the number-two Ferrari, was going to run interference. He wasn't going to let Will by. He would have been signalled not to, but also he had it in for Will, because he had been humiliated at the test session. Will wasn't about to trail him looking for an opportunity to pass; he was going to blast past as soon as he caught up, come what may. Will came up behind him on the fastest section of the track, a long sweeping left-hand corner, and tried to drive around the outside of him. He almost made it; he got up alongside, wheel to wheel, Will on the outside in a monumental drift. It was now his corner. The other guy should back off and let him go.

Carlos didn't back off. There was no room left for both of them. Will's inside rear wheel ran over the outside front wheel of the Ferrari, and he was launched, airborne. The car did three complete somersaults before it hit the ground. Flicking end over end, throwing off wheels, the engine and gearbox unit, and then bursting into flames. The press later said it was the most spectacular crash seen in years. Nobody could believe it when Will walked away from it.

Ray was not happy, "Why the hell did you do it? The car totally destroyed, no points, a third of the race still to run; why didn't you wait? What's the matter with you?"

Will couldn't take it any more, he was at his wit's end, finally breaking down and told him the whole story, every bit of it. Ray had been his friend and he had just cost him a whole heap of money. It was the least he could do to come clean.

"Will, you have a penchant for getting yourself in the shit, don't you? What were you trying to do, kill yourself? I have never seen anything like it."

"I guess I had been so frustrated with not being able to control the situation there or here, that I just decided the hell with it, and go for broke."

"You certainly did that. You are making me broke: you destroyed a brand-new car."

"If I had got away with it, think how much more valuable the team would have been. In fact, you will gain more than you have lost, even without the win."

The motor sport press were lined up outside: "No ill effects from the crash, Will?"

"Only from the bollocking I got from Ray for wrecking his nice new car."

"That was the most spectacular crash that I have ever seen, and you have no ill-effects whatsoever?"

"Oh, of course there is some bruising. Tomorrow I will be suffering from aches and pains that will last about a week; and I am sure the chiropractor will be pleased to see me."

"That was an incredible performance, coming from tenth on the second lap to third by the twentieth; and to overtake the second-place car by driving around the outside was incredible. By the way, he is saying it is your fault."

"He would, but remember my inside back wheel ran over his outside front wheel, which should tell even him that it was my corner, because I was ahead."

"But to overtake there!"

"It's been done before, in the same spot."

"When?"

"In the fifties."

"That's completely different, they weren't doing a hundred and seventy."

"It's all relative, really."

"But the old timers wouldn't have walked away from a crash like that. Do you still think that you're going to win the championship?"

"Who knows? I can but try," Will laughed.

"Phone for you, Will," called out one of the mechanics.

"Tell them I'll call back."

"I think that you had better take this one."

"Who is it?" Will asked.

"A very angry lady. A very, very angry lady.

"Hello," Will said cautiously.

"How could you do this to me?"

"Do what?"

"I am watching you die live on television, and you don't even call me when you are not."

"I'm sorry, I just got back from the hospital," Will lied.

"Are you all right?"

"Yeah, I'm fine. They always insist on taking you to the hospital."

"But how could you live through that, the fire and everything?"

"I guess I was going too fast for the fire to catch up."

"Will, do not joke. How can you joke, after what I just saw?"

"I guess because I haven't seen it."

"This is worse than the corrida, much worse. It is going to happen again, the same that happened to my brother, and I can't allow this to happen to me, or to my family."

"Isobel, what are you saying?"

"I don't want this to happen again. It is too much, too horrible. Goodbye, Will."

"But—." Then he realised he was talking to a dead phone. Why would she do that, with only three races to go? Then he remembered. Her brother had been talking about stopping after a few more bullfights, before he was killed.

What should he do? Leave it till after the season, call her back now, go to see her, or what? He had too much on his plate, without hysterical women to deal with. No, that wasn't right. She wasn't hysterical; he had gone out and gone insane to blot out other problems, much like somebody getting drunk, and now he had stuffed up the best relationship he was ever likely to have.

He tried calling her back. No go, continually busy. She probably left the bloody phone off the hook, he thought. Now he had another problem. What should he do? She won't talk to him on the phone, and you can bet she will not be home. If she says that's it, she means it. Will remembered when they first met, and her reaction to the similar fate of her brother and the effect on her family. This was serious — what should he do? He couldn't just leave it, but calling or going to see her wouldn't work either. He thought about writing her a letter, but then maybe the best was to let it go. See how the whole thing panned out.

"Will, phone."

Oh, good. "Hello."

It wasn't Isobel, it was her father. "Will, how are you?"

"Just fine, Don Alphonso, just fine."

"I saw it on the news. Horrible. How did you escape? The flames, everything, impossible. You must be hurt. How can I help?"

"Thanks, but I'm fine. Just dumb luck, I guess."

"They say the last time anybody overtook at that spot was in the fifties, yet you did it. Why?"

"It was one of those days when nothing went right. In fact, it was one of those weeks, and I just decided the hell with it, I was going to make it work. I almost did."

"You are very lucky. You almost lost your life."

"Yes."

"You do not seem concerned."

"It's not that. I am being distracted when I should be concentrating on the championship, and I guess I just got so fed up, I ended up taking too many risks."

"Are you having problems on the island?"

"Yes, but I can't talk about it over the phone. Do you have some time tomorrow?"

"Of course. Do you want to come here, or do you want to meet me somewhere?"

"I don't want to put you to any trouble. Look, I can get a jet charter out of here, and be at your local airport in two hours."

"I will pick you up on my own. We can talk in the car."

Will wasn't sure this was the greatest idea in the world, going to see Don Alphonso. He did not want Isobel to think that he was trying to return through the back door. He was also worried about the number of people who knew about his problem. As far as he knew, the only person who knew the whole story was the chief of police, whom he was sure knew far more than he admitted.

•

Don Alphonso and the immigration captain met him at the step of the Learjet. As usual, there was instant clearance. As they left, Will started to relate the whole tale, including his deal with the chief.

"Why did you not tell me about this before?"

"I am not sure. Maybe I didn't want to involve you."

"I see. I think that you may have approached it the same way I would have, except that I would have done some checking first, which could also have been the wrong thing to do. This situation is not unknown. The policeman could be on, how do you say, a shakedown? Or somebody may be seeking to put you at a disadvantage."

"A disadvantage? That's the understatement of the year."

"You say that he asked for more, if he could show you that the man that you suspect was your problem?"

"Yes. He looked me in the eye, which seemed to mean that he knew who I was talking about, but that could be a scam as well."

"Si, it could be. Does Isobel know that you are here?"

"No, she doesn't. She gave me the message."

"What message?"

"Don't come back."

"Don't come back; what does that mean?"

"Finito, the end."

"But why?

"Because she thinks I am going to kill myself."

"It certainly looked like it today. How you could have survived a crash like that seems impossible, the flames also."

"The cars are very strong; the capsule that we sit in is extremely strong. The rest of it, wheels, suspension, engine, gearbox, break off and leave the tub, the chassis."

"But to just walk away from it, that seems impossible."

"It's the sudden stop that kills you. There was no sudden stop; the car just kept rolling."

"More about it has been on the news, a lot more than is usual. They are talking about the crowd standing on their feet, and also about you going to Ferrari next year; very exciting. But Will, I don't want anything to happen to you."

They pulled up under the porte cochère and climbed out. Isobel came rushing out of the house, but came to a screeching halt when she saw Will. "What are you doing here?"

"He came to see me on business," said her father. "We had much to discuss."

"Oh Will, are you all right?"

"I am fine really, not a problem."

"Nothing?"

"No, they checked me out at the hospital and couldn't find anything wrong. I know my back's out, but I didn't tell them."

"Why, because they might keep you in?"

"No, because they don't know anything about backs. I have my X-rays with me. I'll find a chiropractor here or wait till I get back."

"What are you really doing here?" For the first time since Will had met her, she looked vulnerable.

"I have a meeting with your father."

"I could not believe what I saw, it was a nightmare come true, a ball of fire rolling and bouncing with you in it. You know what I thought? How could you do this to me, to us? You and my brother with your macho disregard for life, your lives and ours. Then the press coverage on the heroic drive, it made me sick. You destroy your life if you want, but what about the ones you leave behind? You and your macho bullshit!" She was really angry now, and getting angrier.

"Whoa," said Will. "Calm down. I did not have the best day of my life today. Just because I am not belly-aching, doesn't mean I am not hurting."

"Enough, Isobel. There is more to this than you know," said Don Alphonso.

"What do you mean?"

"There is intrigue on the island. Somebody may be trying to make big problems for Will."

She looked from one to the other. "What has that got to do with him trying to kill himself? Did he have to pass when it was impossible? No! Did Juanito have to turn his back on the bull? No! They are the same, no brains, only cojones."

"Isobel," said Don Alphonso, "such language is not acceptable. Control yourself."

"Control myself? The moment I met him I knew what he

was, another one who will bring us heartache. Why are we not grieving again now? A miracle is why, a miracle." Her emerald eyes were so bright in her rage that they glowed.

Will tried to put his arms around her to calm her down. It didn't work. She pushed him away with enough force to make him stumble backwards. "Get away! You think you can kiss and make up, like I am one of your stupid women. Kill yourself if you want, but you will not kill me as well."

"What women?" As the words left his mouth Will knew he should have kept it shut.

"That stupid bitch that you got pregnant for one, and all the others."

It was Will's turn to start getting angry now. "Since I have met you there has never been anyone else, and you know it. As for the pregnant one, that is rubbish and you know that too. For me there is no one else, and there never will be. I am sorry about today. It was a weakness; I allowed myself to be overcome by circumstances, trapped in a situation of my own making. I couldn't concentrate. I became frustrated, and tried to cure the problem by lashing out, nearly paying the penalty for it. Now you are lashing out at me."

"Of course I am lashing out at you. I do not want you destroying our lives. You are selfish. You are only concerned with your own ego, and you only care for yourself. When you are dead, you will be a dead hero. What about us? What about me and my family?"

What could he say in his defence? It had been proved beyond doubt that he was a selfish pig. The prosecutor, judge and jury had pronounced him guilty. What could he do? Throw himself on the mercy of the court? Plead insanity and hope for a lesser sentence?

"Don Alphonso, may I borrow your telephone?"

"Of course. If it is private, use the one in my office."

"What do you want a phone for?" snapped Isobel. "We haven't finished."

"Yes we have. I'm leaving."

"You mean you are just going to walk out of here, and go back to England, just like that?"

"Just like that."

She turned to her father. "What did I just say? Selfish, arrogant, ego-driven."

"Isobel, enough! Will is my guest, and I will not have a guest in my house treated in such a manner. Stop."

She stalked off. A few minutes later she came storming back in, and threw the Porsche keys at Will. "These are yours. You can drive it back to London."

Will had had enough. He was really beginning to hurt now. He had a massive headache and was starting to stiffen up. "I will use your phone if I may."

"Certainly. In the office."

Will rang the pilot. "Can you be ready to leave in an hour?"

"Departure at 2300."

"That's fine."

"What are you doing?" Isobel stood at the door with her hands on her hips.

"Going."

"When?"

"Now."

"You can't just leave like that."

"What the hell do you want me to do? I came here to talk

to your father, to seek his advice, but I can't do that because you haven't stopped yelling since I got in the door, so I might as well bugger off."

"What's gone wrong?"

"Ask your father. I have a plane to catch."

56

THREE RACES TO go, and nine points behind. They were one car short; the situation on the island hadn't changed; and there were ten days to go till the next race. Don Alphonso had driven him to the airport, but had no answer to the problem. It wasn't something that you could just pick up the phone and ask someone about. It was a dangerous situation; he could be in serious trouble. Isobel was on his mind. Now with another race coming up he had two things to not think about. Great. That was all he needed.

The test programme with Jean-Claude had come to a grinding halt, because there weren't enough cars. They were also short of two engines because he had blown up one and wrecked the other with the gearbox. On the good side, but of minor importance, he was getting along really well with Jean-Claude, and everybody else on the team. His relationship with Ray would probably never be the same again, but it was not too far off what it had been.

Will had heard nothing from the chief of police, and didn't expect to hear anything.

One thing about the break-up with Isobel — it served to take his mind off the other problem, but it didn't help concentrate it on the championship either. His normal cure for any woman problem was simply find another one, and as he was usually running more than one, it never was a problem. This time he had no stock; he had to start from scratch. The trouble was that he wasn't interested. He wanted his emerald-eyed lady back. But he was damned if he was going to go crawling. Even if he did, it wouldn't make any difference. It was all tied up with her brother's death, and a bunch of hocus-pocus.

He spoke to the guys on *Imperialist* a few times and everything seemed to be going fine. The foreman was showing up for work on time, and they were finishing off the dock.

And then a phone call. "Hello, Isobel?"

"Yes." The line wasn't very good.

"Where are you?"

"I can't say much, but the problem has been solved."

"What do you mean?"

"Just what I said. I will call again." Click.

Will wasn't sure what to think. He couldn't believe it was that easy. It didn't put his mind at rest; in fact it made it worse. If she had sorted it out, did that mean he had been on the wrong track? He had no idea. She had called him; she was trying to help. But knowing her, it probably didn't make a scrap of difference to their situation. What he should do was get the boat out of there, forget the dream, sign with Ferrari for next year and get on with what he knew best. Right now he had a test day tomorrow, and he had to get his head clear for that.

•

Test day was a disaster; he couldn't get the tyres to heat up. Sure it was overcast and the wind was chilly, but it wasn't that. It pushed the front in the tight stuff, and oversteered in the fast sections. "Ray, it's doing the exact opposite of what it is supposed to do. It won't turn into the tight corners, and the rear end feels really loose, as if the ride height is too high."

"I don't know," said Ray, "the settings are exactly the same. You've had a hell of a crash. It's pretty hard to come back immediately from something like that. Look at you; you're still bruised — it must still be hurting. I know what you are going to tell me, that you have had big crashes before and they didn't make any difference, but that was then and this is now. You have never had a crash like this before. Neither has anybody else and walked away from it. And on top of it all," he said, looking around to see whether anybody was listening, "you have this other thing hanging over your head. I haven't heard a word about Isobel. The silence is deafening.

I don't like this. There are media around and you know what they are like. If he goes faster, it will be in tomorrow's papers."

"Ray, let's get to the bottom of this. It's either me or the car. Stuff the media; let's find out."

Jean-Claude went nearly a whole second faster. It was difficult for Will to swallow, but to give Jean-Claude his due, he was almost apologetic about it.

The media weren't too bad: some made a meal of it, but most were almost understanding: "Will gun-shy after crash? New boy quicker during testing."

That night Isobel rang from Miami. "It is all fixed. You don't have to worry any more. The chief of police has been arrested.

It seems that it was a simple extortion attempt."

Will didn't know what to say. He was pleased to hear from her, but he didn't believe the outcome, it was too easy. "How did you do it?"

"I got the right people on to it. You have more friends down there than you realise."

Will had a gut feeling that it wasn't as simple as that, but sometimes the simple answer was the right one. "How did they know it was the chief?"

"They found the money that he extorted from you."

"They found cash?"

"No, they found the bank deposit slip."

"What about the dead man? Who killed him? And what about the witnesses?"

"I don't know. It's not your problem any more. You have three races to go. Finish them without this hanging over your head."

"But Isobel?" She had hung up.

She had gone down there to sort this out, so he would be able to concentrate on the job in hand. How had she managed it? Somehow she had short-circuited the system. That the chief was involved from the start, Will was quite ready to believe. But the chief wasn't stupid; he was unlikely to have tried this stunt on his own. Or was he? Isobel must have somehow kicked up a stink, and the chief was the fall guy, which meant that the big dog behind it was still out there. How could Will find out the true story? His only contact was in jail. But it sounded as though he was safe from this problem for the moment. He had a feeling that it would leap up and bite him, and that it would be much worse next time.

•

They went out the next day with new tyres and a new engine. Several teams were testing and the place was crowded with the motoring press. Some were quite solicitous. "How are you feeling Will? You must still be a bit shook up," said one reporter he had known for years.

"Not half as shook up as when Jean-Claude blew me away yesterday," Will replied. "He's going to be good, that kid."

"What do you expect, Will, after a crash like that? Nobody has ever walked away from something like that before? Just a couple of years ago you would have been toast."

"I thought the expression was brown bread?"

"Brown bread is without the fire; with the fire it's toast."

Will spent the morning diving in and out of the pits, trying to get to the bottom of the problem. He wasn't trying to go for a time; he was trying to fix it. "The front feels stiff, Ray, and the rear feels as though it is jacked up too high. It feels as though it doesn't have enough rakes in the tight stuff, and too much in the fast sections."

"Wait a minute," said Ray. "We put new shocks on, non-adjustable Bilsteins, gas ones. Jean-Claude tested them and liked them, so we put them on this car."

"Why didn't you tell me? You always tell me when you make a change like that."

"With all that's been going on I clean forgot. We'll change them now."

Will left the pits with the old shocks on the last settings that had been used. The car felt totally different, not good, but different. He was back in the pits two laps later. "We're back in business, just need to adjust the settings."

"Good. What's it doing?"

"It's bottoming under brakes into the hairpin. Its turn-in is really sharp, so I suspect we should go up on the bump for a start. I think it's too soft all around, but let's do one thing at a time."

They worked together, as they had so many times in the past. Will encouraged Jean-Claude to be involved: he had to learn, and he was a good kid. Ray was grateful for that, and for the first time in months, everybody was pulling in one direction. By close of play they were back on track. They had set the fastest time of any of the teams testing, a whole two and a half seconds faster than the day before.

●

"Señor Will, this is Clementina, wife of Jorge, Chief of Police."

"Señora, I am glad to hear from you. I heard about your husband, but I didn't know how to contact him."

"He say no contact him, he contact you. He will finish contract. He say he's the goat."

"I understand. They have made him the scapegoat. I hope he is well?"

"It is not a nice place where he is, but it could be worse."

"How will I hear from him?"

"People in the prison pass message to me. I visit, but he not tell me then."

Will was now thoroughly mixed up in Central American politics, a subject that he knew less than nothing about. Worse yet, he had tied up millions of dollars in it. He could end up spending time in jail with the chief, or worse. Isobel had thrown the cat among the pigeons, trying to sort out his problem, but he wasn't sure of the result. He couldn't just leave the chief to take the rap, even if he'd been involved to start with.

●

"Hello Will, can you hear me? Okay good; this is Hernando Solis. I have been trying to contact you, but it has been very difficult. We saw your accident on television. Horrible, unbelievable. How did you survive?"

"Too many sinners in heaven, Hernando, and the devil doesn't need the competition."

"Right. Now, that problem of yours has become a very big problem."

Will's heart started to race. What next, he thought. "How big a problem?"

"The Chief of Police is in jail, but there is more. The other two men cannot be found; the witnesses have disappeared. There is a rumour that somebody high up was involved."

"Involved how?"

"In the cover-up."

Will was starting to get really angry now. What the hell was this guy up to? "What cover-up?"

"We understand these things; we are not norteamericanos. There was what you call an accident, a misunderstanding — a thief got shot trying to escape, and died later of his wounds. Embarrassing, but not a major problem. Some money to his family, some to the police, and everything is as normal. But now the president is involved and he wants answers."

This is probably being recorded, thought Will. This guy is no bunny. They are all running for cover now. What the hell did Isobel do? I have to be careful here. "First of all, Hernando, when this incident occurred, I fired warning shots at some men who boarded my yacht in the middle of the night. Three men left in a motorised canoe. We shone a searchlight on them, and they were alive and well when we last saw them."

"I understood that these men were trying to steal an outboard motor from you, and you fired at them."

"At the time we could only guess what they were up to. We didn't take it too seriously, but now we don't know what they were up to, or who sent them."

"What are you saying?"

"I'm saying that what looked like a simple burglary attempt may be more than that."

"Then why did you bribe the Chief of Police?"

"I didn't bribe him. I hired him to find out who had sent these men to commit an act of piracy."

"Piracy? They were only thieves."

"Maybe, but I don't know that." Watch for the sum-up now, thought Will. If this is taped, he will try to package it.

"You are saying, that you only fired warning shots at some men who had boarded your yacht in the night, and they left in a canoe."

"That's it."

"So why did you hire the Chief of Police to, as you say, find out who was behind it?"

"Because afterwards he told me that one of the men was dead, and the others were saying that I had killed him. It seemed to me that I was being set up by somebody for their own purposes, and that the chief was the only person I could think of who might have any idea who that was."

"Who do *you* think is behind this?"

"Maybe you."

"Me! You can't really believe that."

"Then why are you recording this conversation, Hernando?"

"I am not recording it."

"Maybe you aren't, but someone is."

"I tell you, this is not being recorded."

"Hernando, I have a device that protects me from being misquoted by the media that tells me when there is a recording device in operation. And there is one on." That sounds like a good story, thought Will — let's see how he reacts to that.

"If it is being recorded it is not by me. Why would I record our conversation?"

"You tell me, Hernando."

"I give you my word."

"That doesn't mean a thing to me. You may not be, but somebody is, which means that maybe you have a problem as well."

Will was pretty pleased with that. He had rattled him. He was sure that Hernando was recording the conversation, probably to protect himself more than anything else. But if he wasn't, he would be even more rattled.

All this wasn't contributing to Will's state of mind as he needed to concentrate on the next race, at the same time this business was uppermost in this mind. Isobel had helped in one way and created chaos in another. God knows what she had done, but it looked as though everybody was running for cover.

•

"Señor Will, this is Jorge. I am out."

"Escaped?"

"No, no, released. They have nothing to hold me on. I showed them the contract; which means that I lose my job, maybe, but they cannot touch my pension. I have done nothing illegal — just, as you say, a conflict of interests. Maybe improper conduct, no more. But I know too much, so maybe I will still be chief."

"What happens now, Jorge?" They had moved to a first-name basis, Will thought; he might as well use it for what it was worth.

"I am on suspension, so I will be able to spend more time on the problem, which has now become our problem."

"I had a call from Señor Hernando Solis. I am sure that you know him."

"I know of him, but I do not travel in such circles."

"He says that the president is involved, and wants the matter cleared up. He also says that the two witnesses have disappeared."

"Yes. They are all running for cover. It is very political. I hope that in a few days the witnesses may reappear and tell a new story."

"Do you think that will clear the matter up?"

"No, but it will release you from the first problem. Not the second. That will take more time."

57

WILL WAS IN his London house, wishing that he could call Isobel. He had never liked the place from day one. Normally he would have been out on the town, but he hadn't felt like going out. Then again, the phone had hardly stopped ringing. Now that the situation on the island appeared to be over the worst, he was worried about the media.

The phone rang. "You are an ungrateful pig. Look what I have done for you, yet you don't even say thank you."

"Good morning, Isobel, so nice of you to call. You really did me a big favour. The Chief of Police is in jail and Hernando Solis is trying to entrap me. I fully expect the CIA to be after me next, with the IRA putting bombs under my house. Still, I miss you, I need you here, or I need to be there."

"Get here then." BLAM.

•

Will levelled off at 10,000 feet after climbing on instruments through dense cloud. He was in bright sunshine, above a solid base of cumulus. He checked all his instruments and relaxed. The Beech Baron had served him well: it was four years old and a major overhaul was coming up. Most of his compatriots had gone onto jets, but Will didn't think that he flew enough hours to warrant the time to convert. Which meant that he would have to hire a pilot, so he might as well charter a jet when he needed it.

Two hours into the flight, the cloud base had disappeared. Isobel had arranged customs and immigration at a little grass strip near the beach house. How she managed all this stuff was still a mystery. Better not to ask. There were no navigation aids so he had to take a back bearing on the ADF or Automatic Direction Finder from a local airport, as it had no radio control, just a windsock and a couple of buildings.

What was that? A light flashing? A mirror? Bet it is her with her compact. There it is, where is the windsock? Got it. Late. Too much altitude. Power right off, mixture full rich, turn for a long downwind, rate of descent 1000 feet per minute, speed too high, pull the nose up, ears popping. Exaggerated yawn, good, ears clear. Okay, gear down, turn in on base leg. Half-flaps. Final, full flaps, props fine, bleed off some more speed, hold the nose up. Okay, 90 knots, whoops, cross-wind gusting, windward wing down, cross-correct with rudder, rate of descent good, nose right on the end of the strip. Perfect, bam on the ground, aileron to windward rolling, flaps up, brakes on, cowl flaps open, turn off into the parking area. Park into wind, instruments off, engines off, brakes locked.

She was on the wing, wrenching open the door, into the passenger seat, arms around his neck, big electric kiss, sending shivers down both their backs, come up for air, and back into it. "Never do this to me again. Never, do you hear?"

"Yes'm. Never again."

She grabbed him again. It was like the first time all over again.

"When do you want to get married?"

"Not until I know that you are not going to kill yourself."

"What about jail?"

"Let me worry about that."

The next morning out on the terrace with the deep blue ocean on one side, red bougainvillea against the cliff on the other, Will broached the subject of what had happened in Central America. "I went to school with the president's daughter," she said. "She was always a hopeless romantic, so I embellished the story a bit and she arranged a meeting with her father. Her mother was also there. I think she is worse than the daughter."

"What did you tell her?"

"You don't want to know, but what I told the president was true. That you were a famous racing driver who would more than likely win the World Championship, and that you had had this huge crash, which nearly cost your life. That you could not get on with the job of racing, because you were being blackmailed by the local police chief, in league with some politicians, because you had fired at some thieves. That they were trying to get you to believe that one of them was dead, so that you would pay them off. And you had already paid off the policeman."

"Oh shit. What happened then?"

"He called one of his aides and told him he wanted an answer that afternoon. They found out that the policeman had been out of the country, they searched his house and found the deposit slip hidden."

"So they slammed him in jail."

"Yes."

"Well, that certainly got some action. By the way, the chief is out of jail."

"Why?"

"Because he showed them the contract that I had with him. Also I got a call from Hernando Solis, which I suspect he was recording, trying to implicate me in the death. The funny part about the whole thing is that I suspect the chief was mixed up in it to start with, but is now motivated by vengeance and greed. He may very well come up with the answer."

"What answer are you looking for?"

"I think the minister of mines has something to do with it. To get even, and perhaps a bit of graft."

"Oh, come on. Why would he go to those lengths?"

"He didn't have to do much, it was so easy. I tell the chief what happened, he knows of the grief we had with the minister; he goes to him and puts the scenario together, the final squeeze play, far better than a mining licence. Plus an opportunity to brag, "I told you so," to the other ministers. "Arrogant gringo can't go around shooting our citizens.""

"What an incredible story. Did you make this up all by yourself?"

"If it's so incredible, why did Solis call this morning to try to entrap me?"

"Do you think he is involved?"

"No, he doesn't have the guts. But I'm not sure what he's really up to."

"You're saying that the police chief was the instigator, but now you are protecting him, and have entered into some sort of contract with him to hunt down his accomplice, who you believe is the minister of mines?"

"Yes."

"Why?"

"Because the son of a bitch pissed me off."

"Are you certain that you didn't shoot that man?"

"No, but I didn't kill him. According to the chief, he was shot at close range with birdshot. I fired at him from long range with heavy pellets. If it's the same man, which may or may not be the case, he was murdered to implicate me. I don't believe the chief was involved in that."

•

There was an old rowing boat, in a boat house at the bottom of the cliff. It must have been used as a fishing boat in the distant past. There were some rotten old canvas sails on a boom hanging up in the rafters. But the oars were good and it looked sound. Isobel sat in the stern with a big straw hat like some lady from the nineteenth century, while Will pulled on the oars with sweat pouring down his chest. It was heavy, it was leaking, and it was never made to be rowed by one man. But it felt good.

He rowed right up the coast to the next village. It was like a picture postcard, whitewashed houses against the cliffs, covered in bright flowers, with a small restaurant, bar and an old stone dock. They wanted to go ashore but didn't have an anchor and there was too much swell against the dock. But they were in luck; a man was beckoning them to come closer. As they got up to the wharf he hopped aboard with a length of rope and pointed to a mooring buoy afloat fifty yards out. They tied up to the mooring and backed the row boat up the sea wall, tying it off. Will thanked him profusely and tried to offer him money, which he waved away, instead, inviting them into the restaurant. They dined in front of the little restaurant by candlelight on the best paella he had ever tasted, washed down with a huge jug of sangria. By this time the villagers had worked out who Isobel was, and the local bullfight experts had gathered. Then she let the cat out of the bag, by explaining who he was. Of course he wasn't as important as a bullfighter, but he was not a bad second.

●

Practice went well, and he was quick all weekend; if not fastest in any of the practice or qualifying sessions, then close to it. Race day dawned bright and clear. He was second on the grid, beside Flint in the Ferrari, with the Lotus third. Will talked sternly to himself: "Three to go. You don't have to win this one, just finish it where you are. You don't have to win; there are two more after this."

Will stalked Jackie Flint for the entire race. Move, countermove. Sometimes Will would come up the inside with a passing move, and no intention of carrying it off. It wasn't as though he could pass at will. He couldn't — the cars were so close in overall speed that it was down to a game of tactics. It was like a tennis match rallying back and forth, back and forth. Move, countermove. But with an iron ball that could kill you.

Will could see that Jackie was worried, not sure what Will might do. Suppose he tried another kamikaze move and took both of them out like he took out his Argentinian teammate last time? Will knew what was going through his head. Jackie, the odds man, would be thinking, "Should I let him go before he takes both of us out? Better to take points for second, than none." But he wouldn't want Will to get the nine points for first either.

To get back to even in the points, Will needed to win, and he had to finish out of the points. Jackie knew Will was trying to wear him down. To win wasn't enough. Will hounded him, nose to tail, lap after lap, a two-car high-speed train.

Because Will was right behind, he could read Jackie's pit board, not that it told him a hell of a lot, but the guy was under some serious pressure. Will was pushing him. He wanted to see him locking his fronts, flat-spotting his tyres so he'd have to pit. At the same time Will was wearing his front tyres out in the turbulence off the Ferrari, and overheating the engine, sucking the hot air from the exhaust. The Ferrari pits were warning Jackie about backmarkers. They would soon start lapping the slower cars; Jackie would have to start taking some chances to maintain his lead, as he came upon the backmarkers, who might not be expecting him. If Will could force Jackie to give up the lead, even if he still finished second, he would have a valuable psychological advantage for the rest of the season.

Will was sure Jackie let him pass; they were lapping backmarkers, and he delayed overtaking. Will had virtually no choice. He popped out of the slipstream and went for it. He talked to himself: "Put as much distance between them as possible, walk away into the distance."

He finished more than ten seconds clear of the Ferrari, with nine points as against six for second. So he was now six points behind, with two more races to go.

Ray was thrilled. "You hunted him down till he broke. He let you go, didn't he?"

"Yes, but he did it discreetly. Few people will realise."

"Well he knows, and his team knows. They probably told him to do it."

"I don't think so. I was reading his pit boards. He realised I was pushing him, hoping that he would take himself off. When we got among the backmarkers he realised he was more at risk than I was, because he was onto them first, and they might not be expecting him. He knew I was going to capitalise on that."

The media was out in force: "You seem to have recovered from your accident rather well. Was he holding you up? Once you were past, you simply drove away."

"He let me by, which I thought was real decent of him," said Will. "There aren't that many gentlemen left in the sport."

"Was he a bit concerned that what happened to his teammate last time might happen to him?"

"No, I don't believe so. He was holding me up, so he let me go."

"Will, you are only six points behind, with two races to go. Do you think that you will win it?"

"It looks a reasonable possibility, but that's all I can say at this point. Thanks, guys, I have a plane to catch. Must run."

"Going to Spain?"

"Could be. See you guys next time."

•

The Santiagos picked him up in Isobel's Mercedes and headed for the hacienda. "Good race," said Don Alphonso. "Merciless. Same as the bull. You have to break his spirit to be able to turn your back on him."

Will smiled. "You have it exactly. I can't let him finish second in the rest of the races or we will tie. He has to finish further down than that, and his teammate has to be afraid of me, because he is going to be used to protect the number one."

"If he is not afraid of you by now, he never will be," said Isobel.

"I need a bit of respect every now and then."

"How are you making out on the island?" asked Don Alphonso.

"It's pretty hard to tell. Isobel stirred up a hornet's nest going to the president. The Chief of Police is out of jail, the two men are missing, and Hernando Solis is trying to cover himself, for what reason I have not been able to work out. Whoever killed the first one is just as likely to have killed the other two as well. The chief seems pretty sure of himself. If he collects all the bonuses in the agreement, he won't have to work again. But I probably will."

"If he succeeds, you will either have made yourself a lot of enemies, or they will never try anything like that again. When are you going back?"

"Tomorrow afternoon."

"So soon?"

"There isn't much time. I have to be back by the middle of next week."

"You be careful. Trust nobody. Is Isobel going with you?" Don Alphonso looked amused.

"No. She created enough havoc last time."

58

As WILL STEPPED off the aircraft, he was greeted by a blast of hot air and the glare from the sun. Apprehensive, he hoped the air conditioning was working this time. His stomach was in a knot. He had no idea what was awaiting him.

The air conditioning was still not working, and the immigration line was long. Nobody to greet him this time. What does that mean?

"Good morning Señor, please come with me."

"Oh shit," thought Will, "here we go."

"Where are you taking me?"

"There's somebody here to see you."

"Who."

"You will soon see." Which didn't help Will's nerves.

It was Jorge. "Chief, it's good to see you."

"Señor, I thought it was better to see you here than in town."

"I was hoping you would show up. You got my message then."

"It was very discreet, but I understood it."

"Have you made any progress?"

"Yes and no. It is very political."

"I don't understand how it can be. The object was graft, using the mining licence as a lever. It was blackmail, pure and simple. Not politics. It may have become politics, but it didn't start out that way. And when it backfired he resorted to politics.

"Si, but you will have to be very careful. He has many friends, and perhaps more that he has made promises to."

"What about the two characters?"

"Characters?"

"The ones that boarded my yacht."

"Oh, them. I have them under control."

"You mean they haven't disappeared?"

"No. I know where they are."

"Do you know who killed the other one?"

"Oh yes, but I don't know who paid them to do it. They don't know either."

"So what happens now?"

"We have to wait, Señor. We have to go back to the beginning."

"What do you mean?"

"Señor Will, you fired at these men, which gave your enemies an opportunity. An opportunity, how do you say, to put you in a compromising position, by making it appear that you had shot the man. By involving me, they increased your problem. Although we know how it was done, we cannot prove it. We can prove that you did not kill the man, but we cannot prove who did. So the first thing to do is to get you off the hook. We have the killer but he doesn't know who paid him. We know who ordered it, but he is muy importante, and we cannot charge him, unless we have complete proof."

"Okay, I got you — we may never be able to prove it, but we can use what we know to put pressure on him. Use the whisper, spread the word that he committed murder to try to steal the island."

"But, Señor Will, he had no desire to steal your land. What would he do with it? It is purely revenge for you shaming him when he lost out on the mining licence."

"So, what happens now?"

"It's no longer a problem for you, so that is the end of phase one. We know who did it, that's phase two. We think we know who ordered it, but we can't prove that yet. So you are in the clear. I have completed the first two parts of my contract, and here is your invoice with the expenses attached. I will now concentrate on trying to get proof on who ordered it."

"But chief, you know who ordered it."

•

Outside the boys were waiting in the Suburban. "That was slow. What happened? We thought they had taken you off to jail."

"No, that problem has gone. The next issue is to get to the source, without kicking over the dolly house."

"How are you going to do that?" asked Graham.

"Set a thief to catch a thief, without catching too many other thieves in the rush."

"What do you mean?"

"There is so much corruption, that there is corruption within corruption, and it's not in our interests to go too far. We just want to park the bastard who has been giving us trouble, without it spilling over into something else."

"Way too complicated for me," said Peter.

"Anyway, how are we going?"

"We have some really good guys, some so-so ones, and some we should be getting rid of."

"Start at the bottom. Who is the worst?"

"The foreman."

"Okay, let's get rid of him. Who is the best one?"

"The grader operator. He doesn't speak English, but he has the respect of the others."

"So you take him off the grader. Who operates that when he has gone?"

"There isn't anybody. Maybe we should keep the foreman."

"No, we've settled that. He goes immediately. Does he have any support?"

"None."

"Then the minute we get back, draw a cheque for three months' pay, and get rid of him."

"Three months! No way, that's ridiculous."

"It is, but it's our own fault. We shouldn't have hired him in the first place."

"He came highly recommended."

"Yes, by some politician, which means that we shouldn't have hired him."

•

Will sat alone in the little skid-mounted porta-camp construction office down by the dock. The air conditioning was humming, the coffee was percolating and there were drawings and aerial photos on the walls. Out in the bay *Imperialist* was lazily swinging at anchor. What did he need all this for? Why take on a project that was almost destined to fail? With a little bit of intelligence he could spend the rest of his life cruising on

Imperialist. What could be better? Instead he had put himself in hock, and gambled the lot on some crazy scheme that was going to cause him nothing but problems and probably drive him broke. At worst he could end up in prison for the rest of his life, or at the end of the hangman's noose.

Jorge had made it sound as though the situation was under control, but was it? Was it too late to pull the plug? Lose the money and keep racing for another couple of years? If he won the championship, he could probably double his income. In two years he would make back what he had lost. Perhaps the island was a distraction he didn't need.

Will got up and walked out of the site office. He was struck by the glare of the white limestone that had been spread down towards the dock. He could barely open his eyes. He had forgotten to bring his dark glasses. He turned to go back to get them, then realised they were on his head. "Dumb shit," he muttered to himself, putting on his glasses, almost sticking an arm into his eye. He was really getting agitated by all this business; he was down the hole millions of dollars with no end in sight. Once the glasses were on, and the glare no longer a problem, he could look out and see the blues and greens of the bay, to the darker blue of the deep. Coconut trees waved in the breeze; with white clouds scudding by. The air was just the right temperature, cooling the heat of the day. It was beautiful. Just looking at it calmed him right down, reminding him why he had got involved in the first place. One day he would build a house here, an old-fashioned upstairs house with louvered windows, high ceilings and big verandas, looking out to sea. He could almost see himself and Isobel sitting on the veranda in rocking chairs, watching the sun go down.

"Shit I must be going senile," he thought. He was in no hurry, and he had *Imperialist*, which was better than any house. But where would he build, on the beach or on the hill? Not a problem he had to face right now.

His mind flicked to the championship, and his retirement. Ray knew that he intended to retire, but Will had kept that information pretty much to himself. If he won the championship, that would be the ideal time. But if he won, he could earn a lot more, particularly if he replaced Ken with one of the aggressive managers some of the others had.

Would he stay with Ray? The question had never come up before. He would have felt disloyal; however, after the dust-up he didn't feel that committed to him any more. Besides, if he stayed on, it would be for the money to replace what he had lost on the island. He really didn't want to continue, didn't want to drag every ounce of effort and concentration out of himself. It was just too difficult. Just keeping fit was hard enough.

But he must be a sucker for punishment: here he was going from one extreme to the other. On the one hand, the risks of Formula One; on the other, the risks of doing business in Central America and losing all he had earned the hard way. He had a big grub stake — why didn't he put it into something safe? He didn't need to gamble any more. Yet here he was tossing the lot into the pot with a good chance of losing it. Too late, he was already in it. He had three choices: go for it, forget it, or split the risk by bringing others into it. If he split the risk, he would lose control; the concept would change. It would end up a tourist resort, just like a hundred others. He might as well quit, try to sell it and recover what he could.

•

On the plane back, Will was no further ahead. But one thing he did know — he had to get it out of his head completely, before he was back in Europe. He couldn't race with all this rubbish going on. He tried to sleep, pushing the seat right back. He even covered his eyes with one of those masks that they handed out. More as a device to keep people away than anything else, but he still couldn't sleep. The food was good, but as always, he was conscious that he had to fit into the seat at the next race, that had been made to fit him exactly, with no room for weight gain. When he got out of the airport, it was raining. This was England: it always rained. Nobody had recognised him besides the immigration man, and he hoped to make it to a taxi unnoticed. He was in luck. The taxi driver paid no attention to him, delivering him to his front door with hardly a word spoken. Will walked into the empty townhouse and threw his bags down. The wooden floors echoed as he walked towards the kitchen. The fridge was stocked as usual by the housekeeper. He needed some milk. All this stuff was churning up his guts.

He sat the glass of milk down by the phone, and started dialling. Jesus, it was freezing. Why couldn't she leave the goddamn heater alone? It was on a thermostat. Why did she have to turn it off? He knew the answer already: to save money, it's a waste heating an empty house. But Will didn't give a damn about the waste. He hated coming into this miserable, cold, damp house.

"Ray, it's me."

"You're back. How did it go?"

"At least I'm not in jail. I hope to be getting to the bottom of it, if that's possible in that Central American pest-hole."

"Good. Test day is Thursday, practice on Friday, Saturday

qualifying only, but three sessions. We have three cars and six engines, so we're looking good."

"One of the cars for Jean-Claude?"

"No, not yet. Next season we'll run him. He's ready now, but we don't need the distraction. Let's win the Championship first, and then worry about how to run a two-car team next season."

Will could read Ray like a book. He was asking Will to stay on, telling him that it would be a two-car team but with Will as the absolute number one. Will didn't answer. Answers were unnecessary. In any case, Ray knew that Will didn't have an answer.

"Will, there is a cocktail party on Wednesday night at the chateau, which you should attend."

"You remember what happened last time?"

"How could anybody forget? How could you do a thing like that? Even you."

"Hey, take it easy, it was a long time ago. Maybe they won't even recognise me."

"For God's sake, Will, I don't know how you get away with half the things you do. None of the other drivers do things like that. You are a throwback."

"Like a dinosaur who has outlived its usefulness, a relic from a bygone era?"

"Not quite. You still have some spark left in you, too much spark. Try to behave yourself."

59

Will sat in the hangar, at the small grass strip from which he had just taken off. He held a mug of sickly-sweet milky tea that some kind soul had foisted on him in a misguided effort to make him feel better. Will had had the most prolonged fright of his life. It was different from racing cars, which happened quickly. This had taken too long, maybe a couple of minutes, a lifetime in the world of absolute fear. He had taken off from the little grass strip that was used by the local glider club and the usual collection of single-engine light aircraft. It was too short for the Baron, because there was a line of tall pines not far from the end of the runway. The main runway was fine, but the secondary one, which was used when there was too much cross-wind for the main one, ended in the pines. He shouldn't have attempted to use it in the first place. But he had to get to the next race, and the plane was the easiest way.

After going through all his checks, Will pushed the throttle levers forward to full takeoff power, letting the toe brakes off.

As the airspeed indicator read 90 knots, he eased back on the control column, and the nose wheel lifted, followed by the main wheels. The pines towered in front, dark and menacing. Will wasn't worried — in seconds he would clear them and be on his way.

Swing left, right foot stamp on the rudder to keep it straight, shit! Engine failure! Nose down, keep it level, aileron to the right, gear up, flaps up, level off, still veering off to the left, dead foot, dead engine, confirm. Left fuel mixture pull back, fuel off, no change, confirmed. Dead foot, dead engine had been part of his flight training in twin-engine aircraft; when an engine failed the plane swung away towards the dead engine, driven by the good engine. To correct that, the pilot stamped on the opposite rudder pedal, to keep the aircraft straight. Hence the term dead foot, dead engine. It was drilled into a pilot's head, so that he could react instantly to an engine failure.

Left engine dead, left propeller pitch control, full feather angling the propeller blades into the wind to reduce the drag and stop the windmilling propeller turning, creating drag. Still flying, got that right, what about the damn trees? Altitude 200 feet, rate of climb 300 feet per minute, speed 90 knots, is that the optimum rate of climb on a single engine? Can't remember. Too close to turn, and rule one, never turn back. With the dead engine propeller fully feathered, the drag is reduced with the blades turned sideways into the wind. If he has to fly it through the top of the trees he will, but what happens then? Prop stationary, fully feathered. Close the cowl flaps, anything to reduce drag. Would half-flaps help? Don't know. A pro would.

Would he clear the trees? Altimeter 320, rate of climb 300, don't know, temptation to pull back on the wheel overpowering, speed still 90, still climbing at 300 feet per minute. Still looking at the top of the trees. Dark wall of pines reaching up to snare him? How high are pines?

It seemed like ages, slow motion, creeping towards the trees. Can't turn back, trees staring him in the face. This was like slow motion, not like the cars. Oooh shit! Crashing into the treetops, windshield full of branches and leaves. Stall warning horn blaring, clear, no trees, huge vibration. Jesus, push the controls forward; build air speed, massive vibration. Both props bent. Rate of descent 300 feet per minute, no air speed indicated. Must have knocked off the pitot tube. Huge vibration. Fuel off, full feather on good engine. Got to land straight ahead, lucky, farmland. Altitude 100 feet, rate of descent 300 feet per minute. Prop stopped, Jesus H Christ, a whole blade missing. "Mayday, mayday, November 6834 engines out, gear up, landing south of airfield in one minute."

Will had no airspeed indicator. As long as he kept the rate of descent at 300 feet per minute, the airspeed would look after itself. Full flaps; wait for the last second to turn off the master switch. Lucky, cornfield, no trees, thank God; I might walk away from this yet. Will flicked off the master switch. Nothing. No airspeed indicator, no stall warning. Switch it back on. Rate of descent 300 feet per minute. Careful, don't stall it. Wait till the last second to turn off the master switch. Will had to watch himself. Off with the master switch. Hold the nose up, but for God's sake don't stall it. Settling into the corn, shit flying everywhere, hold it off, hold it off, good, good. Will pulled the wheel right back into his stomach. Hold it off, hold it off. Keep it straight; work the rudders, nothing else mattered.

The crash landing was almost gentle. As the plane settled

down in the corn, Will lost his vision: all he could see was corn. He had expected that, so focused on the compass — don't let it go sideways; don't let the wing dig in. Keep it straight. It started to tilt forward, shit, it's going to flip onto its back and catch fire. He was terrified of fire. He always had been. Being trapped and burnt was his greatest fear since he had been driving. Now he was about to be fried in a goddamn aeroplane with roast corn. That he hadn't bargained on.

Finally the plane stopped moving. Open the door; out as fast as you can. Shit, the frigging door is stuck. You stupid bastard, why didn't you open the door before? The common-sense bloody obvious thing was that the blasted door was going to be stuck because the airframe would twist. You should have opened the damn door and stuck your damn shoe in it to prevent it jamming closed, idiot. Flick the passenger seat forward, into the back; should be able to kick the double doors open even if they were stuck. They weren't, and Will was out. He fought his way through the corn to get clear of the plane, and then stopped. Use your head you silly bastard, you'll get lost. Stay here, let them come to you. A sea of corn — there didn't seem to be any gaps in it.

Will could hear a helicopter heading straight for him, or rather straight for the crash site. He thought he had better head back to the plane as they probably couldn't find him. Obviously they could, as they were right above him, clattering away, the blast blowing the corn around. Will was trying to look up to see what they wanted him to do, but he couldn't see with all the wind and dust. His eyes were now full of all this shit flying around. The hell with this, he thought, if the plane hasn't caught fire by now it won't. I'll go back and use the radios if they are functioning and find out what their intentions are.

Will had never been so frightened for that long in his life. In the cars it was over quickly, either you're dead or not, over in an instant, not this prolonged agony. He was wet through with sweat.

He had had no time to ponder the situation; he needed an air taxi to Heathrow and a jet charter. He was going to be late for practice and Ray was going to chew half his arse off. Will sat nursing his foul mug of tea, surrounded by people from the local aero club. "I don't give a rat's arse about the plane; it's the insurance company's problem now. I don't have time to wait for the air inspector, I need a charter, and I'm late."

"We don't have an aircraft that can take you to Belgium immediately."

"That's fine. I only need to go to a place where I can hire a jet."

"But what about the air inspector of accidents? He will need to see you," said a man with an RAF moustache.

"Look, people, thank you for your help, I really appreciate it. I will leave a contact number, but I gotta go. Somebody fly me, or lend me a phone, please. I don't have time for this."

60

"You crashed the plane," said Ray, "and walked away from it. Now I have heard it all. What have you not crashed? Last year you wrote off my brand-new Mercedes. This year you wreck an aeroplane. What next? You crash my racing cars with impunity, but that doesn't even count. You destroy women's lives without a backward glance, and now you are probably planning to destroy the economy of some poor Central American country. You are a modern-day Attila the Hun," said Ray, laughing and shaking his head.

Jean-Claude was watching the two of them as though he were at a tennis match, his head swivelling back and forth. He was not sure what to make of these goings on. He didn't know whether they were serious; his English could not quite cope with it. However, he was impressed that Will could destroy such a wide variety of equipment, and get away with it.

"Enough of this bullshit," said Will. "My feelings should be hurt. Here am I risking life and limb to bring bread to your table in fact so you can live off the fat of the land, as is obvious by the size of your belly hanging over your belt and all you do is try to embarrass me in front of this young fellow here."

"Okay, okay, enough already. Are you fit to drive?"

"Of course, or I wouldn't be here."

"Don't say anything to anybody about the plane crash. They might just use it as an excuse to force a medical report or some bureaucratic nonsense."

"That's fine with me. I can't take any more harassment anyway."

Will stepped over the side of the car and stood in the seat. He lowered himself down, taking his weight on the side pods, and twisting sideways to get his shoulders through the bodywork. He wriggled himself into the seat, pulling the crotch strap up between his legs, so his mechanic could hook up the six-point harness. Will wriggled and twisted as they pulled the shoulder straps as tight as possible. No matter how hard they pulled, it was never tight enough. It was a brand-new car, no different from the one he had destroyed last time, but new. The steering wheel was slightly different; it was suede-covered, but everything else seemed the same.

Will flicked on the master switch, followed by the ignition switch. On came the outsized oil-pressure light, the one that looked like the rear light off some old car, he couldn't quite remember what make. "That's new," he thought, "that's to prevent me blowing up the engine again."

He pumped the accelerator pedal twice to prime the fuel injection, and pushed the starter button. A couple of turns and the engine rasped into life. The oil-pressure gauge jumped off its peg, reading sixty pounds at idle. Will blipped the throttle so that the plugs wouldn't oil up, pumped the clutch a couple of times, slapped the gear lever over towards him, pushed the clutch in, and pulled the lever back into first. Blipped the throttle again and eased the clutch out. He got it rolling without too much trouble, and headed out onto the track.

•

"Heard you had a crash, Will."

"No, I've only been out for a few laps. Maybe later."

"Not a car crash, a plane crash."

Jesus H Christ, he thought. How the hell do they find out so fast?

"Oh, you mean the plane. "'Twern't nothing."

"So you *did* have a plane crash," said the reporter.

"Only a small one."

"How did it happen?"

"An engine stopped running."

"What did you do?"

"Landed it."

"Will, this is like pulling blood out of a stone. Where did you land it?"

"In a cornfield."

"Did you hurt yourself?"

"No."

"Is the plane wrecked? Were there any passengers? Were they hurt?"

"Yes, no, and no."

"The plane is wrecked and there were no passengers."

"Roger that, over and out."

Will was dying to get away from the reporter. This wouldn't do him a bit of good. It would only foster his playboy image, which usually caused him problems. But too late, he was surrounded. He could just imagine tomorrow's news. Now he was going to have problems with track officials, who would want medicals at least. Then there was civil aviation, leaving the scene of an accident. He was going to be showered in crap if he was not careful.

"Look, guys, an engine quit, and I couldn't clear the trees at the end of the runway."

"The report said that you used a runway that was too short."

"Nobody told me it was too short."

"But that is your responsibility. The pilot is responsible."

"What about the trees? Who left them there at the end of the runway? Why weren't they cut back? *That* is the question. I have a motor race to run. I walked away from the goddam aeroplane; it's now up to the bureaucrats and the insurance company. Nobody got hurt and I couldn't give a shit. Over and out." With that he walked off.

"They know?" asked Ray.

"Everybody does."

"Oh well, I suppose they'll just require a medical before you go out again."

"At least."

Five minutes later the officials arrived and banned him from driving till he had been to see the chief medical officer. It was all a pain, but the amusing bit was the nurse, who looked as though butter wouldn't melt in her mouth, rested her pubic area on his knee as he sat on the bed in the examination room. Will thought she expected him to rub his knee against her parts. When nothing happened, he got the impression she was a bit put out. By the time he had been discharged, Will had missed the second practice session, and by the third session it was raining, and continued raining till early Sunday morning. He hadn't gone out because he would have learnt nothing, and there was no way that he could have gone as fast as in the first session.

Will was nineteenth on the grid. He had never been this far back in his entire life. With two races to go and his main opposition for the championship on the front row, it looked as though he had blown it again.

The warm-up was at ten and Will was the first car out. It was clear and cool and he got right into it. By the third lap he was going full blast. The car felt fantastic; he was going like the last laps of qualifying, smoking the inside fronts into the corners under brakes, hanging the rear out with bags of opposite log. Will was enjoying himself.

"Don't do anything stupid," said Ray. "You can't win it on the first lap; just take your time and try to get into the points if you can."

"Yeah, sure, but I can't just sit back and wait. I'll have to go for it and the best time is at the start. There are plenty of turkeys between me and the bastards at the front."

"Yes, but for God's sake use your head, not your nuts this time."

He was so far back on the grid; he would need a neck like a giraffe just to see the front. But he could see the starter on his little podium. He knew there was no point in trying to jump the start too soon, but if he could just squeeze up the pit apron, he might be able to nail a few without getting tangled up in a crash.

Will watched the little man climb the starter's box with the flag under his arm. He felt himself go tense. He couldn't hang back; he wasn't made that way. The flag was up, the left shoulder went up; Will dropped the clutch and dived for the pit apron. He was in second gear before anybody around him had moved. Into third, quick, look for a hole, jink left. Everybody in front was twisting and turning looking for holes. Fourth gear; leave it there, no point going for fifth. Check the mirrors, nobody up the inside. No space in front, just gearboxes and wings staring at him. Try for the inside, no room. Wait; there is nothing you can do, no room, just wait. Position yourself to be on the throttle first. Leave a little space in front and try to slingshot out of the corner. Turn in, boot it, boot it. Away, great, where the hell am I, must have knocked off a half a dozen at least. Settle down; don't panic, one at a time.

Will kept talking to himself. Watch the revs; don't blow the bloody thing up just because you can't hear the engine. That's it, stick the nose under his wing, get a good draught, that's it, go.

He popped out of the slipstream. Jesus, the car feels great. Open your hands, push yourself back into the seat, relax, don't get all bound up. Get yourself positioned for the corner onto the straight. Should be able to pick off two more. Must have got five or six on the first lap. Ray will be crapping himself. If I crash, I'll never hear the end of it.

By the end of the third lap, Will was ninth. They had flattened out the wings to reduce drag and it was paying off big time. But he had to keep lecturing himself: don't kill the tyres, use the straight-line speed. Pick them off one at a time. Don't kill the tyres, take it easy, pace yourself, don't panic; it's not over till it's over." Will kept talking to himself, "Don't get carried away. You can't win from nineteenth but you can pick up a few points.

But what good were a few points? Finishing second again in

the Championship was useless. He had done that twice before. The season was coming to a close, and he had to finish at least third to have a solid chance. But if he got no points, he had almost no chance.

Shit, the car was great. He wished he could start pitching it around, he would really chew these bastards up, but he had to save the tyres. He could feel the rears going off already. Take the pressure off the rears, let the fronts work some more, stop stamping on the throttle, you jackass, use your bloody head for once in your life. You can pick up a few points if you think. Just don't kill the blasted tyres.

Will's instinct was to pitch it into the corners and stand on it. It felt so chuckable, there was so much more speed that he could get out of it. But he knew it was short term. The soft-compound tyres would not last. He had to preserve them. As he progressed up the field, it became harder and harder to overtake. People fought harder to hold their position, but Will kept using that straight-line advantage that they had planned on. He made sure that he was under the wing of the car in front, as they came onto the main straight. Then he would stay in the slipstream till he got into the braking area for the hairpin. Then pop out of the slipstream, run up the inside, and Bob's your uncle, another one was gone. Simple as that, Will was knocking them off lap after lap.

He could see Ray with the pit board. Somebody was going to run over the silly prick again one of these days; he was leaning so far over the pit counter, he was going to fall over onto the track. Will knew that Ray was beside himself with excitement. He would be in the pits changing every gear, leaping up and down like a man possessed.

It started to dawn on Will on about the fifty-fifth lap that he could win this. He was fourth and could see the three in front. He kept talking to himself: you don't have to win this, fourth is enough, and fourth keeps you in contention. He could hear Ray in his head, "Take it easy, fourth is good, don't throw it away now."

But there was Ray hanging over the pit wall giving him the time to the lead. Silly bastard, thought Will, he's gone mad. He's telling me to do exactly what he told me not to do. "I have two choices, go for it and blow the tyres, or try and pick them off one at a time, and not make it." The decision was made for him. On the pit board with Ray hanging it out further than ever before was "Go, go, go."

"He has gone totally demented this time," thought Will. "Silly bugger." He was sorely tempted to go for it, but talked to himself: use your head; don't follow that silly bastard, use your head; take one at a time, don't get carried away. Do what you've been doing; use your straight-line speed. Don't go for a win; just knock off one at a time."

Smoke! Thanks, old buddy, a freebie.

Will was now a podium candidate if he kept running. He was closing at half a second per lap. To win, he needed a second per lap. But if he pushed that hard, the tyres would be gone in five laps. If he didn't, he would end up third. If he stuffed the tyres, he might still be able to hang onto a distant third. So the answer had manifested itself: he had nothing to lose if he didn't totally kill the tyres. "I'm thinking like an odds man," thought Will. Maybe he had grown up.

In one lap, he had lowered his lap time by a second. He was using the tyres, pitching the car into the corners and standing on it. Use your head, use your head, Will kept telling himself. What are they up to? Are they fighting among themselves? Holding each other up? They'll soon know, I'm closing at a hell of a rate. What will they do? Stop fighting, or keep on? Time is running out, and so are the tyres. What is the closing rate? It has to be a second and a half. What about the clown behind, what is he doing?

The closing rate was still a second per lap, but the car behind him was not being left behind either. He was on the move as well.

Five laps to go and three seconds to do it in. The two in front were still fighting for track position and holding each other up. This was going to be tricky; if they held him up they could all get done by the fourth car. Four laps to go, and Will was just out of touch, but closing fast. One more lap and he would be onto the gearbox of the Lotus. If the tyres lasted that long. He was no longer closing at a second: he was down to half a second and the Menendez Ferrari was closing on him. Three laps to go, and he wasn't close enough; it would take a lap longer, and the fourth car would be right with them. His palms were sweating in his gloves; he was tensing up. Think, jackass, think. Don't throw this away. It is yours to lose or win. *Think*. His mirror was now full of the Ferrari; and he was just in reach of the one in front, who was still trying to get by the Brabham.

"How the hell is this going to work? Two laps to go, everybody is up everybody's arse like a dog jamboree and there are two laps to sort it out. My tyres are stuffed. Menendez behind is going to make his move on the main straight this lap, he can't afford to wait. The Lotus in front of him is waiting for the next lap to make his move on the lead Ferrari, but is going to try to stuff me up this lap. So how does this pan out? Think, think."

They came onto the straight like a four-car train, nose to tail. "Who makes the first move? The leader is panicking; he is weaving about trying to throw the second car off. Think, *think*; the leader is panicking, the guy in fourth thinks he can do it, the one in second is trying to stuff me up and get by the leader at the same time, and what am I doing — sitting here thinking."

The end of the straight is coming up fast. It's like a bomb burst, four abreast. The leader is stuffed. He is now on the outside, the fourth is on the inside, and here I am piggy-in-the-middle with the other idiot. What happens now?"

Will breaks early and slots in behind the fourth, sticking his nose right up his gearbox. There is no space for the other two. Musical chairs; the roles are reversed. The other two are duck soup. They pass the pits nose to tail. Careful, your tyres are stuffed. Don't stay too close or you'll understeer off. Save it for the corner onto the straight. You have one shot and one shot only.

"Let the guy go, he's not a championship contender. The other two were, but not this one. Let him go." But Will wouldn't listen to himself. He had to have a go. "What stunt is this guy going to pull? He won't let me draught him onto the straight? What is he going to do to break the tow?" The guy was smart. As Will came rushing up to make sure he got a good tow, he banged the brake going into the corner onto the straight. Will had to brake, losing the tow. That's torn it, Will thought, but he'll be panicking now; he has everything to lose. A small voice in Will's head said, "You have even more to lose, you fool. You are far further ahead than you had any right to expect, and now you're planning to pitch it away."

419

Menendez, the new leader, was weaving, hoping to throw Will off, but Will kept going straight. He had no chance of passing; his only hope was to get close enough to have one more go on the fast right-hander onto the pit straight. He went for the inside, hoping that the other guy would fall for Will's move. He did, and cramped himself by entering the hairpin too tightly.

Will ducked for the outside, exiting the hairpin with good speed on the right line. He was now closing fast as they crested the hill with the almost flat-out right-hander leading to the flag. Will had more speed from the hairpin exit, and there was nothing the Argentinian could do. Will was up the inside, with wheels within wheels, inches ahead.

As he crossed the finish line, Will threw up his hands. He screamed and yelled in his helmet, kicking his feet and pounding on the steering wheel. The crowd was waving, jumping up and down, and chanting. By the time he got to the parc fermé, Will was exhausted. He felt drained, as though somebody had taken a big syringe and sucked him dry.

Ray went mental. He threw his hat in the air, jumped all over, threw it up again and when it landed, jumped on it all over again. Silly bugger, thought Will, that's his new hat.

61

THE BAY WAS almost landlocked, with steep bush-clad hills on three sides. It was extremely deep, so anchoring was a problem; they'd had to drop the anchor on a four-fathom ledge close up to the north-east corner. Just out from the ledge it was fifty fathoms, too deep to anchor.

The waiting was the worst bit. They had done everything that they could, but the apprehension was palpable. The forecast was for storm conditions. Sure, they were anchored in a bay, but space was limited, and they were on a short scope. They could not let out as much anchor as they would normally have. There was just not enough room. *Imperialist* was too big and drew too much water; also the little bay was full of fishing boats waiting for the big blow.

They had been through a hurricane some months previously, and now this. They had deployed their biggest anchor, a huge Bruce, and had let out eighty feet of chain in twenty-four feet of water. Not nearly enough, but that was all the room they had to swing in. They had considered deploying a second anchor, but Will hated laying two anchors. It always led to grief when the chains got tangled up.

It was still, very still, with some rain but no wind. The fishing boats had been pouring in all afternoon, some large, some small, some middling. There were some Florida shrimpers, about 80 feet, with high bows sweeping down to a low, wide transom, a small deckhouse up forward. Will watched the fishermen to see whether they had any better ideas than he did. However, aside from sticking their noses right up under the cliffs where *Imperialist* couldn't go, they didn't seem to have anything new to add. Some seemed to be getting ready to party down. Music was blasting out, and there was a fair amount of shuttling back and forth between them. Will wondered what they must think of this huge sailboat in the middle of their world, but nobody approached them.

"Do you think any of those guys might want to sell us some lobsters?" Will asked.

"You want me to go and ask?" said Graham.

"No, I'll check it out myself."

"Oh shit, we stowed the dinghy."

"I know what," said Will," I'll try them on the VHF. Maybe they'll bring some over."

"Yeah, great. How are you going to do that? You can't speak Spanish," laughed Graham.

"I'll just try spinglish and see if that works." So Will got on the VHF and broadcast, "Anybody got any crawfish that they want to sell?"

The response was immediate and in a good old southern drawl. "No, we ain't got no crawfish for sale, but we got some we'll swap for beer."

"Sounds like a good plan to me," says Will, "If you deliver them, we'll throw in some fried chicken as well."

"You got yourself a deal, mister. We'll be right over."

Will dug two dozen Millers out of the chiller, and a bag of fried chicken pieces, and went on deck.

The fisherman was an old redneck, sunburnt to a white blond; wrinkled, scrawny, blue-eyed. A toothless, dried-out shell of his former self. Will looked down into the bottom of the old dory. "You got a heap more crawfish than I bargained for, old buddy. We don't have enough beer to swap, so we can either give you money or whisky."

"Man oh man, whisky! Now that will keep us safe and sound in the blow."

"How bad is it going to be?"

"I's been fishin' these waters man and boy from just after sail. I reckon I ought to know. But this one has me fooled. I ain't never seen one like this, at this time a year, so I cain't rightly say." He looked around at *Imperialist*, along the hull and up the rigging. Will watched him without a word; waiting for the comment he knew was coming. "My daddy told me about these. He fished the Newfoundland banks for codfish in ships like these. Wooden ships and iron men, he said. Not like nowadays. No fish any more, all fished out. Japanese, Chinese, Taiwanese, Korean. They work for nothing, they strip the sea clean. Fishin' for things we ain't never heard of. I fight them in Korea, I fight them in Vietnam, and still we lose. If the Chinaman don't get you, the bank will. All we do is fish, buy diesel, and pay the bank. What little we take home, my fat old lady takes to the casino."

"What do you say to a man like this," thought Will. "The world had passed him by. How could you help him? What could you do for him? Would he be better off working for a wage in a factory somewhere? Would he have been better off staying in the military, where his life would have been organised for him?"

They worried about dragging. If the anchor didn't hold, but slid off the ledge that would have been it, a 100-foot boat skidding out the bay backwards or, worse yet, into one of the vertical rocks that came straight out of the water astern of them. It blew like a bastard all night. *Imperialist* heeled right over in the gusts and dived to one side or the other. The anchor chain popping and banging in the fair lead. The wind howled through the rigging, moaning like a thousand banshees. And the rain — they had never seen anything like it. They dragged and dragged, and kept resetting the anchor all night. In the pitch-black they couldn't see the other boats; most were black anyway and their pathetic anchor lights were invisible in the torrent that was coming down. Each time they dragged, somebody had to go up on deck and raise the anchor, and then they had to motor back up to where they thought they had been, and reset it. But where had they been? They couldn't see. There were no visible reference points. The most they could do was to use the depth sounder and searchlight, trying to reposition themselves relative to the fishing boats. It was not exactly science, but what choice was there? Go out to sea in this shit, or take the risk of running aground, or into a fishing boat. And they weren't the only ones dragging; a couple had come skidding backwards past them in the dark.

Next morning the wind was mostly gone, and the scenery was dramatic — new waterfalls thundering down where there had only been small streams before. Some were hundreds of feet high, others not as high but wider. The dark green mountain rose vertically out of the deep water, fjord-like; mist poured through a saddle between the hills, almost like smoke. It was still overcast, and Will was pretty sure it wasn't over yet. One thing he did know — he didn't want a repeat of last night. Nobody had got any sleep. It had been nerve-racking.

Imperialist rolled gently, in the slight swell left over from the gale they had just been through. Will stood up in the cockpit looking around. He hadn't seen the sun for days. It had been nothing but wind and rain, eventually culminating in a full gale. The forecasts had all been hopelessly optimistic; one system after another had marched through bringing worse and worse weather. Now all the crew wanted to do was dry out.

They sat under the deckhouse having breakfast, looking at the dramatic scenery, the rain starting again with gusts of wind. In a few minutes the rain was lashing down, and the wind was blowing *Imperialist* around her anchor. They couldn't afford to stay here long, but they were sick of beating into a head sea for days on end. They hoped for a break in the weather, or a wind shift, but it didn't look good. They couldn't motor as the engine was overheating; all efforts to find the problem had failed. They could charge the batteries and run the refrigeration but it would overheat when they tried to motor up into a head sea, which required much more power. Will had run out of books to read. There were two left, but one was too technical, and the other was a novel so badly written he couldn't bear to read it. He had persevered with it, not believing it could be that bad, finally giving up.

With nothing else to do, Will started to analyse the

season, and his chances of winning the Formula One World Championship. What had he done wrong? Was it the car, the organisation or himself? Or was it a combination of all three? If he could rerun the season, what would he do differently? Could he have done it better? Was the island distracting him? No matter how many times he ran through the year up to this point, he always arrived at the same answer. Of course he could have done better. If he hadn't had the distractions, he wouldn't be asking himself these questions now. He would be way ahead.

The island had definitely been a distraction, especially shooting at the clowns who tried to board *Imperialist*, and all the other foolishness with the politicians and the police. To get the whole thing going had been hard enough. But to put up with all that other stuff, and trying to win a World Championship at the same time was just too much. He had bitten off more than he could chew. So, what else was new? He was always going over it in his head. Whether trying to pass where nobody had ever done it before, on the outside of some 150 mph corner, or out-braking somebody else into a hairpin, when the odds of pulling it off were against him,

Will was a gambler. He had got himself in more trouble over women than he cared to remember. He'd even had to jump out of a window once. That was an experience — an irate husband with a double-barrelled shotgun yelling, "I'm going to shoot the blackguard!" He had landed on the roof of the husband's new Bentley, leaving a large dent, which annoyed the cuckolded man far more than Will's taking a slice off the wife.

62

EVENTUALLY THEY GOT totally fed up with the weather. They had dragged several times, and the perpetual rain was depressing them, so they up anchored and headed out into a lumpy sea. Just getting the main up had been a nightmare, motoring slowly into the enormous, steep swells that were breaking right across the deck, as they hoisted the heavy mainsail. They had had to continue motoring right into a head sea, with the main strapped in and water washing over the deck, until they cleared the island, when they could turn south. But once they had passed the island, it was going to be a lot worse, as they would be fully exposed to the open sea.

Finally, they made the turn and hoisted the staysail. *Imperialist* heeled to the wind, starting the long beat away from the lousy weather, trading it for hours of bashing to windward. The motion was terrible — up, down, up, down. Soon Will started to feel sweaty, the first sign of sea-sickness, nauseated, though not enough to throw up, which would have been preferable. With the rain and the poor visibility they were on dead reckoning. They couldn't get a decent sight with a hand-bearing compass, so they used the RDF, taking some bearings off a local coastal station.

Will was a bit worried about shipping; the radar had a proximity alarm that should alert them to anything within a ten-mile radius; however, with a closing speed of thirty knots, ten of his and twenty of the ship's, it wouldn't take much time. Every time he went down to the nav table, he would feel worse, but it had to be done. He could feel the cold sweat on his forehead. He didn't want to be the first one to barf, but it looked as though that was exactly what would happen. *Imperialist* ducked her head into the sea like an enraged bull digging in a pasture, flicking the water over her shoulder to let it roll down the leeward deck. It was miserable, grey, raining, uncomfortable, and he felt sick. He wished he could just throw up and get it over with, but he wasn't sick enough for that, not even if he stuck his finger down his throat.

Imperialist pounded her way down the coast, up the wave, over the top, slamming down the other side. Will wondered what he was doing there. He felt just plain rotten. He desperately wished to vomit, but no such luck. At lunch time all Will could get down was some plain white bread and a little Coke. Anything else just made his nausea worse. Peter and Graham felt a lot better than Will, and weren't backward in letting him know.

It was just on dark when they reached the channel. The entrance was wide, but it had rocks in the middle and rocks on either side. There was a lighthouse on the starboard cliff and a leading light where the channel made its first turn. Will did not like it, but the thought of carrying on for another fifty miles to the next anchorage was not particularly inviting either. Worse, the channel was directly into wind so they would have to drop the sails and motor in. Dropping the sails on a 100-foot yacht is not easy, particularly when you feel like shit. But it had to be done.

Will went downstairs and started the engine. They rolled up the flogging staysail, which shook the whole boat as they brought it in. Luckily the main was on lazy jacks, but they still had to furl it and tie it down. A great way of ripping out your fingernails. They got it all done in the end, beginning the harrowing business of taking bearings with a hand-bearing compass, checking their heading and depth, and running back and forth to the chart table trying to make sure that they were in the channel, and not heading for the rocks. Eventually they made it into the anchorage. The wind was still howling as they dropped anchor. The wind immediately caught *Imperialist*, swung her sideways and pushed her back as the chain rattled over the bow roller. Will slowly applied the windlass brake to allow the anchor to dig in, before he put too much load on it. Finally he locked the anchor off.

He stood on deck taking bearings, making sure that the anchor was holding. The last thing he wanted was to have to reset the anchor because it was dragging. There were a couple of houses up on the hill he could use as bearing markers when fixing his position, and what seemed like a pine forest, hearing the wind roaring through the trees. Satisfied, he headed below. The stove was going and the guys had a large pot of hot chocolate ready, and dinner in preparation. "That's the great thing about misery," said Graham. "It feels so good when it's over."

Next morning the world had changed: the wind had dropped, and the sun was out. They had to get moving, Will needed a telephone. There was one race to go, and he was equal on points. He just had to finish ahead or at least end up with more points. Technically, he would be champion if this was the end of the season, because he had won more races, but that wouldn't matter unless both he and Jackie Flint finished out of the points in the last race. Or the unthinkable: Jackie got one point for finishing sixth and Will got none. In which case, there would be a dead heat. The pressure was on; Will's guts tightened up at the mere thought of it. So close so many times before, but this was closer than ever, and in the middle of it all the other grief. The island, the politics, the murder, all self-inflicted.

63

HE WAS IN first class on a 747 again, heading for Heathrow, as scruffy as he had ever been. Unshaven, sunburnt, salt-encrusted deck shoes, jeans, and a dirty T-shirt. There was the usual crowd. A few businessmen in suits, some bureaucrats. One or two looked to be deadbeats like him, but not quite as bad. Probably musicians. He was hoping to get straight to sleep, and prayed nobody would sit beside him. No such luck.

"Are you an entertainer?"

Will thought for a while and came to the brilliant conclusion. "In a way."

"Are you a musician?"

She wasn't bad-looking. Sort of Swedish, not really his type, but not bad. "Why do you ask? Because I look scruffy?"

"No, because you look familiar."

"And because I look scruffy?"

"And because you look scruffy."

Will had to smile. "I'm not a musician, I'm just scruffy."

"I didn't really think you were a musician. I thought you might be some kind of weird military type, but military don't fly first class. But you look familiar. You said you were an entertainer?"

Will laughed. "Are you hitting on me?"

She went bright red, sat up straight in her seat and huffily replied, "Of course not."

"As I thought, you *were* hitting on me."

"I just told you I wasn't!"

"Then why did you turn bright red?"

"I didn't."

"You did, and I'm glad you blushed."

"I didn't, and why are you glad? Are you trying to embarrass me?"

Will laughed. "No — if I have, I apologise. I was only having some fun with you."

"You don't want to tell me what you do, do you?"

"No, it only leads to more questions."

"Are you married?"

"My answer should be, do you want to marry me? But I won't because you will only start getting red all over again."

"You don't answer questions, do you?"

"Not if I can help it."

"Are you some kind of spy?"

Will cracked up. "I have been called every name under the sun except a spy. But wait a minute; I *was* accused of spying the other day."

"Spying on what?"

"There you go again."

The stewardess showed up with champagne, canapés and a

432

knowing look. "Good to see you travelling with us again, Mr Archer. Would you like some champagne?"

"Of course we would, we are on our honeymoon."

"We are not! I am a married woman. I mean, married to somebody else." Turning red again.

"Jeez, I wish you had told me that before, dear."

"You are insufferable. Stewardess, can you find me another seat?"

"I am sorry," said the stewardess, stifling a laugh. "The flight is full."

"Why are you like this? Why can't you act like a normal person?"

"It's my defence mechanism."

"Defence against what?"

"Predatory women."

"I am not predatory. I was only trying to make conversation. Besides, as you can clearly see, I am married." Wiggling her finger with a huge engagement ring and matching wedding band.

"That's no proof you are not predatory."

"I am not predatory. You are only trying to embarrass me."

"Agreed, predators don't blush, not for real anyhow. Not *real* red."

"There you go, embarrassing me again."

"You are not really embarrassed."

"Yes, I am."

"I have proof."

"What kind of proof?

"You only went slightly red."

She settled back in her seat and took a sip of champagne.

"You have not answered one single question, but I do know some things about you."

"Like what?"

"Like you say you entertain, which could be taken many ways. You imply that you are afraid of women, which I don't believe for a minute, and you didn't answer when I asked if you were married, which means that you probably are."

"Do you think I am a porn star?"

"No." She laughed.

"Why, do you thing I am incapable?"

"No, nothing like that," blushing again.

"You know what I think? I think you are somebody's trophy wife."

She jerked upright. "That's rude. How can you say something like that?"

"It's true, isn't it?"

"No! Why do you say that?"

"Because you are an unfulfilled innocent. You look at me as if I'm a snake. You would like to pet me, but you are afraid."

"I am not unfulfilled, I am not afraid and I certainly don't want to pet you. How can you say that?"

"Because snakes know these things."

"You are so aggravating. You are just making this all up to try to embarrass me."

Will looked at this perfectly dressed young matron, probably out of the Midwest somewhere, the wife of a VP of some big company. "I told you I was an entertainer. When last have you had this much fun?"

"You are exasperating." But she was forced to smile.

Will leaned back in his seat, taking a sip of champagne, and swallowed the canapé.

"At least you are not boring. Most men are boring. Where I come from, they are *all* boring."

"Oh, I knew that."

"How?"

"It's the snake thing."

"What are you implying? Is the snake some kind of phallic symbol?"

"Oh no, a snake's a snake, not some psychiatric thing."

She was quiet for a while but couldn't help herself. "What do you do? And I don't want some smart answer."

Will considered it for a while, and eventually said, "I race cars."

"Please, for once give me a straight answer."

Will looked at her and thought about his answer for some reason he decided he needed to tell her.

"No, really, that's what I do. Have you heard of Grand Prix racing?"

"Yes. I saw this horrible crash on TV a few weeks ago. Is that what you do?"

"Yes."

"Did he die?"

"No."

She looked at him intently. "It was you, wasn't it?

"Yes."

"I remember now, you were the one who got that poor woman pregnant and left her in the lurch."

"Told you I was a snake."

"So you are not married."

"I am worse than married."

64

"THIS IS THE last one. You are either going to be remembered as the champion, or as the man who finished second. What's it going to be?"

They were in Ray's office and the race was ten days away. This was the closest they had ever come to winning the championship. It had been close before, but not this close. Certainly not a dead heat with one to go. Will didn't answer. There was nothing to say, nothing more to do. This was it.

"If you win, are you going to quit? If you lose, what then? Stay with me — go to Ferrari? What about the island? Are you just going to drop out, and turn into some kind of farmer-hippy? And what about Isobel — is she going to put up with another season, is she going to be a landed gentry-hippy too?"

"Ray, too many frigging questions. Right now I don't know whether my arse is punched or bored. I have to work on one problem at a time, beating that goddamn Scotsman in a car that's ten miles per hour faster at the end of the straight. That's it. No island, no murder, no woman, no plane-crash inquiry, no next season and no tomorrow. That's it, finito. So if you have any more questions, go down to the pub and ask the barman."

"Don't turn shitty on me. I need to know what you intend to do."

"There is only one thing to do. Win, that's it. Nothing else. The car is perfect as it is. There is no point going testing with it. We won't achieve anything, unless we can get out on this track. And we can't, so all we can do is make damn sure that it doesn't quit."

"Okay, I won't belabour the point. One thing at a time. What's happening on the island?"

"Not bad, the boys are doing well, but they are not tough enough. The supervisor needs firing, and they haven't fired him yet. The police chief knows who killed the thief in the canoe, and thinks he knows who ordered it, but he can't prove it. The chief was involved; or rather he was bribed to implicate me. But Isobel stuffed that up by going to the president, so the chief is now working for me. A bit convoluted, but that's how things work down there. Anyway, we believe it is the minister of mines trying to get even after we fingered him for trying to extort money for a mining licence."

"So, have you sold anything yet?"

"Well, sort of, no money yet, but it all looks good."

"Remember how many times we thought a sponsorship arrangement looked good, and then it fell over at the last minute?"

"Yeah, that keeps running through my mind."

The phone rang and Ray picked it up. "It's yours."

Will took the phone and listened. "What the fuck are you

talking about? Who says the takeoff distance for the plane is longer than the airstrip? Don't you even know that the takeoff distance is calculated on a full load? There was only me in the friggin' plane, nobody else. I am not shouting, this is all bullshit. Use your head. First, the plane was light. Second, the airstrip people allowed the trees to grow too high. And third, the damn engine quit. There is enough there to put the kibosh on the thieving insurance company. Do your job, man, and don't come whining to me. Who the hell are you working for, me or the fucking insurance company?" Will slammed the phone down.

"What was that all about?"

"The insurance company being an insurance company and the dickhead broker doing what a broker does, which is just doing whatever the insurance company wants, so he now has a flea in his ear and he might just go and do his job."

"Is the plane repairable?"

"Probably, and that's the next stunt they will pull. I want a new one."

"You will never get a new one out of them. Wasn't it due for an engine overhaul?"

"Yes; it has less than a hundred hours to go, and no, I don't expect them to give me a new one, but I expect them to pay out."

•

The turning point in Will's life was five days away. If he won, there was one set of circumstances, and if he lost there was another. The common denominator was *Imperialist* and the island, which remained the same, win or lose. Isobel was an enigma. She might walk if he didn't quit, but then again she might not. If he lost, would Ferrari still want him? If he won, would he want to go to Ferrari? What about Ray; if he won, would he stay? If he lost, would Ray still want him? And the big one, either way, if he won or lost, would he want to continue?

The short answer was: win the race and worry about the rest later. But what to do in the meantime? There were five days before the track would be open. There was no point going testing, and he didn't want to get distracted by any of the other issues. There was no sense in looking for trouble.

Will had just walked into his London apartment when the phone rang. "He wants to see you."

"Who?"

"Enzo Ferrari himself."

"When?"

"Tomorrow."

"Shit."

"What do you mean, 'shit'? This is what you have been waiting for all your life."

"True, but your timing is shit."

"What are you talking about? You have a couple of days, and you are not going testing."

"All it's going to be is a 'what if?' visit."

"What the hell are you talking about?"

"What if I win is one price, what if I lose is another. And since we don't know, then we throw in a maybe price."

"All you have to do is to get on the big iron bird. They will pick us up at the airport. The least you will get out of it is a great lunch, so just come for the lunch."

Will pondered this for a moment. "Look, I don't want to start something I can't or won't finish. I'd rather just leave it till the show's over."

"You won't know any more then than what you know now,

except that you've either won or lost. That's it."

"That's the most sensible thing you've said all day, but the situation remains the same."

"Will, my friend, this is the big opportunity you have waited for all your miserable life, and now you are going to blow it away. This could be your swansong, the mega payout. Just think of it, you might be able to do the island debt-free."

"You think I haven't thought of that? I'm not going to keep racing for money alone, as silly as it sounds. It's not the risk. Without the will to win I'd end up looking like a jackass. And I'm not prepared to do that."

"So what do you want me to do?"

"Tell them there is no point in talking till the season is over."

"Do you want me to set up a meeting for right after the last race?"

"You are not hearing me. After the last race, I'll make up my mind if I want to continue, and with whom I want to continue. And before you ask, it won't be immediately after. I'll need a couple of weeks."

Will was in a quandary. Was he biting off more than he could chew? What if he ended up broke if the island didn't work out the way he planned? It could suck him dry. What if he had to go back racing to recover — would he get the kind of deal that he was being offered now? Not a chance.

If he didn't have the island he could really sit on the fence, but he wasn't a fence-sitter. He was a balls-to-the-wall idiot, who took risks that no sane person would even consider.

The phone rang. Ray. "What are you doing?"

"Agonising."

"Over what?"

"Life."

"Want a beer?"

Have a beer, or go for a run? What a decision. "Where?"

"The usual."

Will knew immediately that Ray had something big on his mind, and hoped it wasn't about next season.

•

Ray went up to the counter, returning with two beers.

"Spit it out," Will said. "I've known you long enough to know that you are freaking out. Has the bank got you by the balls again?"

"No."

"What then?"

"It's Shirley."

"Has she caught you with your dick in the maid again?"

"Will, be serious. I have a problem."

"Like I said, spit it out. Is she having it away with the gardener?"

"For Christ's sake, Will, be serious for once in your life."

"Okay, serious. Lay it on me."

"You remember Amanda?"

"The receptionist with the goo-goo eyes, and the big tits?"

"Jesus, Will, this is serious."

"You've knocked her up, haven't you? You dirty bastard, and I suppose she wants to have it."

"Well, yes."

"Oh boy, can I get you a deal on a Ferrari."

"What the hell are you talking about?"

"Think about it. It's a cheap way out, a multipurpose cure-all. You can give it to Amanda to change her mind, or to shut her up, or give it to Shirley to pacify her."

"Can't you be serious for once in your life? This is a major problem."

"Does she want the baby because she has gone clucky, or because she thinks she can get her hooks into you?"

"She has always wanted a baby."

"Well, why didn't she have a baby with the plasterer down the road? She doesn't want you to leave Shirley, does she?" Silence.

"Oh for fuck's sake, Ray, you are a first-class mug. She sees herself turfing out Shirley and becoming Mrs Ray Milligan, the lady of the manor."

"No, she isn't like that."

"No? That's exactly what she is like. She is a dumb bitch who has got her hooks into the cookie jar. End of story."

"What do I do?"

"Tell her you are going to tell Shirley, and that Shirley will sort it out. If that doesn't put the frighteners up her, nothing will."

"I always knew you were crazy. How do you think Shirley would react?"

"She's going to find out anyway, because little Miss Big Tits is going to make sure she finds out, just like she made sure she got pregnant. But if she knows she has nothing to gain except an illegitimate kid, she might just back off."

"It's a huge bluff."

"In for a penny, in for a pound, Ray. Do you remember that old joke you told me about not screwing around with something that you don't know anything about?"

•

Will was jumpy, his stomach was tied up in knots, and he felt like a juggler. There was the island and all the political rubbish still hanging over his head. There was the championship, there was Isobel, and there was the primary decision. Whether he won or lost, did he stop at the end of the season?

The phone rang. It was Ray. "They've stacked the grid."

"What the hell do you mean?"

"They have three cars entered, and the story goes that two of them will have qualifying engines and tyres for the race. This means that two have no intention of finishing, with the high-horsepower qualifying engines, so they will block you, and let the other one get away."

"Oh yeah?"

"Yes."

"What are you going to do about it?" asked Will.

"There is nothing that I can do. There is nothing to stop them running a third car, and there is nothing to stop them running hand grenades."

"No, they'll do whatever they think will give them an advantage, and there is not a goddam thing we can do about it. How did your little drama pan out?"

"Turns out she is not pregnant after all."

"Yeah, right. After you told her you were going to tell Shirley, she must have had a miscarriage."

65

THURSDAY WAS THE first day the track was open for testing. Will did the usual cruise around, getting a feel for the car and the track. Some sat it out waiting for the track to get quicker, as rubber was laid down; others pounded around as fast as they could go. Will was happy with the feel of the car at low loadings, but it could be a different story when they got going.

Isobel had arrived the night before and was in the pits. As usual, she had the mechanics eating out of her hand. She was wearing jeans like nobody he had ever seen before. It was not that they were that tight, but with high-top riding boots and a long-sleeved silk shirt she created an image of classy, slinky sexiness.

Ray was hyper, worrying about the stacked grid. Everybody knew it for what it was. Will was questioned by journalists asking how he felt about being set up. He just laughed. "It takes the pressure off me. If I don't win, I have a good excuse."

"I don't believe that for a minute. Aren't you going to protest?"

"Can't. Ray has been down that road."

"So what are you going to do?"

"It all depends where I qualify. If I am on the pole it might not matter, if I am behind them, I may be able to wait it out till they pop. There's no point worrying about it till it happens."

"Will, what happens after the race?" asked Isobel when they were alone.

"Win, lose, or draw I am out of here to the island, and I'd like you to come with me."

"Yes I will, but what happens after that?"

"What do you mean?"

"You know what I mean." The green eyes lit up.

Will knew he was entering troubled waters. "Whatever happens, I am not going to lose you. And that's all I know for now."

"They say that they have put in extra cars to block you, and perhaps run you off the track."

"Yes I know."

"So what do you do about it?"

"There is no point worrying about something that may never happen. They might not even qualify up front, and then it means nothing.

"Will, I know you, and this is not like you. What are you planning?"

"Isobel, there is nothing to plan. Yes they are stacking the deck. They probably have other plans as well, but it means nothing. They can't set the grid. Only the qualifying times apply."

"I understand, but you are telling me that you are taking this, how you say, lying down. I don't believe it, and I am worried what you are going to do."

"Okay, let me put it to you this way. They will have two cars with qualifying engines and one with a race engine. The qualifying engines and tyres will give them more speed, but they won't last the race distance, so they intend to make their third driver as fast as their first, for enough time to hold me back while Flint gets away. Their qualifying engines will give them over a second a lap with half-tanks and race rubber. Another second on qualifying tyres. But what if I start on half-tanks and on intermediate or soft-compound tyres. What then?"

"You will run out of gas."

"And tyres — but if I could come into the pits and get new tyres and fuel, what then?"

"But it would take too long, and so could they."

"Why? They do it in the long-distance sports-car races all the time. They run up to twenty-four hours."

"But you have never done it."

"True, but the boys are practising it right now back at the workshop. So the only thing different from the qualifying setting is a race engine. If we are two seconds faster per lap, we will pull out a big enough gap to come in and do a pit stop, and still be ahead."

"Ah, comprende, Señor. Now I understand why you are as cool as a cucumber."

"No problemo."

"Shit," Will thought. He hated lying to her, but she was like a dog with a bone. She wouldn't let it go until she got an explanation for his faked relaxed response to stacking the grid. It was true that they were practising pit stops, and they did have an intermediate tyre, but there were too many ifs. If he ended up on the front row alongside bloody Jackie Flint for the Formula One World Championship, what was his risk? Jackie couldn't afford to run into Will, but Will could afford to run into him because if they were both out Will would win. But what about the stacked grid — what if they were behind him and they took him out? Or if they were running light, as they might be, they could pass him and just hold him up long enough. But if he was running light as well, chances were they couldn't.

The more Will pondered the situation, the more questions there were; what if this and what if that? No matter how much planning he did, there were too many permutations. So go for pole as normal and then work it out. He had to remain flexible. The one thing that kept nagging him was: could he drive for a team that would pull such a stunt? He didn't have an immediate answer. The issue was, he supposed, whether he was the screwer or the screwee.

66

PRACTICE WENT WELL. Will was as quick as anybody, and he wasn't at a hundred per cent. He needed wiggle room to manoeuvre tactically; he had to hold something back to see how this game would play out. Ray was like a cat on a hot tin roof. He kept going over what ifs, time and time again. Nothing Will did or said seemed to make any difference. Ray was a nervous wreck.

"Ray, get a hold of yourself. You need to be calm. We can't blow this. We don't know how it's going to play out. We don't know what tactics we will use. We can't even make a decision till after qualifying is finished. Suppose we are on pole and they are not close, what can they do? Wait for me to lap them, and then run me off the road?"

"Yes, I know all that but—."

"Hang on, Ray. I want two things: the best car you can give me, and the potential for a pit stop. That's all, nothing else. We have to act absolutely normal; they could just be trying to rattle us."

"Or they could be dead serious."

Will was playing it as quietly as possible. He had the doomsday plan in his head. He knew that Ray suspected that he had, and that Isobel smelled a rat. He had to play calm because if he pulled the doomsday stunt, it had to be a surprise. What was the penalty if he pulled it? He didn't know, and he couldn't ask anybody. He kept talking to himself: "Stop trying to second-guess; you have already made up your mind. It will either be straightforward or it won't, so stop agonising over it. Put the damn thing on the pole and walk away with it. It's that simple."

●

It was breathtakingly beautiful driving up the freeway through the tunnel of trees in every colour from red to silver. It was a crisp but clear morning but as they headed into the track they saw a huge column of smoke and a traffic jam. People were out of their cars and running. Will jumped out, trying to see what the problem was, but all he could see was smoke.

"What is it?" asked Isobel.

"It's the bog. They are probably burning a car."

"Pardon?"

"They've been doing it for years. It's a big draw card. It started out years ago. It's a mud hole, and the idiots used to jump into it and cover themselves with mud. I once saw a big fat guy, stark-bollocky naked, and the only thing you could see were the whites of his eyes, starkers in the freezing mud. Then they started bringing old wrecks and burning them. The latest thing was rolling any car into the bog that was left nearby. It's a great crowd draw. Some of them never see the race. I guess that's why nothing has been done about it."

The traffic started to move again, and then Will saw it. "Holy shit, they've burnt a bus." He laughed. "Christ, that's torn it. They'll put a stop to it, and you know what? The attendance numbers will drop, and the best race track in the country will be kaput."

"Why? It's only a bunch of idiots. What difference does it make?"

"Because idiots pay money to get in. In this country even idiots can have money. The race isn't the only attraction. Beside this, there is a huge camping area where all kinds of shenanigans go on. One guy told me that while they were sleeping in their tent a bunch of clowns rode trail bikes through the tent. So the next night he parked his Jeep in the tent and slept under it. He said he heard the bike coming and the crunch as it hit the Jeep. Busted guy, busted bike. He hasn't stopped laughing since."

●

It was cool and clear for the first qualifying session. As usual he started out slow, letting it all warm up. First one Ferrari then the other went by him, followed by their test driver in the third car. Will just let them go, as well as a few more that didn't concern him. By the second lap he was hard on it. The cool air made a difference too — he was pulling at least another couple of hundred revs at the end of the straight. It all felt really good. He kept it smooth, but continued pushing on. He kept checking the pit board and when his times stabilised he shot into the pits.

Ray instantly plugged in the intercom. "How's it going?"

"Everything is A-Okay. How are they doing?"

"Not so hot. One went off, and the other is nearly a second slower. Your buddy is about a half second off the pace."

"Yes, one, but it doesn't matter. I think you should sit this one out and see what happens."

"Okay, I'll get out."

What now? Will thought: if this was the grid, I would be on the front row and their number one would be behind the pole-sitter. He can't afford to run into me. But what about the other two? If he was on pole then he would go with the race set-up, but the other two would be using qualifying engines and tyres. Could he keep ahead of them on a race set-up? But then, did he need to keep ahead of them? It only mattered that he finished ahead of Flint; the other two didn't matter. There were so many scenarios that it made him giddy. Trying to second-guess it was hopeless, but he couldn't take his mind off it. It was difficult to relax; the tension was starting to affect his guts. It felt like acid indigestion.

The final qualifying session was at two-thirty. Will had won the race here at the end of last season; all he had to do was to win this one as well. Easier said than done. By two-thirty it was almost warm. He had a fresh qualifying engine and a set of scrubbed-in tyres. He started off in his usual manner, slow and easy, gradually winding it up, but he just could not find the speed he'd had that morning. No matter what he did, he couldn't get rid of the understeer. They tried softening the front by easing off on the roll bars, then the shocks, even the springs. Finally they tried the wings. Whatever they did upset something else. They tried different tyres but it made no difference. It was only when they went to the hard-compound tyres for the race that the car was balanced, and the understeer disappeared. So the problem was tyres again. Not in race set-up, but the qualifying tyres, the soft-compound stuff. There was nothing to do but try to drive around the problem. It was too late to do anything else. Will ended up third on the grid, totally bottled up. The Ferrari number one was on pole with his number two beside him, and the test driver was alongside. All his nightmares had been realised: they had him boxed in. Ray was in a state and Will was pretending there wasn't a problem. The qualifying set-up option had gone. It wasn't fast enough, unless they could get new tyres in time.

"What are they going to do, Ray? Run me off the road? We have lost the option of the qualifying tyres, as the damn tyres don't work, the same bloody problem we have been having all year. The only other option is refuelling. If we do, we should be quicker, but we'll need a pit stop with all the risks. If we don't, I'll get held up by the other two till one gets so far in front that I can't catch him. What do we do? Are you happy that we can make the pit stop in less than five seconds?"

"No, I'm not. Yes, the boys have done better than that in practice, but in the heat of the moment anything could happen."

"Okay, so we go with the race settings and hope to get by them or hope that he breaks."

"I suppose that's about it."

67

WILL WAS ON the grid in the same race that he had won last year. Last year he hadn't had a chance of winning the championship and he was on the front row of the grid, though not on pole. Here he was tying for the lead, but on the second row, and thoroughly boxed in. This time, Will not only had to watch the starter, but also had to watch those who had him boxed in. He still didn't know how this was going to play out, but he was certain of one thing: nobody was going to make a mug out of him. He had one valuable advantage: if neither of them finished, he would win. This was his secret weapon.

The starter mounted his rostrum, the same little fat man as last year. The starter held the flag up, the engines raised to a crescendo, he raised his left shoulder; Will dropped the clutch and jinked right. But the two front rows had moved as one, and their test driver had jinked right as well. They had expected him to jump the start so they had also jumped it. Something was up.

Will was inches apart from the test driver alongside and

right on the gearbox of Flint. He changed up early to ensure that he didn't over-rev. The last thing he needed was to blow the engine. He was completely boxed in and the test driver was pushing him up against the Armco. They were going to be in the braking area in a moment, and he figured the test driver would have to move left to line himself up for the steep right-hander at the end of the pit straight. But no, he kept moving over. Either he wanted Will to brake so that he could go in front, or he was trying to push him into the wall. Will feinted to the left a couple of times, but it didn't work. Shit, the guy was going to push him into the Armco.

"Fuck this," thought Will; he was inches from the one in front and the one beside him. The guy was moving over on him. There was no doubt he was going to get taken out in another second and they were into the braking area. The guy's front wheel graunched Will's side pods. "Stuff you," yelled Will, banging the brake. The test driver's front and rear wheels rode up over Will's and launched him into space. The steering wheel was almost torn out of his hands. He saw the underside of the car out of the corner of his eye as it flew by.

They were into the braking area. Will's left front suspension was stuffed; there was no way he could race with that. Jackie Flint, the pole-sitter, was a few yards in front. His gearbox kicked up as he braked hard for the corner, but Will kept his foot in it. He didn't try to brake; he didn't lift his foot off the accelerator pedal. He piled right into the back of Flint, riding up over the gearbox, tearing the wing off. Flint T-boned the other car and they all slid across the track, and down to the catch fencing, in a huge cloud of dust.

Shit, that's it, thought Will, as he flipped off his seat belts and ripped out his oxygen tube. What a dumb stunt to pull. They had given him the championship and he had proof, his wheel marks on the Armco, and the test driver's wheel marks on his side pod. But he needed to play his part now.

Marshals ran towards them and the drivers headed towards each other. Will thought that attack was the best form of defence, so he went after the test driver. "You crazy, thieving son of a bitch! Pushing me into the wall, you dumb shit! What did you think you were doing?" Will turned to the marshals. "You saw what happened, didn't you? This dumb shit shoved me into the Armco."

"Whoa, you calla me dumba shita?"

"You, you dumb shit, you just cost your boss the championship. He's going to cut your balls out, and shove them down your neck, you stupid fuck."

The test driver had looked aggressive, dancing around on his toes, looking for a fight, but now the result of his effort had started to dawn on him. His hopes for a permanent Formula One drive had just gone out the window. "No, no stilla even."

"Yeah? Read the rulebook, asshole." And Will walked off.

The race had been stopped because the track was full of wrecked cars. Red flags were out. Ray came running over. "What happened, Will? Jesus Christ!"

"What happened? What *happened*? You dumb shit, we just won the championship. The dickheads gave it to us. Keep a straight face; we've got to play this right. Play the part. Go look at the right-hand back wheel and the left-side pod. Make a fuss. We have to be the innocent party."

Ray charged up to the marshals. "I need you to witness this. See the damage to the side pod. Look at the circle from the wheel rim, and look at the right rear wheel. See the marks on the rim and tyre. Come with me. I want you to see the Armco where it hit. Anybody actually see what happened?"

"Yes," said a marshal. "I saw Will hit the back of the other car."

"Everybody saw that," shouted Ray. "I want to know what caused it. Not that it matters anyway because the evidence is there for all to see."

"What difference does it make, Mr Milligan? Will has already won."

"Yes, but I don't want somebody saying Will took him out when it wasn't his fault, and I want that guy banned from Formula One. We don't need idiots like that."

Isobel and some of the mechanics ran up. "We saw it all. The bugger pushed you into the wall," said one mechanic.

Isobel looked at him with those green eyes and whispered in a tight voice, "How much of this did you plan? You lied to me. You knew exactly what you were going to do."

"Isobel, drop it. This is no place for this discussion."

"You lied to me!" she hissed.

"Use your head. How could I have set this up? It's impossible."

"Impossible maybe, but you did it — you lied to me!"

The pace car was out as the field trundled along behind. Five laps later the pace car pulled in and the race was on again. Will found himself with a very strange feeling. This was his last race and it had lasted only a few hundred yards, ending in a very weird way. At least they hadn't made a mug out of him.

They walked back to the pits and went into the motor home. Ray could barely contain himself. "We won, we won."

"Just calm down, Ray. We still have to face the stewards."

"You knew exactly what you were doing, you bastard. No wonder you were so calm."

"Exactly," said Isobel.

"Look, there was no way that I could have engineered being third on the grid. There is no way that I could have engineered having him push me into the wall. And there is no way that I could have engineered him putting his front wheel into the side pod."

"Agreed," said Ray, "but who sent him into orbit, and then who drove into the back of the pole-sitter?"

"Well," said Will, "that's another story. They sent a boy to do a man's job."

68

"Let's go," said Ray," it's time for the emergency stewards' enquiry, and I smell a big fat rat."

Walking over to the stewards' office, he felt the same as when he was at boarding school being sent to the headmaster's office for a caning. The difference would be that the stewards' meeting was going to be full of waffle before they beat you, instead of getting straight into it. Bend over boy, whap, whap!

They called all the participants in one at a time. Will was last. He didn't know any of the stewards — they were locals. He just hoped they had a sense of humour.

"Gentlemen," said the chief steward, "we are here to determine fault or not in this accident at the start of the Grand Prix. You are charged with deliberately ramming the car in front of you, so as to put him out of the championship. You are also charged with deliberately ramming the car beside you, causing him to be launched, taking out the entire Ferrari team at one blow. These are serious charges. We have been looking at your record, and found that you have been involved in many accidents involving other cars. We believe it is entirely possible that the ramming of your fellow points leader in the championship, to win it by default, was deliberate."

Ray was going redder and redder. He looked as though he was about to explode. Will grabbed his leg and shook his head. He stood up. "Sirs, I will answer your accusations in reverse. First, true, I have had many accidents; I haven't had the luxury of going back though my career, determining how many accidents I have had over the many years that I have been racing. Nor have I had the opportunity to work out the ratios between solo accidents, and accidents involving other cars. Nor have I had the time to work out how many were injury accidents, or how much time I spent in hospital." He looked from face to face. "Did any of you see the accident I had this year? How many accidents worse than that have you seen when the driver walked away from it? Do you really believe that, after that, anybody in his right mind would deliberately get himself into another one? Does that make sense to you?"

Will looked at them, trying to read their minds. Were they more or less hostile than when he came in? "Have you seen the physical evidence? Would I drive my car into the Armco? Did you see the right rear rim on my car? Did you see the rim mark on my left side pod? How do you think that happened? If you have seen the marks, you will have seen exactly what happened."

"Yes, we have. That, and the evidence we have heard from the other drivers involved led us suspect that it is possible that it was deliberate."

"Okay," said Will, feeling his stomach tighten up. "Did he not move over on me?"

"Yes."

"Did I not touch the Armco trying to get away from him?"

"That we are not sure about."

"You are saying that I did not touch the Armco?"

"No. I did not say that. We are not sure whether you were pushed into the Armco or whether, in feinting to gain space for yourself, you hit the other car and bounced into the Armco."

Will felt his blood boil. Now it was Ray's turn to grab his leg. Will sat down as Ray stood up. "We would like to see the TV coverage please."

"It is not available."

"Then please reconvene when it is."

"We can't do that."

"Why not?"

"Because we need to have a champion before the race is over."

Will leapt out of his seat before Ray could stop him. "So this is a kangaroo court. You want to make the announcement at the prize-giving, and it's too hard to explain to john public that we are tied, but that because I won more races, I have won. Is that because you think that they are too dumb to understand that I am the champion? It's much easier to tell the punter that I have been disqualified for deliberately taking out the competition."

Will was fuming, but he could see that he had struck home. Two stewards looked decidedly uncomfortable. "You guys want to sacrifice me because it's easier to explain, plus there's just a tiny weenie bit of pressure from the big boys. I don't believe it."

"No, this is not true."

"If you saw the TV coverage, and I am sure that at least one of you actually saw what happened, you know exactly the sequence of events. You know that the test driver moved over on me and squeezed me up against the Armco. You would have had reports from the marshals. You also knew when the third car was entered what their plan was, so don't treat me like a dummy. Stick to the facts. I was pushed into the Armco, then he had another go; the wheels tangled and he flew. We were already in the braking area. How do you think he flew? I braked, but it was too late. I couldn't brake before — the wheels were interlocked."

A steward who hadn't spoken before said, "My problem with this is that you didn't appear to brake. You just drove into the back of the other car."

Will thought that he might have found an ally, somebody who didn't want to be part of a set-up. "Sir," he said, "I was being penned up against the wall. I was about to crash. I was trying to get out of the hole I was in. I had nowhere to go. As you said, I had plenty of experience crashing, so I knew I was going to crash. I was set up, and there was nothing I could do. I was along for the ride, and it ended up the way it was going to end up, no matter what I did."

"Please give us a few minutes," the chief steward said, and led the others out of the room.

"What now?" said Will.

"They are under a lot of pressure to settle this by prize-giving," said Ray, "and the whole Ferrari organisation will be putting pressure on them, plus the FIA and everybody else you can think of. We are a small organisation without much clout, so we are getting railroaded. We would be done for, but they will be afraid of the TV coverage and anybody with a movie camera."

The stewards walked back into the room. "We have considered the situation, but we are still not satisfied that you didn't deliberately drive into the back of the other car, to put him out because your car was already damaged."

"Gentlemen, you can't have it all your way. First, you accuse me of deliberately launching one car, damaging my own, which made no sense when I needed to finish ahead of the car in front. And then you accused me of deliberately ramming Jackie Flint. The first accusation made no sense, which I believe you now agree with. Second, if he wasn't trying to put me out, why did he push me into the wall? And you have to ask yourself this, what was he doing in the race in the first place? And, finally, how did you expect a car with a damaged front and rear suspension to be able to stop as fast? It was a set-up that went wrong for them — end of story."

"Still, we think there was enough time."

"Everybody uses brake markers. Not only couldn't I see my brake marker, I couldn't see anything. I was jammed up against the wall with his wheels inside my wheels, which meant I couldn't brake even if I wanted to, and when I did, both front and rear suspension were damaged. What do you expect?"

"We will take this under consideration."

"What does that mean?" said Ray.

"It means what it says, that we will announce the Formula One World Championship winner at the prize-giving."

"If I don't know now, I am not waiting around in suspense like some quiz-show contestant. I want to know now or I am gone."

"If you go, we will award it to the other."

Will was really angry, and before Ray could stop him he

shouted, "I'm not going to play your silly games. We will sue."

"We don't like to be threatened."

"Believe it, it's not a threat. It will happen."

Will got up and grabbed Ray by the arm. "Let's go. I'm done here. I have to contact the lawyers."

"Hang on a minute," said the chief steward, "this is no way to behave at an investigation."

"This is not an investigation, this is a kangaroo court, and I am not being part of it."

"Okay, okay, give us a minute."

"No. I want an answer now or I am done."

The stewards went into a huddle for a few minutes. Then the one who Will thought might be an ally said, "All right, we agree that there is insufficient evidence to prove that you rammed the other car deliberately. We agree that the car beside you did not give you sufficient racing room, causing an accident."

"Okay," said Ray. "We will accept that, but I want it in writing now."

"Don't you trust us?"

"Of course. Just making sure."

"We need to get it typed up."

"We are all friends here. Just write it by hand and you all sign it."

"We need to confirm it."

"No, we just agreed, and you are already welching. Write it and sign it, as you just said."

"All right, we will do it. But in return we want an undertaking that you will come to the prize-giving."

"Okay, you have a deal," said Ray.

69

THE SUN WAS out, the sky was cloudless, the fluffy cumulus clouds drifted by. Coconut trees waved in the light offshore breeze. The beach was white; the sea was green and blue. *Imperialist* swung slowly back and forth on her anchor. The boom cover was up covering the deck, shading the boat from the midday sun. The boys were ashore. Will sat in the cockpit sipping an espresso, deep in thought. Isobel was asleep beside him on a bean bag; a book had fallen out of her hand.

Will was World Champion, and everybody was after him. The media, Ray, his manager, his lawyer, his accountant, Ferrari, the politicians, everybody. They all wanted answers. Will didn't have any. As long as he stayed where he was, he didn't have to.